MY ENEMY, MY FRIEND

My Enemy, My Friend

▼

Jack Nadel

Writers Club Press
San Jose New York Lincoln Shanghai

My Enemy, My Friend

Writers Club Press
an imprint of iUniverse.com, Inc.

For information address:
iUniverse.com, Inc.
5220 S 16th, Ste. 200
Lincoln, NE 68512
www.iuniverse.com

ISBN: 0-595-14516-7

Printed in the United States of America

Contact:

    Jack Nadel
    1187 Coast Village Road
    Suite 106
    Santa Barbara, CA 93108-2794
    805-565-1438
    Fax-805-565-1430

For Elly
my wife, partner, guide
inspiration, critic and best friend

CHAPTER ONE

▼

The shrill shriek of sirens pierced Yukio Matsuda's ears and his eyes immediately snapped open. Sitting upright in bed, he stared into the darkness and listened to the distant roar of the B-29 bombers, approaching like a thunderstorm, growing louder with each passing moment.

Groping in the darkness for the nightlight, he flipped it on and looked at the clock in disbelief: 2 A.M. The incessant bombing of Japan had been going on since November of last year. But the attacks had always come in the daylight hours, aimed at factories and military targets. Never before had there been an assault at night. Yet, he could now hear the low rumble of planes as they rolled across the sky, seemingly headed straight for the heart of Tokyo.

Yukio sprang out of bed, grabbed his robe and wrapped it around his powerful body in one swift motion. Forty-eight years old, he still moved with the grace and agility of his Samurai ancestors.

A sharp knock sounded at the door and as he opened it, he came face to face with Hito, his manservant. Bowing awkwardly, Hito pointed his finger toward the sky. His hand shook and there was panic in his eyes.

"The devils have now come at night, Matsuda-San!" the old man gasped, his voice laced with fear. "There is no time to lose! We must go to the bomb shelter!"

"You go and take the others. I will follow later," Yukio commanded, watching the old man as he quickly shuffled away.

Pausing only long enough to put on his slippers, Yukio hurried out into the night. His family's low, polished wood home sat atop a small hill just five kilometers from downtown Tokyo. From this vantage point, he could view the city. Giant searchlights now probed the cold, dark sky. They swept across the high ceiling of clouds, as the sound of plane engines grew to a powerful, deafening roar.

A bright explosion lit up one area, followed by another and another as dozens and then hundreds of small wooden houses burst into flames. He watched the giant spotlights race across the sky until they caught one of the offending B-29's in the center of their glare. A barrage of anti-aircraft guns zeroed in on the lumbering plane until it exploded and hurtled down like a shooting star into the blazing inferno below.

The night was filled with smoke, flames and sounds. Wave after wave of bombers soared through the skies, dropping thousands of incendiary bombs on the now helpless city. Through the light of the fires and the haze of smoke wafting through the air, the lone figure of Yukio Matsuda was illuminated in an eerie glow. He stood with his feet planted firmly on the ground, his fists clenched in rage, as the pungent aroma of burning flesh and wood stung his nose and brought tears to his eyes.

With the break of dawn, the last of the B-29's began to depart. With anger still burning inside him, Yukio shook his fists at the sky. Then, with his head down, he walked slowly back to his home.

Daylight draped the smoldering city as the servants wearily returned to their quarters. Yukio's wife and daughter were visiting relatives in Kyoto. He picked up the phone to call them but found the line was dead. He closed his eyes and sent a silent prayer up to the gods, asking them to protect his family. When he opened his eyes, he saw that Hito had returned and was hovering anxiously, awaiting instructions.

"I will walk to the city," he barked at the old man. "I will return in a couple of hours. You check to see if any damage has been inflicted on my home."

Yukio returned to his room and quickly changed his clothes. With his jaw set and his eyes bleary and bloodshot, he began to walk toward the city. The scowl that had appeared earlier that morning, had not left his face.

All around him, the streets were filled with refugees streaming out of town. In carts, on bicycles or on foot, their meager belongings were strapped to their backs and held in their hands as they headed for the relative safety of the countryside. With each step Yukio took, the smell of the dead and the dying became more intense.

The roads were littered with bodies, charred black beyond recognition. It seemed that the closer he got to the center of town, the more corpses blocked his way, creating an obstacle course of death. Bile rose in his throat as he stepped over remnants of disfigured humanity, trying hard not to look.

From what he could see, everything on both sides of the Sumida River had been incinerated. The land was as bare as an empty table, except for the few telephone and power poles still left standing. Gone was much of his beloved city. The Ginza, once teeming with life, was now filled with dazed, desperate people picking through the debris, carrying off anything they were able to salvage.

Walking on, Yukio came upon the site of the beautiful Asakusa Buddhist Temple. That, too, was gone. The sloping, deep-red roof, the beautiful, ornately carved walls, even the giant ginkgo trees surrounding it, were nothing but ashes.

Yukio continued on in shock and disbelief. He turned and began to head toward the river but an old man stopped him on his way. "There is nothing for you there," the man told him, his eyes glazed. "The river has almost stopped its flow. It is filled with bodies of those who jumped in to escape the flames."

By now Yukio's face wore an expression as dazed as that of the refugees he'd passed on his way into the city. Like a robot, he walked slowly, mechanically, aimlessly along.

Rounding the corner, Yukio realized he was near the home of Senji Watanabe, his trusted assistant for the past twenty years. Yukio was the fourth generation Matsuda to head Tosui, the huge, international trading company founded by his great-grandfather. And although he had many employees, Senji was his right-hand man—totally irreplaceable. With a new sense of purpose, Yukio walked quickly to his confidant's home. But where Senji's comfortable home had stood, there was now just a pile of ashes and rubble. Anxiously, Yukio's eyes sifted through the wreckage. At last, they came to rest on a solitary figure, sitting in the middle of the devastation, staring vacantly at the nothingness surrounding him—as still as a tombstone marking the spot.

"Senji?" Yukio whispered as he crouched in front of the man and peered into his eyes. Oblivious, Senji continued to stare into the ashes, his face lifeless, his eyes without expression. Finally, placing both of his hands firmly on his assistant's shoulders, Yukio raised his voice and commanded, "Senji, look at me!"

The vacant look began to fade and a wan smile appeared on Senji's face as he recognized his employer. His eyes, however, did not blink. "My family is gone, Matsuda-San. My wife, my two beautiful daughters—burned beyond recognition. I cannot even give them a proper burial." He sat quietly for a moment and then, as if speaking to himself, said simply, "My life, it is over. My family is with my ancestors now and I must join them."

A picture of his own wife and daughter, smiling happily at him across the dinner table, flashed through Yukio's mind. He thought, too, of his son, Yoshikazu, fighting the enemy on the island of Iwo Jima.

Lifting Senji gently to his feet, Yukio's eyes narrowed as he said, "All your family is not lost, Senji-San. Your son, Takei, is fighting the honorable fight against the demons. He will help to right the wrongs. Your ancestors are crying out for revenge and you must live for that. I will help you. Come with me now to my home for there is nothing more you can do here."

Senji's grief-stricken eyes met his. "Is it not ironic, Matsuda-San, that my son, who faces death every day, remains alive and well while the rest of my family, whom I vowed to keep safe, is nothing but dust?"

As they made their way through the rubble of the city, Yukio suddenly stopped and cocked his head. From somewhere in the distance came the strained sound of music. Looking in the direction of the sound, he saw an army military band, sixty strong, in full color regalia, parading down the street. While the music swelled, refugees, numb with shock and despair,weaved in and out amongst the band members, unseeing and unhearing. The sight chilled Yukio to the bone.

The music seemed to shake Senji back to his senses, however. "It is Armed Forces Day " he said, quietly. "This military march was planned many weeks ago."

"Those damned fools!" Yukio growled. "Don't they realize Tokyo has been burned to the ground? Did no one have the sense to change the orders?"

In that moment, Yukio realized the war was lost. He stared, frozen in his tracks, at the macabre sight before him. Finally, he turned to Senji and said in a gentle voice, "Do not worry, my trusted friend. The murder of your sweet wife and children will be avenged."

Only a few office buildings remained standing in downtown Tokyo. One of those, a tall, chrome and glass tower, was the headquarters of the Tosui Trading Company. Inside this building, in a tenth floor conference room, seven men, dressed in traditional kimonos, were seated around a large, round glass table. Outside, the constant wail of sirens could be heard but the seven most powerful men in Tokyo seemed oblivious to the sounds.

The past month might well have been the worst in thousands of years of Japanese history. The Imperial Army was retreating on all fronts and many army units had been returned to Japan to prepare for the impending American invasion.

The seven men finished their tea. Putting down his cup, Yukio Matsuda, representing the Tosui Trading Company, called the meeting to order. "I want to welcome you and to apologize for the condition of my humble office.

"This is a sad day. our country is in ruins and our military is faltering. It appears that it is not time for victory for Japan."

Yukio looked around, eyeing each of the other men at the table. He depended on their support to set his plan in motion. "It is now up to us to restore dignity and pride to Japan. We may not win this battle but, if we work together, we will ultimately win the war."

Several of the men looked up at him, puzzled. "Please understand," Yukio continued, "the war I refer to is not this one of military might but a new war—one that will be waged starting today, March 1, 1945. This will be a war that will require great patience and wisdom, but it is a war that we must win."

By the looks on their faces, Yukio knew he had their complete attention. Smiling, he went on. "The war in which we will be victorious is an economic war. If we all work together, following the plan, we will bring the Americans to their knees. We will succeed in taking over the United States of America. The next millennium will belong to Japan."

Mr. Nakamura rose and, in a shaky voice said, "With all due respect, Matsuda-San, our country is in ruins. Our factories have been destroyed by American B-29's. There are people starving. Many of our young men have been killed and others are committing sepuku. Perhaps we will survive—but can we rise and conquer?"

Yukio nodded patiently. "Not only will we survive, but we will spring back stronger than before. We Japanese are like the bamboo—pliant and supple—while the Americans are like the oak—sturdy and strong. In the greater wind, the bamboo will only bend…while the oak will eventually crack and break."

"We will rise from the ashes!" cried Mr. Yamamoto. "If we are defeated, we will appear to become subservient. Then, the Americans will help us to restore our factories so that we can supply them with cheap labor. We will learn from them how to make things better. We will take their inventions and their technology and produce their products better and cheaper than they can. We will harness all the power of our government, our banks and our workers. We, the great trading companies of Japan, will lead the way!"

"We will be the wolf in sheep's clothing!" another of the men shouted.

"Exactly!" Yukio told them, the passion in his voice growing stronger. "The words that have been spoken are the truth. By working together, we will once again make our nation the most powerful in the world."

Yukio stopped for a moment, calming himself. When he spoke again, his tone was solemn. "To accomplish our goal, we will need total allegiance from every man here. Please indicate if we will have your full participation."

One by one, he looked into each man's eyes. Without hesitation, they met his gaze and gave a slight nod of the head.

"Arigato. We have unanimous approval," said Yukio with a satisfied look. "Know now that we cannot defeat the United States militarily but eventually, we will own it!"

CHAPTER TWO

───────────▼───────────

"Men, every Jap home is a war factory, and we're gonna have to treat them as such. We're gonna start hitting them with incendiaries—all of them." The speaker spat out some tobacco juice and smacked his lips. "And what we're gonna do tonight is to fly in at 5,000 feet and surprise the livin' hell out of em!"

Hank Marshall laughed until tears came to his eyes. Bubba Rice, Hank's burly co-pilot, had his imitation of General Curtis E. LeMay down pat.

Next to Hank, Howard Rogers, their wiry navigator, slapped his thigh repeatedly. "But General, at that altitude our B-29's will be sitting ducks!"

"Well, son," answered Bubba in his Curtis LeMay voice, "then we'll just have to get us some more B-29's. It takes a brave man to send brave men to their deaths!"

"Yes, sir!" said Pat Patterson, the co-pilot of another one of the planes in Hank's squadron, snapping off an exaggerated salute. "Whatever you say, sir!"

The four young men erupted in another wave of laughter, gradually slowing long enough to catch their breaths. Still chuckling, Hank studied the other men. All of them—Bubba Rice, Howard Rogers and Pat Patterson—wore enormous smiles, as though they were the happiest they'd ever been. It was always like this, Hank knew, before they flew out on their most dangerous missions. The thin veneer of humor and toughness covered the doubt and fear that lay hidden below.

A loud, sharp voice cut through the maze of conversations. "ATTENTION!" Six hundred men leaped to their feet and stood silent and motionless as the wing commander and the two generals strode briskly down the center aisle to the front of the room. A stage with a large screen awaited them. After the generals had seated themselves in the front row, the group commander turned to face the combat fliers. "At ease!" he shouted. As they sat down once again, he added, "We will be briefed by Captain Gold."

A short, stocky man with a hairline that had receded well beyond his twenty-seven years approached the stage from the side of the room. Next to the trim young men around him, his uniform looked rumpled and unkempt. He held a long, thin pointer in his right hand, and, by the smile on his face, it was obvious to all he enjoyed occupying center stage.

The lights dimmed and the image of an aerial photograph of the Mitsubishi aircraft plant was now visible on the large screen.

"The target for today is…" said Sandy Gold, pausing for dramatic effect while lifting the pointer to the screen. "The target is…3-5-7." A gasp was heard throughout the auditorium and all traces of the earlier gaiety disappeared.

"Gentlemen," he continued, "we have visited this factory on six different occasions, and the Japs have been very inhospitable. In fact, they've shot down a lot of our B-29's while we have been spectacularly unsuccessful in knocking them out. The truth is, they're now producing more planes than ever before. And this will contribute to our casualties in the future unless we destroy their factory today.

"The enemy now has a 50% greater concentration of antiaircraft firepower than our comrades in Europe are facing over Berlin. Plus, they have moved in additional fighter squadrons whose job it is to protect the plant and to blast you out of the sky. I'd now like to turn the briefing over to

General O'Donnell. Sir…go." Handing the General the pointer, Sandy Gold moved to the front row.

On stage, the General stood tall and trim. At the age of forty, he seemed almost a fatherly presence amidst this group of men whose average age was twenty-two. "Gentlemen, this is an historic mission. On all of the previous B-29 missions from Mariana Islands—Guam, Saipan, Tinian—you have flown over Japan. You have had to take on the whole Japanese air force as well as antiaircraft fire from the ground. Today, for the first time, you will have a fighter escort.

"Up until now, we have not had an air base close enough for our fighters to use. You are aware of the great battle that has been waged for Iwo Jima. This strategic island lies halfway between Saipan and Japan. It has now been secured at a very heavy price. We have already moved in several squadrons of P-51 Mustangs. They will rendezvous with you off the coast of Japan and provide fighter cover for today's mission."

Putting the pointer down, he turned and looked squarely at the men. "Mark this moment in history, gentlemen, April 4th, 1945. In February, we burned Tokyo to the ground. Today, we will destroy their most important war plant. History will record this moment and your part in defeating Japan. Captain Gold will now supply you with all the details."

Once more, the orderly shouted, "ATTENTION!" and as the six hundred men sprang to their feet, the Generals walked back down the aisle and out of the hall.

Before the door had closed, the briefing room erupted into bedlam. Hank Marshall turned to face his crew, seated around him.

"Holy shit!" exclaimed Mike Monroe, the radio operator. "This is just great! We were expecting to go home after twenty missions. Now, we're flying number twenty-one over a target that scares the shit out of everyone here. Hell, I don't wanna go back! We've already been there six times before."

Hank bit his lip and spoke in a quiet voice that belied the churning in his gut. "Then I guess we're going back for lucky number seven. You know what they say—if you don't do the job right the first time, you keep on trying till you get it right."

Captain Gold walked back to the stage. Again, the room became silent, more out of fear than respect. "Okay, men, this is the seventh round and we're going in for a knockout. We'll be taking off at four minute intervals. Rendezvous point is fifty miles off the coast of Japan. We'll fly over the target information.

Timing must be perfect 'cause it's gonna be a crowded sky: thirty squadrons of ten planes each. This means there will be three hundred B-29's up there. "We'll be met by about sixty P-51's from Iwo Jima, who'll be flying top cover. We are expecting at least one hundred Jap fighters and plenty of flack from landfall—increasing in intensity as we zero in on the target.

"You had all better fly your formations asshole tight or you're gonna end up as statistics. Remember, the point of this story is to get to the target and drop your bombs right down the smoke stack. After that, you're expendable.

"Stay in formation after the bombs are dropped. As you fly over the water again, you're on your own. Today, for the first time, Iwo Jima is not only a base for the P-51's, but an airfield that can be used for emergency landing and refueling. Remember, though, this is only for extreme emergencies. There's still fighting on the island even though we're told the air base is secure.

"For you replacement crews who are flying your first mission, this will be your baptism by fire. Let's hope you can all tell your grandkids about it."

Hank glanced over at his crew. Bubba Rice's jaw was clenched. The knuckles on Howard Rogers' hands were white as he gripped the back of the chair in front of him. Pat Patterson's face was drawn and pale. "I'm glad to see I'm not alone," Hank thought grimly to himself.

Seemingly oblivious to the mood of his audience, Sandy Gold continued on. "Rendezvous point time is six hours and ten minutes. You have your schedules. First plane takes off at 0900 hours. Now, let's synchronize our watches so we're all lined up to the second…and good luck."

The B-29 cruised on autopilot at 10,000 feet. It was noon, the day was crystal clear, and the Pacific Ocean below looked placid and serene. The peacefulness of the scene created an almost surreal background for the violence to come.

"Hey, what's this?" Hank asked, looking over at his copilot. "I thought you were an atheist."

Bubba looked up from the Bible he was reading with a sheepish grin. "I got a letter from my wife tellin' me she expects me home for Christmas—safe and sound and all in one piece. I wrote her and told her, don't worry, darlin', they ain't gonna drag the Pacific Ocean to send me back."

Hank looked at him quizzically. "So what's with the Bible?" Bubba's jovial expression faded from his face. "To tell you the truth, I'm scared. And I ain't never been scared before. This Bible is just a little insurance policy. Sorta wanna cover my bet, know what I mean?"

Hank nodded and a smile crossed his face.

"And what about you?" Bubba added, seeing Hank's smile. "Tell me how can you be so fuckin' cool all the time. Ain't you ever scared?"

"Sure I am."

"Then how come you act so relaxed? Like nothin' bothers you? Is it because everything comes so easy to you? I mean, you play football, you make All-American. We hit the bars, you walk off with all the best broads. Shit! It's too easy!"

Taking off his headset slowly, Hank turned to face Bubba. "As long as this is show and tell time, I might as well tell you something. I've been scared shitless on every one of these missions. And don't ask me why, but for some reason, I just know we're going to come out of this in one piece."

"Yeah, well, I just hope you're right", said Bubba, halfheartedly. "But I'll tell you one thing—if you got that kinda attitude, I'm damn glad to be on your side! See, I figure it this way—long as you're the captain of this ship and you feel like you do, then I ain't gonna get hit."

Hank grinned. Then his face became serious. "I wish it was that easy, Bubba. I know it may look that way sometimes. Playing football was a great time for me. It's probably the only thing I didn't really have to work hard at—it just seemed to come to me.

"But as far as women are concerned, you don't know the half of it. I really blew it before I enlisted. You have a wife and son that you love, waiting for you at home. There's no woman waiting for me. I've had a lot of time to think since I've been in combat and I keep thinking about the one I let get away. I just can't get Ruth out of my mind. Ruth was my girl—before we broke up…before I broke us up. But, hey, who knows?

Maybe when I get back…."he hesitated, "if I get back…" Hank looked at Bubba, thoughtfully. "See, you're the guy who truly has it made. Soon, you'll be heading back to Virginia, back to your family. And, Bubba, that's gonna happen whether you read the Bible or not. 'Cause you're a helluva good man and that's what you deserve.

"Now, take over the cockpit," Hank told him, brusquely. "I'm going back to talk to the other guys. I'll bet they're nervous as hell about this mission."

As Hank's plane closed in on the rendezvous point, other B-29's appeared magically out of nowhere. Hank was always amazed at the navigator's skill—how each plane could fly its own separate course and yet somehow, they would all arrive together at exactly the right time, according to plan.

The squadron maneuvered quickly into a tight formation, with Hank piloting his plane alongside the right wing of the lead bomber. He could now see the whole squadron, fore and aft, as they flew towards landfall and on to the target.

Looking up, Hank saw the P-51's, flying in from Iwo Jima. The Japanese pilots, flying at a lower altitude, hadn't seen the P51's yet and never knew what hit them. As they zoomed in to attack the B-29's, the

P-51's came swarming down at them like avenging eagles, attacking their prey.

"Pilot to crew!" Hank barked into the headset, his adrenaline pumping. "Prepare for action!" Suddenly, the stillness of the skies was shattered by the burst of machine gun fire and the lights of tracers, illuminating the bullets deadly passage towards their targets.

The skies were now filled with fighter planes. The B-29's droned laboriously ahead, straight and level, like slow-moving monsters zeroing in for the kill. Bomber guns blasted the fighters continuously while they dove in and out. As the B-29's flew over land, anti-aircraft guns joined the battle, sending huge shells into the skies that exploded in black puffs of ominous smoke.

Hank's intercom crackled. "Watch it! One o'clock high!" An enemy fighter was coming straight at them with guns blazing. Suddenly, at the last second, he peeled off right before impact. Without missing a beat, another one appeared. The B-29's guns blasted it until it exploded in mid-air.

While Japanese fighters darted in and out of the blackened skies, the squadron continued on course as it approached the bomb run. Looking to his left, Hank waved and gave a-thumbs up sign to Pat Patterson, the co-pilot of the lead plane. Pat returned his greeting with a lopsided grin. Suddenly, a burst of flak exploded and Pat's plane, belching smoke, began to spin out of control.

"No!" Hank cried helplessly, as he watched the plane plunge to the ground. Then, gritting his teeth, he maneuvered his plane into the lead position as the rat-ta-ta-tat of machine gun fire slammed against the fuselage.

"Bombardier from pilot," he shouted into the intercom, "you are now lead bombardier. Make those bastards pay!"

"Pilot from bombardier," the excited voice answered, "I read you loud and clear. We are three minutes to target."

Through the smoky haze, they were able to make out the huge aircraft plant ahead and below. Bursting shells from the ground below seemed to fill every inch of space as the planes moved steadily ahead.

Off to Hank's right, he saw that a P-51 was hit. The American pilot bailed out of the fighter right before it went into a spin. His chute had just opened as one of the enemy fighters flew by. With tracers blazing, the Japanese fired on the defenseless airman. Hank watched as the body stiffened, then hung suspended, as it floated to the ground.

"Bombs away!" the bombardier cried exultantly, snapping Hank back to attention. The squadron released hundreds of bombs, sent hurtling down at the target.

At that same moment, a shell burst against Hank's plane, rattling it severely. Hank could feel the plane start to slip out of control. "We're hit but we're gonna be okay!" he shouted, trying to keep his voice confident. "Stay at your stations. We'll have everything under control in a minute. Keep calm and keep those guns going!" As pilot and co-pilot fought with the controls, the aircraft finally began to level off. Hank and Bubba's eyes met in a moment of silent thanks before returning to the action outside.

As they left the target area, the severity of the battle was beginning to subside. Ten B-29's had flown over the coast of Japan twenty minutes before. Seven flew out the other side. Breaking formation, Hank and his crew began heading toward the base on Saipan.

As the wounded B-29 made it's way through the now lonely sky, flying out over the sea, all signs of combat disappeared. An anxious calm had settled over the ship. The crew moved from one section of the craft to another, reporting to the pilot as they moved along. An hour later, they had finished their inspection. Miraculously, none of the crew had been hurt but the aircraft had suffered severe damage.

"Pilot from flight engineer. The last hit pierced the gas tank on the left side. We're leaking badly. Our best air speed to conserve fuel is 290 knots. I figure at that rate, we'll have about four hours of flying time."

Hank looked at his watch. "Roger. Navigator from pilot, give me a direct heading to Iwo Jima. We're going to have to make an emergency landing to refuel before heading back to Saipan. Over." "Wilco," shot back the voice of Howard Rogers. "Will comply."

Hank turned to Bubba. "You take over here. Remember to keep the nose slightly down—we'll get better mileage that way. Looks like we're just going to have to nurse this baby in."

Unstrapping himself from his seat, Hank removed his headset and stretched his long, lean frame. Every muscle in his body ached. As he stood, they seemed to cry out from the tension of the last two hours. Shaking off the discomfort, he said, "We're going to have to bail out all the excess weight we can. I'm going in the back to inspect the damage and see what we can get rid of.

A twilight of startling color had given way to a cover of inky darkness. It seemed there was nothing else alive except for the huge, ghostly plane, cutting its way through the silence.

Hank entered the cabin and saw Howard Rogers staring intently at the radar screen. Without looking up, the navigator said, "If my calculations are correct, a dot indicating land will materialize in just a moment." Beads of sweat appeared on his forehead as he moved his lips in silent prayer.

"There it is!" he cried out excitedly. "About forty miles at twelve o'clock. We're heading right for it, Skipper!"

Hank placed a hand on Howard's shoulder. "Congratulations! You hit it right on the head." Leaning over the intercom, he said, "Radio operator from pilot, can you pick up their signal?"

"Got it loud and clear," came back Mike Monroe's reply. "I have the tower on the headset." Flashes of light appeared on the radar screen as the small island came into view. "Calling Iwo tower. This is Dumbo 15, returning from 3-5-7. We are low on gas. Need instructions for landing and refueling. Over."

"We read you, Dumbo 15," a voice answered. "We'll light up the runway. Circle the landstrip and stand by for landing instructions. Looks like you're our first customer."

Hank glanced out the window as a straight line of lights appeared, lighting up the runway below. "Roger, I read you," he responded. "What are those flashing lights at the other end of the island?"

"We're still fighting for this fucking rock. Keep circling. I'll give you landing instructions as soon as possible. We'll have the fuel tanks ready to gas you up so we can send you right out again. When you land, the crew should disembark and take positions around the plane. Have your guns drawn and ready to fire. There are lots of snipers down there—enough Japs to mount an attack. How much fuel do you have?"

"Just enough to feed this tin can to the fish. Request immediate landing instructions."

"Roger. Here are your instructions."

Hank sighed with relief as he eased the big bomber onto the newly prepared airstrip. The plane screeched to a halt at the very end of the runway. Tanker trucks and ground crew were waiting as he cut the engines. The aircrew tumbled quickly from the exits, guns drawn and ready for action.

The field was brightly lit and the area was wide open except for the thick bushes on both sides of the runway.

Hitting the ground, Hank motioned to the trucks to move in and start filling the tanks. A burly tech sergeant let out a long, low whistle as he inspected the battered plane. "You must have at least a hundred holes in this baby," he said, shaking his head. "All we can do is fill it back up and hope it holds together long enough to get you back to your base."

The sergeant looked around cautiously. The glaring lights against the black sky made the airfield foreboding. "This place is still lousy with Japs," he told Hank. "Every time we think we've finally got the island secure, another batch of Kamikazes come running out of the rocks, firing. Just keep your eyes open and your guns drawn. We should have you ready to take off again in about twenty minutes."

A humorless smile crossed Hank's face. "Thanks. Without you guys, we'd be dead meat."

Peering into the foliage along the strip, Hank thought he saw movement. I know we're being watched, he thought, grimly. His body was tensed, coiled and ready to spring. Had it been his imagination or had he seen movement? The crack of a branch? His trigger finger tightened on his pistol.

The lone Japanese sniper, his body and face caked with mud, squatted in the bushes. His eyes turned to steel as he saw the pilot walk around the B-29 and take a position, staring into the bushes. The sniper lifted his rifle to his eyes and peered down the barrel. He had the enemy's head in his sights. His finger started to squeeze the trigger. Suddenly he froze, unable to move, unable to shoot.

The gas line was removed. Hank climbed back into the cockpit and the rest of the crew returned to their positions.

The sniper's shoulders slumped as he watched the giant aircraft lumber down the runway and take off.

CHAPTER THREE

▼

Ruth Morris received the letter on April twenty-first, the same day she started her new job at the Los Angeles Chamber of Commerce. It was also the first day of spring and there was a noticeable chill in the air.

The letter was the first thing she noticed as she bounced through the door of her family's large, comfortable home. It was lying on the little, round table in the hallway where the mail was usually placed. Ruth's father, Dr. Edwin Morris, was still seeing patients in his office adjoining the house. She could hear her mother in the kitchen preparing dinner. For once, she was glad to be standing all alone in the dimly lit hallway.

Ruth stared at the letter for several seconds before cautiously picking it up. She recognized the handwriting immediately and the return address in the left hand corner confirmed its source: Lt. Hank Marshall— Somewhere in the Pacific. Underneath was a stamp indicating the letter had been censored by the War Department.

After holding the envelope tightly in her hand for several minutes, Ruth reached down and picked up the small silver letter opener that was lying on the table, and neatly slit the envelope open. As she began to read, the hand holding the letter began to tremble slightly.

April 5, 1945

Dear Ruth,

I am writing this letter in care of your family's address because it's been almost four years since we last spoke. You've been on my mind constantly over the past few months but today, especially, I had to write to you. I had to feel some kind of connection.

This is a particularly difficult time for me as I have just received the saddest news of my life. There is no easy way for me to say this. I was called into the chaplain's office this morning. He's a wonderful guy who tried hard to be gentle when he told me that my brother, Peter, had been killed in action.

I couldn't believe it at first. It just didn't seem real. For most of the day, after that, I've been seeing Peter's face in front of me. You know how close we were. (It's tough to write the word 'were'.)

It's so strange. I keep feeling like Peter's reaching out to me—trying to tell me something—but I have no idea what that might be. I only wish there was some way I could tell him how much I love him, how much I'll miss him.

We had such a great time together, the last time we saw each other. I never believed this could happen. We always seemed so indestructible. I feel such tremendous sadness for Peter. And for my parents: they had such high hopes for us both.

It's strange how everything seems to happen at once. Yesterday, I came closer to death than I had on any of my other combat missions. It was xxxxxxxxxxxxxxxxxxxxxxxxxxxxxxxxxxxxxxxxxxxxxxxxxxx xxxxxxxxxxxxxxxxxxxxxxxxxxxxxxxxxxxxxxxxxxxxxxxxxxx xxxxxxxxxxxxxxxxxxxxxxxxx (CENSORED), Anyway, after so many close calls, I feel I must have survived for a reason. There wasn't an explosion in my head and I didn't suddenly find religion but I know I am changed forever—and that I must make my life mean something.

Ruth, if I survive this war, I need to see you again. For all I know, you may be married and might even have kids, but one way or another, please write to me. Let me know how you are -and if you think of me once in a while. I have never forgotten you and hope that you can forgive me for any pain I have caused. So much time has passed and we were both so young then.

Preparing for combat provides lots of time for reflection and I find I can't get you out of my mind. There's something very important and unfinished between us, Ruth. Something that needs to be addressed. I needed to talk with you so much today and while this letter is a poor substitute, I guess it'll have to do for now.

I hope you will write to me. And please, give your family my best.

HANK

Ruth stared blankly at the pages in her hand, unable to move. Finally, she made her way into the living room, past the overstuffed chairs and the couch with its bold floral print. As though drawn by a magnet, she seated herself on the shiny, black piano bench standing in front of her Steinway piano. Without thinking, her fingers ran over the keys, playing the haunting melody of "Stardust"..

Without warning, tears began to stream down her face and she was startled by the sounds of sobbing that escaped her lips. Laying her head in the crook of her arm, she continued to cry.

Finally, Ruth looked up and saw her father staring at her with a worried look on his face. Before he could speak, she waved the rumpled letter in her hand at him and said, "Can you believe this? I haven't heard from Hank Marshall in four years and this letter arrives. He says he has to talk to me...needs to see me again...has to share his pain." She stopped for a moment, trying to collect her thoughts. A sigh involuntarily escaped her lips and deep sorrow filled her eyes.

"Oh, Dad! I feel so bad for him! His brother, Peter, was killed in action in Europe. It's just so sad!" Tears began rolling down her cheeks once again.

Dr. Morris reached over and took her hand in his, knowing there was nothing he could say or do to ease her pain. He was the kind of father who loved everything about his daughter. Even now, as he looked at her he thought: she's smart, she's beautiful, she's talented, but most importantly, she's a good person with a big heart.

"Ruth," he said at last, "are you still in love with Hank?" She hesitated a moment. "No, Dad. I've had a lot of time to get over him. Besides, I have David now."

She laid her head against her father's shoulder. They remained that way, quietly holding hands, until Mrs. Morris, voice broke the silence with the announcement of dinner.

"Do you want to eat something?" Dr. Morris asked.

"No thanks, I'm not hungry. I'd just like to go to my room." Seeing the troubled look cross her father's face again, Ruth added, with a forced smile, "Don't worry, Dad, I just need a little time to myself, that's all. I'll be fine. I promise."

The evening darkness had set in and the only light shining in Ruth's room came from the street lamp outside her window. Slowly, she rocked back and forth in the chair her grandmother had given her. She watched the shadows of the trees on her wall, swaying gracefully to a peaceful rhythm in the moonlight.

The letter from Hank and the talk with her father left her feeling confused and sad. Her mind drifted back to her father's question: Are you still in love with Hank? Leave it to Dad not to beat around the bush, she thought.

She had been devastated when she and Hank had first broken up; but eventually, she'd jumped back into the swing of things and had gone on with her life. There'd been a few relationships along the way, one in college in particular, but nothing serious had developed—until recently.

David's face appeared before her. Sweet David. Such a wonderful, caring, compassionate, man. The man she intended to marry. David had received a serious leg wound while serving in the army and had been given an early discharge. He returned home to continue his medical practice. Mutual friends had introduced them and right away she could tell what a steady, responsible, committed man Dr. David Phillips was. With him, her life was consistent and secure. He was someone she could count on.

Suddenly, Hank's face appeared before her. She smiled, recalling how they'd met in her junior year of high school. It was fall and Los Angeles was experiencing one of those blazing hot, Indian summer days. Hank had just transferred from a school in New York and for an entire month, all anyone on the high school campus could talk about was the All-City quarterback from back east.

When Ruth first heard about Hank, she was prepared not to like him. She was sure he had to be conceited and muscle-bound between the ears. But all those preconceived notions went out the window when they came face-to-face for the first time. Ruth had looked up at Hank's tall, well-built frame and had batted her eyes in mock admiration. "So you're the big football star from New York," she said with sarcastic innocence.

He looked down at her, knowing she was putting him on, and liked what he saw. With a charming smile he asked her, "Would you like to feel my muscle or would you like me to talk 'New Yawkese'? Or, better still," he said, in a serious tone, "would you like to join me for a Coke so we can get to know each other better?"

Looking at him, Ruth's heart began to beat faster. How handsome he was! He wasn't pretty like Tyrone Power. He was more rugged -like Gary Cooper. With a nod, she stuck out her hand and he shook it enthusiastically. From that moment on, Ruth and Hank were a couple.

Quiet crept in with the night as she continued rocking slowly, lost in her thoughts. Somehow she knew she had to sort out the past to understand what she was feeling now.

One night, after going to the movies, she and Hank decided to go to C.C. Brown's for ice cream sodas. Ruth was still giggling over a scene from the film 'It Happened One Night', starring Clark Gable and Claudette Colbert.

"I loved it that he couldn't hitch a ride with his thumb but when she lifted her skirt, the car came to a screeching halt!" Laughingly, she imitated the sound of the squealing brakes. Getting no response from Hank, she asked in a puzzled voice, "Didn't you think that was funny?"

"Yeah, I did. I thought the picture was great. I just keep thinking about that newsreel they showed." She looked at him blankly, so he continued. "You remember it, don't you? They showed pictures of the Spanish Civil War: the rebels bombing Madrid. All those innocent people getting killed and we could actually see it happen!"

"I agree it's very sad, but that's in Europe—thousands of miles away. They're always fighting with each other over there. It's got nothing to do with us."

"But it has everything to do with us!" Hank shouted, grabbing her arm. "Those German bombers are killing innocent civilians. Don't you see? Adolph Hitler is testing his war machine. And General Franco is his stooge. If they keep this up, how long do you think it will take before he starts shooting at us?"

"Hank, that's ridiculous," Ruth said, shaking her head dismissively. "That funny little man with the stupid moustache, attacking the United States? Come on!"

Hank's expression remained serious. "You can think what you want, but if we don't do something to stop him, he might very well come over here. Did you ever hear of the Abraham Lincoln Brigade?" She shook her head. "Well, it's a group of Americans in Spain, fighting alongside the Spanish Loyalists against Franco and the Fascists. I've been thinking about joining up with them."

"Oh, no!" Ruth gasped, grabbing him by the shoulders. "Are you crazy? You're only seventeen. You have a great future ahead of you. We plan on going to UCLA together, remember? And not only are you going to make the football team, but you're going to be an All-American. Besides, you're a brilliant student. And on top of that, I love you! How can you even think of going to fight in some foreign war?"

Hank's jaw was obstinately set as he listened to her, his eyes avoiding hers. Not getting any response, Ruth wondered if she'd made her point and threw out her trump card. "And furthermore, you are underage and your parents would never give you their consent."

His blue eyes were shining when he turned to face her and she could see he was touched by her passionate outburst. "I love you, too, Ruth," he said in a quiet voice. "It's just that I feel I should be doing something to help. But it's okay. We can talk about this later."

Professor Charles Burkhart cleared his throat, trying to call his Modern History class to order. All semester, he had been battling to keep their interest. Looking around the room at the 36 bright-eyed sophomores, he was finally satisfied that he had their undivided attention.

Speaking in a deep voice that belied his slight build, Prof. Burkhart told them, "History was made yesterday, January 20th, 1941, with the inauguration of President Franklin Delano Roosevelt for an unprecedented third term. War is raging in Europe and the Japanese have stepped up their aggression in the Pacific. The Soviet Union is also under attack. We're sending ships and arms to Great Britain, and many think that Roosevelt is going to lead us into war.

"I'd like to get your thoughts on these current events. But I'd like to have them presented to the class in this way: If you were President Roosevelt, how would you handle the present situation? Please remember to keep your comments brief." Professor Burkhart paused and looked up. "Okay, who'd like to go first?"

Several hands shot up in the air. His eyes rested on the first student to raise his hand. "All right, Mr. Dalton, what would your policy be?"

Fingering his tie and running his hand through his crew-cut hair, Roger Dalton stood up. "I would immediately make Charles Lindbergh my Secretary of State. I would then adopt the platform of 'America First', a patriotic organization that believes in America for Americans. There are two great oceans separating us from the war. I would declare the United States to be neutral and stipulate that we intend to avoid any and all foreign entanglements. We do not need other countries. We're Americans and we should worry about our own country. We should not be fighting for the sake of the communists and international bankers."

The pencil Hank Marshall was playing with snapped between his fingers and he leaped angrily to his feet. "Damn it!" he shouted, his face flushed. "You isolationists! You talk about bankers and communists as though they're one and the same. Don't you know that crazy-man Hitler is saying basically the same thing about those bankers and communists? The only difference is, he calls them Jews, Catholics and gypsies. At least he's open about his hatred!"

Regaining his composure, he turned to the class. "If I were President Roosevelt, I would bring everything out into the open. The Nazis are fighting for world domination. The Italians and Japanese have joined that battle. If we don't fight back now, they'll become much stronger later. What I would do is arm our country to the teeth and declare war on the Axis powers."

A hush had fallen over the room. The other students only knew Hank as the star quarterback of the UCLA Bruins. They never expected to hear such passionate oratory from a man who normally saved his dramatics for the football field.

Professor Burkhart was obviously enjoying the heated exchange from his place at the lectern. His eyes flashed and he tugged at his bristly red beard with a jerky motion. All across the room, hands shot up requesting equal time. But the Professor's eyes searched the room until they came to rest upon the only student not seeking recognition.

"Mr. Matsuda," he said, looking pointedly at his prey with a mischievous grin. "You are an exchange student at our university. Would you care to share your thoughts on this dynamic issue? Perhaps you'd like to comment on what Mr. Marshall had to say."

Yoshikazu Matsuda rose slowly, drawing his slender body to its full height. He looked first at the Professor, then at Hank, his face dispassionate, his eyes blazing. In a clear, controlled voice, he began. "I am here to learn. I am not a political person. But since you have asked me to speak, I will respond.

"Japan is a small country with few natural resources. We are, however, determined to lead Asia into a new era of prosperity. We have no desire for conquest, but we must fight against the colonialism of the Western powers.

"Although Japan and the United States have their differences, there is nothing that cannot be resolved diplomatically. I have come to this country not only to study, but to better understand the United States and its people. All the Japanese people ask is that you make the same effort to understand us.

"If I were your President Roosevelt, I would initiate strong diplomatic action. Then, the problems of the world could be resolved through cooperative negotiation.

"I appreciate the hospitality you have shown me and have great respect for your country. I ask only that Mr. Marshall and the others who think as he does try to understand us and our problems." Bowing slightly, Yoshikazu Matsuda sat down.

Professor Burkhart's eyes roamed the room again, eventually falling upon Ruth's raised hand. "Let's hear what a columnist for our school paper has to say. Miss Morris, if you were President Roosevelt, what would you do?"

Ruth hesitated for several seconds before speaking. "I would not lead the country into isolationism," she said, looking directly at Roger Dalton. "I don't think it's possible for countries, or people, to hold that kind of position in a modern world like this. But I would not declare war either, until I had exhausted all other options.

"I want to know more about the outside world than I do. So, for starters, I would like to interview you, Mr. Matsuda, and find out more about what you have to say."

Sitting down, Ruth looked over at Hank. He stared at her, than shook his head in disapproval.

More hands shot up, some waving anxiously from side to side, begging to be noticed. The Professor beamed. "Well, this has been the best session we've had this semester. It looks like we have opened Pandora's box. Our time is just about up but we'll continue this topic at our next meeting."

Before leaving the classroom, Ruth stopped to talk to Yoshikazu. "Okay, Mr. Matsuda, when can we get together for an interview?"

"Oh, Miss Morris. I appreciate your interest but I do not think the words of one man are important enough to make a difference."

"But Yoshikazu," Ruth said gently, "that's where you're wrong. How will Americans understand your views—and the views of the Japanese people— if you don't express them? Who is going to make your feelings known?"

Yoshikazu looked at her thoughtfully. "Yes, I see your point. And I will agree to do this."

Outside the classroom, in the hall, Ruth found Hank in an animated conversation with Betty Riley and Helen Hunter. Both of whom were giggling over something he'd said. As she approached, she heard Betty say, "0h, Hank, you're really so clever! And we thought you just played football. How come you've never thrown a pass at me?"

"I just did," he laughed.

Walking up behind them, Ruth startled Hank with her acid-toned voice. "Has the pass been completed yet?"

Hank turned to Ruth with a guilty look on his face. Recovering quickly, he said, "Hey, Ruth, do you know Betty and Helen?"

The exchange was awkward and brief. After a few minutes, Helen looked at her watch and said, "Oops, gotta run!" and the two girls retreated down the hall, laughing.

Ruth and Hank walked out of the building and onto the campus in silence. Suddenly, he turned to her and blurted out, "That was a hell of a thing you did!"

"What did I do?" she asked, puzzled. "I thought I was very pleasant to those two floozies."

"They are not floozies and that's not what I meant. I'm talking about your little speech in class—when you spoke up against me and sided with that Japanese guy. I mean everybody knows you're my girlfriend."

"I may be your girlfriend but that doesn't mean I don't have my own ideas."

"Not if they disagree with mine!" he retorted belligerently. "Hey, wait a minute," she countered angrily, "Women got the right to vote years ago. Or is it that I've suddenly become your personal slave? And by the way, which one of those lovely 'ladies' have you been seeing on the side?"

"What are you talking about?" he stuttered.

It had been a shot in the dark but his reaction gave him away. Like a knife aimed at her heart, his next words tore right through her.

"Look, Ruth, he said, his voice sounding strained as he shifted uncomfortably, "You know what I think? I think we need a break from each other."

"Why? So you can share your charm and wit with all the lovely young things at UCLA? Does your ego need that much stroking? I can't believe that because some silly girls paid attention to you, you don't know what to do with yourself. Don't you think guys put the make on me? Because they do—all the time. But I handle it."

"Well, aren't you great," he spat out. "But you know what? You don't have to 'handle it' anymore. You can just do it. In fact, you can do any damn thing you want! Because you and I are finished. Kaput. Done. I feel like I'm suffocating. And I'm gonna get some room to breathe."

Ruth's eyes opened wide and tears stung her eyes. "How long have you felt this way?" she asked at last.

"Long enough," Hank snarled. "Too long, in fact."

A feeling of nausea swept over Ruth, making her feel faint. Taking a deep breath, she turned and with her head held high, walked briskly away.

Ruth's head was throbbing and she realized she was crying just as she had four years before. Squeezing her eyes tightly shut, she tried to block out the memories, but they lingered on.

"Damn you!" she cried out aloud before falling into a dreamless sleep.

CHAPTER FOUR

▼

When Ruth awoke several hours later, it was 2 A.M. and her whole body ached. Easing herself out of the rocking chair, she stiffly made her way to the bathroom, massaging her aching neck and back. Walking over to the sink, she turned on the water. As she waited for it to get warm, she peered at her reflection in the mirror. Ugh, she thought, looking at her swollen face and eyes, this is not a pretty picture.

After washing her face, she changed into her most cuddly nightgown and slid into bed, hoping a comfortable sleep would transform the monster in the mirror back into a normal person. But sleep wouldn't come. The images from the night before kept racing through her head. Now though, it was Yoshikazu Matsuda who took center stage in her thoughts.

About a week after the interview, Ruth had run into Yoshikazu in the library. He was standing at the end of a stack of magazines, holding a book in his hand, frowning down at the title. His American-styled gray slacks, white shirt and black shoes were not enough to disguise the stiff, foreign look about him.

Ruth had walked over to him in her usual straightforward way. "Hi! Nice to see you again," she said, holding out her hand.

Looking up with a startled expression, he fidgeted uncomfortably. Then, recognizing Ruth, he made a half-bow and said shyly, "It is good to see you again as well, Ruth." She looked so cute and friendly in her bobbysocks, pleated plaid skirt, fuzzy white sweater and blond page-boy hairdo. It made him smile.

"Thank you, Yoshikazu. Boy—Yoshikazu, is such a long name. Would it be all right if I called you 'Yoshi' for short?"

"Of course," he smiled.

He's such a nice guy, she thought, studying him from behind her own ready smile. I'd like to get to know him better.

"You know, Yoshi, I was just leaving to grab a bite to eat. If you have time, why don't you come with me to Arnie's hamburger stand. I also have some more questions I'd like to ask you."

Yoshi frowned and looked at her without speaking. Finally, he said, "I thank you for the kind invitation, but I generally bring my own food to school."

Ruth was puzzled. Maybe he couldn't afford to eat out. Or maybe he just wasn't used to the food. "Are you on a special diet of some kind? Or don't you like hamburgers?"

When Yoshi smiled this time, his face went through a remarkable transformation. It was as if a veil had been lifted to reveal an unsuspected warmth.

"To be very honest," he said, "I think they are terrible."

"I knew it!" she laughed. "Not exactly Japanese food, huh?"

"Far from it," he said, joining in her laughter.

"Do you miss being away from your home?"

"There are times that I do," he admitted.

Ruth felt a sudden rush of affection for the young man in front of her. "It must be hard for you—so far from home and in such a different environment. Do you get lonely?"

"Sometimes." Changing the subject quickly, he said, "Your boyfriend, Hank Marshall, is on the football team, isn't he?"

"Well, yes and no. Yes, he's the quarterback on the football team, but no, he's not my boyfriend. Have you ever been to a football game?"

"No, I haven't. I don't really understand the game. And it seems quite brutal."

Oh, but it isn't. I'll tell you what," she proposed. "If you'll promise to take me for a real Japanese dinner, I'll promise to take you to the first football game of next season. Deal?"

"I would be greatly honored. When would you like to have this dinner?"

Thinking of all the lonely nights she'd been spending at home, Ruth said impetuously, "How about this Friday night? Do you know of any restaurants in this area?"

"This Friday would be excellent," he said shyly, looking away. "However, the only restaurants with authentic Japanese food that I know of are in what you call the 'downtown' area."

"That's fine."

"We,ll need to take the trolley,"

Oh, don't worry about that…I have a car. I'll pick you up outside the library at 7:00. Is that okay?"

"That will be fine," Yoshi said with a bow.

"Swell!" she said flashing her biggest smile. "So, I'll see you on Friday, Yoshi."

As they drove downtown from the UCLA campus, Ruth took on the duty of tour guide.

Driving along Sunset Boulevard through Beverly Hills, Ruth said in a nasal tone, "On the right, ladies and gentlemen, is Tyrone Power's house. And on the left is Joan Crawford's." With a quick, sidelong glance, she added, "And immediately in front of us is the home of Mickey Mouse."

"I believe that you are joking with me," Yoshi said.

"Well, his creator, Walt Disney, lives there. Same thing," she grinned.

Ruth turned on Highland Avenue, continuing east on Wilshire Boulevard. Driving through mid-Wilshire area, Ruth pointed out the Coconut Grove nightclub in the Ambassador Hotel. "They have live palm trees with real coconuts growing on them…inside the hotel," she told a fascinated Yoshi. "And the inside of the club is so elegant! There's a stair-case leading down to the dance floor. And they have the most spectacular shows. All the big name talent appears there—Frank Sinatra, Sophie Tucker—you name it!"

Further down the street, Yoshi stared at a large brown building in the shape of a hat. "What does that big hat represent?" he asked, incredulously.

"Why, that's the famous Brown Derby Restaurant," Ruth laughed. "All the stars and show business people eat there. They serve wonderful food—like Waldorf salads and Cobb salads—and there are caricature portraits of their famous customers on the walls. Someday I'll take you there."

As they approached downtown L.A., Yoshi directed Ruth to a small, unpretentious restaurant off First Street. Walking in, Ruth was taken with the strange and exotic odors coming from the kitchen. Inhaling deeply, she told Yoshi, "They sure aren't cooking hamburgers back there!"

The room was already crowded with Japanese patrons. Most of them sat at a long counter, behind which three chefs worked with lightning speed, preparing tantalizing platters.

Ruth noticed all the men were dressed like Yoshi in dark suits, white shirts and thin ties. The two busy waitresses wore plain, dark kimonos. There were only a few other women in the restaurant and most of them wore kimonos, too. Seeing the other patrons made Ruth very conscious of her bright blue pleated skirt and oversized sweater with its large gold "U", set against a white background.

"Yoshi," she said as he led her to a table in the back, "I didn't know I was supposed to dress up."

"I am very pleased with the way you are dressed," he told her gallantly.

Reaching across the table, she took his hand. "Listen, if you and I are going to be friends, we have to level with each other. I know you don't really think I'm dressed properly, but I promise you, the next time I will be."

He gently eased his hand from hers and said, "No, please. I am honored that you are dining with me."

"All right, have it your way," she laughed. "Now, let's get to the important stuff. What are we going to eat?"

"Do you know anything about Japanese food?"

She shook her head. "No, I'm afraid you're going to have to help me."

"Then, if you do not mind, I will be pleased to order for both of us. Are there any foods you do not like?"

"Okra, definitely okra."

"I am not familiar with okra but I don't think it's on the menu." He spoke with great seriousness. "Have you ever eaten raw fish?"

"Raw fish?" she said, crinkling up her nose.

Yoshi smiled indulgently. "I think it will surprise you. In our culture, it is a great delicacy. There are two kinds: sashimi and sushi. Sashimi is the fish by itself. Sushi is fish placed on rice and wrapped in seaweed."

"Seaweed!" she gasped.

He smiled again. "It would please me if you would try a small piece. Then, if you do not like it, we will order something more to your liking."

"Well, I'll try anything once."

"Perhaps you'd like to start with sake, which is a hot wine." As she nodded her consent, Yoshi signaled for the waitress. He spoke to her quickly in Japanese, after which she bowed and left.

"Tell me something about yourself," Ruth said, after Yoshi finished ordering.

"There is not much to tell, really. My father is second in command of the Tosui Trading Company, which was started by my great grandfather. At the proper time, it will be my destiny to take my place within the company."

"Wait a minute. What do you mean, 'destiny'? What if you want to do something else—like become a doctor or a fireman or whatever?"

Yoshi smiled politely. "That is not the way it works in Japan, Ruth. It is destined for me to follow in the footsteps of my family, and I am honored to do that. To better prepare me for that purpose, I have been sent to learn and study at your great university, UCIA."

Ruth giggled. "Great university? Golly, nobody studies here. We just have a blast!"

"What do you mean, a 'blast'?" he asked.

"Well, you know—fun, excitement, parties. Yoshi, this is Los Angeles…Hollywood. We don't take life too seriously here."

The waitress returned and placed a small jar with a little cup in front of each of them.

Oh, how pretty!" Ruth said.

"It is the sake. Allow me to pour it for you. But be careful—it's very hot."

Ruth took a small sip. "It's very interesting."

"Perhaps it is a taste you must get used to," he said. "It is made from fermented rice. It is a little stronger than your grape wines, but not as strong as your liquors."

Yoshi took a sip from his cup. "You said something that I must ask you about. You said you don't take life seriously. But how can that be? Life is a very serious matter. We have many things we must do in this world, and only moments in which to do them."

Before Ruth could respond, the waitress returned, carrying a long, wooden serving block laden with sushi, which she placed on the table.

Wide-eyed, Ruth looked at the feast in front of them. "I guess we have a lot to learn from each other. And I think I'd better start with: How do I eat this stuff?" She lifted the chopsticks next to her plate and stared at them.

"Like this," Yoshi said, reaching over to place her fingers in the proper positions. "Now watch me," he told her as he expertly picked up a piece of shrimp from the platter and popped it in his mouth.

With great concentration, Ruth tried picking up a piece of the tuna sushi. Her hand wobbled and the food fell to the floor.

Laughing, she said, "I sure hope they have plenty of food here, because I think I'm going to waste a lot more than I eat!"

Yoshi smiled. "Perhaps you should eat it the Japanese way, which is to pick it up with your fingers."

She looked at him blankly for a moment before saying, "Oh, you!"

"But I am serious," he told her.

He then showed her how to mix Wasabe, a strange green horseradish paste, with soy sauce and dip the fish into it. With great anticipation, he watched as she tasted the first piece, cautiously lifting it to her mouth and then taking a small bite.

"Why, it's wonderful!" she cried as he smiled with pleasure.

They sat in silence, enjoying their food, until Yoshi spoke. "Forgive me for asking this, Ruth, but in the library, why did you ask me to have lunch with you?"

"Because you are an interesting person, Yoshi, and I'd like to get to know you better. I think it's important to learn about other people -so we can respect each other more. Maybe then, there wouldn't be wars, like the one in Europe."

Ruth hesitated a moment. "Now I have a question for you. Do you think Japan will withdraw from China, like the United States is asking?"

"No, I do not think so."

"But don't you think it would be terrible if our countries went to war?"

He didn't answer, and she wondered if she had offended him.

"I'm sorry," she said. "I don't usually get this serious. Smiling brightly, she added, "So let's move on to more important stuff. Tell me about your love life."

Yoshi's face turned red. "I beg your pardon?"

0h, come on, Yoshi. Tell me about your girlfriends and the kinds of things you do for fun in Japan."

"We, in Japan, do not seek fun. The pleasures we enjoy are those that happen. What we try to do is to bring forth the feelings of tranquility that make one happy. We find contentment in the honor of doing well. It is also of the utmost importance to please one's parents and ancestors."

"Well," she said with a shrug, "East is certainly meeting West. I see it's going to take time for us to really understand each other." She studied him quietly for a moment. "How long have you been at UCLA?

"This is my third year."

"Did you learn to speak English before you came here?"

"I learned at school in Japan, but I've become much more proficient here. I have a real understanding of the language now. And my experiences have been wonderful. I am most anxious to return to Japan and put to use the many things I've learned at UCLA. Your engineering and technology are far more advanced than ours. I am certain that the skills I bring back will be most beneficial to our company and country."

"You're such a responsible person, Yoshi," Ruth said admiringly. "I know my father would like you. He's a doctor and he's always telling me that I should be more responsible."

She drained her cup of sake and held her hand out for a refill. "You know, this stuff is pretty mild but I like it."

"To be truthful, you must be careful. It may seem weak but it is very strong," he said, pouring her more.

Soon Ruth began to feel lightheaded. That, along with the delicious meal and pleasant conversation made her feel very relaxed. Looking across the table at Yoshi, she smiled contentedly as their eyes met. But Yoshi looked quickly down at the table.

"I want to thank you for welcoming me," he said with great politeness, "and for making this one of the most enjoyable evenings I have spent in Los Angeles."

Seeing the embarrassment on Yoshi's face, Ruth thought that perhaps she'd made a mistake or that he'd misinterpreted her friendliness. "Well, I've enjoyed this evening, too. And I know we're going to be great friends."

"I am sure we will," he replied.

Ruth smiled as she remembered that first Japanese dinner they'd shared. A new world had opened up for her. It was as though she had peeled an orange for the first time and once past the bitter outer skin, she could enjoy the sweet fruit concealed inside. The better she got to know Yoshi, the more depth she found within him. Her mind traveled back to that last day they'd spent together.

It was the second week in June and California was experiencing its first heat wave of 1941. With their last class of the day ending at four in the afternoon, Ruth and Yoshi had made plans to catch a five o'clock movie. A new Fred Astaire and Ginger Roger film was showing in Westwood.

"You know what?" said Ruth, after meeting Yoshi in front of Seaton Hall. "It's so hot, let's go to the beach instead. You and I have never been to the beach together."

"To tell you the truth, I have not been to the beach since I have been here. But don't you think it will probably be cooler in an air-conditioned movie theatre?

Ruth took Yoshi's arm and turned him toward her. "What happened to the serious Japanese student I first met? Suddenly, all you want to do is see Fred and Ginger movies. To me, all their movies are the same: boy meets girl; boy loses girl. Then, they kiss and make up with a hundred piece band and a big production number."

Yoshi smiled sheepishly. "You do not appreciate how good American films are. Fred Astaire and Ginger Rogers dance better than any other people in the world. I find it pleasant to escape with them from the harsh realities of the world."

Ruth knew that it was difficult to get Yoshi to change his plans but the hot, steamy day was just made for the beach. "I understand that, Yoshi, but today is such a clear, beautiful day that I'll bet, if we stand on the beach, we'll be able to see Japan from this side of the ocean."

Yoshi burst out laughing at Ruth's outrageous exaggeration, and shook his head in disbelief.

"Well, all right," she continued, "but we will get to see a great sunset. Come on, go put your bathing suit on under your clothes. I'll get the car and pick you up in thirty minutes."

Still, Yoshi hesitated.

"Now, Yoshi, "Ruth teased, "Don't you think it's time I saw your manly physique?"

Yoshi muttered something in Japanese.

"What does that mean?"

Grinning, he said, "It is better that you do not know. Okay, I will be waiting for you in thirty minutes."

Ruth rolled a giant beach towel out on the sand. She quickly removed her wrap-around dress to reveal a form-fitting one-piece bathing suit. Her skin glistened in the sun against the green print swimsuit.

Sitting on the towel, she saw that Yoshi had been admiring her while trying to avert his eyes. And he was still standing stiffly, next to the towel, as though nailed to the sand.

"You are wearing trunks under your pants and shirt, aren't you?" she asked, her eyes dancing.

Looking embarrassed and unsure, he took off his slacks and unbuttoned his shirt, his eyes never leaving her body. Muscles rippled across his wiry frame, revealing a strength that was not visible with his shirt on.

They lay next to each other quietly, letting the warm rays of the sun, penetrate their skin. Ruth had selected this secluded spot between Sunset Boulevard and Malibu Beach for its tranquility. Alone on this section of the beach, their silence was broken only by the sounds of the ocean and the cries of the gulls.

For the first time since she'd broken up with Hank, Ruth felt a deep sense of peace. Lazily, she turned on her side to face Yoshi, who remained on his back. Her eyes ran slowly down his body. Not an ounce of excess flesh, she thought to herself.

Gazing back at his face, she admired his high cheekbones and the creamy brown color of his skin. He blinked as he opened his eyes and turned his head to look at her. Their eyes met.

"You look so peaceful," she said softly.

"This is a most serene moment," he replied.

"Are you in love with the girl you're engaged to marry?" Ruth heard herself asking.

Yoshi looked surprised at this personal question. "Love has no bearing on our marriage. Our match was arranged many years ago by our fathers. It will unite our two houses and produce one of the most powerful companies in Japan."

"But don't you feel any…passion for her?" Ruth persisted.

Yoshi thought for a moment before answering slowly. "There is an old Japanese proverb: "Those who came together in passion, remain together in tears. Passion, like love, is a transitory emotion."

Lifting himself up on his elbow, Yoshi faced her squarely. "Are you not still in love with Hank?"

"Whoa! You sure come back fast," Ruth said, shaking her head. "But that is a fair question. I thought I was."

She placed her hand gently on Yoshi's shoulder and let it slide slowly down his arm. "But now I'm not so sure."

Jumping to her feet, Ruth said, "Let's go in the water."

Reaching down, she pulled Yoshi to his feet, and they ran into the ocean, splashing through the waves.

With powerful strokes, Yoshi swam out from the shoreline. Looking over his shoulder, he saw Ruth matching him stroke for stroke. They cut through the water in silence for about a mile until he noticed that Ruth had begun to lag behind. With a smile, Yoshi turned back toward the shore, slowing his pace so she could keep up.

When they returned to where they could stand, Yoshi turned to Ruth and said, "You are a very good swimmer."

"You're not so bad yourself," she panted back.

They stood in the wet sand with the water frothing above their ankles. Suddenly, a giant wave cascaded around them, knocking Ruth off balance. Yoshi grabbed her, lifting her easily above the swirling water. Ruth felt as if she were on air. She put her arms around Yoshi's neck as he carried her back to the towel, gently laying her down. Gracefully, Yoshi lowered his body and lay down beside her, smiling. Ruth searched his face. What strength it showed, what confidence, she thought.

Finally, in a tiny voice, Ruth asked, "Yoshi, how can you marry someone you don't love?"

"It is my duty," he replied. "One's loyalty is to one's *ie*."

He paused, drawing circles in the sand with his finger.

"*Ie* is a difficult word to translate. It is like a house, in that it means both family and dwelling. The same way the English refer to the House of York, for instance. It is our duty is to honor our ancestors through our deeds and to provide children to carry on our traditions."

"But what if your choice is different than your parents? What if you love someone else?"

"Those things do not matter. It is my duty to honor my father's commitment."

The sun had begun to set, casting a torrent of colors across the sky. Slowly, the light began to disappear, giving way to the insistent darkness.

Ruth sighed as she looked out at the shimmering ocean. "It must be so easy when everything is planned out for you."

"It is easier than your way," he whispered, as he looked into her troubled eyes. "Your way is very confusing. Being in love seems to be so exhausting. Strong emotions like that must be difficult to keep under control."

"Well, I guess you'll never know," Ruth said with a shrug. "You don't believe in love."

"No, I did not say that. I said it is not considered to be a sufficient enough reason for marriage. I am a first son in the house of Matsuda. In turn, I must produce a son with a bloodline that will do honor to my ancestors. Someone who will carry on our traditions."

"That's the way we breed our dogs," Ruth snapped.

Yoshi leaped to his feet, his eyes blazing.

Jumping up beside him, Ruth cupped his face in her hands. "Oh, Yoshi! I'm so sorry!" she said in a pleading voice, pain evident in her eyes. "I don't know how I could have said such a thing. Please forgive me!"

Gliding his face toward hers, she kissed him on each cheek and then on his forehead, before letting her warm, moist lips settle on his mouth. Drawing her close in a fiery embrace, Yoshi's lips hungrily met hers. With his hands, he slid the straps of her bathing suit from her shoulders, lowering them until he could feel her cool, firm breasts against his chest.

Ruth sighed deeply. She opened her mouth and slid her tongue into Yoshi's mouth, searching until it found his. Roughly, he guided her down on the towel beside him, slipping her bathing suit down below her waist, her knees and finally, pulling it from her feet.

Breathing harder, she reached for him, pulled his trunks off, and then drew him inside her with a low moan that turned into a long sigh.

The full moon shone brightly on the horizon, caressing the dark and quiet ocean. A line of the moonslight reflected off the water and seemed to make a path to the two solitary figures lying on the beach. A warm breeze ambled over them as they held each other, talking quietly.

"Oh, Yoshi," Ruth whispered, "I wish I could hold this moment forever."

"But we know that is not possible," he answered as he stroked her hair. "The tide cannot be reversed and time cannot be stopped. Everything must change. It is the way of nature. There is a Japanese haiku—a short poem—that explains it well: The morning glory, even as I paint, it fades away."

Oh, how beautiful! And how sad!" Ruth cried.

"Beauty is as fleeting as life," he said, lifting a handful of sand and tossing it into the air. "Each moment is important, because a moment later it is gone, never to return."

Holding her more tightly in his arms, he kissed her gently.

Ruth felt as if she were floating in space. Sitting with Yoshi in the shelter of his arms, made her feel that at last she'd found safety in her world. But that feeling of security quickly disappeared with the next words he spoke.

"Ruth," he said in a quiet voice, "I must return to Japan tomorrow."

She repeated his words, incredulously. "Return to Japan tomorrow? But why?"

"Because those are the instructions from my father, and I must obey."

"But why must you go? Why now?"

"Because I must," he answered, his face taut and determined. "It is very difficult for me to leave you now but there is nothing that I can do."

Ruth struggled to keep back her tears, but it was impossible.

"But you haven't answered my question. Is it because of what's going on between America and Japan? Are we going to war with each other? Is that why you have to leave?" There was a desperate sound in her voice as tears streamed down her cheeks.

"We cannot speak of this," Yoshi said, stiffly. "I cannot predict what the future holds. Until this day, I had no doubts as to my destiny. My future was determined long ago."

Ruth looked at him as though he were a stranger, but Yoshi did not seem to notice.

"I must follow my father's instructions," he continued. "The arrangements have been made. I will leave tomorrow."

That was the last time Ruth saw Yoshi. But the memory had not dimmed.

CHAPTER FIVE

▼

"At least the ones I had to fight was white and Christian," the elderly driver said, hunching over the steering wheel, his scraggly gray beard almost touching it, as he squinted at the road ahead. "Vicious bastards! Gimme the Germans any day. With these yeller Japs, ya can't know what to expect. Can't trust em. Pearl Harbor proved that. Sure did."

Hank said nothing. His blue eyes remained transfixed on the road ahead, wavering in the headlights.

"You shipping out soon?" asked the driver with a sidelong glance at his passenger.

"Can't say."

Lifting his watch, he saw it was 8 P.M. His orders told him to report to Air Transport Command on August 10th, 1945, at ten o'clock for a flight back to Saipan.

"Here you go," the driver said, pulling to a stop outside the Hickham Field gates. "You go get em, Lieutenant."

"Thanks for the ride," said Hank. He gave a little salute as he got out of the pickup. Standing in the road, he watched the car's tail-lights disappear as it pulled away.

Hank had been on leave in Honolulu since August 1st and had just started to unwind. But now he felt the familiar knot forming in his stomach, just as it always did before he flew. He dreaded the thought of going out on another mission. It brought forth the same anxiety pangs—only worse. He had survived twenty-seven missions, but time was running out. It was like he was speeding along a highway and fate, like a highway patrolman, was waiting to pull him over.

Hank thought about the woman he'd been with the night before—a little redhead with an infectious giggle. Helen or Helene, something like that. He'd taken the wings off his chest and handed them to her, not telling her he bought them by the dozens for just that purpose. She'd been appropriately touched and had led him by the hand to the hotel across the street. There, he made love with a desperation he hadn't felt before. She delightedly mistook his ardor for passion, not realizing he was driven by the fear of not knowing the soft, tender flesh of a woman again.

At one point while she slept, her hair brushing against his neck, Hank stared up at the moonlit shadows on the ceiling and tried to picture every woman he'd ever been with. It was as if he was telling himself he was lucky—that at 22, he'd had more than his share and should be satisfied, even if he died tomorrow.

As far as his buddies were concerned, Hank carried on the barrack's tradition. Women were there for one purpose only. Each time he returned from a foray in town, Hank was met with the inevitable question: "Did you get laid?" He played the game by remaining silent, allowing a blissful smile to cross his lips. This would bring on a series of raucous sounds, knowing winks and slaps on the back.

In truth, however, after his conquests, Hank felt drained and empty. Once, he'd thought he was in love, but that was a long time and twenty-seven gut wrenching missions ago.

Well, he thought, moving on at last, a two-mile hike across the base to the Bachelor Officer's Quarters should give plenty of time for depressing thoughts. He nodded at the guards, showed them his pass, and walked through the gate with his valise swinging lightly in his hand.

Gravel crunched beneath his feet and the sweet smell of flowers thickened the humid air. This leave had been a welcome relief after the last seven months. The beauty of Hawaii with its festive luaus and sensual music had been a breath of fresh air after the drabness of the base in Saipan. How they all loved it when the beautiful native girls rushed up to them on the beach, placing sweet-smelling leis around their necks as waves lapped against the sand.

Hank had first arrived in Saipan in January. He recalled an experience he'd had right after he was assigned his bunk. While unloading his gear, travel-lagged and bleary-eyed, he'd noticed a note on the wall. The inscription, in big, loopy handwriting, said:

"Arrived—November 15, 1944. Departed—?"

Hank remembered looking at the navigator lying on the bed next to his. The man's hands were clasped behind his head and he was staring up at the ceiling. "What happened to him?" Hank asked, nodding toward the note.

The navigator turned his head and looked briefly at the wall before resuming his upward stare. "Departed," he said.

"Home?" asked Hank hopefully.

Nope, just departed."

A jeep shot past him and the sound of lighthearted laughter drifted back in the clouds of dust. Stepping off the road, Hank began to walk across the field. This is Hawaii he reminded himself. This is a lifetime away from Saipan and the skies of Japan. And I still have a couple of hours left to enjoy it.

Suddenly, Hank was engulfed in light. He became disoriented for a moment, then realized that all the lights on the base—floodlights, barracks, mess lights—had come on, all in the same second.

A booming voice shot over the loudspeakers: "Attention all military personnel! Attention! The war has just ended! The Japanese have surrendered. All orders are canceled. Stay where you are. Repeat. The war is over! All orders are canceled. All military personnel stay where you are and you will be given new orders."

Hank stayed where he was as ordered. He stood on the closely cropped, brightly illuminated grass and he felt his shoulders begin to shake. It took him a minute to realize he was crying, but he couldn't stop the tears. The face of his brother, Peter, flashed through his mind and a sob escaped his lips. A stab of pain shot through him when he remembered he would never see him again. But Hank was going to live, by God! He was going to live!

He brushed his tears away and with a jaunty step, walked back along the road, wondering how long it would take-to be demobilized so he could go home. He could see himself back in Los Angeles, enjoying all the luxuries of home. He thought about good food, a comfortable bed, privacy, his family and friends—a world without fear.

His reverie was quickly shattered by the squealing tires of a jeep pulling up beside him. Burning rubber was accompanied by hysterical laughter.

"Hop in, Lieutenant. We're off to a celebration party!" said the Colonel behind the wheel. A beautiful blond nurse sat beside him, her red lips curved in a welcoming smile.

"Boy, am I ever ready!" Hank said, clambering in and sitting down behind the nurse.

From the flush on the Colonel's face, Hank could see that he'd already had a fair amount to drink. This was confirmed when the colonel handed Hank a small silver flask with one hand while driving with the other. "We sure beat the sons-of-bitches!" the colonel exclaimed exuberantly.

"It's the best news I've heard in all my life," Hank answered, uncapping the flask. He recognized the smell of good scotch and took a healthy swallow. "Hank Marshall's my name," he said, passing the flask back.

"John Foxboro. And this is Mary Beth Page. Say hello to the nice man, Mary Beth."

"Hello, nice man," Mary Beth said in a sultry, husky voice. Looking at Hank more closely, she asked, "Did you say Hank Marshall?"

"Yes."

"Oh, no," she said excitedly. "Did you play football for UCLA?"

"Yes I did, before the war."

"Oh, God! I can't believe it! I saw you play! The game against Oklahoma in 1941!"

"You're kidding!" he said feeding on her enthusiasm. "Well, I'm very pleased to meet you."

"What a small world," she said, extending her hand.

As Hank took it, she wiggled her index finger against his palm—an encouraging sign, Hank thought.

"He was a quarterback," she said, turning to John Foxboro. "An All American at UCLA. Really great!"

"Well, I don't know..." Hank began, modestly.

"Are you going to play football when you get back?" she interrupted. "You could probably play in the pros now."

"Well, I'd kinda planned on that. Unfortunately though, I had to make a forced landing during training in Texas and my back and knee aren't football material anymore."

"Oh, I'm so sorry!"

"Thanks," he said, twisting in his seat to get a better look at her. She appeared to be in her late twenties, tall,—maybe 5'9" or 10", with legs like a colt and a sensuous, wide-lipped mouth. Foxboro seemed to be about her height, in his thirties—thickening around the middle and thinning around the forehead. He drove with total disregard for the road, turning his head constantly to talk to them.

"I don't think I'm looking forward to civilian life," Foxboro announced. "After four years in the service, I don't think I'll be able to stand it."

"Well, I can't wait," Hank and Mary Beth said in unison, looking at each other, smiling conspiratorially.

"Think about it," Foxboro said, hardly hearing them. "No more Uncle Sam telling you what time to get up, what time to go to bed, what time to die. No more Uncle Sam feeding you, clothing you, paying you. Guy's gonna have to think for himself!"

He shook his head sadly, swerving over to the center of the road before righting the jeep again.

"Well, you could stay in the army," Hank suggested.

"Believe me, I'm thinking about it. There'll always be something for us to do." He swerved again, this time onto a road leading past a row of bungalows.

He quickly stopped in front of the largest one. "Son-of-a bitch!" he shouted. "They started the party without us!" He jumped out of the jeep, leaving Hank to help Mary Beth out.

Hank's assessment of her height had been accurate, he noticed as she stepped out and thanked him with her wide-lipped smile. He also noticed that she outranked him. She was a captain.

Light poured from the windows of the bungalow. Big band swing played on a radio or phonograph, and every now and then a female shriek or a burst of laughter would rise above the sound.

These bungalows, Hank knew, were reserved for Washington brass—State Department officials, generals and other high-ranking officers—flying between Washington and Honolulu.

Going inside, they saw a dozen or so men and women, dancing or just talking. The women in attendance were civilians, except for one other nurse. And aside from Hank and Mary Beth, the lowest ranking officer there was Foxboro, a colonel.

As Foxboro towed Hank towards the bar, Hank noticed with an appreciative eye that the scotch was Haig & Haig Pinch. He poured a glass, took a sip and savored it slowly and appreciatively. Only after they both had glasses in hand did Foxboro introduce him to the others.

A stocky general in his fifties with closely cropped gray hair introduced himself as Parker. Looking at Hank's pilot wings, General Parker asked, "What kind of plane are you flying?"

"B-29, off Saipan."

"That's a pretty shitty place."

"Well, General, you can be sure that we don't get good scotch like this!" said Hank, lifting his glass.

"Did you fly in the February raid on Tokyo?" the general asked.

"Yes, Sir. We could see Tokyo burning from 250 kilometers out at sea."

"Curtis LeMay's brainstorm," the general said to two desk-bound officers who were listening. "Caught the Japs sleeping, right, Lieutenant?"

Hank nodded. "I heard that something like 25 square miles of Tokyo disappeared."

Mary Beth and another woman joined the group. "Did you ever get hit, Hank?" Mary Beth asked.

"The plane always got hit," he said casually, "but I never did."

"Was Tokyo the toughest target?" another General asked.

"No, Sir. I would say that had to be the Mitsubishi Aircraft Plant, eight miles outside of Tokyo," Hank answered without hesitation. "Number 3-5-7."

"Number 3-5-7?" Mary Beth questioned.

"Targets have numbers—code," General Parker explained.

Hank sipped at his scotch. Men had actually fallen to the floor when 3-5-7 was announced as the target.

"But it's all over now, no need to think about it anymore," said Hank, draining his glass. "But even if I do forget the number, I'll never forget the song we used to sing. It went to the tune of 'Meet Me In St. Louis, Louie'."

"Let's hear it!" said the General.

Hank made a half-bow toward the two women. "You'll have to excuse me, ladies," he said, before launching into song:

"Meet me over 3-5-7. We will soon be there. Don't tell me the bombs are falling any place near there. We won't get back to Saipan 'Cause Wing fucked up the flight plan. So meet me over 3-5-7. We will soon be there."

Everybody clapped loudly and there were whistles and foot-stompings.

Mary Beth had been hanging on his every word. Impulsively, she touched his hand and said, "Well, I for one am glad you made it, Hank."

Hank smiled but noticed John Foxboro watching her with narrowed eyes and tightly-pursed lips.

Hank looked at his empty glass and said disarmingly to Foxboro, "Join me in another drink, colonel?"

Foxboro gave him a hard stare. "You fly boys sure like taking center stage, don't you?"

"We're just here to entertain," Hank answered lightly. He put his arm around the colonel's shoulders. "Now, how about that drink?"

Foxboro's face softened. "Sure, why not? War's over, right?"

"Sure thing," Hank replied.

At the bar, he poured a scotch for Foxboro and another for himself. Looking up, he saw General Carter making his way over.

"Don't put that bottle down," the general commanded.

Obligingly, Hank poured him a drink. Lifting his glass, Carter toasted, "To the next war!"

Mary Beth had just joined them. She listened, not saying a thing.

"What war are you talking about?" Hank asked.

"The Commies, son, the Commies," Carter said. "We've beaten the Japs and the Germans. Now, we have to go after the Russians—show them who we are."

"I thought they were our allies."

"Obviously, son, you don't understand. They've been the problem all along. Still are. They're next in line: the next enemy."

Hank placed his glass carefully on the bar. "General, this soldier doesn't want another enemy."

"You don't have a choice, soldier," Carter replied.

"Well, general, this soldier's had it. I don't know where you're headed but I'm getting out of the Air Force and into civilian life. I am not looking for another war. In fact, I plan on trying to forget about this one just as quickly as I can."

"You don't have to go looking for a war, son, because it's staring us right in the face."

Hank fought down his anger. It was over, goddammit! And the sooner everyone realized it, the better. "You know, general," he said, his voice sounding calmer than he felt, "when the Japs attacked Pearl Harbor, I hated every one of the bastards. I flew twenty-seven missions against them and nearly got killed every time. And one thing is for certain—I am not gonna turn around and start fighting Russians. As far as I'm concerned, they're our allies. And I am going home!"

The general listened to Hank's comments with surprising good humor. "Look, son, nobody's denying you did a helluva job, but you've got a lot to learn."

"General, perhaps you should go take a look at the boys I'm nursing. Or what's left of them anyway," chimed in Mary Beth, unable to control her anger any longer. "You might just learn something."

The general held up his hands in mock surrender. "I believe I'm out-numbered," he laughed.

"And I believe we should dance," Hank said, taking Mary Beth's hand and leading her to the dance floor.

"I'm sorry," she said as he took her in his arms. "It's over, isn't it? So it doesn't matter what he says."

"Yes, it's over," Hank whispered in her ear.

"I'll Be Seeing You" came on the record player. Almost immediately, Mary Beth began to relax, losing herself in the music's slow rhythm. Hank could feel her hair upon his cheek, her warm body moving sensually against his. Cupping her hand between their chests, he felt the top of her soft breast. As they moved together, Hank was filled with an indescribable sense of well-being. Yes, it was over, and he was about to start a new life. There was a whole world out there waiting to be conquered—and he knew he could do it. In fact, he could do anything!

Lowering his head, he whispered in her ear, "I think we should go out-side and see what the stars look like."

Mary Beth glanced over her shoulder and saw that John Foxboro had his back to them. "Okay, soldier!" she said, giggling delightedly.

They'd hardly made it down the hallway and out the back door when Hank took her in his arms. He kissed her fervently on the lips, his hands running down her back, tracing the lines of her body.

"Hey, hold on," she said, breaking away, her breath ragged. "You know I came with John."

"Yes, I know," he said.

She smiled up at him. "And you know you can't use that old line about going back to war and maybe not coming back."

Hank laughed. "I'm afraid you're much too sharp for me."

Then, cradling her face in his hands, he said, "You know, I may have been pretty damn sure of myself before, but I don't feel that way right now. Would you like me to tell you how I feel?"

But instead of answering, Mary Beth placed her hand behind his head and gently guided it down to meet her upturned face. As they kissed, her mouth opened and her tongue moved slowly and invitingly between his lips.

When they finally parted, she looked at him for what seemed to be a long time. Then, taking his hand, she led him back through the house into a small bedroom just off the hall.

Locking the door behind them, she leaned against it, her pretty face flushed, and said, "Okay, soldier, let's see how well you fly."

An hour later, Hank peered out into the hallway. Seeing it was empty, he stepped out of the room, closed the door behind him and walked briskly back to the party.

At least a dozen more people had arrived. The room was filled with smoke and the smell of cigars. And the music was louder, the dancing more frenetic.

Shouldering his way past two generals involved in an energetic, arm-waving discussion, he leaned against the bar and poured himself another scotch-on-the rocks.

"Hey, good-looking," said an attractive brunette standing next to him, "I'll take one of those."

She appeared to be a civilian. And although she was already slurring her words, Hank poured her a drink.

"I'm Janice," she said after a healthy swallow. "And who in hell are you?"

As he was about to answer, John Foxboro appeared on his other side. "Hey, Lieutenant," he said in a belligerent tone, "where have you been? I haven't seen you or Mary Beth for quite a while."

"You haven't?" Hank replied, smiling innocently. "Well, Colonel, I'm sorry I can't help you. I've been out looking at the stars. Hey, this is some kind of party, isn't it?"

Foxboro swayed drunkenly as he glared suspiciously at Hank. He was about to say something else when he caught sight of Mary Beth on the other side of the room. She was laughing animatedly at a burly general.

"Oh, there. Never mind," Foxboro muttered, heading off unsteadily.

"So, who are you?" Janice repeated.

"Oh, sorry. I'm Hank Marshall."

She gave him a blunt, appraising look. "Here alone?" she asked seductively.

For a moment, Hank was tempted. But looking at his watch, he saw that it was 3 A.M. "Just leaving," he said, pleasantly. "Enjoy the party."

"Cheers," she said, lifting her glass to hide her disappointment.

Walking across the room, Hank saw that Mary Beth was still talking to the general, but had her arm entwined with John Foxboro's. Hank waved to her as he headed toward the door. She winked back.

Outside it was still warm. The night was clear and filled with what seemed to be a million blinking stars. Although it was a three-mile hike back to his quarters, Hank didn't mind. In fact, he couldn't have felt much happier. The future seemed to stretch out ahead of him as limitlessly as the stars. He was now ready to resume what he called his "real life."

The next day, the Officer's Club at Hickham Field, Hawaii, bore the signs of the wild party the night before. Hundreds of glasses and bottles littered the tables, floor and bar.

Huddled in a corner of the Club were four of the airmen who were to have reported back to Saipan. Although it was only noon, the table in front of them held fourteen empty beer bottles—the contents of which had been consumed within the past hour.

Hank looked at his co-pilot, bombardier and navigator as if for the first time. A year of training and almost another full year of combat had welded them into a finely tuned machine. And now, after all they'd shared together, they'd soon be parting ways.

"You guys are the greatest!" Hank sputtered, his speech slurred.

"Let's not get fuckin' sentimental," called out Bubba Rice, the burly co-pilot from Alabama. Using the back of his hand, he quickly wiped a tear from his eye, hoping no one had seen him.

"You're right on target again, Bubba," said Howard Rogers, the tall, thin navigator. "Hey, Bubba...remember when the chaplain came to see us before we left the States? He offered to bless the plane and you said, 'Ain't no one gonna bless my fuckin' plane except me!' Remember the look on his face?"

They all laughed, remembering the look on the poor, bewildered, chaplain's face as he stuttered for an answer to such an outrageous statement.

Rick Smith, the little bombardier, stood up to his full five foot frame, and aimed a mock machine gun around the room. "How 'bout when I strafed our own airfield while we were sitting on the ground? I was only testing the guns. Didn't know the fucking things were loaded"

"Maybe you thought the guns weren't loaded, you little asshole, but you definitely were," Bubba chided.

"All right, all right," said Rick, laughing. "Let's get serious for a minute. Now that the war is over, what are you guys gonna do? For me, it's the family plumbing business in good old Cleveland."

Bubba stretched out his arms and grinned from ear to ear. "First, I'm gonna go home and shack up with that little old gal I married. Then, I'm gonna tie one on for about two months. After that, I'll start my own flying business…probably crop-dusting."

Howard straightened up and looked imperiously at the other three. "I am going back to Boston, the birthplace of civilization. Then, on to Harvard and to law school. They're talking about free education for G.I.'s…sounds real good to me. And what about you, Hank?"

Hank thought for a moment. "You guys wanna talk seriously? Okay, I'll tell you exactly what I think. I think we are the luckiest guys in the world—just to be alive. Right now, I hate every Jap in the world, but I expect that will pass.

"I've been thinking that I might want to get into international business. Maybe travel around the world. I expect it'll be a lot more fun to do it as a civilian than it was in uniform."

Looking around the table again, he added, "And I want to say something else: I love each of you guys. Thanks for keeping me alive."

And before any of the others could respond, he called out, "Let's have another beer!"

CHAPTER SIX

───────────▼───────────

1946

Hank Marshall sat quietly at the bar of one of his favorite hangouts, the Melody Lane. The somber look on his face belied the party atmosphere taking place around him. The room was centered around a large, seductive circular bar. Bright white stars danced on the sky blue ceiling above. The walls, painted the same shade of blue, were highlighted by a series of white musical scales. Big Band music played loudly in the background while the bartenders, moving to the rhythm, mixed standard and exotic drinks with equal flair.

Hank lifted his glass to indicate he was ready for a refill.

"Hey, Captain, what happened to that great uniform of yours? The one with all the ribbons?" asked the slender bartender as he placed a fresh scotch on the rocks in front of Hank. "And that hat? With the fifty mission crush?"

"I'm just a civilian now," Hank answered, taking a sip of his drink. "Just another face in the crowd. What's wrong? Don't you like my civies?"

Extending his arms, he showed off the bright colors of his new Glen Plaid suit. His voice was far less enthusiastic than his attire.

It had been a tough day for Hank. His first two job interviews had been disasters. For the past seven years, he'd grown used to being treated with instant respect. As the star quarterback at UCLA and an

All-American in his last year there, he had been the toast of the campus and the sports world.

Then, as a highly decorated B-29 pilot, he'd arrived home in a wave of adulation. His first four months in Los Angeles following his return had been a blur of heavy drinking parties and heavy-breathing women.

But coming home had been a tough experience. After those first jubilant days, Hank had quickly realized that staying with his parents for any length of time was not an option. His father, Sid, was hoping that Hank would be joining him in the family business. He was proud of every woman's blouse he manufactured.

Although Hank loved and admired his father, he knew he could never find fulfillment in women's blouses. He chuckled inwardly as he thought of what a transition it would be to go from flying combat missions to making ladies ready-to-wear. He'd felt a pang of regret though, after telling his father he wouldn't be joining him in the business and seeing the look of disappointment in his father's eyes.

All through Hank's homecoming, Sid and Shirley Marshall had tried their best to act cheerful. But there was always an underlying sadness behind their smiles. The loss of Peter, their firstborn, was almost more than they could bear. The shock from the War Department's dreaded telegram was still too fresh to fade—if it ever would.

Hank sipped his drink slowly, letting the liquor's warmth flow through him. He loved his family and was proud of what they'd achieved. Sid Marshall had long been a shining example to his two sons. Immaculate and stylishly dressed, he stood tall at 5'8", sporting a rakish, well-waxed moustache.

Sid made the long journey to the United States on an immigrant ship, never letting the dirty, crowded, wind-tossed conditions overcome his optimism. He often spoke of the lump that had come to his throat when the ship had passed the Statue of Liberty. The hunger and discomfort he had known were no longer important as he anticipated the great opportunities that were waiting for him in America.

As Sidney Moskovitz was processed through Ellis Island, an immigration official renamed him Sidney Marshall. He was just sixteen years old and barely understood English. He happily accepted the name change with a grateful smile: anything for the privilege of gaining admittance to the United States of America.

Hank tilted his glass and the hawkeyed bartender immediately poured him another drink. This was his first day out of uniform. His long anticipated joy at shedding his military clothing had quickly faded. The glamorous war hero had quickly become just another guy in civilian clothes, hardly distinguishable from the millions of other veterans flooding the schools and job market.

For the first time since entering the bar two hours before, Hank took notice of the other patrons perched on stools around him. The Melody Lane had a well earned reputation as a great pick-up joint. In uniform, he'd been the center of attention. Now, he realized, none of the women seated there had approached him. Since he wasn't much interested in striking up a conversation, it didn't really bother him. Tonight, for the first time in years, he wanted to be left alone.

Hank felt his face starting to grow numb—a signal that it was time to stop drinking. Without a glance or word to anyone, he paid his bill and left.

The next morning, Hank woke up squinting at the bright sunlight streaming through his window. "Another great day in paradise," he muttered through puffy lips. It was one of those glorious, Los Angeles winter days when the sun sparkled and the air was crisp and clean.

As usual, Hank had not slept well. He kept falling asleep, than waking with a start, his body bathed in sweat. His dreams were filled with whining engines and B-29 formations cutting through the Japanese sky. Enemy fighters would follow him, darting in and out with guns blazing. Huge bursts of flak exploded closer and closer to his plane. He heard eerie noises resounding from the explosions—like whispers saying, "I wantcha…I'll getcha."

In his dream at the height of the action, Peter's face appeared. "Everything is under control, little brother. Stay cool. You'll make it," his brother had said with a smile.

Then, suddenly, Peter had shouted, "Hard right!" Hank yanked at the controls—but nothing happened. He could feel himself losing control as the plane plunged downward. It was his own screams of anguish that awakened him, causing him to bolt upright in his bed. With shaking hands, he reached for a cigarette.

Later, feeling calmer, he put out his cigarette and fell into another restless sleep. A procession of women now paraded in front of him. He rubbed his eyes as he recognized each one—remembering the time they'd spent together. They all looked so sexy and smart, he wanted to reach out and touch them. But when he tried, he ended up with only a handful of air.

In his dream he tried to talk to them, but no sound came out. They just continued walking by, eyes staring straight ahead, neither seeing or hearing him. Reaching for the last girl in the line, he was surprised he could feel her soft flesh. She turned and looked him in the face.

"Hank," she whispered.

"Ruth," he cried out, realizing he had a voice once again. "I can see and feel you!"

"I've always been near you, Hank. I've been able to hear you, but you could not hear me."

"Ruth!" he shouted, as she faded into the night. "Come back! It was all a mistake!"

Again he awoke, shaking and sweating.

Without thinking, Hank reached for the phone on the nightstand and hastily dialed the number he hadn't called in four years.

"Hello," answered the male voice at the other end of the receiver.

"May I speak to Ruth, please?"

"Ruth doesn't live here. Who's calling?"

Hank paused for a second. "Is this Dr. Morris?"

"Yes," was the stern reply. "Who is this?"

"This is Hank Marshall, Dr Morris. It's important that I get in touch with Ruth."

"Why?" asked the voice on the other end. "Haven't you done enough damage?"

"Dr. Morris, that was four years ago. And I really must speak to Ruth. Please tell me how I can reach her. It's very important."

There was a long pause. "O.K., Hank, it's not up to me to monitor her calls. Give me your number and I'll pass it on to her. But if she does call you back and you do any thing to hurt her, you'll have to deal with me."

"I understand, Sir,"

Dr. Morris' voice softened. "I heard you flew combat in the Pacific. Are you all right?.

"It depends on what you mean by 'all right'. But, yes, I'm okay."

He gave Ruth's father his number. "And please, Sir, tell her that it's important that she get in touch with me right away."

CHAPTER SEVEN

▼

The sharp ring of the phone pierced the stillness of Hank's room. He had been daydreaming—lost in the memories of his carefree days at school four years before. Though it seemed like a century ago, he could picture those days so clearly, they could have been just yesterday.

Once again, he was playing football on strong knees. Later, he was holding Ruth's hand under the table at Arnie's as they sipped hot chocolate. He could see her watching him, her big eyes absorbing every word he said. Their talk would range from football to their plans for traveling around the world together. They both wanted to see all the far-off places they'd read about or caught glimpses of in the movies. Hank loved watching Ruth. Her whole face would come alive when she spoke.

On the third ring, Hank picked up the phone. A familiar voice echoed in his ear.

"Hank, how are you? Are you O.K.? My father phoned me at work and told me that you called."

"Ruth!" Hank cried, "It's so good to hear your voice! Yeah, sure, I'm okay. I'm not in any trouble but I have to see you."

"If you're okay, why do you have to see me? Why now? After all these years? What do you want? What's the point of…"

He interrupted her with urgency in his voice. "I must see you as soon as possible. Please, can we meet for lunch? Some place where we can talk? I'll even buy." He hoped his attempt at humor would bring back memories of happier times.

"Well," she said, beginning to yield. "Okay, 12:30 on Third and Bixel. It's a small restaurant—called Dave's Place."

At 12:15, Hank was waiting in a small booth at the back of the restaurant. He was dressed in his uniform, replete with shiny captain's bars, wings and battle ribbons. He'd agonized all morning over what to wear: his Glen Plaid suit or his form fitting uniform. Knowing how imposing he looked in his military regalia, he had decided on that. Besides, he reasoned, it would give Ruth a chance to see him in uniform.

This was one of the few times in his life that Hank felt insecure. He wasn't sure how he was going to handle things. He sat at the table, deep in thought, staring at his cup of coffee.

He looked up and suddenly, there she was. she was wearing a trim business suit that couldn't hide her feminine softness. Dark blonde hair cascaded over her beautiful but unsmiling face.

Hank jumped from his seat to shake her hand, touching her shoulder softly. "Ruth, it's so good to see you! You look great!" he told her, as she sat down quietly across from him.

Looking at her, a torrent of words came to his mind, but he was unable to say anything. Instead, they both sat and looked at each other curiously, for the first time in four years.

After what seemed an eternity, Ruth said in a cold, steady voice, "Hank, why did you call me?"

"Because I had to see you," he replied. They were interrupted by the waitress who'd come over with menus in hand. "Would you like coffee?" she asked Ruth.

"Yes, please."

They waited quietly as the waitress poured fresh coffee for Ruth and refilled Hank's cup. She stood there waiting as their silence continued, rolling her eyes and tapping her foot.

"Are you interested in ordering anything else?" the waitress asked.

"I'll have a fruit salad," Ruth said.

"And I'll have a hamburger," said Hank.

"Well, that's terrific, isn't it?" the waitress said, with a sarcastic smile before retrieving the menus and walking away.

At last, Ruth spoke. "All these years, not a call, not a letter." Her tone was icy. "On December 8th, the day after Pearl Harbor, I called you. I felt I had to talk to you because I knew you'd enlist. You told me you had joined the Air Force and would leave after the semester ended. Then, I never heard from you again, only silence." Her composure began slipping as painful memories came flooding back.

Hank reached across the table and took her hands in his. "What I did was wrong. I admit that. But please, just hear me out. I knew that the only way you and I could be together was if I was able to make a permanent commitment to you. But we were both so young and I was going off to war. And to be perfectly honest, I felt I needed my freedom to explore the world. And if I had to die…" his voice trailed off. Shaking his head, he tried to drive away the tears that were struggling to break through. "Ruth, the war is over and if I'm not a lot wiser, I'm a hell of a lot older."

Ruth withdrew her hands from Hank's while keeping her eyes fixed on his face.

"You can't do this to me now," she said. "You can't suddenly come back and disrupt my life. When you called, I thought that you might have been wounded. But I can see that you're all in one piece. And I'm glad that you've gotten on with your life…because so have I. I'm engaged to be married."

"Congratulations!" he said, trying not to let his disappointment show. "I'm glad that you're happy. But this doesn't mean we can't be friends, does it?"

Hank felt his world was crumbling. Now, more than ever, he knew he had to be with her.

Flashing a disarming smile, Hank said, "I want you to tell me every-thing you've been doing. What your life is like now. It's important to me that we can talk like good, old friends once again."

Ruth allowed herself a smile for the first time. "Okay, let's try it. Let's start by your telling me why you think I don't trust you."

"It could be," Hank answered thoughtfully, "because the last time we were together, I was cruel and stupid. But I'm not the same Hank Marshall I was then. I've been put through a meat grinder for the past four years. I may look the same but what's inside has changed. On every one of the twenty-seven missions I flew, I

was convinced I wouldn't come back. Each time, I would think about you and all the wonderful things we never got to do together…

"Hank, please," she interrupted with a catch in her voice. "Don't do this to me. I've thought of you thousands of times. Had you been killed? Were you wounded? It took me a long time to get you out of my system."

"I'll never be out of your system!" Hank cried without thinking.

The shocked look on her face made him realize what he'd said. Catching himself, he said quickly, "Hey, I'm sorry, Ruth, I did not mean to say that."

She looked at him as if for the first time. How handsome he is, she thought. His strong face, framed by wavy black hair, and his athletic body—powerful and lithe. She pointed to the ribbons on his chest. He saw her look and welcomed the diversion.

"This is the Air Medal," he said, "with four oak leaf clusters. This is the Distinguished Flying Cross and this one is for just staying alive." He smiled a humorless grin and paused. He watched her face, but was careful not to make eye contact.

What a great looking woman she is, he thought. More beautiful now than she was before. The food sat on their plates, barely touched.

"Hank," she said suddenly, "I must get back to work. I manage the for-eign trade department of the Chamber of Commerce and I have a meeting with a delegation from China."

"That sounds very exciting. Well, then perhaps we can have dinner tonight?"

"Sorry, I have a date."

Searching her eyes, he thought he saw a flicker of hesitation. "Can we have lunch tomorrow then? Same time, same place?" Nodding at the food sitting untouched on their plates, he added, "Maybe we'll even eat."

She glanced at her watch and got up from her chair slowly. "I really must be going."

"Please, Ruth," he repeated.

"Okay. Same time tomorrow." And turning quickly, she left.

Hank spent another fitful night. Was she engaged? And, if so, was she really in love? Ruth's image stayed in his mind. She hadn't changed much from the pretty, peppy college girl he had known though the years had given her beauty a more classic look. Instead of a pageboy bob, her dark blonde hair made the most of its natural wave and delicately framed her face, accentuating her clear, smooth complexion. But one thing hadn't changed. Her dark, expressive eyes still lit up when she smiled and were unable to hide whatever she was feeling inside.

Although it was late, Hank had no appetite. Earlier, he'd decided to have a couple of drinks before dinner, but he'd never gotten around to eating. The role of the silent drinker was strange to him. Yet, the more he had to drink, the more he wanted to be alone.

He had no answers. All he knew was that he was not enjoying his new-found freedom.

At noon the following day, Hank was sitting in Dave's Place at the same booth he'd been in the day before. He watched Ruth hesitate at the door before walking in, then cross the room with her purposeful stride she slid into the booth facing him.

"What happened to your uniform?" she asked.

He stood up and modeled his bright Glen Plaid suit. "I'm a civilian now," he said with mock seriousness. "One of our nation's heroes, joining the vast army of the unemployed." He pointed to the emblem in his lapel. "With this 'Ruptured Duck' and ten cents, I can get a seat on the bus."

Sitting back down in the booth, he continued. "On my last interview, I was asked about my qualifications. I can throw a perfect spiral to an End, running down field but when I step forward, my knees fold and I fall flat on my ass. Now, that's good for a comedy routine, but it's no cigar with the pros."

"I can also fly evasive action and drop my bombs right on the target. I'm just chock full of talents a prospective employer can't use.

"And, the uniform? It's hype…yesterday's news. I just wore it to dazzle you with the glamour."

Hank sat back heavily. The fear he'd felt in combat combined with the indifference that had greeted him on his first interviews had just boiled to the surface.

Ruth stared at him, a puzzled look on her face.

"What's happened to you, Hank? Why are you so angry? You seem to have come through the war in pretty good shape. So what if you can't play football any more? You don't seem to have any problem walking. As you know, I work for the Chamber of Commerce. We've been knocking ourselves out to help ex-G.I.'s, most of whom have a lot more problems than you do."

The same waitress who'd served them the day before came over to them. "Would you like to order something you might possibly eat today?" she asked, tartly. "The food here is pretty good.'

Then, with a sly look at Hank, she added, "Hey Captain, I love your new suit—real groovy."

Ruth and Hank looked at each other and burst out laughing. Just as before, Ruth ordered the fruit salad and Hank the hamburger.

"Like they used to say in all those corny old movies, I needed that," Hank said, giving the waitress a wink. She winked back and attempted an awkward curtsey as she left them.

"It's kind of hard to explain," Hank said, turning to Ruth. "And this is the first time I've felt like talking about what happened. I spent four years in the Air Force. The first three were a ball: learning to fly and command; meeting some really terrific guys; lots of parties and good booze; the civilian population at your feet. We were the cream of the crop—the highest of the high. And then came the year in combat. Three out of four of the guys I went over there with were killed. They were wonderful guys and now they're gone. And each time, I kept wondering when it was gonna be my turn to die."

Ruth's eyes never left Hank's face as she listened to him. She had to fight the urge to run over to him, put her arms around his neck and hold him close. More than anything, she wanted to comfort him and shelter him from the anguish he held inside.

Unaware of her feelings, Hank continued. "Then suddenly, it was all over. I come back to the United States and get caught up in the wave of patriotic excitement that was made even sweeter by our victory. We were the kings of the hill. We could get away with anything short of murder. Then, without warning, the crash comes. The party's over. You're expected to go back to school or get a job. Gotta do something to get on with your life. Maybe there should be half-way houses to ease the transition."

The waitress returned and placed the food in front of them. "Now eat," she commanded.

For the first time in a long time, Hank felt hungry. Taking a giant bite of his hamburger, he muttered, "Mmmm," in satisfaction, enjoying the rich taste of the red meat.

"I'm engaged to a doctor," Ruth blurted out. "We are going to be married in June. I dated a lot during the war—entertained the G.I.'s at the Stage Door Canteen with my music, and thought I would never hear from you again.

"After you left me, I remained good friends with Yoshikazu Matsuda. He was so sweet and gentle, so understanding. Then suddenly, his father called him back to Japan, before the school year even ended. I think he must have known something about what was going on. For years I felt guilty. It was as though I should have passed on some information—like I was a traitor or something. How could I have been such good friends' with the enemy?

"About a year ago, I met David. He had just been discharged from the medical corps. Recently, he started his own medical practice."

They continued eating silently. Hank now felt that Ruth had loved him all those years. If only I'd contacted her when the war had ended. Or when I arrived home from Hawaii, he thought. Then, perhaps it would be Ruth and me who were planning our wedding.

It can't be too late, he thought, realizing how much he loved her. I'll just take things slowly and make them right!

Changing the subject, Hank asked, "Have you heard from your friend Yoshi?" putting emphasis on the word 'friend'.

"No, not a word. But I really don't expect to. It's strange, isn't it? How you can be such good friends with someone and then all of a sudden, he becomes the enemy—turning into some sort of inhuman monster. If Yoshi's still alive, he's probably hard at work in his father's company. But who knows? In a few years, our countries will begin to forget how much we hate each other, even why we fought. Then, Yoshi might be part of one of the trade delegations who visit here, ready to resume business. It's really a weird world."

"Yesterday you were talking about meeting with a Chinese delegation," Hank said, thoughtfully. "How did that go? The last intelligence I heard was that the Communists are very strong in China now and might well be taking over. Even as the war was ending, there was active combat between the government and the Communist rebels."

Ruth's face lit up. "Then that explains it!" she said. "This delegation has come here to purchase a number of things. But the biggest item on their list is navy blue woolen material, to make uniforms for their army. Everything's in short supply here, though, as you well know."

Hank laughed. "I can get them all the woolen material they need. There's thousands of yards sitting around in army surplus."

"Yes, but it's all O.D. material—olive drab."

"All we have to do is dye it navy," he said, jokingly.

Ruth almost jumped out of her seat. "That's one hell of an idea. They want it. Why not sell it to them?"

Hank's eyes opened wide. "Why not?" he said. "When I was a kid, I worked in my father's blouse factory. I remember that he often dyed materials from one color to another."

The old familiarity and excitement came back in a rush. Once again, they were finishing each other's sentences. Ideas burst from one while the other added something until neither knew or cared who'd had the original thought.

"You always wanted to travel and work in foreign countries," Ruth said. "This could be the place to start."

Hank's excitement was growing. He felt as he had at the start of a football game. Or when he taxied down the runway before a mission. The only difference was, if he got shot down this time, he could walk away.

With eyes aglow, Hank reached over and placed Ruth's delicate hands in his own. He felt a ray of hope when she didn't resist his touch. "Let's be partners," Hank said eagerly. "You have the buyers. I'll find a way of getting the goods and dyeing it to their specifications."

Gently easing her hands from his, Ruth said, "I couldn't do that, even if I wanted to. I work for the Chamber of Commerce. We supply a service and as individuals, we can't get involved in the deals. It's our job to bring the exporter and importer together, than walk away. But..." she added with a sly grin, "I don't see why you can't do it."

He looked at her for a long time. "Okay, have it your way. We can talk more about it later. But right now, how do I get to meet your Chinese friends?"

"I might be able to introduce you to them as soon as tomorrow. But remember, Hank, this is strictly a business proposition. I am engaged and I am going to marry David."

The next two weeks were a blur of activity for Hank. He met with the Chinese importers—three very serious looking men, all of whom wore dark blue suits and spoke not a word of English To communicate, they used an interpreter from the Chinese embassy.

Ruth had told the Chinese that Hank was a veteran who had fought in the Pacific against the Japanese, their common enemy. This, and Hank's winning manner, made him an instant friend. They had not yet found a good source for the blue serge woolen material they needed and welcomed an offer from him.

Hank talked the idea over with his father, who thought it was fantastic. Sid Marshall had been going through a period of disappointment, bordering on depression. The ache in his heart over Peter's death was constant. And it hadn't helped matters when his dream of Hank joining the family business had faded. He worried, too, about Hank's heavy drinking and his lack of direction. But now his son was coming to him for advice and this lifted Sid's spirits.

Sitting down, facing Hank, Sid looked proudly at his handsome son's excited face. Thank God he's not wearing that ugly Glen Plaid suit, he thought to himself. Dressed casually in an open neck shirt and a smart looking sport jacket, Hank looked strong and confident.

"I really think this is my big opportunity, Pop. The Chinese are looking for good quality material at the right price and no one has been able to supply them with what they need. In the meantime, right under everyone's noses are thousands of yards of the army's war surplus O.D. material. I still can't believe that I'm the only guy in the world who's thought of dyeing the O.D. to their specifications!"

Sid was thoughtful for a moment. "It's entirely possible. Many people don't see what is right in front of them. But, by the same token, you should keep in mind that it's not as simple as you make it sound. First, you have to buy the goods from the government, which is not like buying from Johnny Sanders Piece Goods House. Then, you have to give them a sample of the material with the exact color they want. Luckily, I know just the right dye house to turn out the job."

He looked at the ceiling as though studying a script. Ticking the words off on his fingers, Sid went on. "Buying, financing, quality control…and how about getting paid? You can't go after them in China to collect so you're gonna have to get a letter of credit."

"I see I'm going to need your help in launching my career in the Export business, Pop."

Sid rejoiced inside. This son of his, the All-American quarterback, this war hero pilot—he needed his father's help! "And who else would you ask?" he grinned happily. "I will do whatever it takes."

The men stood up and Hank extended his hand. Instead of taking it, Sid reached out to hug his son. When Hank responded, they held each other closely. Four years of anxiety and hurt quickly melted away.

"So, you'll need a place to work. I'll clean out the office next to the bookkeeping department. It has its own entrance, which will give you more privacy. Of course, you will have to pay rent."

Sid looked up at the ceiling again, as if expecting to receive a message from above. "The rent will be…that you'll have to take me to lunch at least once a week."

Grinning in agreement, Hank reached out and shook his father's hand.

CHAPTER EIGHT

▼

The Chamber of Commerce was headquartered in a small, nondescript building on the edge of downtown Los Angeles. The organization had recruited Ruth Morris out of UCLA, where she'd majored in Foreign Trade. After being with the Chamber for only four months, her supervisor was promoted to General Manager and Ruth was offered his job. The challenge was an exciting one and she was still a little in awe of her new position.

Ruth had only been at her new management post for one month when Hank suddenly reappeared, bringing with him all the old memories she thought she'd left behind.

Her school years and the war years had been a period of intense activity. Many of her evenings were taken up by her music, entertaining the enlisted men at The Stage Door Canteen. Ruth's "girl next door" looks were the kind service men longed for. She'd smile, play the piano and accompany them in community sing-alongs while they became her willing captives.

And she could dance, too! Whenever Ruth did the jitterbug with a nimble G.I., a crowd would encircle them—jumping, clapping, swaying and tapping to the beat.

But now, Ruth was all business as she sat at the conference table with the three Chinese delegates and their interpreter. She had already introduced them to Hank as well as two other potential suppliers.

"We have received a very attractive offer from Mr. Marshall for navy blue woolen material." Mr. Chen, the interpreter, paused for a moment. "Mr. Marshall is very young but he is also very aggressive. He seems most confident that he can fill our needs."

Ruth was tingling with excitement but her face remained composed. "Of course you realize that The Chamber does not get involved in the deal itself. Our function is only to introduce you to qualified parties. We make no guarantees. I can say, however, that I have known Mr. Marshall for a number of years. He was a highly decorated combat pilot. His family has been in the garment business for many years and therefore he has a strong familiarity with all kinds of piece goods."

The four men began speaking in Chinese, engaged in animated conversation. After several minutes, Mr. Chen turned to Ruth and smiled for the first time. "We will place our initial order with Mr. Marshall," he said.

Ruth felt exhilarated. It had all happened so fast! She'd just met with the Chinese delegation for the first time two weeks ago. Now they were ready to place a huge order with the man she'd been trying so hard to forget. Calmly and professionally she informed them, "I'm sure Mr. Marshall will be delighted with your decision."

The insistent ringing of the phone jarred Ruth from her sleep. She rolled over, rubbing her eyes, and stared vacantly at the alarm clock next to her bed. The phone kept ringing, even though it was only 6:30 A.M. Yanking the receiver off the hook, she heard Hank's voice bursting with excitement on the other end of the line.

"Ruth, Ruth, are you awake?"

"I am now," she mumbled, her voice still heavy with sleep. She was accustomed to waking up slowly and grudgingly.

"Excuse me for calling this early but I've been sitting here, staring at the phone for the past fifteen minutes…waiting to call and tell you. I have it! It's in my hands!"

"I'm almost afraid to ask," she said, still groggy, "but what do you have in your hands?"

"A cablegram from China!" he shouted. "They are opening up a letter of credit for seventy-six thousand!" Almost in a whisper, he repeated, "$76,000.00 bucks!"

Now, she was wideawake. Sitting up in bed, grinning broadly, she said, "Oh, Hank, that's great! I'm so happy for you!"

"This never could have happened without you, Ruth. Please, have dinner with me tonight. You must help me celebrate!"

Ruth was surprised that the Chinese had acted so quickly. It was unusual in business deals of this type. Yet, despite her excitement, she knew she had to keep her distance. "Oh, I'm sorry, Hank. I can't. I…." she began.

"But you must!" he said, cutting her off. "It's really important that I share this first deal with you. Please…." he implored. "Look, there's a fantastic new pianist appearing at Ciro's on Sunset Strip. I met him in Saipan when he came through with one of the U.S.O. shows. I know you'll love him.

"And besides, I have a big surprise for you. Come on, Ruth, what do you say?"

Not waiting for her answer, he said, "Look, I'll pick you up at seven."

Ruth shook her head at the phone as she heard herself say, "Make it seven-thirty."

It was a beautiful, star-filled night as Ruth and Hank drove up glittering Sunset Boulevard. They passed the famous nightclub, Mocambo's, on the right and classy LaRue's on the left before pulling up to Ciro's. The large neon "Ciro's" sign flashed proudly as a handsome, broad-shouldered attendant opened the car door for Ruth.

They walked through the noisy, crowded bar toward the main room where they were greeted by a maitre'd in formal attire. Slipping him a five-dollar bill, Hank said, "Reservations for two, Hank Marshall."

Hank held Ruth's arm as they followed the maitre'd to their table. He couldn't help noticing the admiring glances Ruth received as they made their way across the room. Even in glamorous Hollywood, Ruth was an outstanding looking woman.

Hank had never seen her in evening clothes before. The straps of her emerald green, satin gown lay just below her shoulders, revealing her long, graceful neck. She wore very little make-up—just enough to enhance her smooth complexion and high cheekbones.

After they were seated at their table, Hank looked across at Ruth and said, "You are truly lovely this evening."

"Thank you. And so are you," she said, gazing at him appreciatively. She was happy to see he had discarded his Glen Plaid suit, replacing it with a finely tailored gray, sharkskin, double-breasted one. The suit, combined with his bold, black and white tie patterned with circles of various sizes, only heightened his attractiveness.

Their table for two was on the left side of a small stage, which featured a shining black grand piano at its center.

"You remembered I like to sit on the keyboard side," she said with a pleased smile.

"I remember everything you like and a few things you don't," he replied.

A bottle of Mumm's champagne sat in a silver ice bucket alongside the table. A tuxedoed waiter approached them. "May I serve the champagne now?" he asked.

"It's as good a time as any," Hank answered, "since this is a very special occasion."

Ruth watched Hank as though he were a champion chess player about to make his next move. "Well, I'm impressed," she said. "And when do you do your magic act?"

"I've already done it," he said. "Just having you here next to me is magic."

"You still have a great line."

With a grin, he said, "Why do I get the feeling you that you still don't trust me?"

He raised his glass of champagne and she slowly lifted hers. Their two glasses clicked with a clear "pinging" sound. Looking into her eyes, he toasted, "To success...to us...and to magic, wherever we may find it."

They sipped their champagne as Bobby Short made his way to the stage. His round face was cherubic and impish at the same time, especially when he flashed his gleaming, broad smile at the crowd. His debonair white ruffled shirt, black satin bow tie and elegant black tuxedo complimented his dark skin.

When he reached the piano, he posed at its side, bowing to his audience as they applauded in an enthusiastic welcome.

"Good evening, ladies and gentlemen," he said warmly, "I'm Bobby Short."

Taking his seat at the piano, he began to play and sing a Gershwin medley. The rich, seductive tones of his voice were reminiscent of a mellow trumpet.

As the music changed from lively "swing" to a romantic ballad, Hank reached for Ruth's hand. The words of the song were as warm and caressing as her hand laying quietly in his.

"...I saw a man with his head bowed low, his heart had no place to go. I looked in his eyes as I said with a sigh, there but for you go I..."

"That song is about me—without you," Hank said softly.

"Oh, Hank," she said, starting to protest and slowly withdrawing her hand from his.

"Shh, wait, don't say anything now—not until you hear me out," he told her.

When Bobby Short ended his set, they joined the rest of the audience in enthusiastic applause. As the room quieted down, Hank said, "Now for the surprise!"

With the flourish of a magician, he flicked open his hand and presented her with an engraved business card. It read:

TRANS-PACIFIC TRADERS
HANK MARSHALL, PRESIDENT

"How do you like the name of the company?" he asked, eagerly. "Now that we have our first export order, we're really a trading company. Notice I've rented a new office on Wilshire Boulevard."

"That's terrific, Hank," she said, excitedly.

"But wait a minute," he added hastily, his face flushed. "Here's the real surprise. Ta da da…he sang like a musical introduction. Once more he produced an engraved card and handed it to Ruth. Lifting it, she blushed as she read:

TRANS-PACIFIC TRADERS
RUTH MARSHALL, VICE PRESIDENT

Ruth was unable to speak as Hank took her hands in his once again.

"Say yes and there will be no conflict of interest," he told her. "And please understand, this is not a proposition. It's a proposal—for life." Hank's voice held no trace of the lightheartedness they'd shared earlier.

"I love you, Ruth. I have always loved you. I need you and this time, I promise I'm not going to do anything stupid. I don't know David—and I'm sure he's a fine man. But what I do know is that he couldn't possibly love you as much as I do. You and I will never be as close to anyone else as we are to each other." He stopped just short of running out of breath.

Ruth's mind was racing. Hank was saying all the things she'd wanted so desperately to hear—a long time ago. Could she really give up the peace and security she'd found with David? Or was it Hank she truly wanted? From the moment he had come back into her life, she'd worked hard not to let her emotions run away with her. Four years of hurt were not easy to forget.

Ruth looked up at Hank, waiting eagerly for her answer. And in that one blazing moment she knew. She wanted to be with him—forever. Her body grew warm and her heart seemed to overflow as tears filled her eyes and ran down her cheeks.

Smiling joyfully, Hank removed the handkerchief from his breast pocket and tenderly wiped her tears away. Then, standing up, he took her hands in his and gently brought her to her feet. As they kissed softly, the people at the adjoining tables applauded. Flushed, they took a mock bow and sat down, as their waiter approached their table. He stood there, grinning broadly, as they ordered dinner.

The walls had come down. There was no more guarded conversation, no more choosing of words. They talked about anything and everything that came to mind. They spoke of the past: remembering good friends and funny events. They planned the future, charting the course for the business. They even discussed the number of children they would like to have. They agreed on two for sure, but left their options open just in case.

As they finished their dessert—a rich chocolate eclair filled with whipped cream Ruth took the last spoonful and fed it to Hank.

"This is magic, Hank," she murmured with a contented sigh. "And you are a magician."

CHAPTER NINE

▼

The Tosui Trading Company was buzzing with activity. Every foot of space in the twelve-story building was filled with the sights and sounds of deals being made and executed.

The building was one of thousands being built over the rubble created by the terrible B-29 bombing raids. The company's world headquarters had just been completed and on the top of the building flew a huge flag with the Tosui trademark: a single bamboo swaying in the wind.

General Douglas MacArthur himself appeared at both the ground-breaking ceremony and the grand opening. In a speech to 1500 employees and the press, he heralded the return of the great trading companies of Japan to the world of commerce.

Yukio spoke a few words in Japanese. He told of his gratitude for the help extended by the man who was the U.S. Supreme Commander. The spirit of the new Japan would work in close cooperation with the United States, he assured them. He then introduced his son, Yoshikazu, who would speak to them in English.

Yoshikazu stood at the microphone. He bowed to General MacArthur and thanked him. "General Douglas MacArthur has shown his determination to help us on the road to full recovery and prosperity through his encouragement and his many wise decisions.

"We are rebuilding our country," he went on, "so that we may take our place in the modern world. We will, however, never forget our honorable ancestors nor the thousands of years of tradition, which have helped to keep us strong. The building of the headquarters of Tosui Trading is just one step on our road to recovery. We will work with great dedication towards success in the world of commerce and to regain our position of respect. This is the beginning of a new era for Japan and for Tosui."

With the opening ceremonies over, every division of the vast trading company began to operate with purpose and efficiency. Once a month, the heads of the various departments met at a huge oval table. Yukio Matsuda sat at its head. on his left was Senji Watanabe, his administrative assistant for the past thirty years. On Yukio's right was his son, Yoshikazu, and seated next to him was Takei Watanabe, Senji's son, who had recently been appointed Yoshikazu's assistant. The other seats were taken by the division heads for automotive, steel, oil, chemicals, plastics, food products, consumer products and electronics.

The meeting lasted for ten hours. The men took infrequent breaks when fresh tea or food was brought in. Each executive's presentation conveyed a similar tone as most of Tosui's production facilities had been destroyed during the war. Before the war, the majority of manufacturing was done in small factories. Then, during the war, parts began to be produced in almost every home. This led the Japanese high command to believe that they were insulated against attack. But, when the Americans began dropping incendiary bombs on heavily populated areas, all the "factories" were burned down. Now, ironically, their former enemy was helping them to build new, larger factories with state of-the-art equipment.

The electronics division chief reported that General MacArthur had been frustrated in his efforts to speak directly to the Japanese people due to the poor quality of Japanese radios. So, MacArthur brought in a team of engineers from the United States to teach the Tosui engineers how to manufacture radios with quality control. The division chief reported that great progress had been made.

The report on chemicals was similar to the other departments except that the department manager expressed concern over the shortage of some key industrial chemicals. He was in desperate need, he said, of caustic soda and other essential products. He reported that he had sent inquiries around the world and had recently received a positive response from a trading company in Los Angeles.

"Yoshikazu-San," Mr. Takeshita said, "I would like to meet with you personally to discuss this."

Yoshikazu bowed and set a time to meet the following morning.

After the meeting ended, Yukio and Yoshikazu walked down the hall to the Chairman's office. They had fallen into the habit of privately discussing the events and decisions of the monthly meetings. This day had been a particularly productive one and Yukio was extremely satisfied. He'd been driving himself mercilessly for over two years to bring the company to this point. Now, at last, Tosui Trading had offices in each of the industrial capitals of the world once again.

Arriving at his office, Yukio moved gracefully into his chair and said, "This is only the beginning, my son. The next ten years will be crucial. We must speak softly as we regain our economic power. Time will show that strength in business is far more powerful than military weapons. And, Tosui will lead the way."

Yoshikazu nodded. With a slight bow to his father, he said, "You are the greatest strength of all, Father. I have watched you work endless hours with unrelenting intensity. I humbly hope I can follow in your footsteps. I would like to make one suggestion, however. It is an idea to which I have given much thought."

Yoshikazu paused for just a moment before continuing on.

"The most important part of Japanese business has always been the great trading companies, exemplified by our own great company. We have bought and sold merchandise from all around the world because very little has been produced in Japan. The products we do manufacture are handmade silk dresses, inexpensive toys and paper parasols. our nation has become known for its cheap products and poor quality.

"My belief is, Father, that while we continue the great trading tradition, we should also begin to concentrate on the emerging technologies. The computer, for example, will soon revolutionize the way we think. Univac, the first of its kind, has just emerged, developed as a result of war technology. The Univac computer takes up a great deal of space and is currently very expensive but the general principles for its design are sound. It is just a matter of time before its design and capabilities are vastly improved and its price is dramatically reduced.

"To establish our credibility in this market, we need to take full advantage of our capacity for miniaturization. We should start to concentrate on finding ways to reduce the bulk of the computer and increase the power. I humbly believe that if we turn sufficient attention to these new areas, we will begin to manufacture the most innovative and best quality products the world has ever seen."

Yoshikazu settled back in his chair, awaiting his father's reaction.

Yukio stroked his chin as he listened. "The truth is, my son, we did not lose the war because we were less brave but because we were less resourceful. The Americans overwhelmed us with mass production and superior technology. I have heard what you said and am impressed by the truth of your words. If the gods spoke to us, they would awaken us with your words."

Yukio shifted his weight so he could look into Yoshikazu's eyes. "We can and we will produce the products of the future right here in Japan. You, with your technical education and keen insight, will lead our efforts. I am going to place you in charge of all product development. At the same time, you must coordinate with the trading end of the business. It will remain the foundation of what we do.

"Along with development and production distribution must come. Our offices around the world will be useful for these plans. Remember, good business remains good business whether the data comes from a computer or an abacus."

Yukio stroked his chin, thoughtfully. "The biggest market for this kind of merchandise will be the United States. We must saturate that huge country with quality products at low prices. This strategy will discourage the Americans from continuing their own production."

As Yoshikazu listened to his father's words, he could almost see his father's mind working.

"In the United States, the Marshall Plan has been approved," Yokio continued. This means the Americans will now share with us the technology they have developed. The only secret they will keep will be the production of the atomic bomb. That is because of its military significance. The United States will aid us in building new factories that will manufacture the products of the future. Our chief competition and biggest customer will be the same foreign devils who destroyed our cities.

"The terms of our surrender prohibit us from making guns or maintaining an army. This is not a problem. Yokio emitted a wry laugh. "The Americans now feel a massive threat from Russia and will continue investing the bulk of their resources in building an even greater military machine. We must remain patient in order to rebuild our economy. That, my son, is the power of the future. I will not live long enough to witness our ultimate victory, but you will. And you will oversee our dominance in the world markets."

Yukio sat back heavily.

"Now, let us retire," he said. "Tomorrow is another day in which to move ahead with renewed energy."

Yoshikazu was filled with admiration for his father and excited by his words. "I commit myself to this victory," he said, bowing respectfully as he backed out of the room.

The next morning, Mr. Takeshita, the managing director of Tosui Chemicals, arrived at the appointed time for his meeting. Yoshikazu had gained the respect of all of the company's department managers by being a war hero who had adapted effortlessly to the ways of commerce. He seemed to be knowledgeable in all areas of the business, having grown up living and breathing the company tradition. Everyone knew the first son of Yukio Matsuda was destined to lead Tosui.

Entering Yoshikazu's unpretentious office, Mr. Takeshita bowed respectfully. Yoshikazu motioned for him to sit, and after the tea was poured, Mr. Takeshita got right to the point.

"As you know, Yoshikazu-San, many important chemicals are in short supply. None are more necessary or harder to find than caustic soda. The United States is the biggest supplier but even there, it is most difficult to find. Prices are high and quantities are limited. If we are to deal with the Americans, we will need a special import license. An export license is also required on the other side.

"We have recently been contacted by a trading company in Los Angeles. They are offering us two thousand tons of caustic soda at an affordable price. This amount is equal to the entire allocation to Japan for the next quarter. If we make the purchase, it will be most profitable for us and will allow us to control the market. We will, of course, have to open a letter of credit in U.S. dollars—after we have been assured that this company can fulfill its commitment."

"I am planning a trip to the United States in two weeks," Yoshikazu said, thoughtfully. "You continue negotiations for price and delivery. Before we open a letter of credit, I will visit this company to determine if they can fulfill their promise. In the meantime, we will run a check on them through our Los Angeles office and through Dun and Bradstreet. What is the name of this company?"

Looking at his notes, Mr. Takeshita peered through his glasses and said, "The supplier is called Trans-Pacific Traders."

CHAPTER TEN

▼

Yoshikazu called Takei Watanabe into his office. Takei bowed as he stepped inside to await instructions. The perpetual smile he wore could easily turn into a scowl when he was puzzled or angry, neither of which happened with any great frequency. And Takei's pleasant disposition could not hide his steeltrap mind, which observed everything and committed it to memory.

Takei always seemed to be in perpetual motion. His short, powerful, compact body, with its low center of gravity, allowed him to move swiftly with little effort. Because it was impossible to find a standard shirt or jacket that could contain his barrel chest, his clothes always seemed to be a size too small, which added to his appearance of haste.

Takei sat down across the desk from Yoshikazu with a long note pad in one hand and a bulky fountain pen poised in the other, ready to take down the rapid instructions he knew he would receive.

Without taking time for pleasantries, Yoshikazu began. "We are going to the United States next month and there is much to do in preparation. Bell Laboratories has just received a patent on a new invention called the transistor. I am very interested in this. I would like you to schedule a meeting with their top people. If it is as powerful as I think it is, we must make a licensing agreement with them before the invention becomes common knowledge.

"There is also a company in California called Ampex. They have invented a device that allows one to record an event on tape and then play it back on a television set. It makes great sense for use in studios. Although they are not thinking this way, it could become a large volume consumer product. Our own brand of wire-audio products are selling very well. I would like to find distribution in the United States.

"I would also like to see the file on the company offering us two thousand tons of caustic soda. We should make arrangements to meet with them while in Los Angeles."

"I have already checked on Trans-Pacific Traders," Takei said, separating one file from the rest of his papers. "They are a new company—just two years old. They started in 1946, selling large quantities of woolen material to China. This year, they have been actively selling industrial chemicals. They have successfully supplied large quantities of caustic soda and soda ash to the Phillipines and India. This is our first contact with them. The principles are a husband and wife named Hank and Ruth Marshall."

Yoshikazu felt his face flush and quickly looked away. He had always prided himself on his ability to appear unruffled under any conditions. And he would not let his reputation be compromised.

Turning back to Takei, his face was expressionless. In a calm voice, he said, "Very well, leave the file with me and start working on travel arrangements."

With a nod, Takei left the room.

With Takei gone, Yoshikazu rose and walked to the door, locking it. He then buzzed his secretary on the intercom. "I do not wish to be disturbed," he told her.

In the now silent office, Yoshikazu sank softly into his big leather chair and closed his eyes.

She was standing before him once again, teasing him, challenging him—her eyes warm and inviting. He watched as she unwrapped her dress, unveiling the wonders of her body. He tried to control his desire for her but he was boiling internally like the inside of a volcano, ready to erupt.

Holding her tightly in his arms, he lowered her slowly to the towel, gently kissing her forehead, cheeks and eyes. As their lips met, he heard her sigh softly and felt her melt into his arms. Her warm, pulsating body pressed harder against his own. His very soul seemed lost in space as he drifted in and out of time—without control, without caring. It was the only time in his life he had felt vulnerable, yet safe and secure.

And then he told her he had to leave. The look of pain and hurt in her eyes still burned in his memory. It had taken everything he had within to walk away. Not seeing her again had made the burden lighter. But that was about to change.

Suddenly, the picture in his mind shifted. It was now April 4th, 1945. He was on the island of Iwo Jima, hiding in the bushes surrounding the airfield. His battle fatigues were tattered and caked with mud. He'd eaten the last of his rations that morning, and his stomach was growling with hunger. Although the island had been lost to the Americans, scattered Japanese forces still engaged in sniper operations, intending to make the Yanks pay dearly for every inch of soil they'd gained.

Yoshikazu felt himself cursing, waving his rifle when first he heard, then saw, the huge silhouette of a B-29 descending from the sky. He could hear the engines sputter and his trained ear told him that the big bomber was in trouble.

The giant plane was now landing on the pockmarked runway.

"What great fortune!" Yoshikazu thought, as the plane came to a stop less than twenty yards from his hiding place.

He watched as American fuel trucks raced to the monster's side to load it with gas. As the motors were cut, the taxiing plane came to a halt. The doors opened quickly. A crew of eleven men jumped out—pistols drawn, ready to fire. As they stood around the refueling aircraft, their eyes darted into the bushes. They'd obviously been warned about Japanese snipers.

Yoshikazu looked on silently. He saw the tall, lean pilot drop gracefully to the ground. He, too, had his pistol drawn and ready.

Yoshikazu brought his rifle to his shoulder and sighting down the barrel of the gun, brought his finger to rest on the trigger. The American's head was directly in focus. Then, the pilot turned and looked directly into the bushes where Yoshikazu was hidden.

The shock of recognition paralyzed Yoshikazu for a moment. He realized he was staring into the face of Ruth's All-American boy friend. Beads of sweat appeared on his forehead as he began to pull the trigger. His gun suddenly felt like it weighed a thousand pounds. Then, slowly and deliberately he lowered it, without firing the shot that would have surely killed Hank Marshall.

The aircraft finished refueling and the crew returned to their stations. The big plane's engines started up and it taxied out for the take off. The moment had been lost.

Yoshikazu sat back in his chair with his eyes still closed. He pondered the dilemma that continued to haunt him. Why hadn't he fired that fateful day on the island of Iwo Jima? Was it because of some inner feeling he had for this enemy flier? Or was it because he knew that after he fired, he would be discovered and killed instantly? Had it been an act of compassion for an enemy with a recognizable face? Or had it been an act of cowardice?

Soon, he would be meeting once more with these two people who filled his thoughts. These people who had become husband and wife.

"I will be ready," he promised himself as he rose to resume his duties. "I will be ready."

CHAPTER ELEVEN

▼

Hank had begun to think that April 4th always brought some event of great significance. Although he didn't believe in astrology, he couldn't help but wonder about the coincidences.

It was on April 4, 1945 that the skies over Tokyo were filled with more bombers and enemy fighters, locked in mortal combat, than ever before. It was on that day, just three years ago, that he'd faced almost certain death. His continuing nightmares served as a constant reminder of the fear he had felt.

And, it was on April 4th, just one year later, that he and Ruth had eloped to Las Vegas. The date hadn't any significance for him then. He hadn't related it to his most dangerous day in combat. Perhaps he had just blocked it out.

Hank remembered that April 4th two years ago very well. He and Ruth had just received the profits from their first shipment of navy blue serge to China. They were floating on air as they drove back to the office from the bank. The euphoria from their first successful deal was a unique sensation—never to be felt in exactly the same way again. Doing business was no longer just a theory or an idea that might work. They had done it. And the money was in the bank—theirs to spend any way they saw fit.

They turned up Wilshire Boulevard and stopped at a red light. Impulsively, Hank took his hands from the wheel and turned to face

Ruth, who, at that exact moment, had turned to face him. As if drawn together by a magnet, they leaned toward each other and kissed quickly and passionately.

The loud, blaring sound of a car horn jolted them back to reality and they laughed as they realized they were holding up the rush hour traffic. Throwing the car into gear and stepping on the gas, Hank's face was flushed with excitement. "Let's go to Las Vegas!" he shouted.

"When?" asked Ruth, caught up in the giddiness of the moment.

"Right now," he answered without hesitation. "Let's pick up some clothes, drive to Las Vegas and get married."

"Just like that?" she laughed.

He snapped his fingers. "Just like that. I can't think of a better time. We're a team, we're in love and I want the whole cockeyed world to know it!"

"Are you sure about this, Hank?" she asked.

"I have never been more sure of anything in my life. Now, let's do it!"

The two years since they'd eloped had passed in a blur of excitement. The joy they'd experienced in their relationship was almost matched by the thrill of completing one successful business deal after another. The company grew so quickly they were soon forced to move into larger quarters.

Ruth decorated the new offices of Trans-Pacific Traders in a combination of contemporary style and efficiency. She and Hank occupied adjoining offices. A smaller office housed Bea Stein, their new, full time bookkeeper who'd come to them with excellent references and ten years of experience in the foreign trade department of the Bank of America.

Short and squat with steely gray hair, Bea Stein was devoted to the art of bookkeeping and records. She took great pride in her accuracy. She had become the company's technical expert as well as its chief negotiator with banks and freight forwarders. After the terms of a deal were agreed upon, it was turned over to Bea for execution.

She'd also taken on the role of office manager and kept a watchful eye on the two secretaries and the switchboard operator/receptionist who rounded out the small, efficient staff. Bea's days were long as she attended to the many details of the rapidly growing export company.

The company filled five more large orders from China before the government of Chiang Kai-Shiek fled to Taiwan. It was during this period that Hank and Ruth began to deal in industrial chemicals.

The worldwide demand for caustic soda and soda ash, necessities in the manufacture of soap and glass, was very high and in short supply. Soon, Trans-Pacific Traders was actively involved in buying and selling these commodities. They paid premium prices but were still able to sell them at a profit on the export market. The need was so great, they had no problem selling whatever quantities they were able to find. The only difficulty was in finding reliable sources to supply them.

American exporters thrived in the post war era. And as Trans-Pacific's reputation as a reliable source for "hard to get merchandise" grew, so did their volume of inquiries.

Incoming inquiries were placed on Ruth's desk each morning. One day, a request arrived from the Tosui Trading Company in Japan. Tosui was looking for two thousand tons of caustic soda—an order ten times larger than any they'd handled in the past. Ruth recognized the name immediately when she saw the letterhead.

"Tosui," she said aloud. "Yoshi," she whispered to herself, grateful to be alone in her office.

There were only four men in Ruth's life who had been truly important to her. First, was her father: gentle and protective. He showed her unconditional love. Then, there was her husband, Hank: so handsome, strong and full of life. His intense ambition was masked by his easy manner and sense of humor. One moment, he could be inconsiderate and full of himself. Then the next, he'd be tender and compassionate. He was always fair and honest, though. And he could negotiate the toughest deal. A competitor had once described him as "the iron fist in a velvet glove." Ruth liked that description.

Next was David: sweet and lovable. Blessed with the compassion of a true healer, he had been destined to be a doctor. He was also one of the few people in the world who could have made the transition from fiance to friend without losing his dignity. Luckily for both of them, she'd realized early on that she'd never be satisfied being a doctor's wife.

And finally, there was Yoshi. More than six years had passed since that night on the beach yet, she remembered every word, every movement. Hours, days and years could pass by in a blur but those few exquisite moments would linger on for a lifetime.

She recalled every detail of his face, his slender body, his strong arms holding her so gently. She could still feel the frustration she'd felt at his unwillingness to break the bonds of his tradition. The dynamics of war and peace might shake the world but Yoshi would keep his commitments to his family, his company, his country and to his promised Japanese bride.

And now, after all this time, she was going to meet him again, face to face.

"Here it is," she said exuberantly as she walked into Hank's office, waving a piece of paper in her hand. "Our ticket to fame and fortune. Two thousand tons of caustic soda! That has to be more caustic than there is in the world!"

"If it's a real deal, at the right price, I'll find it," Hank told her with a confident smile. "But most of these huge inquiries are just giant wheel spinners. It depends on who wants it and at what price."

"It's from Tosui Trading, one of the largest companies in Japan." She paused, hoping her tone was normal before she gave him the next bit of information. "It's controlled by the Matsuda family."

"Your old friend Yoshi, is it? Well, well, something from the small world department. And now, folks, a really big inquiry from those wonderful people who brought us Pearl Harbor."

"The war has been over for three years," replied Ruth. "And Tosui's money is as good as anyone's. Besides, I have no idea if Yoshi is still around nor do I care. Their opening offer is ten cents a pound but I'll bet they'll go higher. More importantly, their letter says they're confident that they can get an import license, which means they also have the dollars to pay for it."

"Ruth, you know the going export price for caustic soda is sixteen cents," said Hank, all business now. If he had anything further to say about Yoshi, he decided to keep it to himself.

"We're going to have to come up with an entirely different source for this kind of price and quantity," Hank continued. "I don't know if it's possible but, what the hell. If it was easy, than everyone would be doing it. There's no such quantity available from the jobbers or distributors. For a deal this size, we'll have to contact one of the major alkali mills. And probably, everyone in the world has been after them, including Tosui."

A month later, they made the deal, settling on a price of twelve cents per pound. Ruth now brought in a cablegram, which said that Mr. Yoshikazu Matsuda and Mr. Takei Watanabe wanted to meet with the principles of Trans-Pacific Traders to finalize the details. This was polite language for, "We want to make sure you can fill this order before we open a letter of credit committing to $480,000."

Hank continued to have an uneasy feeling in the pit of his stomach. Ever since Ruth had shown him the cable from Tosui, he had wondered how he would handle the meeting.

"I'm sorry, Ruth," he whispered later that night, after she awakened him from a fitful sleep. It hadn't been one of his combat nightmares that had disturbed him this time, though. And all he could remember was making a speech and waving a pistol over his head. Bubba, his co-pilot, had been standing next to him with a gun in his hand, ready to fire. Hank sensed there was a presence out there but in the fog surrounding them, it was impossible to see anything.

He was fully awake now. The clock on the nightstand read three A.M. as he turned to Ruth who was sitting up, wide awake, beside him.

"Today's meeting is really bugging me," he told her. "I'm prepared to meet the Japanese and I'm confident I can answer all their questions. But

I can't get rid of this feeling of anger. I keep thinking about my buddies who died over there…and I feel guilty."

He pointed to his head. "Up here, I have no problem. We're all friends now and, like you said, their money is as good as anyone's. But down here," he said, pointing to his heart, "I'm having a real tough time. I've tried to make peace with it but the ache just won't go away. And I don't know if it ever will."

Ruth cupped her hands lovingly around his face and looked into his tortured eyes. "The friends we have today can be our enemies tomorrow. Last year, we loved the Russians. Now, Winston Churchill is talking about an iron curtain and others are calling for an atomic showdown.

"Today, the Japanese are our friends and tomorrow, Tosui will be our customer. We're all people. Let's try giving them the benefit of the doubt. You never really got to know Yoshi. And I think if you do, you'll like him." She kissed Hank tenderly on both cheeks. And locked in each other's arms, they fell asleep.

Yoshikazu Matsuda and Takei Watanabe arrived at the offices of Trans-Pacific Traders promptly at ten A.M. They were immediately ushered into a large, square conference room with plush, dark blue carpeting. A round, glass-topped table with four iron gray upholstered chairs stood in one corner. Against the adjoining wall, was a large, brown leather couch with a teakwood coffee table in front of it. Two more gray chairs sat behind the coffee table. The setting gave the room a comfortable, yet businesslike feel.

Ruth and Hank were seated on the couch, and rose as the two men entered the room. Ruth walked over to Yoshi and with a soft smile, extended her hand. Bowing stiffly, he took it. Takei bowed, too, as he simultaneously offered each of the Marshall's a pair of engraved business cards.

The room was charged with the silence of unreleased energy. Finally, Ruth broke the stillness with a nervous laugh. "Just look at us!" she gushed. "Acting like total strangers. Hank, this is Yoshi. Do you remember meeting him at UCLA?"

"Yes, of course," Hank said, shaking Yoshi's hand firmly. He then turned to Takei and returned his bow. "We welcome both of you to the United States and to our offices. Did you have a pleasant trip?"

Yoshi realized he had been staring at Ruth, and turned quickly to Hank. "We have enjoyed an excellent trip, thank you." Looking back at Ruth, he added, "And you are looking very well, Mrs. Marshall."

"What is this 'Mrs. Marshall' It's Ruth and Hank. And, if you don't mind, I'd still like to call you Yoshi. Our days at UCLA seem like a long time ago, don't they?" she asked, hoping her nervousness didn't show. "Hank and I have been married for two years now. In fact, our marriage and our business are the same age."

"And both are doing just great," Hank added, countering the edge in his voice with a quick smile.

They both looked at Yoshi and waited for him to offer some personal information. "I am married to Kimi," he said simply. "Now, perhaps we should review our transaction."

"Yes, please," said Hank. "Have a seat and we'll get right down to business.

"As you undoubtedly know, we have concluded the deal with your Mr. Takeshita. We are prepared to deliver two thousand tons of caustic soda in six months or less, at twelve cents per pound, F.O.B., our port. We have asked that you open an irrevocable letter of credit for the entire amount."

Takei gave them his best wide smile before saying in a serious voice, "There is currently a worldwide shortage of caustic soda. We have had great difficulty finding much smaller quantities from our regular suppliers. we have sent inquiries to your major producers, all of whom were unable to fill this order. Please, Mr. Marshall, can you tell us how you can fulfill this commitment? Please understand, I ask this question with the utmost respect," he added hastily.

Yoshi waited patiently for the answer while Ruth sat perched on the edge of her seat. Hank sat back comfortably, his body relaxed, as if storing up energy for an attack.

"Let me set your mind at ease," he began. "We understand that you need to be assured of delivery before making a commitment of this size. Therefore, we're going to take you into our complete confidence, with the understanding that it will remain confidential."

"Agreed," said Yoshi.

Hank glanced at him appreciatively. He liked his quick response and his economy with words. I can do business with this man, he thought.

"The problem with caustic soda," he said aloud, "is not that it's in short supply." He looked around, savoring the curiosity he had piqued with his bold statement, which was seemingly at odds with the facts.

"The shortage lies in the containers needed to hold the caustic. Caustic must be packed in steel drums because steel is the only material that can't be eaten through by this chemical. So you see, the real shortage is in the steel needed for the drums. The mill price for caustic soda is only four cents per pound. The mills would gladly supply you with all you want if they had the steel drums in which to pack the materials.

"We, at Trans-Pacific Traders, have come up with a solution to this problem," he announced proudly. "We've contracted for the necessary steel drums at a high price which we will sell to the caustic mill below market price. In return, they'll sell caustic soda to us at mill prices. When we factor in the loss we take on the steel, we're able to sell you two thousand tons of caustic soda."

Yoshi's eyebrows lifted. "At a big profit to you," he added.

"At a reasonable profit to us," Hank replied. "The important thing is that you can be assured of delivery." With a twinkle in his eye, he added, "At a big profit to you."

"At a reasonable profit," Yoshi returned, smiling for the first time.

Ruth was enjoying watching the exchange between the two men. She knew they'd each emerge from this meeting with new respect for each other. Seeing that an understanding had been reached, she pounded on the edge of the table like an auctioneer responding to a winning bid and called out in a booming voice, "Sold! Looks like we have a deal here."

Glancing at her watch, she looked at Yoshi and said, "Now, may we buy you lunch? We have a very good Japanese restaurant on the corner or a great steakhouse a block down the street."

"Thank you very much. We would love a good American steak. But you must be our guests."

"We'll consider that part of the negotiations," she laughed as they got up from the conference table.

The restaurant was a short distance from the Trans-Pacific Traders' office. The foursome chatted amiably as they strolled along La Cienega Boulevard's Restaurant Row. The restaurant's maitre'd greeted them warmly upon their arrival, and led them to a quiet booth at the back of the restaurant.

The room was elegant with its mahogany walls and warm, subdued lighting. And the specialty of the house was stated simply in the restaurant's name—"Stear's For Steaks."

"California is now producing excellent wines that rival the French," said Hank, glancing over the wine list that had been delivered with the menus. "This Cabernet Sauvignon from the Napa Valley in Northern California goes very well with steak."

Takei's wide smile signaled his acceptance. In his position as Yoshi's right-hand man, he'd done a considerable amount of traveling and had come to appreciate the fine wines of Europe, not available in Japan. He nodded his head approvingly after first sniffing, then tasting the deep, red wine that was brought to their table.

Yoshi and Ruth sat back, listening, while Takei and Hank engaged in small talk. "If you enjoy the wine, then you must try the new salad they recommend with the steak. It's called a Caesar Salad. They make a big production when they serve it, mixing the dressing with fresh ingredients right at the table."

Takei nodded and smiled in appreciation as the waiter wheeled a large serving cart over to the table. With the precision of a surgeon, he began to perform. First, he rubbed fresh garlic along the inside of a large wooden bowl. Then, moving to a rhythm only he could hear, he cracked the eggs, separating the yolks from the whites.

Next, he poured in oil and vinegar, chopped anchovies and, with a flourish, sprinkled grated cheese and croutons over the lettuce leaves. Takei's smile grew wider as he tasted the salad and wider still as the steaks were brought to the table on sizzling platters.

The waiter served them as Ruth spoke for the first time. Looking across the table at Yoshi, she said, "When we first met, you wouldn't eat a hamburger. You told me it was because you didn't like red meat."

"That is true," he replied. "But since that time, I have learned to appreciate different cultures and the foods that go with them. It is important to learn the ways of the world outside of Japan. And that begins with speaking different languages and eating different foods. In Germany, I eat sausage and drink beer. It is all part of working in the world market."

Ruth thought about that for a minute. "So what you're saying is, even the food you eat is part of a plan." Her voice grew sharp.. "Tell me, do you ever act on the spur of the moment? Or do something spontaneous?"

Yoshi continued to eat as if she hadn't spoken.

Feeling the tension in the air, Hank jumped in. "Are you here on business other than finalizing the caustic deal with us?"

"Yes," said Yoshi. "We are investigating new technologies in electronics that have originated in the United States. Our company is also a manufacturer of radios and wire recorders and we are seeking distribution here in America. Do you have knowledge in this area?"

"We're very interested in expanding beyond export," Hank replied quickly. "We realize that supply will meet demand in the near future and our sources will soon begin to sell directly in the foreign markets. Before that happens, we've begun to investigate import opportunities. I must tell you, however, with all due respect, the merchandise that is now being imported from Japan, consists mainly of cheap novelties and toys."

Yoshi placed his knife and fork down on his plate and looking at Hank, said softly, "You have been kind enough to confide in us as to how you will acquire the caustic soda. This was an excellent decision on your part. The logic at once assures us you will be able to fill our order and it shows you have the courage to reveal just how you will do this. I appreciate your honesty and your ingenuity. Few people have original ideas and even fewer have the ability to execute them.

"We, too, have great plans that defy traditional thoughts. We are aware that the rest of the world does, indeed, look upon us as a source of cheap labor and cheap merchandise. Tosui, however, will soon be leading the way to advanced technology in Japan. We have already achieved great success with our wire recorders and our small, portable radios. Would you be interested in importing them into the United States?"

Hank looked at Ruth, who nodded enthusiastically. It was now his turn to be brief. "We would be delighted to examine your products and to research the marketplace. In short, we are definitely interested."

CHAPTER TWELVE

1952

Hank sank into the soft leather seat in the first class section of the Japan Airlines flight. He was headed to Tokyo, with a refueling stop in Honolulu. Marveling at the comfort of the reclining seat, he stretched out his long, lean frame until he almost hit the seat in front of him.

The DC-4 even smelled new. He watched appreciatively as the graceful Japanese stewardesses glided down the aisles serving drinks and exotic hors d'oeurves. The seat next to his was empty, giving him the luxury of spreading out and enjoying a few hours of solitude. It also allowed him the opportunity of reviewing his notes for the important meeting that would take place upon his arrival in Tokyo.

As the big ship sailed smoothly through the air, Hank couldn't help but compare it to the B-29 he had piloted seven years before. He remembered that as soon as his plane had taken off, he'd opened his sealed orders. Reading them over quickly, he'd announced over the intercom, "Well, men, you all know that we're going into combat on sealed orders. From here, we go to Hawaii where we'll stay the night at Hickham Field. They'll load us up with fuel and the chaplain will bless our plane. Then the good ship, Miss M'Nookie, will proceed to Saipan in the Mariana Islands. That's where we'll join the 73rd bomb wing in bombing the shit out of the Emperor. Now you know as much as the Japs, who've probably had a copy of these orders for a week. Who knows? Tokyo Rose might even welcome you personally."

He smiled, remembering all the raunchy remarks that came back over the intercom. And now, here he was, a passenger in a plane that was probably being piloted by someone who'd been shooting at him just a few short years ago.

The four years since his first meeting with Yoshi and Takei had flown by. They had completed the deal for the two thousand tons of caustic soda on schedule. It had taken tremendous skill and effort on the part of Hank, Ruth and Bea Stein to get the order filled and financed. Due to a late steel delivery, they'd had to get an extension on the letter of credit but Tosui had cooperated and eventually, it had all come together.

Chuckling to himself, Hank recalled those crazy, frantic days. You learn by doing, he thought. There wasn't a textbook written anywhere in the world that could have given them instructions on how to swing a deal as complex as that one. Maybe one day I'll write a book, he mused, but who'd believe it?

Little Trans-Pacific Traders had done what no other company had been able to do. And what followed had been equally exciting. Tosui had begun to supply them with radios and wire recorders of equal or better quality than R.C.A. or any of the other domestic manufacturers—at half the cost. At first, the department store buyers had scoffed. "Japan cannot produce quality," they told him, "and certainly not at those prices." So Hank had created the hearing test. He would blank out the manufacturer's name on each of the products. Then, he would have the buyers listen: first to the tone of the R.C.A. radio and then to its Japanese counterpart. Invariably, they would choose his radio because it sounded better—and the sale was made. Just one year ago, he had cracked Sears & Roebuck, the world's largest retailer. After extensive testing, Sears had placed a huge order with the provision that the product was manufactured under the Sears name. Hank continued to marvel at the fact that there was never an order too large for Tosui to fill on time.

Neither Hank nor Ruth had spoken to Yoshikazu Matsuda since their initial meeting. All the company business was being handled through Takei. As the business continued to grow, Takei and the Marshall's came to understand and trust each other more and more. Then suddenly, last month, Yoshi contacted them directly.

They could hear the excitement in his voice through the telephone wire. "We have made a major electronic breakthrough!"

Then, in a calmer voice Yoshi told them, "We would like you both to come to Tokyo to discuss the possibility of American distribution for our new product. You will, of course, come as our guests."

Ruth felt her heart begin to race when she first heard his voice. After composing herself, she said, "Oh, Yoshi, I'd love to come but I can't. Hank and I are expecting our first child in about two months and I just can't make that kind of trip right now."

"My congratulations to you both," he answered solemnly.

Listening to Ruth, Hank felt a warm glow. It happened every time the baby was mentioned. He particularly appreciated the way she'd said, "Hank and I are expecting" rather than, "I'm going to have a baby".

"Hank," Yoshi was saying, "it is most important, then, that you come."

Hesitantly, Hank said, "I'll have to discuss it with Ruth."

"Of course you must go," she said firmly. "Besides, you'll be back in plenty of time. By the way…Yoshi, do you have any children?"

"Yes," he said, "Two daughters and we are expecting another child shortly. Perhaps this time I will have a son," he added, hopefully. Almost instantly, the softness of his tone changed to a challenging one. "So, what is your decision, Hank?"

"I'll phone you tomorrow around this time, with my answer," Hank replied.

The lush, green stretch that was the Hawaiian Islands could now be seen from the DC-4. They looked as tranquil and magnificent as they had when Hank had piloted his heavily armed B-29 in an almost identical flight pattern on his way to Japan. The difference now was that there was no danger.

He had been hesitant to leave Ruth alone so late in the pregnancy, but she'd insisted that he go. "Opportunity is knocking loudly," she'd told him. Placing his hands on her bulging stomach, she'd said, "Don't worry, he'll be right here waiting for you when you get back." As if on cue, Hank felt the baby kick and laughed, "He or she just gave final approval."

The stopover in Hawaii was only for two hours: just long enough to let the passengers off who were disembarking, to take on those who were traveling to Tokyo and to refuel the plane.

Hank left the plane himself, grateful for a chance to stretch his legs. Walking down the ramp, he saw a welcoming committee of four amply-built native women standing in a row, dressed in colorful printed moo-moos. With a warm smile, the largest of the ladies placed a sweet smelling lei around his neck and wished him a pleasant journey.

Returning to the aircraft, he found the aisle seat next to his had been taken. The occupant was a burly, red-faced man wearing baggy, wrinkled white cotton slacks and a wildly colored, short sleeved Hawaiian shirt. When Hank paused in front of him, he looked up with a big smile. "Is this your seat, pardner?" he asked in a booming voice. Standing up, he stepped aside so Hank could move into the window seat. "I'm Jack Strong," he said, sticking out his hand.

Hank accepted the handshake. "Hank Marshall," he answered, easing himself into the wide leather seat while Jack plopped down noisily beside him. The captain announced they were ready for take off. The passengers fastened their seatbelts as the big plane glided smoothly down the runway. When they were airborne, Jack continued his effort to strike up a conversation. "I'm in Public Relations," he boomed, "one of the great hacks of our time. What do you do for a living?"

Hoping to keep the discussion to a minimum, Hank was brief. "I'm in the import and export business," he told him, opening his briefcase.

"What's your line?" was the next question.

"Industrial chemicals and electronics."

"Well, it's all show business," Jack announced grandly. "I handle a bunch of stars and do a lot of work for the motion picture studios. In fact, I'm working on a picture right now that's shooting on location in Japan. It's called, 'Destination Tokyo'."

He stopped for a breath as a tiny, kimono-clad stewardess approached them. "May I bring you a drink?" she asked in a quiet voice.

"Thought you'd never ask, little lady," Jack said loudly. "I'll have a double Bombay Gin martini with onions and olives. And I'm going to buy my friend here a drink. What'll you have, pardner?"

Hank smiled and ordered a scotch on the rocks. With a resigned sigh, he closed his briefcase and slipped it under the seat.

The stewardess returned with their drinks. Handing Jack his, he smacked his lips as he breathed in the pungent aroma of his martini. Then, after gulping down half the drink at once, he sighed ecstatically, and in a pretty good imitation of comedian Jackie Gleason, said, "Boy, that's good booze!" Satisfied now, he turned to Hank and demanded, "So tell me—what kind of electronic merchandise do you handle?"

"We've been importing Japanese radios and wire recorders into the States."

Jack drained his glass. "The Jap stuff is cheap but it's real crap. How can you sell it when we have all these great American manufacturers?"

Hank was surprised at how offended he was by this off-handed comment. "Our radios are as good as anything manufactured in the States," he said in measured tones, "and our recording equipment is better."

The stewardess returned to their aisle once more. "What will you gentlemen have for dinner?" she asked in halting English. "You have a choice of a typical Japanese meal or we have salad and beefsteak with baked potato."

"Give me meat, and potatoes, little lady," Jack bellowed, "but first, how 'bout another round of drinks. I can't eat on an empty stomach." He laughed loudly in appreciation of his own humor. Ignoring the stewardess, he turned to Hank and said, "Boy, I just can't eat that Jap shit. How 'bout you? You going to eat that raw fish stuff?" A pained expression crossed his face.

"It is an acquired taste," Hank answered pleasantly. Turning to the stewardess, he said, "I'll have the Japanese dinner, please." As he said this, he remembered Yoshi saying, 'When you do business in a country, it is a good idea to understand their culture and their food."

The stewardess bowed and with a sweet smile said, "Hai, thank you," before gliding away.

"Is that cute or what? I could eat her up in one big swallow. But I still won't eat raw fish." Laughing loudly again, he looked at Hank to see if he'd gotten the joke.

Hank sipped his scotch without commenting. Then, more to change the subject than from any real interest he said, "Tell me, whom do you actually represent?"

"Well, I don't want you thinking I'm a namedropper like so many of those Hollywood phonies. I work for the studio that's producing the film but I'll probably wind up representing the stars of the picture. There's Edmond O'Brien, who came from Broadway but has done some pretty big pictures. Then, there's this young, British sexpot named Joan Collins. Every time I look at her, I get crazy! We've also got this new, good looking kid, who's gonna to be a big star. His name is Robert Wagner.

"We'll be shooting in Tokyo for a few days. Then, we move on to Kyoto. Anytime you want to, just give me a call and I'll introduce you to show business. It's all bullshit anyway." He was beginning to slur his words by now.

"I'm at the Imperial Hotel," he went on, "and I'm goin' to give you a slogan to remember so you'll never forget my name—Jack Strong. Just remember, 'A good connection is a strong connection'. Got that? Let me tell ya, public-relations is mostly a question of contacts and I have all the connections. Who knows? You might even want to use me someday."

As the meal was being served, Jack attacked his food with gusto, washing it down with yet another double martini. Hank savored each of his courses and tried not to engage in any further conversation. Luckily for him, no sooner had Jack swallowed the last of his steak, than his head fell back and he began to snore loudly.

Looking out of the airplane's window, Hank caught sight of land. There, on his left, was Mt. Surabachi. For the first time, he was struck by the beauty and majesty of the mountain his combat crew used to call 'Mt. Son-of-a-Bitchi'.

Suddenly, a cold sweat drenched his body. In his mind, he could see Japanese fighter planes swarming in for the kill once again. The air seemed filled with flak, bursting all around him. It was almost as if he was in suspended animation—not awake and yet, not asleep. A stifling fear began compressing his lungs and gnawing at his stomach.

Heavy hands were now on his shoulders, shaking him back to the present. He heard a voice that seemed to come from a great distance away. As it grew louder and stronger, Hank was able to bring Jack's face into focus. He heard him repeating over and over again, "Are you okay? Are you all right?"

"Yes, I'm fine," Hank was finally able to reassure him. "Must have been a bad dream."

"You were sure as hell on a bad trip. And you look as if you've seen a ghost."

"I think I've just seen a lot of ghosts," Hank said as his racing heart slowly began to calm down.

Jack's insufferable attitude had disappeared, replaced by concern. "Where were you just now? You looked as though you were having a nightmare but your eyes were wide open and you were staring out the window."

Although his head was still foggy, Hank found himself thinking of a conversation he'd had with Ruth before leaving home. He had made up his mind not to mention the part he'd played in the war while on this trip. Ruth had agreed that was best, saying it wouldn't be in good taste or good for business.

"I don't think the people you meet will react kindly to someone who, just a few years ago, destroyed their homes and possibly killed some of their loved ones," she'd said. "Besides, it really doesn't matter anymore how the war started. This is 1952, not 1945. We have to look to the future and not let the past screw us up."

He shook his head, attempting to clear it. Seeing the worried look still on Jack's face, he let his guard down. "I've had nightmares since my war days, although they come less frequently now. This is the first time, though, it's happened in broad daylight—while I'm wide awake. I guess being here and flying the same pattern I did during the air raids, triggered it."

Hearing himself, Hank wondered why he had taken this complete stranger into his confidence. It just came out, he thought. I didn't have a choice.

"I have a pretty good idea of what you went through," Jack told him. "I was with Army Information Services—a fancy name for Public Relations. We were the first group to go into Japan after the peace treaty was signed. It wasn't a pleasant sight. Fortunately, now, the only thing we're shooting in Japan is this movie.

"Here, take my card," he said, yanking one from his wallet. "I'll be staying at the Imperial Hotel for at least a week before we leave for Kyoto. Give me a call. You can watch us shoot, meet the stars and then we can go out and have some fun."

"Thanks," Hank said, appreciatively. "I just might do that. It's the best offer I've had all day."

CHAPTER THIRTEEN

The next morning, at precisely eight A.M., Takei Watanabe met Hank in the lobby of the Imperial Hotel. Takei appeared not to have changed at all. His suit was still too tight for his short, powerful body and he wore the same wide smile. Hank greeted him warmly—shaking his hand and offering a quick bow. Takei almost touched the ground as he returned a more formal one. "We are honored, by your presence, Hank-San," he told him.

For the past couple of years, their correspondence had begun with salutations like 'Dear Tak' and 'Dear Hank'. They'd developed a mutual admiration and respect for each other's business acumen. This was due, for the most part, to the successes achieved by the two companies through the constant flow of importing and exporting products.

Takei ushered Hank from the hotel to a shiny black, four-door, Toyota town car. A uniformed chauffeur stood at attention before opening the door for them to enter.

The streets of Tokyo were teeming with activity. Tiny taxis darted through the traffic like little bugs. Hundreds of bicycles intermingled with a massive number of cars and buses. Even the noodle vendors kept up with the flow of traffic, madly pedaling their carts through the maze. Hank watched in awe as drivers kept narrowly missing each other in single-minded pursuit of reaching their destination.

In the middle of this frenzy of activity, construction crews worked at a fevered pace, erecting buildings and shops and paving roads. The city seemed to be rising from its own ashes. It gave Hank a strange feeling to actually be driving through the crowded streets of Tokyo.

The imposing gray granite Tosui Building was distinctive -standing taller than the other buildings around it. A huge red flag with a single bamboo emblazoned upon it, waved from the rooftop. The proud, steadfast structure looked as if it could maintain its dignified stance for at least another hundred years.

Hank was even more impressed when he stepped into the lobby. A fine collection of paintings and drawings by well-known Western artists hung on the walls beside delicate Japanese prints. one wall displayed a series of huge, framed portraits featuring three generations of the Matsuda family. Next to them, was a portrait of General Douglas MacArthur. On a brass plaque near the bottom of the frame was a quote, taken from the speech he'd made at the building's dedication in 1948: "Tosui will help to lead the way to a prosperous and peaceful Japan."

Takei led Hank to the tower elevator. It sped, noiselessly, to the top floor where the executive suites were located. When the doors opened, they entered a reception area of lushly carpeted elegance. Nodding to the pretty receptionist, they walked down to the end of a long corridor where Takei escorted Hank into a large, corner office.

As they entered, Yoshikazu Matsuda stepped from behind his desk to welcome them. Extending his hand to Hank, he bowed. Hank responded with a slight bow of his own as they firmly shook hands.

"Did you have a pleasant journey?" Yoshi asked.

"I did, thank you. I enjoyed flying Japan Airlines. They can certainly teach Pan American a lesson on in-flight service. Ruth sends her best regards and her regrets that she couldn't make the trip." A picture of Ruth in her eighth month of pregnancy flashed in his mind.

Yoshi motioned for Takei and Hank to be seated in the black leather chairs across from his hand-carved teakwood desk, indicating it was time to get down to business.

"Four years ago, on the same trip on which we met with you, Bell Laboratories developed and received a patent for transistors. They felt this major breakthrough could be successful in   the manufacture of hearing aids. We felt it had a much wider application with regard to the manufacture of radios.

We knew that if we could increase the currency, we could produce a portable radio of tiny size with astonishing sound. We signed a licensing agreement for the use of the transistor and now, our engineers and designers have collaborated in producing the first transistor radio.

"In addition to this giant leap forward, we are producing a new generation of television sets. Their sound and picture quality will surpass anything that is currently on the market."

Hank immediately recognized the potential power of the products Yoshi was describing. After the successes he'd enjoyed with other Tosui products, he could hardly wait to see them.

"We are now ready," Yoshi continued, "to create our own brand name for these original products. We will produce a full range of merchandise that will compete with R.C.A. and General Electric, not only in Japan but around the world. The biggest market will, of course, be the United States. That is what we would like to discuss with you.

"Please understand there are other distributors in your country with whom we have worked in the past. But now, we must choose one exclusive distributor with whom to begin a joint venture. Would this be of interest to you?"

Hank thought for a moment before answering. "Television is in its infancy but I know the market will eventually explode. Just how small can you make a transistor radio?"

Takei flashed his trademark smile and beamed. "We plan to make it small enough to fit into your pocket," he said proudly.

"With a sound that will be as good or better than today's full-sized radios," added Yoshi. "We are now researching brand names for this new generation of products. No longer will we sell under someone else's name. And what this means is, we will no longer be involved in private labeling, as we have been doing for Sears & Roebuck."

Hank was stunned. "But Sears represents half of our volume! And you know they insist on using their own brand name. We would lose their business. Are you ready to take that kind of a risk?"

"We are more than ready," Yoshi said with a confident smile. "In fact, it is what we must do. Never again will we allow others to put their name on our products. We will produce the merchandise and we will maintain control."

Despite the risk involved, Hank loved the idea. The challenge excited him. "I understand what you're saying, Yoshi, and I believe that you're right. The next step then, is to come up with a gangbuster name." He spoke as though the decision to join forces had been settled. "You claim your televisions will have superior sound. How about the name 'Telesound?'"

Yoshi repeated the word slowly—TELESOUND. Then he shook his head. "It is not modern or new enough."

"There's nothing newer than television," Hank said, "but we could try another word for 'sound'."

Yoshi and Takei began speaking rapidly to each other in Japanese, Takei making sweeping motions with his arms. When they'd finished, Yoshi looked apologetically at Hank for excluding him. Then, he said simply, "Sonics."

"SONICS," Hank repeated. His face lit up and he said excitedly, "That's it! 'Telesonics'.' No wait…'Telesonic'. The three of them nodded, grinning like co-conspirators.

"The name we choose will be of great importance, for it will also be the name of the joint venture company," said Yoshi. "Let us give this idea time to grow in our minds. What we must do now, however, is decide if it is to our mutual advantage to form a joint venture—with you distributing this new line of products in the United States.

"In order to make this important decision, Hank, you should see the models we have developed thus far. Please understand, we will not be satisfied with anything less than establishing our brand as the world leader in consumer electronics."

Hank was quiet for a moment. In his mind, he could hear his father's voice, 'So all right, already. Let's take a look at the merchandise.' Smiling to himself, he said aloud, "I guess it's time to see the line."

Hank arrived back at the Imperial Hotel later that night, elated as well as exhausted. It was now midnight. They'd worked throughout the day and long into the evening. Hank wondered if Yoshi always worked this hard.

He'd been impressed by what he saw. The television sets had big screens with clear, sharp pictures and magnificent sound. Maintaining his cool had been difficult. This was the new technology! Consumer electronics of the future.

Glancing at his watch, Hank calculated it to be 7:30 A.M., Los Angeles time. After propping himself up comfortably on the bed, he picked up the phone to call Ruth. He had to share his excitement with her.

The voice at the other end of the line was husky with sleep. Ruth still didn't awaken easily. Hank had always been able to jump out of bed at the crack of dawn but Ruth preferred sleeping late. Hank joked that his toughest job of the day was getting her up in the morning. And her response was always the same way: "There are day people and there are night people. I am a night person."

He smiled when he heard her on the other end of the receiver. The delight in her voice made it ring through strong and clear.

"Darling, what a wonderful surprise! How are you? I miss you so much! How's the battle going? How was your trip over? Tell me everything that's going on in the world of international commerce."

Hank laughed happily at the barrage of questions. Just hearing her and feeling the warmth and love in her voice melted away his exhaustion. "I feel great. It was a long trip but very comfortable. I met a funny guy on the plane—public relations type, a real character. The hotel is beautiful and the service is wonderful. Yoshi and Takei send you their regards and I love you and miss you. So much has been happening, I feel as though I've been gone for a year. How's the baby?"

On the other side of the line, Ruth giggled and patted her stomach. "Here, I'll let you talk to him." She put the phone against her round belly, hesitating for a second. "He's sleeping now," she whispered.

Remembering the distance of the call, she sat up in bed and said, "This is costing a fortune. So, what's the deal? Is it worth the trip?"

"Everything is fantastic! This just might be the start of a whole new ballgame," he replied. He proceeded to give her the highlights of the day, summing them up by repeating, "It's a whole new ballgame."

"It sounds wonderful, Hank! I love it and I love you! We'll have to completely reorganize and find some heavy-duty financing. Are the television sets and radios really that good?"

"Better," he quickly replied. "It's going to take a lot of hard work and it could be very risky, but I believe this is the future. You know, Ruth, it's funny. It's a totally different world here but in so many ways, they're just like us."

"Yes, I know. What time is it there?" she asked, quickly.

"It's past midnight and it's been a very long day." A yawn slipped out before he could stifle it. "I'd better catch some sleep now. Take care of the baby. I love you both and I'll talk to you soon."

"Sleep tight" she whispered before gently hanging up the phone.

On his third night in Tokyo, Hank was invited to join Yoshi, his father, Yukio, and Takei for dinner. Takei picked him up at his hotel at eight and they drove to meet the others at their private club.

The City Club was located in the Ginza section of Tokyo. As soon as he entered its quiet elegance, Hank began to relax. The cool, calm atmosphere within was a sharp contrast to the teeming metropolis outside.

Hank and Takei were immediately ushered to a table in the corner of the room where Yoshi and Yukio were already seated. The two men rose and bowed as they approached. Returning the bow, Hank looked at Yukio. He could feel the powerful presence of the man. Although Yukio was wearing a conservative, western-style business suit, his manner and carriage brought to mind visions of a samurai warrior.

"Please be seated," Yukio said in halting English.

"I am delighted that we finally have the chance to meet," Hank told him as he sat down. "I have heard so much about you."

Yukio slipped a silver cigarette case from his breast pocket and offered Hank a cigarette, which he politely declined. He then offered one to Yoshi and to Takei, each of who accepted with a deferential bow.

Yukio inhaled deeply and turned to Hank. "Are you enjoying your trip?"

"Yes, but I haven't had much of a chance to see Japan yet."

Ah, but it is important that you take time to see and feel Japan," said Yukio. "A business trip should always include the sights and culture of the country. Many years ago, when I first visited the United States, the automobile was not so reliable vehicle. Yet, I had the pleasure of motoring across the country."

He paused for a moment, taking a last puff from his cigarette before putting it out in the gold leaf ashtray in front of him. "When it came time to send Yoshikazu to college, we had become familiar with the different regions of your country. We were most happy that he was able to attend the University of California at Los Angeles."

"Yoshikazu and I met in Los Angeles," said Hank," although our meeting was brief."

"Yes," Yoshi added. "I did not understand your game of football but I did see you play. I was very impressed by the way you were able to throw the ball and also run with it. Here in Japan, we are great fans of baseball but know very little of football."

The waiter returned to their table and bowed as he presented them with menus, standing by silently while they considered their choices.

"I recommend our beef steak," said Yoshi. "It comes from Kobe and I think you will find that it compares very favorably with American beef."

"If you wouldn't mind," said Hank, "I would very much enjoy having a traditional Japanese meal."

"Ah, very well," said Yukio with a pleased smile. "We will be happy to order for you and will include a sample of our Kobe beef for you to try."

Yoshi turned to the waiter and addressed him in Japanese. The waiter bowed every few seconds saying, "Hai, hai."

"Would you like some Scotch whiskey to start?" asked Yoshi.

"I'd like that very much," Hank replied.

Again, instructions were given and immediately, a bottle of Johnny Walker Black Label appeared on the table, along with glasses and ice. As the waiter poured their drinks, Hank started to bring up the subject of their business arrangement but the conversation was quickly steered in another direction. Several attempts later, he realized the Japanese did not like talking about business in the evening.

"You see, Mr. Marshall," Yukio explained at last, "in our country, we work very long hours—six, usually seven days a week. When we go out in the evening with an honored guest, we feel it is impolite to discuss business."

"When do you find time to spend with your families?" Hank asked him. "Do you include your wives in your dinners with customers?"

"Almost never," Yukio replied. "We go out to relax. This evening, for example, we will enjoy one of the finest meals you will have in Tokyo or anywhere else. Then, perhaps you young people will go to the Copacabana or another of our famous nightclubs.

"You see, Mr. Marshall, a woman's place is in the home. They must bring up our children and carry on our traditions. They also have the responsibility of caring for our elders, which is most important."

Yoshi looked at his father uneasily before saying with a smile, "It is different in the United States, Father. You must realize that Marshall-San's wife works along with him. She is instrumental in running their business."

Yukio, unphased by his son's remark, looked at Hank and said, "Do you have any children, Mr. Marshall?"

"Not yet. My wife is pregnant with our first child."

"Well, then," said Yukio grandly, "we must toast the mother and the unborn child. And hope it is a son!"

They all raised their glasses as Takei toasted, "Kanpai!"

Hank was familiar with the expression and added the English version saying, "Down the hatch!" as all four emptied their glasses. The waiter, standing near by, quickly refilled them.

"My father is disappointed that so far, I have two daughters but no sons," said Yoshi solemnly. "However, Hank-San, we are comrades in this regard. Kimi, too, is pregnant and we pray that this one will be a son."

Hank was beginning to feel the effects of whiskey on an empty stomach. In a somber voice, he raised his glass high and said, "Let us pray this one is a boy."

In an equally serious tone, Yukio added something that sounded suspiciously like 'Amen' before they downed another glass.

Hank was having a wonderful time. He was enjoying the luxurious service and the feeling of being part of Tokyo's inner circle.

The waiter returned to the Matsuda table with several platters of Japanese delicacies. Before serving these, another waiter placed a small, perfectly grilled steak in front of each of them. Hank cut into his and was amazed at the tenderness of the meat. "You underestimate the quality of your Kobe beef," he told them. "This steak is far superior to any I've ever eaten. Is there a secret to what makes it so good?"

With a smile, Yoshi answered. "You will find this hard to believe, Hank-San, but it is because our cattle are handled in a special way. Before slaughter, they are massaged and fed beer. Then, when the time comes to kill them, they are relaxed. In your country, no such precaution is taken.

At the moment of slaughter, your cattle are tense because they have been led to their death in an unfeeling manner."

They sat quietly, enjoying their food and sipping sake, until Yukio broke the silence by clearing his throat. With as much dignity as he could muster, he staggered to his feet. "I will propose a final toast and then I will take these old bones back to their home. I would like to propose a toast to the growth of Japan and to our continuing friendship with the United States."

Raising his glass in Hank's direction, Yukio continued. "Yours is a remarkable country, Mr. Marshall. At no time in history have the victors ever treated the vanquished with such compassion. Now, in this period of recovery, we can look forward to the future glory of our beloved Japan."

Hank stood respectfully and lifted his glass. "To a lasting friendship between the United States and Japan."

"Kanpei!" smiled Takei, as they emptied their glasses once more.

Yukio bowed to each of the men. Then, with the waiter's hand placed respectfully on his elbow, he left the restaurant.

"I believe we should be going ourselves," said Yoshi. "It is still early and I would enjoy showing you a little of our city's nightlife."

The atmosphere at the Copacabana was vastly different from that of The City Club. To enter the nightclub, they had to walk up a flight of stairs, located on the side of the building, not visible from the street. At the top of the stairs was a long dark hallway leading to a large wooden door. A peephole, similar to the ones used during prohibition, was at its center.

Takei knocked firmly on the door twice. The peephole opened and the doorman, recognizing Yoskikazu, pulled the heavy door aside. Bowing very low, he escorted them in.

Entering the nightclub, Hank felt as if he'd been transported back to a speakeasy of the 1920's—like those he'd seen in the movies. A long, wooden bar stretched across the entire right side of the club. Its gleaming mahogany reflected the dim glow of Tiffany lamps hanging above. Seated in a row, on stools facing the bar, was an outstanding array of beautiful women. Their lovely faces were reflected in the mirror that hung behind the bar, spanning its entire length. There were Japanese women, dressed in both traditional and western-style clothing. There were also blondes from Scandinavia, sophisticated brunettes from Europe and a smattering of red heads with long hair that covered their eyes like the American movie star, Veronica Lake. In all, about thirty women sat, waiting to be chosen.

A six-piece band was playing a spirited rendition of "Won't You Come Home Bill Bailey?" The dance floor seemed to overflow with couples, crushed together, moving as rhythmically as possible.

The male patrons of the club were dressed in finely tailored western-style suits while most of the women wore traditional kimonos. A grayish haze had settled over the room from the hundreds of cigarettes whose smoke curled in and out of the spotlights. Small wooden tables with chairs upholstered with dark green plastic covers sat around the perimeter of the dance floor.

As his eyes became accustomed to the darkness, Hank looked around in fascination. Above the loud music, he could hear snatches of conversations in many different languages, blending together. He saw the continuous parade of men, making their way to the bar to choose a companion. The girls at the bar giggled and talked amongst themselves. Their eyes were glued to the mirror, as they watched the men approach.

Takei's eyes twinkled as he watched Hank taking everything in. "Do not worry, Hank-San," he said, impishly. "Our charming companions are waiting for us at our table."

The headwaiter walked in front of them, clearing a path through the crowd like a blocking fullback. He led them to a round table for six, already set with two bottles of Johnny Walker Black Label, a bucket filled with ice, two bottles of plain soda and a pitcher of water.

"Matsuda-San, you honor us with your presence," the headwaiter fawned. "Please let me know what I can do to make your visit more pleasurable."

Three beautiful Japanese women appeared at their table. The men quickly stood up, allowing them to sit down. Acknowledging the ladies with a slight nod, Yoshi turned to Hank. "These three lovely hostesses are here to provide comfort and relaxation. They will light our cigarettes, massage our necks and they can dance in any style you wish.

"Marshall–San," Yoshi said, motioning to the pretty Japanese girl next to Hank, "this is Susie. She spent several years in the United States and speaks excellent English. We have American hostesses here, but I thought you would enjoy a truly Japanese experience."

Susie bowed respectfully. Raising her head slowly, her eyes fluttered as she said in a sweet voice, "I would like to welcome you, Marshall-San."

Hank was not quite sure of what to do. He looked around the table at the others. Takei was laughing as the hostess next to him whispered in his ear. Takei spoke to her in Japanese and she carefully poured him a drink. Catching Hank's eye, he grinned as he gave the girl a fond hug. "This is Toshiko. On the other side of you is Shikibu."

Hank turned his head and started to nod 'hello,' but found himself staring at Shikibu. Her beauty was breathtaking. Jet-black hair framed a face that looked as if it had been carved in ivory. She wore a rich, dark blue silk kimono that draped her body in soft, flowing lines. Nodding to Hank, she bowed slightly. Her perfect features made her look like a sculpture come to life. "It is an honor," she said with a smile.

Yoshi removed a silver case, very much like the one his father carried, from the inside of his breast pocket. He opened it and Shikibu took out a cigarette, which she placed in his mouth. Taking a match from a silver container on the table, she turned her body slightly from Yoshi, as she struck the match. Turning back slowly, she brought the flame to the tip of his cigarette.

"Arigato," he said, glancing sideways at her.

The band was now playing, "It Had To Be You." "Takei took Toshiko's hand and got up. "Hank-San, why don't you dance with Susie?"

Hank turned and looked at Susie's pretty face. "I would be delighted to dance with you, Hank-San," she told him, sweetly.

The dance floor was crowded, yet Susie expertly followed Hank's steps as he held her lightly in his arms.

"Where are you from?" he asked.

"I was born in Yokohama. I have always lived in Japan except for the short time I spent in America. And you?"

"I'm from Los Angeles" he replied. "So, what are you doing here? What is it you do?"

She looked puzzled. "What do you mean?"

"What exactly do you do?"

"This is what I do," she said slowly. "I am a hostess in this nightclub. I meet very interesting people. I enjoy it very much."

"Well, you are a wonderful dancer," he said, slightly embarrassed.

"Thank you. So are you."

Hank was feeling light-headed. And, he was enjoying dancing with this exotic creature, who seemed to float in his arms. I guess that's where the old expression "feeling light as a feather" comes from, he thought giddily. The experiences of the past week now seemed jumbled in his mind. I've had a few too many drinks tonight, he said to himself. I'm getting punchy.

The music stopped, and with his arm still around Susie's tiny waist, they walked back to their table. Delicately, she moved in front of him to allow him to pull out her chair. Suddenly, he felt a sharp slap on his back.

"Hank Marshall, you old son-of-a-bitch! What the hell are you doing here?"

Turning quickly, he stared at the man before him. It took him several moments before he recognized Sandy Gold, his briefing officer on Saipan. A few pounds heavier and almost bald, Sandy stood unsteadily before him, trying to keep his balance. His face was red and sweaty with his shirt unbuttoned, his tie askew. A cigarette dangled from between his lips. Hank reached out to shake his hand. "Nice to see you, Sandy."

"No," Sandy said, slurring his words, "you heard what I said. What the hell are you doin' here? I never figured to meet you in Tokyo."

"I might ask you the same question."

Hank's question remained unanswered. Standing unevenly at Hank's table, he stared at its occupants until Hank finally said, "Allow me to introduce you to Yoshikazu Matsuda and Takei Watanabe of the Tosui Trading Company."

"Tosui? Shit, I know Tosui. We did a little business with them. But they're too expensive. You've got to be very careful who you do business with," said Sandy, swaying and winking conspiratorially. "I'm an old-timer here, you know. I've been doing business in Japan for the past four years."

A violent cough shook his body and he grabbed the back of Hank's chair to steady himself. After regaining control, Sandy looked up with a crooked smile and said, "Hey isn't this a helluva place?"

Without waiting for an invitation, Sandy pulled out the chair next to Hank's and sat down. Yoshi stared at him without speaking.

"Hey, Yoshi-Kazu," said Sandy with great effort, "you're with Ichiban. I know Ichiban." He motioned wildly with his hand in Shikibu's direction.

"What do you mean, Ichiban?" asked Hank.

"Ichiban is number one. She's the best. Just look how beautiful she is. Everyone in the club wants to be with her so she splits her time between a lot of tables. These broads make three bucks an hour—about a thousand yen. They all make the same pittance but it's a lot of money here in Japan. Ichiban's different, though. She can work two or three tables at a time and charge each one a thousand yen, right, Ich?"

Yoshi's eyes darkened and his mouth grew tight but he continued to say nothing. Hank could feel the tension around him, but he wasn't quite sure of what to do. He knew Sandy had had a lot to drink. He remembered him as being loud and undiplomatic even as a briefing officer. That was how he'd gotten the nickname "Randy Sandy."

"Did you ever think," Sandy bellowed, "that you'd be sitting around, enjoying yourself, in a nightclub in Tokyo? Almost doesn't make sense, does it? Then, Jesus, Hank! I don't see you or hear about you in over seven years and here you are in Japan. Son-of-a-bitch!"

Hank was beginning to feel uneasy but apparently Sandy didn't notice anything peculiar, because he just continued on.

"Yeah, I've been importing a lot of stationary from Japan. Just made a deal for these little notebooks," he said, pulling a small book out of his jacket pocket and thrusting it at Hank. "I bought two million of them at four cents a piece—four fucking cents. Can you believe what these guys can turn out merchandise for? Tosui gave us a quote but they weren't even close. They're too high up there. They don't want to

come down to earth and compete."

Sandy seemed oblivious to his cold reception at the table. "So, what are you doing here," he demanded.

"I'm in the import/export business," said Hank, noncommittally.

"Yeah? Well, remember what I said," Sandy told him, staggering to his feet at last and slapping Hank on the back again. "Just be careful." And he walked away unsteadily.

Hank breathed a sigh of relief. But he wasn't sure of what to say to the others, who continued sitting stiffly at the table. "I must apologize," he said. "He's not exactly a close friend of mine. I knew him a long time ago."

"No apologies are necessary," said Yoshi politely, with a slight bow.

Takei, who had been standing through most of the exchange, returned to his seat. During the conversation, Hank had seen him move quietly between Sandy and Yoshi, his short, powerful body poised and ready for any necessary action. Now, he said with an understanding smile, "Whiskey speaks in a loud voice."

Hank now became aware of Susie's gentle fingers on his neck. Although he hadn't been conscious of it, she had been gently massaging away the tension he'd been feeling.

"I think Susie likes you," Takei told him.

"I like her, too," Hank replied. "And thank you, Susie-San," he said, as he removed her hands. Standing, he asked, "Where is the men's room?"

"I will show you," said Takei, guiding Hank away from the table.

As they walked through the crowded club, Takei said to Hank in a confidential tone, "Hank-San, perhaps you would be interested in taking Susie with you when you leave tonight? If you are, you must not take her to your hotel but to a Japanese Inn."

"Why is that?"

"American hotels, like the Imperial, do not approve of men bringing women to their rooms who are not their wives. It is different in a Japanese inn, however. If you do not go with a woman, they think you are strange. Please understand that a hostess will not go with just anyone who asks her. There must be real feeling. Of course, it is expected that you give her a little gift as a token of your esteem."

"Thank you very much, Takei. It is very kind of you but I'm not interested."

Arriving at the restroom door, Takei gave a slight bow and returned to the table.

Hank walked in and went over to the sink. Turning on the faucet, he splashed cold water on his face. An attendant quickly rushed over with a clean white towel and bowed as he handed it to him. Drying himself, Hank looked at his reflection in the mirror. The numbness in his face made him realize he'd had too much to drink.

Well, Pal, I think you've just about had it, he told himself. The thought of spending the evening with Susie was tempting but a casual sexual encounter held no appeal for him. After four years of marriage, he was still very much in love with his wife.

Looking into the mirror once more, Hank slurred to himself, boy, have you changed! You're gettin' to be a regular old stick in-the-mud.

Returning to the table, he said, "I've really had a wonderful time but I'm about ready to go back to the hotel. I want to thank you, though, for a truly enjoyable experience."

"It is our pleasure, Hank-San, said Yoshi. Calling the waiter over, he gave him instructions in Japanese. Turning to Hank, he said, "This gentleman will escort you downstairs. The car is waiting to take you to your hotel.

"Thank you for joining us this evening. We look forward to seeing you in the office tomorrow morning."

Hank shook hands with Yoshi and Takei and nodded to the women sitting next to them. He then took Susie's hand and brushed it against his lips. "Thank you for being so kind to me," he said.

Following the waiter through the crowded club to the exit, he walked on out to the car.

Chapter Fourteen

$\blacktriangledown$

Hank had been in Tokyo for five days. It was six o'clock on Friday night and he was sitting at the bar in the hotel's lounge feeling mentally and physically exhausted. What had seemed so exotic when he'd first arrived, was all too familiar now.

He had hoped to catch a flight and be home for the weekend, but he still had three more days of work left. There was now no doubt in his mind that he would ultimately make a deal with Tosui, forming a joint venture in the United States. They just needed to agree on the terms of the partnership and on how much financing would be needed. They'd already reviewed the product line and had scheduled Monday to discuss the other items, in various stages of preparation.

Hank was disappointed that he couldn't go home as early as he'd planned. His phone conversations with Ruth always ended with his gnawing desire to be with her. He longed to hold her close and feel the weight of their unborn child push against him as they embraced. He was thankful that the Japanese worked on Saturday. That way, he could finish up by Wednesday and fly home.

Despite the fact that he was feeling lonely, he had no desire for company. And so he did not welcome the sound of the booming voice coming from behind him.

"Hank Marshall! What are you doing sitting in the middle of Tokyo all by yourself?"

Jack Strong had seen Hank at the bar as soon as he'd entered the lobby.

"Mind if I join you?" he asked, sitting down on the stool next to Hank's without waiting for an answer. "Phew", he sighed loudly. "We've been shooting this picture on locations all over Tokyo and I'm whipped."

A kimono-clad waitress silently approached them. "I'll have a double Bombay martini with olives and onions and bring my friend another of whatever he's having." As if they were old friends, he turned to Hank, gave him a wink, a slap on the back and said, "Well, old buddy, how's it going for you in the Land of the Rising Sun?"

Realizing he was stuck, Hank resigned himself. "It's been going real well. I've been busy as hell but I've accomplished a good deal here. I was hoping I could go home today but I've still got a few more days of work in front of me. What's new with you? How's the picture going?"

Jack-picked up the martini glass that had been placed in front of him and ceremoniously brought it to his nose. He inhaled the aroma with a blissful smile. Lifting his glass, he made a toast: "To our wives and sweethearts—may they never meet!" Then, with a conspiratorial wink, he downed half his drink.

"I don't remember if I told you what the picture is about but, hell—it doesn't really matter 'cause it's a real pot boiler. What that means is, it ain't a great picture but it's got lots of scenery, sexy women and a predictable soppy ending.

"Let me tell you this though…by the time I get finished flogging it, you'll think it's an Academy Award contender. But hey, that's enough about me…let's talk about my next picture."

Chuckling in self-appreciation, he took a pack of Lucky Strike cigarettes from his pocket and offered one to Hank, who shook his head and said, "No thanks. I quit about five years ago. Booze is my only vice now."

Jack lit a cigarette, inhaling deeply. "A good smoke helps me to think, an ice cold martini helps me to relax and a hot broad is my ticket to heaven."

Oddly enough, Hank was beginning to relax for the first time in days. It felt good to just to sit there and make small talk, after working so intensely for the past week.

Shifting on his stool, Hank studied Jack's profile. His first impression of Jack had not been favorable. But a picture of Jack's concerned face on the plane from Tokyo flashed in Hank's mind. Was the man really a buffoon? Or was there some substance hiding behind his abrasive personality? The question piqued Hank's curiosity. He wanted to know more about the man sitting beside him.

"You mentioned you've been here before. What was it like right after the war?" Hank asked.

"It was one big mess," Jack answered, somberly. "It was total destruction. There was hardly a building left standing. And the population looked like the walking wounded. They'd taken a helluva beating. They were tired and defeated and relieved the war was over. They'd already been beaten before the atom bomb was dropped. The bomb just helped them to save face when they surrendered."

Jack nodded to the waitress, who promptly brought him another drink, most of which he slugged down before continuing.

"I was in the Army of Occupation so I got to go to Hiroshima. The people would look at you with empty faces—like ghosts walking through a cemetery after they'd witnessed hell." Jack's voice became almost a whisper. "No one who hasn't seen it can ever understand the damage that was caused by those atomic bombs."

Jack stared at his glass as though he could see the horror in his mind reflected there. "Old Douglas MacArthur was pretty wise, though. Most of the American troops occupying the country hadn't been in combat so they felt compassion towards the people. They might not have if they had witnessed the atrocities the Japanese committed."

Hank looked hard at him. There was empathy in Jack's voice. Feelings he kept hidden from his bawdy public relations persona were sneaking through.

As if he'd been reading Hank's thoughts, Jack shrugged, shaking off the past. Finishing his drink, he boomed, "But that was yesterday. It's like living on another planet now. The cities have been rebuilt and are producing more than they did before the war. The nightlife here is like nothing you've ever seen. The nightclubs are reminiscent of the Roaring Twenties, in the United States.

"And they love Americans here! They play all the American music, particularly jazz. They learn to sing American songs phonetically—listening to records and repeating every sound they hear, even if they don't understand a word."

Having returned to his old self, Jack turned to face Hank. With a sly grin, he lowered his voice to a loud whisper and said, "But there is one thing that is strictly Japanese. You don't know what it is to get laid until one of these little ladies takes you to a Japanese inn." He closed his eyes, savoring the memory as a look of ecstasy swept across his face.

When he opened his eyes again, he looked around the quiet bar and said, "Hey, why are we wasting our time here? I'm supposed to meet some of the kids from the cast at Madame Cherry's Copacabana around ten o'clock. Why don't you join us?"

Hank started to decline but Jack wouldn't listen. Checking his watch, he told him, "Look, it's eight o'clock now. Why don't you go to your room, get a couple hours of shut-eye and then meet us? I guarantee you're gonna love this place."

"I'm really kind of beat," Hank protested.

Jack stood up, lifting himself heavily from his seat. "Well," he said, "we will be there at ten and I will have a scotch waiting for you. Straightening his tie, he looked at Hank, gave him a wink and said, "Thanks for the drinks," before turning and walking to the elevator.

Chuckling to himself, Hank asked the waitress for the check.

He had to admire the way Jack had managed to stick him with the bill. He wondered why he found this man, who seemed to be such a complete boor, so interesting.

Leaving the bar, Hank walked to the lobby to wait for the elevator. I am pretty tired, he thought. Maybe I'll just stretch out and relax for a while. See how I feel later. The elevator arrived and just as he was about to step in, he stopped himself. Oh, hell, he thought, who am I kidding? I can sleep anytime. I'm in Tokyo now and I might as well enjoy it.

Two hours later, Hank walked into the Copacabana. Everything was exactly as it had been three nights before. The tables were full, the band was playing Dixieland, cigarette smoke curled in the spotlights and couples were crammed together, dancing on the crowded floor.

When his eyes adjusted to the dim lighting, he saw Jack Strong sitting at a table for four in the middle of the room, his legs propped up on the chair next to him. Behind him stood a tiny, delicately featured Japanese girl, massaging the back of his neck, moving her hands in a slow, circular motion.

"Deeper, baby, deeper, he sighed, his eyes half closed.

Hank stood in front of them for several moments before Jack noticed him. Opening his eyes slowly, careful not to disturb his semi-prone position, he called out gaily, "Hank, baby, I've been waiting for you! Say hello to Mishi."

Mishi started to remove her hands from Jack's neck but he reached back quickly and grabbed her wrists. "No, no, baby, don't stop. Just say hello to Hank-San. Placing her hands back on Jack's neck, Mishi smiled at Hank.

"You can't believe how soothing these little fingers are," Jack purred. "Why don't you go pick out a little 'muchacha' for yourself and bring her back? The girls are the cheapest thing in the joint. They just add them on to your bill."

Ignoring his suggestion, Hank sat down in one of the empty chairs. "Where's the rest of your party?" he asked.

"Oh, hell. They all pooped out. Turns out the actors wound up with a fan club, and now they're being adored by their adoring public. But I decided to come here and meet you instead. Doesn't look like I'm suffering though, eh?" He leaned over and kissed Mishi on the cheek as she playfully pushed him away.

The waitress came over to the table. "Champagne for my little friend, a scotch for my big friend and another double Bombay martini for me. And listen, don't forget the olives and onions this time."

A wisp of silk, brushed Hank's hand and a sweet, delicate scent drifted to his nostrils. Turning his head, he saw Shikibu standing next to him. Recognizing her, he jumped quickly to his feet. A little smile appeared on her perfect face.

"Good evening, Marshall-San. How nice to see you again."

"Please," he stammered, "the name is Hank. And I'm very happy to see you again."

"May I sit down please?"

"Yes, of course." Hank gently touched her arm as Shikibu gracefully slipped into the seat next to his. He could feel the warmth of her body through the softness of her silk kimono.

Shikibu was so exquisitely beautiful Hank could hardly keep his eyes off her. Her dark brown eyes shone above her high, delicate cheekbones. Her luxurious black hair was piled high on her head and her flawless pale skin was accentuated by red lipstick, highlighting her sensuous mouth.

Realizing that Hank was staring at her, Shikibu turned to him. Their eyes met and locked into one other's. It was almost as if they were sharing a private secret, saying things they'd never dare to say aloud. So engrossed in each other did they become, that the sound of Jack Strong's voice startled them both. "Ichibon!" Jack said. He stood up and attempted a low bow but staggered unsteadily and had to grab on to Mishi to keep from toppling over. Regaining his balance, he announced in a loud voice, "It is an honor to have you at our humble table." The word "humble" came out sounding like a burp. "May I introduce Mishi? And I am Jack Strong—'a good connection is a Strong connection'."

"I know Mishi, of course. And I am most happy to meet you," she told him. Only a slight accent was noticeable in her English. Turning back to Hank, she said, "I am very happy to see you again, Hank-San." Bowing her head in a respectful way, a tiny smile crossed her lips.

Her voice was soft and clear and as Hank watched her, the nightclub's noise seemed to disappear behind them. He could hardly keep from staring at her and he didn't know quite what to say. It was as if this beautiful creature had come from some other world. And he was afraid that if he made a wrong move, she'd vanish.

The band was playing "As Time Goes By." "Would you like to dance?" he asked.

Shikibu gave her consent by rising gracefully to her feet. Taking her arm, Hank led her to the dance floor. He could feel the warmth of her skin as he guided her. Resting her forehead against his chin, Shikibu seemed to melt into his arms as they danced.

"You are very tall," she told him.

"And you are very beautiful," he replied.

They continued dancing in silence as a Japanese woman in a low-cut black gown stepped up to the microphone and sang "It Had To Be You" in a seductive voice. Lost in their own world, the club lights seemed to grow dim and the people around them seemed to fade away.

As the song ended, Hank said in a low voice, "She's really good. She almost sounds American."

Shikibu looked up at him and smiled. "Himei listens to American records for many hours. She is repeating what she hears although she does not understand it."

Slowly, they walked back to the table. Jack and Mishi's positions still hadn't changed. Hank turned to pull out a chair for Shikibu, but she leaned against his arm and whispered, "I must leave you for a little while. But I will return soon."

Hank watched her as she walked away. He could feel Jack's eyes on him when he sat down.

"That's Ichibon for you," Jack told him. "She's in such demand, she makes almost three times what the other hostesses make. But I don't care," he said, patting Mishi's hand lightly, "I'll take Mishi every time." Nodding, Mishi continued to rub his neck.

Twenty minutes later, Shikibu returned to Hank's side. "Hank-San," she said in her soft voice, "I am very sorry but I must spend some time with an old customer. The nightclub closes at one. Perhaps we can then go downstairs to Madame Cherrie's restaurant. The food is very good and we will be able to talk without interruption. I hope that will be satisfactory to you."

"That'll be great," Hank replied.

The club had pretty much cleared out by one o'clock. Jack and Mishi had departed half an hour earlier, with Jack telling Hank in a slurred voice, "Well, Buddy, we got us a reservation at a Japanese Inn." He managed to give Hank a cockeyed wink as they left.

Checking his watch, Hank walked down the stairs to Madame Cherrie's. The restaurant was small but well lit, compared to the nightclub. There were four small booths located in the back. And although it was after one in the morning, two of the booths were already taken.

In the center of the room were several larger tables, set up for parties of eight. The majority of the women seated there were Japanese. Hank recognized a few of them from the bar upstairs. Most of the men appeared to be foreigners, businessmen from the United States and Europe. It seemed Madame Cherrie's was the place to be. It had become one of the more popular nightspots among the many that had been springing up around Japan. And it was always filled to capacity.

Walking toward a darkened corner booth, Hank was surprised to find the table had already been reserved in his name. He sat down and a waitress quickly appeared with a scotch on the rocks. His mind began to race.

He tried piecing together the events that had brought him to this night-club in Tokyo—and had him waiting for its Number One hostess.

What am I doing here? He thought. My wife is six thousand miles away, in her eighth month of pregnancy. I miss her so much I ache. I haven't been tempted by another woman since we got back together. Yet here I am, sitting and waiting like a high school kid on his first date. I should really just go back to the hotel and forget about this evening. This does not make sense!

He thought about the first time he'd seen Shikibu. Was it only three nights ago? He'd watched her out of the corner of his eye, sitting close to Yoshi, lighting his cigarettes, listening carefully to his every word. He wondered about their relationship, and why he even cared.

His thoughts turned to earlier in the evening when he had held Shikibu in his arms as they danced. How effortlessly she'd glided across the floor, her slender hand in his. Thinking of her, his heart began beating faster.

Snap out of it! He told himself. This is ridiculous. He stood up and was just about to leave when he saw her—floating into the restaurant. He watched her smile and nod as she passed the tables in front. When she reached the table where Hank was sitting, he offered his hand and she slid in next to him. Her lips grazed his cheek softly in greeting.

"What would you like to eat?" she asked. "They have anything you want, even American hamburgers."

"I'll have whatever you're eating," he answered.

She looked up at the waitress, who had instantly appeared, and ordered for them both in Japanese. As the waitress walked away, Shikibu turned to Hank and said, "I hope you will find the food satisfactory."

Settling back in the booth, she positioned herself so she could see him better. "Are you enjoying your trip to Japan?"

"I am now," Hank said with a surge of confidence. "I've been working long hours and really haven't had much time for sightseeing. And there's a lot I'd like to see."

"How long will you be in Tokyo?"

"Just a few more days. Then I must return to Los Angeles."

Plates and chopsticks were placed in front of them. Three large serving dishes filled with fish, rice and vegetables were set down in the center of the table. Shikibu quickly picked up Hank's plate and began to serve him. "This is a light dish that will rest easily in your stomach. Hope you will enjoy it."

"Domo arrigato," he replied. "'Thank you' are the only words I know in Japanese. Perhaps you'll teach me more. But tell me—how did you learn to speak English so well?"

"We are taught English in our schools at a very early age. Also, in the club, we speak more English than Japanese. And yes, I would be most happy to teach you more Japanese expressions."

Hank put down his chopsticks and looked into her eyes. "How do you say, 'Thank you for inviting me to be here with you'?" She smiled at him, her eyes never leaving his.

"Hank-San, I would like to meet you tomorrow night. But not in the club. It is Saturday night and I will be very busy with old clients. If you will meet me outside the club at one-thirty, after the club closes, we can leave together."

Hank reached under the table and took Shikibu's hand in his. "I look forward to being there."

The next evening, Hank was waiting outside the Copacabana at one-fifteen. He paced the sidewalk nervously, glancing at his watch every few minutes. At exactly one-thirty, Shikibu emerged from the club. Once again, Hank had to catch his breath at the sight of her. He wondered if he'd ever get used to seeing her.

Spotting Hank, Shikibu walked over and whispered in his ear, "I made a reservation for us at a Japanese inn." He hesitated for just a moment. Then, with a nod and a smile, he raised his hand to hail a taxi.

Hank and Shikibu entered the inn through a series of gardens. The fragrance of flowers was heavy in the air.

A middle-aged hostess showed them to a small chamber and left -them in the company of Itsuko, a short, kimono-clad woman. Bowing in greeting, Itsuko offered Hank and Shikibu tea and rice cookies. The three of them sat on woven mats on the floor beside a low, shiny, lacquered table, sipping their tea while Shikibu and Itsuko chatted. As Hank watched them talking, Itsuko stole periodic glances at him. A few minutes later, she rose. Bowing and smiling, she backed out of the room.

Shikibu took Hank's hand lightly in her own and led him into a small, white, dimly lit room with an enormous round wooden hot tub. Next to the tub was a small wooden bench, which held a number of brushes in different sizes and several bars of scented soap.

Hank looked around hesitantly. Seeing his expression, Shikibu said, "Excuse me, Hank-San. But it is customary—to take a hot bath when one first arrives. If you would please remove your clothing and sit on the bench, I will return shortly." With that, she stepped out of the room.

Hank moved about in a daze. It was as if the real world was slipping away. What am I doing here? He thought to himself once again. This is crazy, but I don't want to leave.

With a sigh, Hank began to remove his clothes. After he'd finished undressing, he sat down on the little bench and waited. The room was damp and warm as steam rose from the tub. He could feel the moisture on his body.

Shikibu re-entered the room quietly, wearing a fluffy white terry cloth robe. With a sweet smile, she ran her hands across his muscular shoulders as her eyes ran down his body.

Hank saw that Shikibu had removed her makeup. In the dim light, her face appeared child-like and innocent. And she had untied her hair, allowing it to hang luxuriously down her back, reaching well below her shoulders. To Hank, she looked even more beautiful then she had before.

Looking at him tenderly, Shikibu said, "I will wash you now. It is important that you cleanse your body before entering the tub. Using a wooden bucket, she carefully poured some of the hot, steaming water over

Hank's head. He gasped at first, its fire touching his skin. But the water quickly cooled and Hank began to feel warm and comfortable all over.

Shikibu's hands gently applied the fragrant soap to his head, shoulders and broad back. She touched each of his muscles, caressing them expertly. Softly, she massaged his soapy body thoroughly, carefully avoiding his genitals. Like an artist, she traced the lines of his body, moving her hands over his hips, down his long legs and around his feet.

When Hank's body was covered with the foaming lather, Shikibu again filled the bucket with steaming water. He gasped and sighed in the same breath as she poured it over him.

Hank felt as if he was in a trance and it startled him when Shikibu said, "Please, Hank-San, will you enter the tub now?"

The heat was almost overwhelming as Hank stepped into the water. Slowly, he sank down into it until it reached his neck. Closing his eyes, he could feel the tension slip away as his body became accustomed to the temperature.

When he opened his eyes, Hank watched Shikibu as she slowly untied her robe. She stood motionless as it fell at her feet. Her skin was pale like alabaster in the muted light. Her small breasts with their large, dark nipples were round and firm. Hank's eyes moved lingeringly down her delicate torso as he felt himself becoming aroused.

Shikibu filled the wooden bucket with steaming water once again and poured it over her own body. Then, taking the soap, she slowly, erotically, massaged herself using the same motions she had used on Hank. Her eyes never left his face.

At last, Shikibu picked up the bucket and carefully rinsed herself off. Gracefully entering the steamy tub, she moved close to Hank, who enfolded her in his arms and began kissing her passionately. Shikibu placed her finger to his lips and whispered in a husky voice, "Please, Hank-San, wait."

Rising slowly from the tub, she covered herself with a terrycloth robe and held out another robe to him. Hank stood up and stepped onto the floor. Placing the robe around his shoulders, Shikibu took his hand and led him into a small adjoining room, empty except for a large futon on the floor. Walking over to the futon, Shikibu lay down on it and held her arms out to Hank.

Rational thought left Hank's mind as he moved over to lie down next to her. Drinking in Shikibu's body with his eyes, he began to caress her. Gently cupping her small breasts in his hands, he kissed her hardened nipples. Her body responded as if receiving tiny electric shocks. He could feel the warmth coming through her pores.

Slowly, rhythmically, she began to move while her hands and mouth engulfed him. Their lips touched gently. Opening her mouth, their tongues met in a fiery kiss.

Later, as they lay in each other's arms, Shikibu sighed softly. "You have given me great pleasure and I have infinite love for you."

Hank tried to speak but she put her finger to his lips once again. "Please, Hank-San, say nothing now. It is not necessary. It is I who must express her feelings."

With gentle hands, Shikibu tenderly stroked his forehead, neck and shoulders as Hank drifted into sleep. He dreamed of flowers and Buddhas. In the distance, there were bombs dropping. But when Shikibu embraced him, the bombs disappeared. Suddenly, in the distance, he saw a figure standing in the mist. Straining his eyes, he recognized Yoshikazu Matsuda. He turned to Shikibu. She kissed him and the figure disappeared as they walked away through the cherry blossoms.

At two o'clock on Tuesday afternoon, the final meeting of Hank's trip was to begin. He'd spent the entire morning in his room at the Imperial Hotel pouring over the sketches, photos, blueprints and meticulous notes that had been drawn up by Tosui's engineers and economists. He found it hard to believe that he'd been in Tokyo for only one week. But now it seemed that everything he'd done up to this point, would pale in comparison to this newly proposed business.

Telesonic would be a new line of technologically advanced televisions and radios in a booming market. And Hank Marshall was on the cutting edge! His head was spinning with all that he'd seen. And his gut instinct told him he was lucky to be in the right place at the right time.

Yoshi and Takei were waiting as Hank entered Yoshi's office.

"Do you have any questions concerning the merchandise you have seen?" Takei asked with a smile. "Of course, you realize this is all confidential. Any further discussions you have must be confined to your staff, your banks and the legal and accounting services you retain. Please know that no one outside of Tosui is aware of the extent of our progress."

"Your confidence will be respected," Hank assured him. "And yes, I do have a number of questions and suggestions. I'm also quite sure I'll have considerably more once I've arrived back in the United States and have had time to think about this and discuss it all with my associates. Right now, I have no idea what it will take financially to get things started. Or if we should distribute regionally, or immediately go for national distribution. I'd like to get your ideas."

Yoshi leaned forward from behind his big desk. His hands had been clasped in front of him and his eyes were half closed as he'd listened to Hank. Now, his eyes widened.

"As I have stated previously, it is our intention to create the world's leading brand of electronic products. This is possible because of our high degree of advanced technology and our ability to commit vast sums of money to launch these products. We plan to market our merchandise in the United States and Japan simultaneously—at the earliest practical moment. As soon as we have accomplished this, we will begin marketing in Europe and throughout Asia."

Yoshi sat back in his chair, folded his hands in his lap and looked at Hank. "We propose a joint venture in the United States—Tosui owning sixty percent and the American company owning forty percent. You will have to raise your end of the capital privately, as we strongly feel there should be no public offering at this stage."

"Why is that?" Hank asked.

"When you are involved in the stock market, too much time and effort is devoted to the stockholders," Yoshi replied patiently. "Everything you do is examined under a microscope by the government and by the public. We have superb connections with many banks all over the world. Here in Japan, our Ministry of International Trade helps us to achieve lower interest rates—to encourage the export of Japanese merchandise. Therefore, we can be of great assistance in helping you to find the financing you will need."

Hank sat thoughtfully for a few moments. Getting up, he began to pace the floor. "I'm sure you realize I can't make decision like this at a moment's notice. There are, however, a few comments I would like to make." He turned and positioned himself so he could look at both Yoshi and Takei.

"The picture on your televisions is sharper and clearer than anything I've ever seen—the sound, far superior to anything I've heard. The styling, however, is just a copy of what's already been produced in both the United States and Europe. I respectfully suggest that we retain a top American designer to give both the televisions and the radios, a modern, streamlined look.

"And..." said Hank, looking directly at Yoshi, "a sixty-forty split, with our company taking a minority interest, will not be satisfactory. I am referring only to the American company, of course, which would be the exclusive distributor. It will have no share of the manufacturing. In any event, I will need time to investigate the market and to propose a complete plan."

Returning to his chair, Hank waited.

For the next few minutes, Yoshi and Takei spoke to each other in Japanese. Hank watched them, trying to read their faces. Finally, they were silent. Yoshi sat back and looked at Hank for a moment.

"Hank-San, you have honored us by coming here on such short notice. We greatly appreciate your visit. We must both continue our respective investigations. Let us allow two months in which to put together a business plan. The matter of percentages must be favorably agreed upon before we can proceed as we are both aware of the importance of voting control. I believe we have ideas that may be satisfactory to all." It was obvious by the finality in Yoshi's tone that the meeting was now over.,

"At what time would you like our car to pick you up at your hotel and drive you to the airport?" he asked.

Hank was feeling good about the meeting. He was pleased that so much had been accomplished in such a short period of time. He knew, too, that he had a lot of homework to do before they met again.

After giving them his flight time, the men exchanged pleasantries before Hank was ushered to the door amidst bows and handshakes.

Before Hank walked out, Takei handed him a flat, beautifully decorated box. "It is a small gift for your lovely wife," he said, smiling warmly. Thanking them both, Hank quickly left.

After he had gone, Yoshi and Takei sat silently. Several minutes later, Takei reached into his portfolio and pulled out his note pad. Yoshi immediately began to give him instructions in Japanese.

"Arrange a meeting at nine o'clock tomorrow morning with our head engineer and designer. Have the chief financial officer finalize his report on our financing needs for this project. I also want key financial reports on the Marshall's and their associates.

"And, instruct Jack Strong to meet us in my office at eleven A.M."

Hank entered the lobby of the Imperial Hotel and walked over to the desk to check for messages and to get the key to his room.

"And this letter came for you, Mr. Marshall," said the clerk, handing Hank a small, white envelope with his name written on it in a flowing script. The delicate scent of roses wafted to his nostrils and Hank immediately knew it was from Shikibu.

Moving over to an armchair in the center of the lobby, he sat down and opened the envelope. There were two pieces of stationary inside.

The first read:

> Hank-San, It is most important that we meet today. I will be waiting for you at the rock garden of the Gokoku-ji Temple at five o'clock. Please come—it is most important.

> The second sheet is for you to give to the taxi driver. It contains directions on how to drive there from the Imperial Hotel. It should take about twenty minutes. Shikibu

Hank glanced at the clock on the wall. It was already past four-thirty. He jumped up, walked quickly to the lobby door and handed the door man the instruction sheet. The doorman beckoned to one of the waiting cabs and handed the driver the paper, giving him further explanation in Japanese. Then, grinning at Hank, he saluted and said, "No problem, sir."

Hank handed him a bill and jumped into the taxi. There was no time to lose.

A sense of peace and calm came over Hank as soon as he saw the rock sculpture at the entrance to the temple. Paying the driver, he walked through the garden gate. He immediately saw Shikibu, sitting on a flat rock beside a miniature pond filled with dark green lily pads and fragrant white flowers. She wore a sand-colored kimono decorated with cherry blossoms that could well have been a reflection of the flowering trees that surrounded the rock garden and the pond.

She turned, slowly, as he approached, a smile replacing the somber expression he'd first seen on her face.

"Hank-San, you are here," she murmured. "Thank you for coming."

Hank's heart began beating faster as he held out his hands to her, drawing her to her feet and into his arms. He kissed her lightly on both cheeks.

"When we said goodbye on Sunday, I did not expect to see you again until my next trip to Japan. I am very happy to see you, of course, but is there something wrong?"

"Let us sit," she answered, taking him by the arm and drawing him down on the rock next to her. A tear appeared in the corner of her eye. "It was important that I see you today...for we will never be together again."

Hank turned her shoulders toward him so that they faced each other. "But I promised that I would call you on my next trip. I want to see you again. I must see you! Something happened to me when we were together. Something strange and wonderful. I..."

Shikibu interrupted him by placing her hand on his lips. "Hank-San, please listen and try to understand." Her eyes filled as she looked into his with a pleading expression. Her voice trembled slightly as she said, "When I was a little girl, I heard stories of hearts that touched each other: of love that blossomed from the very first glance. As a hostess, I have met many men: men of power and of wealth, from Japan and from far off lands.

"When I first saw you, all else disappeared. Our night together was as though the gods had dropped a veil down from heaven and spread it in our path."

Hank took her hands in his and tried to calm their shaking. Looking at her pale, delicate face, the same sensation he'd felt when he first saw her, swept over him again: he would never get used to her loveliness.

"Then Shikibu, why is this good-bye?" Hank asked, his throat tight and his voice sounding strained. "I didn't want to feel for you as I do, but when we are together, it is as though we are in another world. A world that has nothing to do with this one, or with any other people. I've tried hard to push these feeling aside, but I can't. It's impossible."

Shikibu cupped his face lovingly in her hands. "You must listen to me, Hank-San. And please, do not think there is any anger in what I say. I was born and I grew up in Hiroshima." Hank's eyes grew wide and his head began to throb.

"I was just seventeen when the atom bomb was dropped. My family lived ten miles from the explosion and we thought we had escaped. But yesterday, I went to see the doctor and he told me that I have cancer. He also said that I have very little time left." She smiled wanly. "And the reason I cannot see you again is because you must never see me other than the way I am right now."

"But I want to help you!" Hank cried. "I'll take you to the best doctors in the United States! There's got to be someone who can do something!"

"There is nothing anyone can do," she said, quietly. "Today, I told Madame Cherry at the Copacabana that I would not be returning. I did not tell her why, however. You are the only one who knows the truth. Tomorrow, I am going away to a remote, but beautiful place. I will not see Tokyo again. But I had to see you again, Hank-San, to tell you what I feel and to thank you for a moment of beauty and purity."

"No, no! This cannot be!" he said, choking back a sob. "There's got to be something I can do. You've got to let me! Can I at least help pay for your expenses so you won't have to be concerned about money?"

She shook her head sadly, her eyes welling with tears. "Hank-San, you must not worry. I have made more money than I will have time to spend."

She stroked his cheek softly with her fingertips while his shoulders sagged with the realization that he had to accept the inevitable.

At last, he pulled her toward him and they held each other for a long time. With tears streaming down his face, Hank whispered in her ear, "I will never forget you, Shikibu-San."

CHAPTER FIFTEEN

───────────▼───────────

1970

It was in June that Michio Matsuda arrived at the Marshall home for the first time. His father, Yoshikazu, drove him there directly from the airport.

Sarah Marshall had been eagerly awaiting his arrival and was pleased when she saw him. From the description her father had given her, he was just the way she'd pictured him. His thick black hair was closely cropped and accentuated his warm brown eyes. Even his nervousness didn't detract from his exotic good looks.

Michio had graduated from his high school in Tokyo at the head of his class. Immediately upon graduating, his father had put him to work at Tosui Trading, the family business. Yoshi's plan was to have Michio work for Tosui for one year, then attend UCLA to formalize his education—just as Yoshi had done. There was no question in anyone's mind that Michio would follow the path of his father, grandfather and great-grandfather by taking over the leadership of Tosui at the appropriate time.

When Yoshi mentioned his plans for Michio to Hank, Hank insisted that Michio stay with the Marshall family while attending school.

"Yoshi, he's a young man and these are turbulant times," Hank had said. "There is great unrest over the war in Vietnam. We'll be more than happy to have Michio stay here with us. He's the same age as Peter and with Peter away at Julliard, I know Sarah will be happy to have the company. Besides, UCLA can be a big, lonely place. It'll be good for him to have family close by."

Hank also suggested introducing Michio to the ways of American business by bringing him into the Marshall-Telesonic fold. "I'll take him under my wing—give him a real education," Hank offered. "Then, he can bring some good old American know-how back to Japan."

The sun was setting as Yoshi and Michio arrived at the Marshall's home in affluent Brentwood Park. On the drive there, they'd passed many estates, all with perfectly manicured lawns and profusions of colorful and unusual plants and flowers. Now, as they pulled up to the house, the neighborhood seemed to shimmer in the soft shadows of evening. Michio looked around and realized he was far away from home.

From a distance, it was difficult to tell the two Matsuda men apart. They were dressed alike—navy blue suits, white shirts and blue ties. And although Michio was taller than his father, Yoshi remained in excellent shape and hardly seemed older than his son.

Before the Matsudas had a chance to knock, the Marshall family met them at the door. Ruth and Hank, radiant and young looking in their knit shirts and jeans, greeted them warmly. Standing next to their beautiful, mini-skirted daughter, they personified the image of a modern California family.

Hank had seen Michio several times on his trips to Japan. Looking at him now, he was pleased at what a fine young man he'd become. Smiling broadly, Hank put his arm around Michio's shoulders affectionately and said, "It's about time you visited our neck of the woods."

Not waiting for an introduction, Ruth took Michio's hand and leaned over to kiss his cheek. "Welcome to our home, Michio. We're happy to have you with us."

"The honor is mine," he said shyly, with a slight bow. "I will try to be as little trouble as possible."

Hank caught Yoshi's eye and winked. Turning to Michio, he said, "Relax, kid. We're all one family here and you're one of us now."

Sarah stepped out from behind her parents, impatiently. Hank smiled proudly as he introduced her. "And this is Sarah. You'd better watch out for her. She's a good student, even if she is a flower child and a peacenik. But Sarah knows everybody, and she can be a real asset in showing you around."

"Oh, Dad," Sarah admonished, glancing down with embarrassment. Raising her eyes again, she looked at Michio. "Don't mind him, Michio,—he likes to tease. Anyway, I'm very pleased to meet you and I'm glad you'll be staying with us."

Michio stared at her, dumbstruck. With her long blonde hair and bright blue eyes, he thought she was the most beautiful girl he'd ever seen. And, in her tiny mini-skirt, her black-patterned stockings and loose-fitting tie-dyed shirt, she seemed much older than her fifteen years. Somehow, he managed to say, "Thank you," while avoiding her eyes. Looking around self-consciously, he was relieved that the others were involved in their own conversation and hadn't noticed his discomfort.

Hank laughed and slapped Yoshi on the back, playfully. "It really is good to see you, my friend. Now, what do you say we go inside and have some refreshments?"

Entering the house, Ruth took Yoshi's arm and said, "Maria made her special quesadillas for you—to go along with our cocktails. She said she remembered Mr. Matsuda loved them the last time he was here."

Inside, Sarah motioned to Michio and said, "I'll show you your room and the rest of the house, if you want. It'll give you a chance to learn your way around."

Michio looked at his father, who nodded his approval, before picking up his suitcase. With downcast eyes, he followed Sarah up the stairs.

The others had just seated themselves in the living room when Maria, the Marshall's housekeeper, came in. She carried with her a large platter of piping hot Mexican quesadillas and placed it carefully on the coffee table, next to a stack of plates and silverware. The tantalizing smell of melted cheese and spicy salsa quickly filled the air.

A wide smile appeared on Maria's round face as she looked up. "Buenas dias, Senor Matsuda!" she said. "It is good to see you again!"

Yoshi returned her smile as he settled into one of the comfortable arm-chairs. "Buenas dias to you, Maria. And thank you for remembering how much I enjoyed your quesadillas."

Maria's face beamed. She'd first come to work for the Marshalls when Sarah was born, and had taken charge from that day on. She now considered the whole family to be her own, and their friends, her friends. Still smiling, as she made her way out of the room, she said, "Gracias, Senor Matsuda."

"Anytime."

Hank opened a bottle of chardonnay from his special stock. He poured the wine into three glasses and handed one to each of them. As they lifted their glasses in unison, he made a toast. "To good friends and great partners." Looking at each other with satisfied smiles, they clinked their glasses in agreement.

Yoshi sipped his wine thoughtfully. "Thank you both for taking my son into your home," he told them. "The university will provide him with his formal education—essential for his success. But more than that, you, Hank, are providing him with an even greater opportunity. From you, he will learn the great marketing techniques that only exist in America."

He paused for a moment. "I was thinking that perhaps it would be a good idea for Michio to work at Marshall-Telesonic before returning to Japan. If you are agreeable, he can begin his apprenticeship by working during the summer months. Then, during the school year, he can live on campus and devote himself entirely to his studies. This would also keep him from becoming a burden to you. And, it will allow him to concentrate fully on acquiring the skills he will need to adequately fulfill his destiny."

Ruth and Hank looked at each other, puzzled. Seeing that they were getting ready to protest, Yoshi added, "The necessary arrangements have already been put into motion—upon your approval, of course."

"With all of the social changes that are going on, I was hoping that I could help introduce Michio to our new American lifestyle," Ruth said, her disappointment visible.

"Oh, but you can, Ruth," Yoshi said with a smile. "From you, Michio can learn all about American politics. And, by the way, how is that new organization you helped to form working out? I believe it is called 'Another Mother For Peace', is it not?"

Pleased that he'd remembered, Ruth grinned. But her expression quickly changed. "Yes, it is. And I have totally committed myself to doing everything I can to help stop this unjust war in Vietnam. American boys are being killed every day for no reason. It is the wrong war, in the wrong place, at the wrong time. If we can shorten this travesty by one month or one day or even by one hour, it will be worth everything we put into the peace movement.

"But you know what really scares me, Yoshi?" she said, with sadness in her voice and on her face, "Our son, Peter, is now eligible for the draft. Hank and I have discussed it and we've agreed that we will do whatever we have to, to keep him out of it."

Yoshi shifted in his chair, uncomfortable with the turn the conversation had taken. Hoping to change it's direction, he asked brightly, "How is Peter doing at Julliard? Is he good enough to concertize yet?"

This was a subject Ruth could smile about. "He's doing beautifully, thanks. And I have no doubt he will be a great pianist. In fact, he's now in a master class—studying with Rudolph Serkin."

Hank's face glowed with pride as well. "We are extremely proud of him," he added.

Maria re-entered the room and whispered to Ruth, who nodded. "Maria has prepared a special Mexican feast in honor of Mr. Matsuda and the food is now ready. I think Sarah's had enough time to show the house to Michio, don't you?"

Two weeks later, Hank called Michio into the den to discuss his career. Sarah came in with him and sat down. "Do you think Michio needs an interpreter?" Hank asked, looking fondly at his daughter.

"No, Dad," she answered seriously. "In fact, he speaks better English than I do. And he's been teaching me some Japanese. "It's just that I know you're going to have Michio working in the office this summer and I thought, well…how about letting me work there, too?"

"Now that's a switch," Hank said, trying hard to suppress a grin. "A couple of weeks ago, you were talking about going to Israel to work on a kibbutz. Before that, you were talking about a commune in Oregon. What have you done to her, Michio? To turn this flower child into a capitalist?"

Michio hesitated before answering, not sure if this was a serious question or not. "We have been having many discussions and I have found that Sarah has a very keen grasp of business. Although she is young, her thoughts are quite mature. She has taught me many things about American habits and has expressed many interesting ideas about marketing and advertising campaigns."

Sarah looked at her father triumphantly.

"Is that so?" Hank said with surprise. "How come I didn't know these things about my daughter?"

"Well, Dad, I guess you just didn't ask," she answered, her eyes twinkling mischievously. "If you'll let me come and work for you, I promise to dress like a real business person," she added, earnestly.

Seeing the dubious look on Hank's face, Sarah continued in a rush. "Okay then, let's look at what's really going on in this house. You work fifty or sixty hours a week. Mom's dedicated herself full time to 'Another Mother For Peace'. When Peter gets home, he's gonna turn right around and go to Santa Barbara—to the Music Academy of the West. And Michio's gonna be joining you at the office."

She paused for a moment, letting it all sink in.

"Look, Dad, I think burning bras is silly. I agree that the war's a mess but I don't want to march in demonstrations. I mean, look what happened to those kids at Kent State! I really do want to be a part of Marshall-Telesonic. Just like Michio wants to be part of Tosui. I know you're proud of Peter but he has no interest in the business." She looked at her father imploringly. "Come on Dad. I am interested in business. And you're stuck with me! What do you say?"

Hank burst out laughing. "If you can sell television sets like you just sold me, you'll be terrific."

Turning to Michio, he grinned and said, "Well, Michio, I'm certainly glad you and I had this discussion."

Jack Strong looked across his desk condescendingly at Sarah. "Now let me understand what you're saying. You want us to reduce our regular advertising budget and put that money into direct marketing. Listen, darlin', we showed record sales last year. My ol' pappy once gave me some good advice. He said, 'If it ain't broke, don't fix it'." Jack's whole body shook as he chuckled loudly.

Sarah was trying her best to pay respectful attention to him. She'd known him all her life and had never appreciated his sense of humor. She'd always felt that Jack Strong's jokes were made at the expense of others and she didn't find them amusing. Besides, she thought, he laughs hard enough at his own jokes.

"I'm not suggesting that we change the way we do things, Sarah said. I'm just saying that we should use a small part of the budget to try some new marketing techniques. The world is becoming much more technological. Someday, computers will be doing a lot of the work we're doing now. Look what radio and television have done for advertising. It may reach a lot of people but it's sort of hard to tell just how many people feel the need to buy."

Jack got up heavily from behind his desk and walked over to Sarah. Placing his hand lightly on her shoulder, he said, "Honey, there's a heap of difference between school and the real world. I appreciate your comments but I'm really busy right now. And what I need to do is look at those press releases I gave you to type. Don't forget though, little lady, I'm always happy to hear your ideas…when I've got time."

Sarah slid out from under his hand and rose to her feet. She noticed she was slightly taller than Jack Strong and wished he wouldn't refer to her as "little lady." Shrugging her shoulders, she said in a respectful tone, "I'll have the press releases ready for you to sign in about twenty minutes."

At lunchtime, Sarah met Michio in the employee's dining room on the third floor. It was a large room with cherry wood picnic tables and benches at its center. A dozen smaller tables, seating two or four, lined the east wall.

The food was served at a long counter in the back of the room. On the left was an array of hot dishes: soups, pastas, vegetables, meats cut to order. On the right were salads, drinks and desserts. Sarah heaped her plate high with sliced roast beef, macaroni and cheese, hash browned potatoes and a slice of cherry pie. Michio settled for a tuna salad, some rolls and a dish of strawberry ice cream.

"Quick! I see a table in the corner," Sarah called out, rushing past him to grab the empty seats. A few seconds later, Michio joined her and for the next few minutes, they ate in silence.

It had been two weeks since they'd begun working at Marshall-Telesonic. Each day, they looked forward to lunchtime when they met, to compare notes on the events of the morning.

"So how's it going?" Sarah asked at last, sopping up the last bit of melted cheese on her plate with a piece of Michio's roll.

"Actually, I am learning a great deal from Milt Samuels. He is a very able and resourceful administrator. I feel I am very fortunate that he takes the time to explain things to me," Michio answered, as he watched Sarah wolfing down her food with gusto.

"You're lucky," she said, heaving an exaggerated sigh. "Jack Strong tells me, 'Just do what I tell you, little lady, and keep your opinions to yourself'. Of course he doesn't say it just like that—I am the boss's daughter. But it pisses me off that I have good ideas and he won't even listen."

Michio's eyes had widened at the language she used. Seeing the distressed look on his face made Sarah laugh. "Loosen up, Mick! Remember, that's all part of what these protests are about—free speech."

He wasn't sure if he liked her calling him "Mick," but he didn't say anything. Instead, he told her in a stern voice, "In Japan, we are taught to respect our elders. We remain silent until we have earned the right to make suggestions or to question their decisions."

"We're taught the same thing," Sarah chimed in, "and look at the mess it's caused. You'll see what I mean when you start at UCLA next month. You'll be right in the thick of things." She stopped long enough to attack her cherry pie. After announcing, "Ummm, good!" she continued.

"Before you came, I started getting into the demonstrations at Palisades High. Man, it was crazy! They'd start off real serious. Then, once you were caught up in 'em, it was like a party. Everyone was smoking grass. And suddenly, everyone's high, singing, dancing, playing grab-ass. It might seem like it's all just about sex and stuff but underneath it all, there's a revolution going on. Only the government doesn't want to hear what we're saying. They see long hair and hear loud music and figure it's a fad and it's all gonna pass. But it's not."

Michio couldn't take his eyes off her. And although he was mesmerized by her enthusiasm, he felt compelled to speak his thoughts.

"Do you not think, Sarah, that those in authority know what they are doing? I find it most difficult for me to level criticism at our elders. In Japan, it is just not done."

"Mick, don't you know that they're lying about our victories in Vietnam? They just want to send in more troops. They try to ignore people like my mother. The male chauvinists in power say these women don't understand that our country is protecting the Asian world against communism. They say the students involved are just a bunch of hippies—drugged out and out of touch with the real world."

Sarah paused and then giggled. "It's funny, you know? Here in this citadel of capitalism, Jack Strong said the same thing to me. He said I don't understand the 'REAL WORLD'."

"In Japan," said Michio, thoughtfully, "there is also a peace movement. But those involved keep a low profile—away from the outside world. I think most Japanese people believe the American government is foolish and irresponsible. But we would never say that publicly. Few people here are aware that while the United States is spending more and more money on arms, other countries are putting their time and money into consumer products. And this gives the rest of us a great advantage in the future. As you may know, we in Japan are forced by treaty not to arm ourselves. But it is a good thing for us."

Suddenly, Michio's face lit up. "Sarah," he said, excitedly. "Would you take me to one of the protest rallies? I would very much like to see what they're like, so I can understand."

It was seven in the morning and the sun outside the breakfast room window bathed the garden in varying degrees of light and shadows. The grass and the trees glistened with the dew that had fallen on the landscape just before dawn.

Hank was already dressed for work. He wore the slacks from his charcoal gray suit, a light blue shirt and a maroon knit tie. He'd grown accustomed to having an early breakfast with Sarah and Michio before they headed off for the day, and was waiting for them to come downstairs. Their summer apprenticeship at Marshall-Telesonic was over and they now had to prepare for the new school year.

They wandered into the breakfast room, one after the other. Michio was bright and cheerful, while Sarah groaned and headed straight for the coffee pot. As they sat down at the table, Hank said, "I can't believe that three months have passed since Michio first arrived. I know that your plan is to move into the dormitory before school starts, but Michio, you know you're more than welcome to stay here with us."

Michio looked at Sarah, who was nodding in agreement. "I thank you very much, Hank-San. Staying in your home has been a rich experience for me. But I must continue as planned." With an impish grin, he added, "You know how we Japanese are about our plans."

Sarah laughed. "You see, Dad, although Mick has almost become an American, he still hasn't learned to go with the flow."

Turning her head toward the door, Sarah saw Ruth walking into the kitchen. "Mom!" she called out, "What are you doing up at this hour?"

Ruth moved over to the counter and poured herself a cup of coffee. She had her full makeup on and was smartly dressed in a soft turquoise suit. Jokingly, Hank dropped his fork in amazement. Ruth's love of sleeping late and waking up slowly was a favorite family joke.

"Ha, ha. Very funny," she said. She seated herself at the table where Maria had already set down a platter of scrambled eggs and sausages along with a basket of warm bagels. "It so happens I have a big day in front of me and I'd appreciate your skipping the usual smart-ass remarks."

Hank got up and stood behind her. Bending down, he kissed her lightly on the forehead. "Why, Mrs. Marshall!" he said with exaggerated indignation. "How you talk in front of the children!"

Maria bustled in once again and placed a stack of hotcakes on the table. "This looks wonderful," Ruth told her. "If you always treat them this well, maybe I'll start getting up early more often."

Reaching for a hotcake, Ruth looked over at Sarah and Michio. "What are you guys doing in jeans and T-shirts? Aren't you going to work today?"

Sarah gave her mother a tolerant look. Swallowing her last bite of scrambled eggs and waving a sausage link in the air, she said, "Mother, Friday was our last day at the salt mines. Michio's packing so he can move into the UCLA dormitory, and I'm getting myself together for the first day of school."

Ruth leaned over and gave Michio a kiss on the cheek. An embarrassed look came over his face, which made her laugh. "Come on, Michio. You're one of the family now. You're going to have to suffer my kisses just like everyone else."

Looking around the table at everyone, Ruth said, "Well, isn't anyone going to ask me where I'm going today? Who I'm going to meet and why I look so gorgeous so early in the morning?"

Before anyone had a chance to answer, she continued, excitedly. "Okay, you give up. I'm going to meet with Paul Newman and Joanne Woodward. They're going to Washington with us—to lobby for a 'Secretary of Peace'."

Ruth stopped suddenly. "Wow, me and Paul Newman! That's a fantasy come true!" Her voice then became serious. "We're going to plan the trip this morning. We've enlisted the aid of the entertainment community, as well as the business community, to join in our efforts."

Hank leaned back in his chair with his arms folded, and nodded his approval. "You'll be interested to know that I've been asked to join a group called 'Business Executives Against the War'. And I have accepted."

"But how can you speak against your own government?" Michio asked, quietly. "I went to a peace rally with Sarah and I was revolted to see them burning the American flag. In Japan, such actions would not be tolerated."

"But Michio," Sarah interjected, "don't forget, the American Revolution got started because of people protesting."

Hank put his hands together, forming a T. "Whoa, time out! This is a pretty heavy discussion for the breakfast table."

Changing the subject, Hank continued, "I would like you to know, Michio, that you made a fine first impression at Marshall-Telesonic. Several people mentioned to me how much they thought of you. And I, personally, enjoyed working with you very much. It's very satisfying to see you picking things up so quickly. Even Milton, who's slow to praise, tells me you have a mind like a steel trap. That once you learn something, you really own it. Your father is my best friend and when we spoke yesterday, it gave me great pleasure to tell him about the progress you've made. I have no doubt you will be a great asset to both Telesonic and Tosui."

Sarah fiddled in her chair impatiently, waiting for her turn at praise, her face filled with anticipation.

"As for you, young lady," her father said, with mock sternness in his voice, "Jack Strong tells me you are a giant pain-in-the-ass. But he also had to admit that some of your ideas for direct marketing were pretty good. He's even proposed putting some of them to work. Bottomline is, I'm very proud of both of you."

Sarah looked over at Michio, gleefully, waiting to catch his eye. When she did, she nodded to him victoriously.

But something in his look made her pause. He was looking at her differently this time.

Slowly, it hit her. He was looking at her like a woman instead of a girl. Blushing profusely, she quickly looked away.

Chapter Sixteen

▼

"But we can't just ignore what's happening. This terrible war will not just pack up and go away. We have a corporate responsibility, as well as a personal responsibility, to do whatever we can to end this miscarriage of justice."

Hank paused and looked searchingly at the faces surrounding him.

The group was seated around the square glass coffee table in the Marshall's living room. Ruth and Hank shared the loveseat located at one end of the table, facing the white marble fireplace. To their left, seated on the emerald green velvet couch, were Michio, Sarah and Jack Strong. Across from them, in a pair of comfortable matching arm chairs, were Yoshi and Takei, who had just flown in from Tokyo the night before.

It was nine o'clock on a mild, summer, Saturday night in June, and the Marshalls and their guests had just finished a delicious dinner of barbecued chicken and steaks on the patio. The talk around the dinner table had centered on the war and the recent revelations concerning the My Lai massacre. Sarah and Michio had been particularly appalled by the events. They brought the conversation back into the house where everyone had adjourned for coffee.

"I can't believe it. It's just not possible. American soldiers could not kill innocent women and children," said Sarah, her voice quivering at the very thought.

Michio took her shaking hand in his and tried to soothe her with his words. "Perhaps it is not true. Or maybe it has been greatly exaggerated. They say they do not have all the facts in yet."

Yoshi watched the two of them, listening and saying nothing.

"Ruth and I feel very strongly that we must do something to help bring this war to an end," Hank interjected. "Thousands of American kids are being killed."

Yoshi raised his eyebrows. "And what of the Vietnamese who are dying by the tens of thousands?" he asked, quietly. "Are their lives any less important?"

"Of course not," Ruth interjected hastily. "This war is a horror for all of us. Hank and I have been doing all we can to try to put an end to it. That is why I joined 'Another Mother For Peace.' Our group speaks for mothers all over the world when we say, 'War is not healthy for children and other living things.'

"I think we're beginning to make an impact, too," she said with a pleased expression on her face. "We've been lobbying in Congress and I think a few important minds have been changed. I'm thrilled by the large number of bright women who've become involved. Their anguished cries are the ones we are hearing when we say, 'enough is enough! We will not send our sons to fight!' Hank and I can't help but personalize it either. Peter is studying music at Juilliard. He could be called up at any time. Not only is his career at stake, but his life as well."

"The point is," added Hank, "we can no longer just sit back and watch. I'm on the board of 'Business Executives Against The War In Vietnam.' We've been campaigning hard and I think we've persuaded the president of I.B.M. to join us in denouncing American policy. We've talked to companies, large and small, in an effort to bring corporate pressure to bear against the war. We're convinced that the war is not only bad for people, it is bad for business.".

Hank looked at the group gathered around him. "This is one of the reasons I wanted us all together tonight. I would like to propose that

Telesonic join IBM and other courageous companies in opposing the official policy of the United States. I must warn you that the risk is great. A lot of people out there believe opposing the war is unpatriotic, so it's possible that Telesonic could lose a sizeable amount of business. And there's no way to predict how much business that might be. But I'm firmly convinced that the only way to put an end to this terrible war is to take risks and make sacrifices."

Hank shifted his gaze to Yoshi. "How do you feel about this, Yoshi?"

All eyes turned toward Yoshi. "I believe," Yoshi answered in a quiet voice, "that it would be a big mistake to take any position in this matter. We must remain non-political. The public will buy Telesonic products because of their quality and price—not because we are for or against the war in Vietnam.

"We have just released our new VHS video system, which is locked in a struggle with Sony's Beta system. It would be very bad business for us to take a controversial position at this time."

Yoshi turned in his chair to look at his son. "And what is your opinion, Michio?"

Michio shifted uncomfortably in his seat. He looked at Sarah, as though hoping she held the key to the answer. She smiled back at him, encouragingly.

"Well, Father," he began slowly. "I have now been in Los Angeles for one year. Living in the dormitory at UCLA, I have gotten a very good sense of what the students are saying. They are primarily against the war. And until recently, theirs were the only voices that were heard. From a business standpoint, I think the younger generation would look kindly upon any company that backed their position. The students have risked a great deal by participating in antiwar demonstrations. As you know from reading newspapers, the rallies sometimes turn into riots, exposing the participants to great physical danger. For these reasons, I believe Hank's proposal is worthy of close consideration."

"Well, I agree with Mr. Matsuda," Jack Strong said firmly, his eyes darting around the room. "We cannot afford to get political. We produce consumer products, manufactured in Japan. The American public would not look kindly on a foreign company getting involved in U.S. politics. Besides, our government has to know what it's doing. I mean, they have information that we don't have. They've been elected to make decisions based on the facts. And Richard Nixon's policies are good enough for me. You don't like 'em, vote for somebody else."

Jack settled back into the couch. "In any event," he concluded, "from a-public relations point of view, it would be a disaster for us to take any kind of a political position."

Takei silently nodded his head in assent.

Yoshi looked at his watch and rose to his feet. "I'm afraid the hour is growing late and it has been a long day. Perhaps we can consider this again at another time. We should all take time to think about it—not act in haste. Our decision on so important a matter should be well considered and rational."

"Well, I'm sorry, but I cannot be unemotional about innocent people being massacred," Ruth blurted out.

Hank reached for her hand and could feel it trembling. Looking up, he caught Sarah staring at him, waiting for him to speak.

"I didn't expect us to resolve this tonight," he said calmly. "Ruth and I have often discussed this issue far. into the night. We just want our feelings known to our friends, our stockholders and particularly, to our children. I'll bring it up again at our board meeting on Monday."

Sarah and Michio sat in her Ford convertible, outside the dorm. Neither of them had spoken on the short, fifteen-minute drive from the house in Brentwood to the UCLA campus. They'd been lost in their own thoughts, digesting what had been said.

As Michio made a move to get out of the car, Sarah grabbed his sleeve and turned him towards her. "Wait just a minute, Mick. I was so proud of you and of what you said back at the house. I know it wasn't easy for you to disagree with your father. I mean, he would have really flipped out if he knew that you and I went to meetings and rallies together. Anyway, I just want you to know I think you're terrific."

Michio smiled. "I said what I did because that is my conviction. I meant no disrespect and I can only hope my father understands that. As you know, in Japan one is taught to accept the judgment of one's elders without question."

He looked deeply and seriously into Sarah's eyes. "I have noticed many changes taking place in my thinking. I have made some good friends on campus. There is much humor there, yet they can be very serious when it is called for." Michio started to leave again, but stopped as his hand reached the door.

Turning back to Sarah once again, his words came rushing out. "You have been the greatest influence on me, Sarah. You can be serious one minute and funny the next. We have discussed many serious problems, yet I have laughed more with you this past year than I have in my entire life. And I have discovered more feelings than I ever thought existed for me."

He paused to take a breath before continuing, but was stopped when Sarah moved closer to him and kissed him on the lips. At first, Michio was embarrassed. Then, he took her in his arms and kissed her again.

Drawing back, Michio studied Sarah's face before whispering, "Good night." Opening the car door, he walked swiftly to the dormitory.

"How about a cognac?" Hank said to Ruth as they turned away from the door. "I'm wired and I need to talk about what happened this evening."

"I feel the same way," she said, walking over to the bar and pouring two Hennesey cognacs into snifter glasses. She carried them back to where Hank was sitting.

Hank sipped his drink, thoughtfully. "I'm not surprised by Yoshi's attitude. He's all business, no emotion. Guys like him piss ice water."

Hank swirled the golden brown liquid around in his glass.

"Michio, on the other hand, is showing a strong American influence," he continued. "You can be sure that a year ago, he would not have dared to disagree with his father. And by the way, did you notice how he looked at Sarah before he gave his opinion?"

"That came across loud and clear," Ruth responded. "There's something going on between those two and I'm sure Yoshi didn't miss it. Do you think it's possible that Sarah and Michio have gone past the 'just friends' stage? I love Michio and I know you do, too, but Sarah is very young. Also, interracial relationships are difficult at best. And I'm quite sure Yoshi would not be happy about the situation."

Hank frowned. "He'd be very unhappy, I'm afraid. He's already chosen Michio's wife. She's the daughter of a very prominent Japanese banking family. They don't believe in love marriages in Japan. They believe in mergers that increase the power of the family."

Ruth's heart skipped a beat. A feeling of deja vu came over her while her mind struggled to free itself of its memories. Changing the subject quickly, she asked, "Did you notice how Jack Strong toddied up to Yoshi? He calls everyone else by their first names but it's always 'Mr. Matsuda.' I get the feeling he'd agree with anything Yoshi says."

"I think you're absolutely right and I'm damned uncomfortable about it. I also now know that we cannot commit the company to any kind of a political position without the unanimous agreement of the principles. But we sure as hell can do or say anything we want to as far as our own personal statements are concerned."

Later that night, as she was falling asleep in Hank's arms, Ruth whispered, wistfully, "Our little girl is growing up."

"Yes, I know," Hank answered, softly.

After returning from spending their evening at the Marshall's home, Yoshikazu Matsuda and Takei Watanabe sat in the living room of their suite at the Bel Air Hotel. Seated on the couch, Takei had his everpresent notebook ready on the coffee table in front of him. Yoshi sat across from him in a red velvet, straight backed chair, stroking his chin and contemplating his thoughts. As was their custom on all business trips, the two men would review the events of the day, and Takei would receive his instructions.

"You will instruct Jack Strong that at no time, under any condition, will Telesonic take any kind of political position. It is also most important that he closely monitor the activities of Ruth and Hank Marshall. Remind him that he must be very discreet. They must not become suspicious. I believe, however, that they now understand the importance of Telesonic remaining non-political."

Takei nodded as he took down his notes. "Matsuda-San, it is important to note that the Marshalls are most observant, and therefore scrutiny must-be exercised with the greatest of care."

"It is noted," Yoshi said, dryly. "I am most concerned, however, with the comments made by my son. I fear that this past year in the United States may have influenced him in the wrong direction. I can see

that he has become very good friends with Sarah Marshall. We must not let their relationship develop into anything more than that. Today's events showed me that Michio's thinking has been affected. It is therefore, my decision that his education should continue at the University of Tokyo. He will now receive his business training at Tosui in Tokyo rather than at Telesonic, in Los Angeles. Michio must be re-immersed in his Japanese culture.

"I believe that it is also time for my son to be made aware of our Plan, as it will be his duty to take my place and fulfill his and Japan's destiny. You will make arrangements for him to accompany us back to Japan this week."

CHAPTER SEVENTEEN

1982

The day was like many Los Angeles days. Rich sunlight enveloped the city with warmth, while a faint ocean breeze drew the smog into a thin brown line that wove itself through the horizon.

Hank was making his way from the parking lot to the front doors of Marshall-Telesonic. In spite of the almost perfect fall weather, he was feeling unsettled. There was nothing he could put his finger on, just a nagging intuition that tugged at his senses. The meeting he was about to attend was routine: the normal review of quarterly performances and marketing strategies. There were, however, a few changes in the routine—small and insignificant perhaps, but they bothered him nonetheless.

Why should I be worried? He asked himself. Business is better than it's ever been. Sales on the new VCR's and television sets have surpassed their projections. Telesonic is on a role, he thought. This is not the time to worry about change.

Before reaching the main entrance, Hank veered to the right. He walked along a concrete path, which led to the side of the building. When he came to a high metal gate, he removed a plastic card from his pocket and inserted it into the key slot. The gate swung silently open.

About twenty yards further, the path suddenly ended, replaced by cobbled stones that were rough but comforting beneath his feet. Stepping through a border of tall, green shrubbery, he felt as if he'd entered another world.

This was the Rock Garden, or, as Hank called it, the earth-sculpture— a perfect harmony of sandy hills and valleys, rocks, trees and ponds, a miniature depiction of nature's glory. When Marshall-Telesonic had first moved into their new corporate headquarters in 1975, Hank had hired a famous Japanese landscape artist to design and build this garden. The designer then handpicked a local Japanese landscaper to maintain the area. Each week, the man came to trim the trees and bushes, remove the dead leaves and weeds, and to rake intricate patterns into the fine white gravel.

The garden was a very special place to Hank. The serenity it provided filled him with the same sense of peace and tranquility he'd experienced at the rock garden of the Gokoku-ji Temple in Tokyo. It reminded him of those few, precious moments he had shared with Shikibu.

Hank knew he would never understand the forces that had brought them together. The brief time he and Shikibu shared had been both beautiful and sad. The memories were now carefully locked away in a secret corner of his heart. This garden was Hank's memorial to Shikibu's short life. Its peace provided Hank with a quiet place to be alone with his thoughts, free from the intrusion of the outside world.

Over the years, Hank had come to believe, as the Japanese did, that the composition of space and matter cleansed the souls of those who contemplated them. While the garden was open to all the staff, there was no smoking, eating or talking allowed within its borders. It was strictly a place for meditation.

Sitting on a stark wooden bench next to the fishpond, Hank's eyes took in the perfect harmony before him. He tried to let it permeate his very being.

Hank learned a number of lessons from his dealings with the Japanese, among them the value of intuition. And right now, his intuition was giving him signals that were in direct opposition to the perfection before him. It was as if he were being cautioned.

The uneasiness had begun when Hank first realized that the routine had changed. It was now Monday and Yoshi had flown in from Tokyo the night before. That was change number one. In the past, Yoshi had always arrived on a Friday or Saturday so he could have dinner with Ruth and Hank at their home on one of those nights. The ritual not only allowed them a chance to go over some of the more pressing business before a meeting but it also served as a courtesy, reaffirming the special relationship between them. Courtesy and ritual were of prime importance to the Japanese. But not this time.

There had been a change in plans once before. Five years earlier, Yoshi had called Hank to tell him that he had to alter his schedule. He had apologized profusely for the inconvenience. But this time he hadn't called. In fact, all Hank had received was a telephone message telling him that Yoshi would arrive on Sunday. It also said he wanted to meet with him privately at eight-thirty Monday morning, before the scheduled nine o'clock meeting was to take place. Change number two.

Usually, Yoshi called Hank as soon as he was settled in his hotel room. This time he had not. Change number three.

Small variations in the normal routine, each with a thousand possible justifications. Nothing to really be concerned about, except that he was dealing with a man to whom order and ritual were a necessity of life. If Yoshi were an American businessman, it wouldn't be bothering Hank. But he wasn't. He was Yoshi. And something was definitely wrong.

Hank rose and stood quietly for a moment, trying to shake off his feelings of foreboding. He didn't have time to continue worrying. Soon enough he would know what was behind his fears.

Yoshi and Hank had worked well together from the beginning. In the 1950's, when the idea of importing high-quality Japanese electronic appliances to the United States had been an impossible dream in the minds of many, they had pulled it off together. Hank had been the marketing man, and Yoshi the ever-practical engineer. Over the years, they made Marshall-Telesonic a multibillion dollar company. By 1982, the name 'Telesonic' had become a household word throughout the United States and around the world.

The relationship between the two men, started through mutual need, had developed into one of respect and trust. Hank had never doubted Yoshi's integrity and liked to think Yoshi felt the same way.

Leaving the rock garden, he walked toward the main entrance of Marshall-Telesonic's modern, five-story office building. He wondered if perhaps Yoshi was having personal problems of some kind. That would account for the change, he thought.

He walked through the large, glass doorway into the main lobby. "Good morning," Hank said, nodding to the pretty young Asian receptionist seated there.

"Good morning to you, Mr. Marshall," she answered with a smile. Picking up the intercom, she told Hank's secretary, Sheila, he was on his way up.

Hank had grown more handsome with age. Tall and erect, he still maintained his athletic physique at the age of sixty. While wrinkles caused the flesh of some men to sag, deep lines had only given Hank's angular face more character. And his thick, gray hair made his piercing blue eyes appear even more luminous and alive.

Walking through the lobby with an easy stride, he exchanged brief greetings with two of his salesmen who were on their way out.

"Hey, Chief, we're going for a record today. It doesn't get much better than this!" the young salesman said, grinning.

"That is what I like to hear," Hank smiled. "Go get em!"

"Consider them got, Boss!" the second man replied.

Hank took the elevator up to the executive offices on the top floor. The fifth floor offices were plush. Unusual contemporary furnishings had been combined with rare antique pieces to create a look of subtle elegance. In front of the elevator, an original oil painting by Leonard

Creo, depicting two salesmen shaking hands, dominated the cream-colored wall. To the left of the elevator was the "second phase" of visitor screening: a large waiting room, comfortably furnished, with another woman seated behind a desk.

"Good morning, Mr. Marshall," the attractive redhead said cheerfully.

"Good morning, Margaret. Is Mr. Matsuda here yet?"

"He's in the Tosui office, Sir."

Hank walked past her through double doors of tinted glass and down the long corridor. Reaching a door marked, "Vice President, Marketing," he opened it and entered his daughter's office. Sarah looked up from the papers she was studying and grinned. "Hi, Dad! "she said, in that tone of pleased surprise she always used when she saw him.

Sarah was twenty-seven years old and had worked for Marshall-Telesonic full-time since graduating from college with a degree in marketing. It was a great source of pride to Hank that his daughter had qualified for an executive position at such an early age. She had an intuitive knowledge of marketing that he liked to think was genetic.

Tall and slender, she had dark blonde hair like her mother's. And although her features were softer and more sensual than her father's, there was no doubting her Marshall heritage.

"I've been polishing up the new digital tape deck campaign," she told her father.

"So you're ready for the meeting?"

"Got all the latest survey data. And we've come up with the new positioning."

"Good," he said. "Get into any trouble on the weekend?"

She smiled playfully. "Of course!"

He raised an eyebrow, mockingly. "See you in a bit," he said as he left the room.

Before reaching his own office, Hank knocked on a door marked "Senior Vice-President" before walking in. Milt Samuels, the chief financial officer of the company, had worked with him since mid-1959, when

Bea Stein had decided to retire. Short and balding, Milt wore thick glasses and a permanently bemused expression.

Looking up distractedly from the printouts he was analyzing, Milt saw Hank and asked, "How was your weekend?"

"Fine. And yours?"

"I was here for most of it," said Milt, without complaint.

"I guess that means all the numbers are ready."

"Yup, and you're gonna love them."

They talked for another minute before Hank continued on to his own office.

His suite was at the end of the long hall, fronted by a smaller office containing the final barrier—Sheila.

Tall, thin, and always moving at high speed, Sheila protected Hank's time and energies like a well-trained watchdog. In the ten years she'd been his secretary, she'd coordinated his schedule and relieved him of details. Her thick black hair and eyebrows, accentuated by thick round eyeglasses, contributed to her intimidating demeanor.

Now, in her late forties, Sheila had been married to the same husband for twenty-five years a man she described as "essentially boring, but reliable." Life as Hank's secretary was not boring, however, and her creativity went into the many hours she spent at Marshall-Telesonic.

As he opened the office door, Sheila smiled in welcome. "You have two call-backs before your meeting," she said, lifting the pile of messages from her desk. "Everything else can wait until this afternoon."

It was a testimony to his faith in Sheila's efficiency that he simply took the sheaf of paper like a relay runner, and continued into his own office.

Hank's office was a series of long angles dictated by a bank of windows that faced the hills of Bel Air and Brentwood on the right side. On the left was Santa Monica and the Pacific Ocean, which presented an ever-changing array of colors and moods. Hank particularly enjoyed the darkening tones of twilight.

The room was furnished simply. There was a desk at one end, a comfortable grouping of chairs and a couch at the other and a small conference table in between. Along the walls was an eclectic array of display cases exhibiting a collection of prototypical Telesonic products, that were almost works of art: an AM/FM radio cassette player as thin as a cigarette case; a small black tape deck with multicolored lights that measured sound frequencies; headphones so light they practically floated; a powerful hand-held portable vacuum cleaner with a tapered nose that made it look like an anteater; bookshelf speakers shaped like seashells, and a host of other electronic gadgetry.

Hank sat at his desk and looked at the top two messages Sheila had given him. One was a call from Senator Harkins, who sat on the House Foreign Trade Committee, and the other, a social call from Carter Robb, an old friend and business competitor. Quickly, he shuffled through the rest of the messages, smiling as he reached for the telephone. As usual, Sheila had assessed the priorities perfectly.

No sooner had he finished making his calls than Yoshi entered the room. Hank rose and met him halfway. Both men bowed and then held out their hands, observing the traditions of the other.

"It's good to see you again, old friend," Hank said warmly.

"As usual Hank-San, it is an honor."

In some ways Yoshi was unchanged from the first time Hank had met him. His hair was still full and black, his body still slim. He was tall for a Japanese of his generation, although Hank dwarfed him by five inches. Yet Hank had never thought of himself as being much taller than Yoshi. Yoshi, with his impenetrable calm, carried himself with a regal air of self-confidence. It added stature to his physical size. Hank had often attempted to analyze this aspect of the man. He knew it had to do with Yoshi's satisfaction of who he was and his place in the world. Call it pride, Hank thought, or perhaps even arrogance. Whatever it was, it was an attitude that had intrigued Hank for decades.

No matter how well he thought he knew the Japanese, there was an intractable element to them. It might have been because they believed themselves to be of divine origin: People of the Gods, living in the Land of Gods. To the Japanese, all others, no matter how distinguished, were either foreigners or 'gaijin'. And while they kept their feelings hidden behind a maze of rituals and manners, the Japanese felt they were superior to every other race. In his early visits to Japan, Hank had been astounded to find that people who seemed so genuinely friendly, could be so xeno-phobic. He still found it difficult to justify the contradictions.

Moving across the room to the round glass conference table, he motioned for Yoshi to join him. "What is it that caused you to call for a private conference?" Hank asked, getting right to the point as they took their seats.

Hank's directness had always been disconcerting to Yoshi. He'd always felt compelled to observe polite repartee before settling down to business. This time was no exception, so instead of answering Hank's question, he asked, "How are Ruth and Sarah and Peter?"

"Very well. And all anxious to see you."

Yoshi smiled faintly, than paused. "Hank-San, I will come to the point. As you are well aware, in all of Telesonic's manufacturing and distribution throughout the world, there is only one area where Telesonic-Japan does not totally control distribution."

"Of course, in the United States," said Hank, wondering where this was leading. "I've always felt it was a testimony to the harmony of our part-nership that for the last thirty years, we've remained on top in such a com-petitive business."

Yoshi inclined his head in a half nod, half bow. "But Hank-San, the realities have changed. Things are different now. We are getting older. As you well know, change is the essence of growth. Although Marshall-Telesonic and Tosui have lived well together for many years, we have no way of knowing what will follow at Marshall -Telesonic when it is time for you to retire."

Shifting in his chair, Yoshi looked at Hank, his face void of expression. "Again, I will come to the point. We feel it is imperative that Telesonic-Japan has total control of Telesonic's distribution in the United-States. It is the only place in the world where we do not have that control and it is our largest market. We cannot allow ourselves to become vulnerable to any management that might follow you."

Hank's anxiety transformed itself into a tightening sensation in his chest. This was no small matter. He knew that whatever the outcome of this conversation might be, Yoshi's words were a signal that there would be a major change in his life, his relationships and in the destiny of Marshall-Telesonic forever.

"What are you saying, Yoshi?" he asked.

"Hank-San, Tosui would like to buy out your interest in Marshall-Telesonic. We..."

"You want to buy me out?" Hank interrupted in disbelief. "Why? Are you dissatisfied with the way we run the business? And if so, why?" He tried to keep the emotion out of his voice, without success.

"Of course not, Hank-San. It simply makes good business sense to us. And, we are prepared to make you a very generous offer."

Hank was stunned. He had never expected this. Never. But at least now he knew what he was facing and what he would have to fight.

"A generous offer?" Hank repeated incredulously, his voice rising. "A generous offer after thirty years of working together? Creating a name that is respected throughout the United States and around the world? A generous offer? There is not enough generosity in this world to offer me. How do you plan to compensate for the creativity, the teaching, the blood and the sweat that's gone into making the name 'Telesonic' one of the most successful manufacturers of television sets in the United States?"

Hank looked at Yoshi, who was sitting stiffly in his chair, eyes straight ahead, unblinking. Hank shook his head in disbelief.

"In your mind, this is a done deal, isn't it, Yoshi? It's been discussed in the boardrooms of Tosui and Telesonic in Japan and has been decided, hasn't it? What I don't understand is why you didn't come to me as a friend and tell me. How can you come to me now, after the decision has already been made?"

Yoshi's voice was steady as he answered. "Yes, the decision has already been made, Hank-San. But I think if you examine our thought process closely, you will find that this change will not only be good for Telesonic, but for you personally. You have worked long and hard. It is time for you to enjoy the fruits of your labor."

"Are you telling me that I should retire?" Hank asked, incredulously. His voice reached a menacing pitch as he struggled to stay in control. Although this had come as a complete shock to him, he knew he had to maintain a clear head, to keep his balance.

Rising to his feet, he paced up and down the deep burgundy carpeting, before stopping abruptly beside the chair where Yoshi was sitting. Hank towered over him as he attempted to keep his voice calm.

"You come to me after thirty years of friendship. After we created a brand name from nothing—a name from my idea! We worked together, side, by side, dismissing those clumsy, awkward first models, and we introduced a superior product to the American market in the face of sarcasm and laughter. Do you remember those first models you wanted to present to the public? They would never have sold, no matter how good the sound and picture were..."

Hank paused, remembering the dozens of meetings he'd had with engineers, designers and marketing people. The end result had been that his ideas had brought style and innovative marketing techniques to the brand name of Telesonic.

Resentment hit him hard. He couldn't help it. Hank had put boundless energy, as well as his heart and soul, into creating a quality image for Telesonic. And this was his reward?

His voice rose again. "We took your son into our home, Yoshi, and into our confidence. We trained him and others in our methods. We built a company that could go on and on. We became bigger and better than all the established companies in the United States. General Electric is nothing, RCA is nothing, Zenith is struggling—but Telesonic prevails. And why is that? Because we were a team. We combined American and Japanese ingenuity and capabilities. We created a success.

"And now? Without warning, without thought—as though everything we created never happened, as though we are strangers—you walk into my office and say, 'Hank-San, I think you're getting old. You might even be starting to lose your grip. And I'm not so sure that those who'll succeed you will be able to maintain our standards'. Well, that's bullshit', Yoshi!"

He bent down and looked Yoshi straight in the eye, "And I will not sell out. Do you understand that?"

Yoshi's face was stoic. Without looking at Hank, he said, "I understand your feelings and I respect them, Hank-San. As you know, a change such as this cannot be accomplished quickly. I think though, that when you reconsider, you will begin to see the logic and the need for what I now propose."

"Possibly," said Hank, thoughtfully. "But my answer will be the same."

Yoshi got to his feet and faced Hank. "There is a saying from the Chinese sage Confucius: 'Only the supremely wise and the abysmally ignorant do not change'."

Without hesitation, Hank replied, "Yes. He's the same guy who said: 'The superior man seeks what is right. The inferior one, what is profitable.' "But, Yoshi, I'm in no mood to exchange proverbs. I'm angry and hurt. You have confronted me with a decision that is going to have a tremendous affect on my life and the life of my family. You see I, too, expected my children and grandchildren to carry on the family business."

Shaking his head, Hank sat back heavily in his chair while Yoshi gracefully returned to his seated position.

"Let's get something straight right now," Hank continued, "I am not ready to retire. I am not ready to play golf every day nor am I ready to rest on my laurels. There are too many new ideas burning in my head. There are still many places I want to take Marshall-Telesonic, especially now, with all the advances in micro-chips and high-definition television. I've always felt that Japanese engineering and quality control, combined with American marketing and creativity made us the force we are today. And that it would continue to make us the dominant force in the electronics industry." Hank shook his head again.

Yoshi put his hands up in exasperation. "Hank-San, I know you are upset. But this is something that must be. The investment in this company is great. The markets of the world are at stake. We came together at the right time. And we have each fulfilled our destiny. But you are sixty years old and I am sixty-two. We are no longer the young men we once were. It is time for us to set the stage for what is to follow. We cannot think only of Hank and Yoshi. There is more to consider. We must now worry about succession."

"My staff is extraordinarily capable and none of them is ready to retire," said Hank with conviction. "Sarah will eventually take over the company and run it as well, if not better than I have, because she has all the benefits of the new technologies, the new ideas, and special training that I never had."

Allowing only a slight movement of his lips, Yoshi smiled for the first time. "Come now, Hank-San," he said, amusement in his voice. "Your daughter is very pretty and clever and certainly very competent. But after all, she is still a woman with a woman's priorities. She could never take over Telesonic in the United States. Women are different than we are. They have different priorities…marriage, children. They make too many emotional decisions where cool logic should prevail…"

"Now just a minute, Yoshi!" Hank interrupted, angrily, "Don't you think it's time you came out of the Dark Ages? I'll put Sarah up against any executive you have. And what's more, no one could be more dedicated."

"Please do not misunderstand me, Hank-San. We will always have a position for Sarah Marshall at Telesonic. She is a very capable woman, indeed. But the head of the company? Never!"

Biting his lip, Hank did not respond. He looked at his watch, than turned his burning eyes to Yoshi. "We're running late," Hank told him. "Half an hour is hardly enough time for me to prepare to face my associates with a proposition of this kind. But, they are waiting for us in the boardroom and we should go meet them."

"Would you prefer to postpone the board meeting until one o'clock?" Yoshi asked.

"No. I think now is the time. I've never withheld anything from my people. And I want them to get this message directly from you. I don't want it to be distorted in any way by time or by my feelings."

Yoshi nodded without comment.

As both men stood, Hank said sarcastically, "By the way, you've already discussed this with your son, haven't you?" For a moment, Yoshi faltered. Then, looking at Hank with a cold expression, he said, "Let us go to the meeting."

Silently, they walked down the hall to the conference room and entered. A gleaming oval walnut table, long enough to seat twenty people, dominated the room. By the time Hank and Yoshi had arrived, some twenty minutes late, the seven other participants were already seated and glancing nervously at their watches.

Hank sat at the head of the table. Yoshi took the seat to his right. On Yoshi's right sat Takei and next to him was Toshiro Saito, President of Tosui Trading Company, USA. Beside him sat the chief financial officer of Tosui Worldwide, Kenji Toda. Last in the row was Yoshi's son, Michio, who had become a younger, taller version of his father.

Sitting to Hank's left were Milt Samuels, Sarah, and Jack Strong, Director of Public Relations and Advertising.

Sarah concentrated determinedly on her father. A small frown began to form on her forehead as she sensed something was wrong. Clearing his throat, Hank began.

"This is going to be an extraordinary meeting," he started. I am setting aside today's agenda due to a meeting I just had with Yoshikazu Matsuda.

In that meeting, he informed me that Tosui Worldwide wants to buy out the American interest in Marshall-Telesonic. This came as quite a shock to me. And I am not easily surprised by the actions of my competition or," he paused meaningfully, my associates."

Yoshi stared straight ahead, impassively. Michio looked down, shifting uncomfortably, making notations on his pad.

Sarah's mouth had parted in shock, while Milt sat stiffly in his seat. Rifling busily through his briefcase, Jack Strong avoided making eye contact. The Japanese executives looked on with interest.

"Yes," Hank continued, "the decision seems to have already been made by our Japanese associates. It appears, then, that the purpose of this meeting is to respond. The meeting is now open for any questions you may have. After that, we will adjourn until we have had a chance to review this new set of circumstances and prepare our answer. I would like to say for the record that I was not happy to be taken by surprise. I have never considered selling my interest in Marshall-Telesonic. Yoshikazu-San does, however, have a legitimate right to make this request and to propose that negotiations be opened for the acquisition of the American interest by Tosui. I would therefore like to have Mr. Matsuda state Tosui's position, so that we're all perfectly clear as to what the proposition is and why this move is being made."

Hank took a deep breath and turned toward Yoshi.

After meeting his gaze for a moment, Yoshi looked at the others and said in a firm voice, "We have enjoyed a long and happy relationship with the Marshall family. We hope this new set of circumstances will only continue the splendid cooperation and understanding we've shared for the past thirty years. But times change and with all due respect, Mr. Marshall is approaching retirement age. Tosui must be assured that the Telesonic brand will continue to grow and prosper in the United States."

For a moment, Sarah looked as if she was going to interrupt, but instead, she clamped her mouth shut and narrowed her eyes.

"As you are aware," Yoshi continued, "the United States is the only country in the world in which Tosui does not have total ownership and control of Telesonic. We have joint ventures in other parts of the world, but nothing that involves distribution of a brand the size and scope of Telesonic.

"In the field of television, VCR's and stereo components, American manufacturers have all but disappeared. The new technologies—high-definition televisions and super-sound—are, for the most part, being pioneered and funded by the Japanese, who literally own this market around the world. Tosui's major competition is not the once-great American companies, but other manufacturers of Japanese electronics—Panasonic, Sony, Hitachi and Toshiba.

"The Japanese manufacturers all have one thing in common," Yoshi added. "They are all controlled by Japanese headquarters. We feel it is essential that Telesonic also benefit by uniform worldwide decisions."

Looking around the table as if to reassure everyone, he said, "There will be no other major changes. We want to keep the same efficient American managers we have now, and the same system of distribution that exists today.

"In making this move," Yoshi continued, looking directly at each of the Americans at the table, "we are prepared to make a very generous offer for the fifty-one percent of stock not currently owned by Tosui. I will now be happy to answer any questions you might have."

Milt put down the pen he'd been clutching and was the first to speak. "I'm as stunned by this announcement as Hank must have been. Still, I do understand your motivations. There is one thing I want to point out, however. We have an entire network of distribution that's been geared to the Marshall-Telesonic'Personalit' for many, many years—and very successfully, I might add. Have you considered just how that network would be affected?"

"It will not be affected at all," Yoshi assured. "All contracts that currently exist will be honored. The only change taking place will be in the stock ownership. As a matter of fact," he said, pausing to look at Hank, "I would be most pleased if Mr. Marshall would continue as President of the company and plan his retirement at his own convenience."

Sarah could contain herself no longer. With eyes flashing, she literally snarled, "Dad, retire? Are you kidding? Why, he's probably the best marketing and merchandising person in the United States! I have a very difficult time picturing him doing anything else."

Taking a deep breath, she regained her professional demeanor. "We have created some remarkable images around Telesonic and, for all intents and purposes, it's as American as apple pie. Will this move change its character? And also, are you considering any changes in the executive personnel?"

As Hank watched her, he realized how alike they were. She was frank and direct, just as he was. Not one to back down from a confrontation.

"Now wait a minute," Jack Strong interrupted. Although the room temperature was set at a cool sixty-eight degrees, the public relations man was sweating profusely.

"We need to remember something," Strong said. "The United States understands that the Japanese have become our trading partners, our financiers, and that they are in the process of bailing us out of all kinds of problems. When I say 'us', I'm talking about the United States as a whole. And, from a P.R. standpoint, I really can't see any big problem here. The American consumer now sees Japanese brands as the ultimate in manufacturing quality. If anything, the news that Telesonic will be entirely Japanese-owned might even enhance our consumer image."

A strange thought struck Hank as he listened. Fixing his eyes on Jack's face, he said softly, "Jack, did you have any idea this was going to take place?"

Shuffling his papers and taking care not to look directly at Hank, Jack responded gruffly, "Of course not."

As the discussion continued, Sarah and Milt asked most of the questions. Hank noticed that Michio kept trying to get Sarah's attention, but she completely ignored him.

Yoshi had just finished answering a question about finances when Hank suddenly stood up. "This has been a very trying day. We are faced with a proposition that, unfortunately, feels to me like an ultimatum. Be that as it may, I would now like to bring this meeting to a close and adjourn to my office with Milt, Sarah and Jack."

Hank looked at Yoshi seated beside him and allowed a hint of sarcasm to surface in his voice. "I am quite certain that our Japanese friends and associates have been aware of this proposition for some time and have therefore had the opportunity to discuss it thoroughly. That being the case, it's only fitting that we be given the same opportunity. I would like to call this meeting to an end and continue tomorrow at nine A.M."

"Of course, Hank-San," said Yoshi, rising and bowing slightly.

Their eyes met and it was as though they were looking at each other for the first time. No masks shielded their faces. Both sets of eyes hardened! Unyielding, while they glared at each other for several seconds. Finally, Hank turned and left the room.

Back in Hank's office, Milt asked, "Why not hear him out? What's the harm in listening to what they have to say?"

"Because I don't want to sell," replied Hank, vehemently.

They were all sitting around Hank's conference table. Milt's sleeves were rolled up, his tie was askew and there was a disturbed expression on his face.

"Well, I'd sure as hell like to hear what he means by 'generous'," he said, thoughtfully.

"What's the difference? I don't want to sell."

"Come on, Hank. You taught me yourself that everyone has his price!"

"I'm enjoying myself, though," Hank protested, hardly sounding that way. "We've worked hard to develop a successful name and a good product line. In fact, we're the best, goddamned product line in the country! Then all of a sudden we sell out? If we do that, we're nothing."

Jack jumped into the discussion, shaking his head. "What do you mean, we're nothing? With a couple of hundred million bucks in your poke, you're nothing? Hey, you're no kid anymore, Hank. You've been in this pressure pot for a lot of years. Maybe it's time for you to enjoy yourself. Go and relax. Have a little fun. Go travel with Ruth. You've been married a long time. Maybe now you can spend some of it with her. You owe her that. Think about it."

"Pressure's never been my problem," Hank said, disgruntled, looking down at the table in front of him. Slowly, he lifted his eyes.

"Jack, do you want to sell?" he asked. "Is that what this is all about?"

"I would like to hear the man out," Jack replied. "Look, you have a partner who wants to buy you out. You say 'no deal' and the partnership continues. But there are sure as hell going to be problems we haven't had before."

"Yes, he implied that," said Hank bitterly. He'd seen a different side of Yoshi today, and it had disturbed him. He'd always been aware of the man's toughness, but it had never been directed at him before. They'd been allies. Now, they were adversaries.

Hank looked at Sarah. He wanted to see if he could get a reading of what her feelings were. But Sarah was sitting across from him, her mouth pursed, and she seemed content to let the others debate the issue for the time being.

"Let's take a look at this," Jack said in a conciliatory tone. "Let's take it all apart. What's the harm, eh? Yoshi said 'generous.' Now, what does that mean? What would we take? If you knew you could get whatever you wanted, Hank, what would you take?"

"I don't like the idea," Hank answered. "I don't like the way he put it. I just don't like the whole thing."

"Well, Hank, you can't always have everything you want. But, hell— money can sure make up for what you don't have. He leaned across the table, his eyes bright. "I think we should give him a number that will knock him on his ass. All right, so you don't want to sell out. Fair enough. Then let's give him a number he won't take."

"What's the point?"

Leaning back again, Jack crossed his arms. "Look, either he's gonna forget about buying the company, or we will be very rich. That's the point."

I'm already a rich man, Hank thought, worth several million dollars. But there was rich and there was very rich. What Jack was talking about was very rich, an amount of money that would assure his future, the future of his children and even his grandchildren.

Jack wanted him to sell. Hank could see that. The son of a bitch is marching to his own drummer, he thought. There had always been something about Jack Strong that didn't sit right with Hank. And his attitude disturbed Hank, now more than ever.

He stood up and walked over to where Jack was sitting and put his hand on Jack's shoulder. "What kind of money were you thinking of?" Hank asked him.

"Off the top of my head, I don't really know. But let's see what we can come up with. This doesn't have to be a disaster, you understand. It could be a hell of an opportunity."

"All right, Jack. Let's try it your way and see what we come up with."

Half an hour later the two men had a figure.

Milt, who had been listening quietly while the two men bartered, estimated the net book value of Marshall-Telesonic at one hundred and forty million. He then multiplied the earnings ratio by a high rate of fifteen, which came to five hundred million. "Just for the hell of it," Milt said, "let's set the value at six hundred million. Tosui owns about half the company. To buy us out, they would have to come up with close to three hundred million in cash."

"It's an outrageous figure," said Hank, dubiously.

Jack smiled wolfishly. "Well, we wanted a figure that would knock him on his ass, and that's what we got."

Sarah broke her silence at last. "I vote that we go ahead and present it to them. They want us out, let's make them pay!"

CHAPTER EIGHTEEN

▼

Hank sat alone in his office and stared at the view of the Pacific Ocean from his window. Usually the calm waters soothed him but on this dreary, overcast day, they didn't have that effect. The shock of the day's events seemed to have obliterated any chance he had of finding peace.

After the others had left, Hank thought about their reactions. Milt, as chief financial officer, was well compensated. Though he owned no shares in the company, his income, bonuses and profit sharing programs had made him a wealthy man. He had recently been awarded stock option privileges that could be exercised upon the sale of the company. If the takeover was successful, he stood to make a huge profit.

Jack Strong would also benefit greatly from a takeover. Hank had hired him to work for Marshall-Telesonic when it had been newly formed. There'd been a real need for the company and their new product line to burst into the publics consciousness in a dramatic way. They needed to overcome the stigma of poor quality that was associated with most imported Japanese merchandise. Jack had ably accomplished this task. His presence had also been instrumental in breaking the only deadlock that had ever existed in the relationship between the Marshalls and Tosui.

In those early bargaining years, both sides had demanded majority control. The issue had finally been settled when each side agreed to take a forty-nine percent share, with Jack getting the remaining two percent as an incentive.

Since that time, there had been no other major problems. All policy decisions had been unanimously approved. It had given Hank a real sense of security to think that Jack would be on his side in the event of a dispute. Now, he realized, this might not be true. Fear began to take root in his mind. Had he made a serious error thirty years ago by trusting Jack and bringing him into his inner circle? Hank's stomach churned, realizing what the consequences of such a mistake might be.

And then there was Sarah. A warm feeling swept over Hank whenever he thought about his daughter. She was so bright and capable. He saw the future of the company in her. Initially, Hank had been disappointed when his son, Peter, had shown no interest in becoming a part of the family business. But Peter had inherited his mother's musical talents and was now a critically acclaimed concert pianist.

Sarah, on the other hand, had an instinctive understanding and love for business that could not be taught. Her natural skills in sales and marketing were further enhanced by her computer literacy. Hank and Sarah spent many hours together, discussing a future that would combine television with computer technology, forming an information highway. Her ideas were so fresh and progressive that thinking about Yoshi's chauvinistic feelings towards women made Hank angrier than before.

Suddenly, Hank felt a burning desire to be with Ruth. Although she'd retired from the business twenty years before, she'd never lost interest in it. She enjoyed the world of business, but they had both decided that after the children were born it was more important for her to devote her time to the family. It had also given her an opportunity to spend more time with her other love, the arts.

But, no matter how many activities Ruth became involved in she always managed to keep up with what was happening at Marshall-Telesonic. This enabled Hank to consult with her on important issues.

Right now, he needed her cool, logical counsel more than ever.

The buzz of the intercom startled him. He'd been so deep in thought that he hadn't heard it until Sheila's insistent voice came through the speaker. "Mr. Marshall, Jack Strong would like to see you. He says it's very important."

"I'm sure it is. Tell him to come in."

The door opened immediately and in lumbered Jack. His shirtsleeves were rolled up, his collar was unbuttoned and his red-and blue-striped tie hung loosely around his neck. The tie appeared almost as wilted as he did.

Hank looked up at him with cold eyes. Irritably, he motioned with his hand for Jack to sit down in the chair facing his desk. Then, he waited impatiently while Jack removed a large, white handkerchief from his pocket and wiped away the perspiration that was dripping down his forehead.

"Rough day," Jack said at last, carelessly stuffing the damp cloth back into his pocket. Attempting to sound lighthearted, he winked at Hank before saying, "Well, it's show time! Boy, that Yoshi's a cool cat. He wants the company badly, too. And he's willing to pay through the nose. His eyes watched Hank, who sat quietly across from him, hands folded against his chin, listening. Beads of sweat began appearing on Jack's forehead once more and, again, he pulled out his handkerchief to mop his brow.

"It's time for the big killing, kiddo," Jack continued, jovially. "They want what we got. It's payoff time!"

A long pause filled the room. Hank's eyes bore directly into Jack's. "You knew about this all along, didn't you?" he asked in a steely voice. "In fact, it wouldn't surprise me if you helped plan the whole thing."

He rose menacingly and moved toward Jack, whose hand shot up as if to protect himself.

"Now just hold on just a fucking minute, Hank. Whatever I did works out in the best interests of all of us. I'm going to level with you. I did help plan it. But believe me, Tosui would have made this move with or without Jack Strong. That's just the way it is." A sweaty grin was stamped across his face as he tried hard to keep his tone light.

"Look, the cards have already been dealt," Jack continued. You're holding a good hand but if you put up a fight, you're gonna lose big time. On
the other hand, if you go with the flow, you can ride into the sunset on the
biggest golden parachute anyone ever saw!"

Hank watched Jack get up and begin to pace the floor. He continued to
watch him for a while before letting his voice cut through the tension like
a knife. "Just how long have you been working for Tosui, Jack?"

Jack stopped his pacing and turned to Hank. "Since day one," he
answered, in a flat voice. "It was no accident that we met on that plane
thirty years ago. They sent you a ticket and placed me in the seat next
to yours."

Hank's eyes grew wide. "So, I was your pigeon all along. And when I
asked you to join the company and gave you a two percent share, it was all
part of the plan, wasn't it?"

He could hardly control himself. "You son-of-a-bitch!" he yelled at
Jack. "You set me up. And you're part of this master plan to control
Marshall-Telesonic. I get it all now. Tosui wants to own the consumer
electronics business, to go along with their computer chip and automobile businesses."

Jack laughed. "Why should I give a shit who controls what? You're
gonna wind up with three hundred million bucks from this deal and Mrs.
Strong's little boy, Jack—will walk away with a cool twelve million. Not in
your league, to be sure, but hell, I ain't no pig."

"Oh, but you are a pig," Hank spat out as Jack's face flushed brightly.
Drawing himself up to his full height, he looked down with rage and dis-
gust at the man standing before him.

Jack laughed again, but this time the sound was high-pitched and nervous, tinged with fear. Backing away slowly, he said, "Hey, I guess I am a
pig, but a very rich pig. And I don't really give a shit what you think of me
now. And I'm willing to bet you that by tomorrow, you're gonna feel differently. You're too smart to blow this deal, Hank."

Abruptly, Jack turned and walked out of the office.

"You're too smart to blow this deal." The words rang in Hank's head. He'd always been an extremely confident man. He was aware of the respect others had for his quick mind and his ability to instantly grasp a situation. In negotiations, he always seemed to have the advantage of instinctively knowing what the other person was thinking. He would act, rather than react.

But now he was on strange ground, caught unprepared for the events of the day. He'd been maneuvered into a corner. And this angered and frustrated him, despite the fact that the corner was lined with gold.

He was mortified by Jack's admission of being a spy. And he wasn't sure if his anger stemmed from being deceived or because he'd been so completely taken in.

Looking at his watch, Hank was surprised to see that it was just eleven-thirty. Only three hours had passed since the start of his meeting with Yoshi. Picking up the phone, he dialed his home number, hoping Ruth was there. Relief filled him when he heard her voice on the other end.

"Hi, honey, I'm glad you're home. There's been some big developments here that I really need to talk to you about."

"Is anything wrong?" she asked anxiously. "Are you all right?"

"I'm fine," he said, trying to sound cool. "But I got hit with a real shocker this morning. Our friend, Yoshi, had a real surprise up his sleeve. Seems Tosui wants complete control of Marshall -Telesonic. They're proposing to buy us out."

There was a long pause.

"From out of the blue, this guy tells me it's time for me to retire. Says the company we built together has to change. Can you believe it?"

"Hank, I don't know what to say. I'm shocked. Why don't you come home so we can talk about it?"

Ruth waited for an answer, but none came. In a softer voice, she tried again. "Come on home, honey. I'll be waiting for you. And Hank, I love you."

No sooner had Ruth hung up then there was a tap on the door and Sarah walked into Hank's office. "Dad," she said in an anxious voice, "I had to see you right away."

Practically running to him as he got up to greet her, Sarah flung her arms around her father's neck and kissed him tenderly on the cheek. Taking a step back, she looked into his eyes.

"Are you okay? This had to come as a complete shock to you."

The concern on her face said everything. "Look, Dad, you just have to know that whatever you decide, I'm right behind you."

Hank smiled as he sat back down behind his desk with Sarah facing him.

"Thanks for the vote of confidence, sweetheart. It's always good to have."

The events of the morning came rushing to him and it took Hank a few moments to sort through them.

"I had a visit from our friend, Jack Strong," he said at last. "And I found out he's not one of the good guys. He was working for Tosui before Marshall-Telesonic was ever formed. In fact, he's been their man from day one." He stopped for a second, seeing the stunned expression on Sarah's face.

"Jack took great pains to let me know just how much we would all benefit by selling out. He's such a phony bastard! It took a hell of alot of will power for me not to knock him on his ass. But, I kept my cool."

"That certainly would have been something to see!" Sarah laughed. "Listen, let's have some lunch so we can talk about this some more."

"I'd love to," Hank said, looking at his daughter fondly, "but I just spoke with your mother and she and I are going to have a quiet lunch at home. In fact, I was getting ready to leave when you walked in."

Seeing the disappointed look on his daughter's face, Hank added, "But I have a few minutes before I have to go. Tell me what you think about all of this. What are your feelings?"

"Well, I'm not worried about losing my job," Sarah answered confidently. "I feel good about the work I've done here and I think I can replace

Marshall-Telesonic easier than they can replace me. Besides, if you're not here, I don't know that I would want to stay."

Sarah paused. "I do have one concern, though. Michio and I have been very close friends for many years. But I am so disappointed in him now! I just can't believe that he'd turn on us this way! I don't know if I'll ever feel the same way about him again. And that upsets me."

Hank got up and perched himself on the edge of his desk, taking Sarah's hand in his. "There's something you must always remember," he said. "Family and tradition are what Japan is all about. Everything else is secondary. Michio is just following his father's orders—and his destiny."

Noticing that Sarah's pained expression was still in place, Hank asked, as an afterthought, "How serious is your relationship with Michio?" Quickly, he caught himself as he stared at his child who was now a woman. It's really none of my business, he thought.

Without waiting for an answer, he stood up. "How about us having lunch tomorrow? I really do have to go now."

"I know you have a hot date!" Sarah laughed, reverting back to her old self. And giving him a peck on the cheek, she left.

The drive from his office in West Los Angeles to his home in Brentwood took just under ten minutes. Hank loved his quiet, tree-lined neighborhood. It was a far cry from where he and Ruth had first started out.

Leaving the car in the driveway, he walked toward the front door, where Ruth was waiting for him. When he reached her, she threw her arms around his neck and hugged him in a warm embrace. Stretching upward, she kissed him gently on the lips. Hank loved the feel of her slender body against his.

"You look like you've had a helluva day," she said, slipping her arm through his as they walked into the living room. "How 'bout a drink?"

Before he could reply, she walked over to the bar and poured a scotch on the rocks for him and a glass of mineral water for herself. And although she appeared to be relaxed, her hands were trembling. She handed him his drink and then seated herself on the edge of the couch. Looking up at her husband, she said, "Okay, tell me everything."

Hank sat down in his favorite chair, facing her. "There's not much to say. Yoshi's proposal this morning hit me like a ton of bricks. He wants to buy us out. He wants total control of Marshall-Telesonic."

"But why? I thought the company was doing really well. Why would they want to change a winner?"

Hank shrugged. "Because they want it all. And, they're willing to pay top dollar to get it. It's like the Mafia says, 'Nothing personal,' but the decision has already been made. The question isn't, "do you want to leave? It's how much will it take for you to go quietly? Imagine, after all these years—there's nothing to discuss."

Ruth shook her head in disbelief. "But how can they do that? They only own forty-nine percent of the company. That's not a majority."

Hank sighed deeply. "Yes it is. I found out that the Japanese own Jack Strong. With his two percent, they have control. It's amazing. I always thought Jack was on our side—that we could count on his shares for a majority. Now I find out we were never in control. It was his goddamn job to meet me on the plane on my first trip to Tokyo. It was all part of a master plan. Jack worked his way into my confidence while doing a spectacular job in publicizing Marshall-Telesonic. But all the time, he was a spy. He kept Tosui in touch with every move we made."

Hank took a sip of his drink and smiled ruefully. "You should have seen him at the meeting this morning. He looked like Judas at the Last Supper. Then, later in my office, he used all his persuasive guile to try and convince me that we should take the money and run."

"Maybe he's right," Ruth said quietly. "You know, Hank, you and I haven't talked or even thought about retirement. We are both young, healthy and full of energy, so why shouldn't we enjoy ourselves? We're at a point in our lives when we can do anything we want or go anywhere we want—without a care in the world."

"Retiring is like sitting in God's waiting room," Hank said softly. "I'm just not ready for that yet. And there's no way I'm going out with my tail between my legs. What troubles me the most is that it was so easy for Yoshi and Jack to fool me. But the fat lady hasn't sung yet, so this show isn't over."

"You're absolutely right," Ruth said. "I never liked Jack Strong—never trusted him. And I always suspected that he might have a hidden agenda but I could never put my finger on what it might be. Well, now we know, don't we?"

It tore at Ruth's heart to watch her husband struggling to find answers. It was as if she was seeing him in a way she never had before. In the past, whether on the football field, in war or in business, Hank had always set the course. He'd made tough decisions and had come out on top. The idea that he'd been manipulated and possibly defeated was hard for him to grasp.

At last, Ruth said, "It seems to me we have two options here—one, we do as our 'friend' Jack Strong, suggests—take the money and run. Or two, we fight the bastards."

Hank looked around their exquisitely furnished home. He saw the paintings, tapestries and objects d'art they'd collected over the years on their many trips to Japan. It was as if everything he'd seen and done in his life surrounded him.

Leaning over the coffee table, Hank picked up a shiny, red, ivory sculpture. Holding it gently in his hand, he stroked its smooth finish with his fingers. At first glance, the piece resembled an ordinary ripe apple. But inside, the ivory had been transformed into an elaborate scene, bursting with life. The artist had carved a perfect, tiny replica of a house with trees and flowers surrounding it. The miniscule setting was alive with intricate detail.

Hank remembered the day he'd bought the ivory apple in Nagoya, almost twenty-five years before. He'd been amazed at how the artist had managed to capture the essence of life in miniature—the smooth, outer surface belying the world of activity beneath it.

Looking at his wife, Hank realized how lucky he was to have her as his partner and how much she meant to him. Standing up, he reached out and took Ruth's hands in his, gently pulling her to her feet. Wrapping his arms around her, he kissed her lightly on the mouth.

Ruth stepped back slowly and asked him with a smile, "What was that about?"

"I just wanted to let you know how much I love you," he whispered softly in her ear.

The loud, insistent ringing of the phone broke the mood. Hank reached over to the end table and picked it up.

"Is this Hank Marshall?" The voice on the other end had an oddly familiar ring—from somewhere in the past.

"Who is this?" Hank asked impatiently.

The husky voice seemed to need further verification.

"Is this the same Hank Marshall who flew a B-29 from Saipan during the Great War?"

This time, the voice did not wait for an answer. "Hank, it's Sandy Gold, your old briefing officer. Remember, we ran into each other again at that nightclub in Tokyo, in 1952!"

A strange feeling came over Hank. Could this call be related to the events of the morning? He put the thought out of his mind quickly. It was too illogical.

"Of course I remember, Sandy. How have you been?"

"Still in there pitching," was the hearty answer. Then suddenly, the voice dropped. "Hank," he said, "I really must see you as soon as possible."

'Randy Sandy' had never been one of Hank's favorite people. "It's very nice of you to call, Sandy," he told him politely, "but it's kind of a bad time right now."

"That is, exactly why we have to get together. . . now. There was urgency in his voice. "It has to do with the meeting you and Yoshikazu Matsuda had this morning."

Hank frowned into the phone. "How did you know about that?"

"I know all about your relationship with Tosui, plus a lot more. That's why you need to see me before you make any decisions. Look, let's not waste time talking on the phone. I can be there in an hour."

"Okay, I live at...

"I know where you live," Sandy interrupted. "I'll see you in an hour."

Hank put the phone down slowly and turned to Ruth. She'd tried to catch the gist of the conversation, but couldn't, hearing only one side.

"This is really crazy," Hank said. "That call was from a guy named Sandy Gold, who was my briefing officer during the war. I ran into him again on my first trip back to Japan thirty years ago.

"During the war, before every mission, a man from Intelligence would brief us. He would tell us about the terrain around the target, the kind of resistance we'd find there—how much anti-aircraft we would encounter. Those guys seemed to know everything. They could even accurately guess how many fighters the Japanese would send up. Now, out of the blue, Sandy calls me and wants to talk to me about the takeover.

Puzzled, Hank shook his head. "How could he possibly know what happened this morning? And how does he know where we live?"

Ruth shrugged. "I guess we'll find out soon enough."

Ruth and Hank sat quietly in the kitchen, sipping coffee and waiting for Sandy Gold to arrive.

"How are you feeling?" Ruth asked, breaking the silence.

"Like I've been hit in the stomach by Muhammad Ali," Hank answered. "I was stunned at first but now I feel sad. I keep thinking about what my father said when I asked his advice before making the deal with Yoshi. I remember the way he looked when he told me, 'I don't trust them and I never will. I hate them from Pearl Harbor. They were in bed with the Nazis from the beginning and never objected to the killing of the Jews. In fact, they clapped their hands because they were, and still are, anti-Semites. And don't forget, at the same time the Nazis were doing their terrible deed, the Japanese were killing the Chinese and committing their own atrocities. Your brother was killed by the Nazis—Japan's allies.' Then his eyes bore into me as he said, 'And you're ready to become partners with them?'

Hank turned his head and looked out at a lush garden, visible from the sliding glass doors. "I listened to every word my father said, convinced he was wrong. Now, I'm not so sure."

"We can't forget that the Americans committed atrocities, too," Ruth said evenly. "Let's face it," she said, placing her hand on his knee. "There are no good guys in war. And I wonder sometimes if there are any good guys in business either."

"Not as we used to know them," Hank replied. "In the old days, you could pretty much tell the good guys from the bad guys—white hats versus black hats. But now the lines are blurred and the enemy you hated ten years ago wants to be your best friend today. It's all so damned cold-blooded!"

Hank paused, gazing out the window again. "There's another issue that keeps creeping into my head, Ruth. I've tried to ignore it but it keeps bugging me. The Japanese want market share, with profits coming in a distant second. We, Americans, want profits, while market share is relatively unimportant to us. The Japanese make plans for the next century while we plan for the next quarterly earnings. If Tosui takes over Marshall Telesonic, they'll completely dominate consumer electronics, here and around the world. And if we pack up and fold, we are contributing to the decline of America's influence. And, damn it! I don't want to be a part of that."

CHAPTER NINETEEN

---▼---

Sandy Gold arrived exactly one hour after his call. The years had not been kind to him. His thinning hair was now gone, and what had been the suggestion of a paunch had turned into a full-sized belly, round and tight as a drum.

Sandy hadn't lost his belligerent look though, and his face carried the scars of numerous physical encounters. His nondescript gray suit, a plain white shirt and dull, thin tie knotted beneath his unbuttoned collar expressed his personal indifference to fashion and style.

Sandy looked at Hank appreciatively as he entered the room. "You look terrific!" he said. "I'll bet you can still fit into your old uniform. And there ain't too many of us who can make that claim."

"Thanks for the compliment, Sandy, but I'm sure you didn't come all this way to tell me how great I look." Then, putting his arm around Ruth's waist, Hank said, "I'd like you to meet my wife, Ruth."

As they shook hands politely, Sandy looked Ruth over approvingly.

"I never did get married," he told them. "Never quite had the time."

Turning back to Hank, he asked, "Is there somewhere we can speak in private?"

"Sandy, anything you have to say, can be said in front of Ruth. Let's go into the living room where we can all sit down."

Waiting until Hank and Ruth had seated themselves on the couch, Sandy plopped himself down in Hank's favorite chair, facing them. But before he could begin talking, Hank spoke up.

"Tell me, how did you know about my meeting this morning? And how did you know where I live?"

"I'll come right to the point and level with you," Sandy said somberly. "But first, I must swear you both to secrecy."

Hank and Ruth looked at each other skeptically before nodding in agreement.

"We know that the two of you work very closely together which also makes Mrs. Marshall essential to our efforts. "You may remember that I was in Intelligence in Saipan and I've been in government service ever since. But now, in order to accomplish my mission, it is necessary that I reveal to you that I am a government agent."

"You mean you're with the CIA or one of the other agencies?" Hank asked incredulously. "I find that very hard to believe."

"Believe it," said Sandy, a hard edge creeping into his voice. "I came to Japan with the first group assigned to General MacArthur's staff—but I never wore a uniform. My cover was to be one of the many importers who used cheap Japanese labor after the war."

Sandy continued, "The Japanese were brutal conquerors but after their defeat, they made a one hundred and eighty degree turnaround. You don't want to know how they tortured their prisoners, particularly the B-29 crews who bailed out during the air raids. But after the truce was signed, it was like nothing had ever happened. They suddenly became meek and submissive. If you told them to jump, they only wanted to know how high."

Ruth and Hank listened in astonishment as Sandy went on. "Now, we come to the part you must never repeat. In March of 1945, months before the peace agreement was signed on the battleship *Missouri*, a meeting took place in the old, bombed out Tosui building. Attending the meeting were the heads of every major trading company in Japan. What I'm going to tell you now is both bizarre and outrageous."

Sandy paused for a moment and looked at Ruth and Hank to make sure he had their complete attention. And he did.

"A detailed economic plan for the takeover of the United States by the year 2000 was agreed upon at this meeting. Each participant pledged his life to accomplishing that goal. Your friend Yoshikazu's father was the driving force behind the plot. His son eventually succeeded him and has now dedicated himself to fulfilling that prophesy.

"These guys have maintained their schedule. They plan to be in control of the U.S. around the turn of the century. And while there are no bugles sounding, they are still marching to the beat set down in 1945. They've risen from the ashes of unconditional surrender to the point where their commercial army dominates world trade.

"Right now, the Japanese own one-third of all American treasury bills. They've purchased key pieces of property in every major American city. In 1941, they bombed Pearl Harbor but they couldn't take it over. Today, however, they own half the Hawaiian Islands and are buying up the rest."

"Hold on for a minute," Hank interrupted. "It's true that the Japanese staged a remarkable recovery. I admire what they've done. But take over the United States? That is preposterous!"

Ruth said nothing, continuing to concentrate intently on what was being said.

Sandy smiled grimly. "You have the vanity of the average American citizen. You think it can't happen here. 'What are we?' you say, 'Some Banana Republic? No! We are the United States of America, the invincible good guys!' Well, my friend, don't forget that we took our lumps in Korea. And we were all but destroyed in Vietnam. We've been caught up with the Cold War and the threat of Communism, so every year we spend hundreds of billions of dollars on policing the world. Meanwhile, the Japanese have been building better automobiles, taking control of the micro-chip market and are now completing the takeover of the consumer electronics industry. Your meeting today was just another piece in the puzzle."

Hank's face grew ashen. Sandy saw the effect his words were having and continued on without missing a beat.

"Do you still think it's 'preposterous' to believe that all of this is not part of some overall plan? We bleed our resources dry and import without restraint. Meanwhile, the Japanese keep on exporting and building up an enormous surplus of dollars. They don't have to spend a dime on defense. The terms of their surrender wouldn't allow it, even if they wanted to, which they don't."

Stopping to catch his breath, Sandy grinned humorlessly. "Hey," he said, "how about an adult drink? I dry up when I talk this much."

Ruth rose from the couch like a sleepwalker, but quickly fell into the role of hostess. "I apologize for our poor hospitality, but I'm just mesmerized by what you've been telling us. Please, what would you like to drink?"

"I'll take anything with alcohol. But if you have it, I'd love a bourbon with one ice cube."

Ruth poured a generous amount of Old Grand Dad into a double old fashioned glass. "Suppose that we believe this whole wild story could possibly be true. What exactly is it you want from us?"

"Before I can answer, you need to know a little more," Sandy said, taking the glass Ruth offered with a nod of thanks. "We send trade missions to Japan all the time who plead with the Japanese to open up their markets to American manufacturers. Even as we talk, we continue to run up bigger and bigger trade deficits. We import their Sonys, Telesonics, and Toyotas while we sell them very little in return.

"Part of the problem is that most of our manufacturers have become lazy and non-competitive. Our quality control stinks. And the few competitive products we do have are shut out by the trade barriers the Japanese have set up to keep us out. American beef, for example, is less than half the price of Japanese beef. Our rice is one-fifth the price of their comparable product, yet, they've successfully kept us out of their market.

"Now, here's the payoff. Whenever the Department of Commerce or trade negotiators put pressure on the Japanese to free up their markets, they go running to our State Department and demand that we withdraw our objections on how they're handling U.S. trade relations. And, because our State Department feels we need Japanese support against the Russians, they order our trade negotiators to back off. Then, with all the surplus dollars the Japanese accumulate, they go out and buy a Rockefeller Center in New York, some state-of-the-art research facility, or billions of U.S. Treasury bills."

Sandy bolted down the rest of his bourbon. "What galls me is, the takeover of the United States of America is in progress and nobody even knows about it!" He banged his glass on the table for emphasis. "We cannot ignore that we are engaged in an economic war and that we must fight the Japanese with the same weapons they are using against us."

Hank sat silently throughout Sandy's monologue. He thought back to the scene in Madame Cherrie's Copacabana, many years before, when Randy Sandy had cast himself in the image of a price-scavenging importer and had deliberately confronted Yoshi and Takei. He now looked at Sandy with new respect. "So that night in Tokyo was all an act," he said.

"Not entirely," Sandy responded with a lascivious grin. "I really do hate the bastards and I enjoy pissing them off. It got to be a kind of game—seeing how far I could push them before I had to back off. But that was kid stuff then. The real battle is being waged right now."

Impatiently, Ruth said, "If what you're saying is true, then the whole country's been brainwashed. How can that be possible? And what I'd like to know is, what do you want from us? Where do we fit in?"

Sandy's voice was soft as he said, "There's a Japanese philosophy called 'Kaizen'. In it's simplest form, it solves big problems through a series of small changes. It's like the Chinese proverb says, 'A journey of a thousand miles begins with a single step'. Changes are made, a little unthreatening bit at a time. It is basically brainwashing."

"That doesn't answer the question," Hank growled. "What is it you are asking us to do?"

"When you understand the problem, you are halfway to the solution," Sandy answered, patiently. "We are at war, although it is an undeclared one. There are no guns being fired and no one is planning to march over our borders. It is not our lives that are at stake here, but our way of life. And we must fight this battle or be conquered."

Sandy continued, "Now, let's get to what we need from Ruth and Hank Marshall. The Japanese have planned the takeover of your company and there's no way you can stop them. You realize now that the guy you thought was your man was working for them all the time. And he's just one of a vast army of Americans who've been bought and think that it's okay."

"Are you saying that you knew about Jack Strong all along?" Hank interrupted angrily. "If you're on our side, why didn't you warn us?

Sandy smiled wryly and shook his head. "It wouldn't have made a difference. He already owned the controlling stock."

"Boy! I don't often make a mistake but when I do, it's a beaut!" said Hank, shaking his head, ruefully. "To think that I actually gave that son-of-a-bitch control."

"What's done is done, but now you know the problem," said Sandy, looking closely at both of them. "And here is how we solve it: We think you should sell out to the Japanese."

Ruth and Hank were shocked. At last, Ruth broke the silence. "Sandy, you've spent the last thirty minutes telling us we're in the midst of an economic takeover. And now you're advising us to surrender?"

He smiled tolerantly. "Look, you have to realize that you can't win this battle—but you can position yourselves to win the war. By fighting the Japanese, you'll just exhaust your resources and minimize your net cash worth. If you decide to cooperate, however, they will pay almost any price to take control of the company without a fight and without adverse publicity. You'll need to put up a struggle, though, to make them pay top dollar to get you out. After that, you'll be in a position to act as major players in an economic counter attack."

Hank looked at Ruth. "Well, what do you think?" he asked.

She smiled, grimly. "I think Sandy's about to tell us what he expects of us."

Sandy grinned. "Once upon a time, Winston Churchill said, 'The side that wins the war is the side that makes the fewest mistakes'. But it's not that simple today. The side that wins this war will be the side that controls the best technology. Right now, America's way behind. But don't forget, we're the people who invented most of the great products we're behind on.

"When the battle for Marshall-Telesonic is over, the Japanese will own it and you will have about three hundred million dollars. That will be enough to plant the seeds for the coming technology. And, with your reputation, you'll be able to raise the kind of money required to develop the products of the future.

Part of our contribution will be in getting the government to cooperate with you on favorable tax treatment. This will substantially increase the value of your investment.

"After this is accomplished, we'll work out a high level appointment for you which will bring you into the realm of official trade negotiations. More needs to be worked out but now you know enough to help you to decide if you are with us or not."

"I have to be going now," Sandy stood up. "I have to be going now but I'll contact you about this same time next week. If your answer is affirmative, we'll proceed to the next step. In the meantime, this conversation must remain confidential. If either of you reveal any part of it to anyone, I'll deny that I even know you. I thank you for the drink and, like they say in Japan, sayonara y'all."

CHAPTER TWENTY

Whenever Yoshikazu Matsuda came to Los Angeles, he stayed at the Bel Air Hotel. Lush, rolling hills surrounded the grounds and the abundant foliage growing around the hotel's entry was similar to that growing on his family estate. Being there filled him with peace and serenity.

The hotel consisted of a series of bungalows. Yoshi's, the largest and most luxurious, was located on the furthest corner of the hotel grounds, hidden from the rest. The suite contained two bedrooms furnished in rich dark woods and warm subtle colors, a small, well-stocked kitchen and a large, comfortable living room filled with antiques and original works of art. Picture windows at each end of the room opened onto a beautifully landscaped private garden.

Yoshi and Michio left the Marshall-Telesonic board of directors meeting and returned to the hotel to share a quiet lunch on the patio. They wanted to privately discuss the events that had taken place.

Michio discarded his jacket and settled into a comfortable, overstuffed armchair in the living room. Yoshi changed from his business suit into a traditional Japanese robe and seated himself across from Michio. The straight-back, Queen Anne-style chair he sat in was reminiscent of a throne, and allowed him to look slightly downward at his son. Michio sat, watching his father closely and waiting for him to speak.

"We have just completed the first step toward total ownership of Marshall-Telesonic," Yoshi said at last. "The next few days will be critical ones."

Michio shifted uneasily. "Please, Father, do not take what I am about to say as a mark of disrespect. I know this move has been carefully planned but I am feeling a deep sense of sadness. I grew up in the Marshall house and cannot help but be aware of the anger and the hurt expressed by Sarah and her father. They have been close friends—almost like my own family."

Yoshi's eyes darkened. "You have only one family, now and forever. We did what had to be done. You should understand that strong moves bring strong reactions. The present structure has outlived its usefulness and must be changed. The 'gadjin', no matter how well they think they know Japan, will never understand. This is a global market and we must have control around the world."

Silence filled the room until Michio said, hesitantly, "I believe we may now be facing a very difficult situation. There will be cries once again of how the Japanese have launched yet another sneak attack. We struck without warning and that could be very bad for us. Although they need our money and technology, many Americans fear that we are taking over their country."

Yoshi rose to his feet, his face locked tightly in anger. "Could it be that my own son believes that we are monsters? Do you have any idea what it is like to swallow your pride and grovel in the dirt? That is what happened to us. From the early days, when the Americans first docked their boats in Tokyo Harbor, and demanded we open our holy lands to them, they treated us like animals. They called us little yellow monkeys and planted their boots on our throats. We were small and helpless and could do nothing as we watched them plunder the land of our ancestors. They called it 'The White Man's Burden' as they raped our land and our women. The war of bitterness we fought ended when the Americans dropped the atomic bomb. We were ready to surrender after Hiroshima but they inflicted a final, unnecessary punishment upon us—they dropped another atom bomb on Nagasaki."

Pain was visible on Yoshi's face as he stared, unseeing, out the window. The horrors he'd witnessed flooded his memory.

Finally, he turned to Michio again. "As you know, there was a meeting in the Tosui building forty years ago. My father—your honorable grandfather—presided over the proceedings. It was decided that Japan would no longer merely survive; we had to achieve domination over the United States.

"If you had been alive in 1945, you would have seen the Americans rush in once again, to exploit the 'Japs'. You would have witnessed the scum who came over from American import houses and department stores. They acted like thieves—demanding cheaper and cheaper prices. Part of their 'deal' required us to provide them with women. These were the 'noble Americans' who helped to restore our country. They each took their pound of flesh. But now, we have regained our independence and our pride. The ancient power of Japan will finally be restored."

Michio was stunned by his father's rare display of emotion. As a father, Yoshi had always exhibited a tender, caring attitude toward his children. Later, over the course of time, Michio also came to know him as a brilliant, yet cold and calculating businessman. But this angry outburst of Yoshi's caught him completely off guard.

"Father," said Michio, cautiously, "please, understand that my comments are offered with the greatest respect. And that I will, of course, obey your orders but I must voice my concern. I have always known you and Hank Marshall to be the closest of friends. His family and ours have worked together in harmony for as long as I can remember. The Marshalls have been good allies, but they can also be tough enemies. I think it is important that we retain their friendship."

Yoshi jerked back impatiently in his chair. Looking harshly at his son, he said, "Our friend, Mr. Marshall, is less of an idealist than you think. He is an honest man but he is also a realist. Right now, he doesn't understand what has taken place. He does not know that we are following a plan—a plan that is not subject to change. In the end, though, he will bow to the greed that motivates all Americans. He will negotiate for a very high price and we will pay him more than the stock is presently worth.

"The stakes are higher than they appear on the surface. We are at the beginning of a new era that will be dominated by whomever controls communications—hardware and software. After this takeover is complete, we will begin to acquire major motion picture studios with their vast film libraries and their broad production capabilities. You will be named as the new Chief Executive Officer. And your first act will be to change the name of Marshall-Telesonic to Telesonic."

Sarah peered at her father over the rim of her glass as she sipped her drink. The quiet table at Alice's Restaurant on the pier in Malibu gave them an opportunity to speak privately.

Hank seemed to be preoccupied as he gazed out the window at the ocean's sparkling water. And concern showed on Sarah's face as she noticed how tired and drawn he looked.

Reaching out, she took his hand in her own and said, "Dad, are you okay?"

"Sure I'm okay," Hank answered with a reassuring smile. "Although I admit I feel like I've been a patsy all these years beginning with Jack Strong and working up to my 'good friend' Yoshi. You were at the meeting. You saw how it was handled. I was as surprised as you were by the outcome. And do you know what the worst part of all this is? I can't believe that I was so naïve. I never suspected a thing."

"We're all still in shock," Sarah said. "You and Yoshi have always been such good friends. You even took Michio into our home. He lived in our house, shared our table and looked up to you as a mentor."

Sarah's anger began to rise. "Well, if you were a patsy, then so was I and so was Mom. I've been working at Marshall-Telesonic since I was fifteen years old, and you've always been the one in charge. You're the one who's looked up to and respected in the industry as the driving force behind the success of the Telesonic brand."

Sarah stopped to catch her breath. "So, what happens now? Where do we go from here?"

As if on cue, the waitress approached their table with her pencil poised and ready.

"How about a big platter of seafood?" Hank asked.

"Sounds great to me," Sarah answered with a grin. "I'm starved."

Ruth and Hank had discussed whether or not they should tell Sarah about the strange visit from Sandy Gold. Although they'd promised not to speak about it with anyone, they weren't comfortable about letting her make new career plans before giving her some indication of their own direction.

Hank watched Sarah attack her plate of seafood with gusto. Proudly, he smiled and thought, she's my kid all right—taking this shakeup in stride, ready to move on to the next opportunity.

He and Ruth had eventually decided that it wasn't necessary to discuss the meeting with Sarah just yet. The news Randy Sandy had given them was too obscure to share with anyone until they'd had time to set their own course.

While picking at the last bit of meat of a particularly obstinate crab shell, Sarah looked up at her father. "I guess I might as well tell you that I had a bad scene with Michio after the meeting," she said. I was really pissed off. I called him some ugly names and told him I never wanted to see him again. Guess I cooked my goose."

Then, smiling conspiratorially at Hank, she said, "Okay, Dad, it's your turn for show and tell. What's the next move?"

Hank didn't hesitate. "I'm not completely sure yet, but it looks like we will sell. I want to keep them dangling for a while, though. Sort of like those people out there," he said, motioning to the fishermen outside. "However, we will be the fish in this scenario, allowing ourselves to be caught only after they've put enough bait on the line. If they really want our share of the company, then I have no problem with making them pay through the nose for it."

Hank looked out the window. "You and I see the enormous opportunities in new technology, Sarah. We're witnessing the beginning of high definition and inter-active television and many other extraordinary products of the future. I'm ready to start moving into these areas without Telesonic. But first, we must make a deal with Tosui that will place no restrictions on our future activities. Frankly, I don't think they'll have any problem with that."

Sarah looked at her father with love and admiration. "You're like an old fire horse who hears those fire bells ringing. I'm with you if you want me, Dad, 'cause I believe that if two Marshalls are tough to beat, three working together will be invincible!"

"You just made the 'A' Team, kiddo!" Hank told her, sounding pleased. He then put his fork down and looked at the empty platter of shells in front of them, without seeing. His voice was serious when he finally spoke.

"You know I'm very proud of you, Sarah, and that I love you very much. I also have a great deal of respect for you and your ability. I must warn you, though, getting started is not going to be an easy task."

"Who said I was looking for 'easy'? All I know is, when this battle is over, we will still be standing!"

CHAPTER TWENTY-ONE

1988

It was eight o'clock in the evening when Sarah Marshall pulled into the parking lot of the International Student Center at UCLA. The building, well worn and in need of repair, was two blocks south of the campus.

Walking purposefully down the corridor, she headed for the dining room where the dinner meeting was already in progress. The room was filled to capacity. Normally, one hundred people could easily be fed there but today there was a surplus crowd, and an overflow of people lined the outside wall.

After the meal had been completed, student waiters and waitresses removed the dishes and began to pour coffee. Sarah excused herself from the table where she was sitting, and slipped quietly to the rear of the room. Sam Davidson, the distinguished professor who taught foreign trade in UCLA's School of Business, stepped up to the podium at the front of the room. He was a tall, slender, distinguished-looking black man with gray hair, stylishly attired in an Italian made charcoal gray suit.

"It is my pleasure," Davidson began, "to introduce our featured speaker for this evening, Mr. Michio Matsuda. Mr. Matsuda has kindly consented to address us on issues regarding business relations between the United States and Japan and the effect of Japanese investments here in the United States.

"Mr. Matsuda exemplifies the many Japanese business people who know and understand our country and, indeed, our city. He received part of his training right here at UCLA. Mr. Matsuda has advanced degrees in electronics and electrical engineering and is the great-grandson of the founder of the Tosui Trading Company, one of the largest and most distinguished businesses in Japan. He serves here as President of Telesonic, USA, a Tosui subsidiary. "Mr. Matsuda will speak to us this evening about the very special relationship between Japan and the United States. Ladies and gentlemen, Mr. Michio Matsuda."

Rising from the table closest to the podium, Michio unbuttoned the jacket of his tailored blue suit as he made his way to the front of the room. Arriving at the podium, he placed his hands on top of the polished blonde wood, centering himself. His eyes traveled around the room panoramically and he smiled at his audience before he began to speak.

"It is a great honor to be at UCLA again, talking to students, graduate students and others interested in a subject that is very important to us all," he began.

Sarah studied Michio carefully as he spoke, aware that he hadn't seen her yet. Her heart beat faster as she watched him. Again, she realized that she'd loved him since the first day he had arrived at her family's home. She and Michio had become very close while he'd attended UCLA—they were almost like brother and sister. In fact, there'd been times that Sarah felt closer to him than she did to Peter, but in a different way. After their last night together, Sarah had thought the fragile wall between them might come tumbling down, that Michio would tell her of his love for her. But it had never happened.

Forcing herself back to the present, she heard Michio telling the audience about the confidence Telesonic and Tosui had in the American marketplace. Of how they had learned the American way of doing things, and had penetrated the market by understanding the American consumer. They had thus perfected the products they first introduced in 1952.

"And because we have worked so hard to satisfy and serve the American public, we are shocked and dismayed at the resentment many American's feel toward the Japanese presence in the United States,"Michio continued. "The Japanese are sincere in wanting to contribute to the U.S. economy. We have brought in new capital, created thousands of jobs in this very community, and are determined to make a permanent impression on the United States."

His smiling eyes surveyed the audience. "As I look around, I see the spirit of internationalism personified in this room. And that is most important for continuing good relations between the United States and Japan."

Sarah watched the faces of those in attendance as Michio spoke with a power and sincerity that held the attention of each individual in the room. Because he'd spent so much time in the U.S., his English had only a trace of an accent. He was also able to express himself with American phrases and form, which worked to his advantage.

Michio finished his speech with a strong statement. "We must face reality: Japan and the United States need each other. As in any close relationship, there are some areas of friction. Japan has been accused of closing its markets to American products, thus causing an imbalance in our trade. It is then Japan's responsibility to correct this misunderstanding and to renew its efforts to encourage the import of American merchandise. But America must also accept her share of responsibility for this situation. American manufacturers must work to correct deficiencies in quality control that inhibit sales, resulting in this stalemate."

Michio's voice took on a lighter tone. "Please believe me when I tell you," he said, "that all of these problems can be solved through the spirit of cooperation between our two great countries. The strong and thriving partnership that has existed between Japan and the United States for the past forty years, can, and will, overcome any and all adversity."

An enthusiastic round of applause was heard as Professor Davidson returned to the podium to join Michio. Shaking Michio's hand, the professor thanked him for his speech, and announced that the meeting would now be open for questions.

A hand immediately shot up in the front row and a short man in a pin-striped suit stood up. "Mr. Matsuda," he said. "I'm a commercial real estate agent in downtown Los Angeles and I'm pleased to say that the Japanese have increased property values by purchasing the best office buildings in Los Angeles. Can you please tell me how big an investment they are planning to make in the L.A. real estate market?"

"I would have no way of knowing how much of an investment will be made," Michio replied, "But obviously, there are real estate investors in Japan who feel confident about Los Angeles and the United States in general, and are investing accordingly. In a free society, there are no set patterns. But I do believe the investments will continue."

Satisfied, the real estate agent sat down.

"Mr. Matsuda," a middle-aged woman from the left side of the room called out. "There seems to be a lot of interest on the part of Japanese investors, in our entertainment industry. I am an actor's agent and funding for some of our motion pictures has started to come from Japan. We know that Japan has already invested heavily in the record industry. Is this going to be a continuing trend? Because if it is, I believe it will bring additional prosperity to this area."

"As far as I know," answered Michio, "Japan is most interested in continuing to invest in the American entertainment industry. American motion pictures are the best in the world and are one of your chief exports. A clear female voice spoke up. "At what point will the Japanese declare the United States of America a possession of Japan?"

Nervous laughter arose from the audience as Michio looked out across the room. There, standing ramrod straight near the rear wall, was Sarah. For a moment, he lost his composure, but regaining it quickly, he said, "I believe that you are joking."

Ignoring his remark, Sarah went on. "Is it not true, Mr. Matsuda, that while the United States is open to Japanese merchandise and welcomes

Japanese investors, products and factories, it is almost impossible for our industries to crack the Japanese market? And, isn't it also true that there are both acknowledged and unacknowledged restrictions with regard to the U.S. shipping merchandise to Japan?"

"No, this is not true," answered Michio, calmly. "We have tried in every way to encourage the export of American merchandise to Japan, but in most cases the Americans have not aggressively sought out our marketplace. They have not come to Japan to do business. If they did, they would find that they are more than welcome."

"Does that welcome apply to the meat industry?" Sarah asked harshly. "American beef is not allowed into Japan even though our product is of equal quality and costs much less. And does that welcome also extend to rice imports? And to our citrus crops?"

The audience was watching the exchange between the beautiful young woman standing in the back and the prominent Japanese business executive with great interest. Hastily, Professor Davidson got up and moved closer to Michio. A low murmur could be heard throughout the room.

Smiling at Michio, the Professor positioned himself in front of the microphone and said, "Miss Marshall, I don't believe we are treating our guest with the proper respect, challenging him with these kinds of questions."

"But they are real questions," she replied, heatedly. "And they need answers. I think it's high time we examine all sides of the trade situation. Part of reason for the problem we have in the United States is that the public is unaware of the many economic threats coming from outside our country. While it's true that we haven't aggressively gone after the export market until recently, we have finally come to realize that unless we become players in the global trade arena, we're going to become a second-rate power."

Sam Davidson smiled uneasily and turned to the audience. "I would like to introduce the second participant of this ...er...debate. She is Sarah Marshall, Executive Secretary of the Marshall Foundation and a generous contributor to the International Student Center, for which we are truly grateful. I suppose this has earned her the right to ask these questions."

"I think every citizen has the right to ask these questions, whether they are contributors or not," Sarah retorted.

Michio returned to the microphone and pressed against Sam Davidson's arm to assure him that he was in control of the situation. Looking right at Sarah, he said, "We, in Japan, have tried very hard to maintain a continuing and fruitful relationship with your country. You must understand, however, that the Japanese consumer has not only become very particular but extremely quality-conscious. The truth is, Ms. Marshall, that much of American industry has forgotten how to produce quality merchandise. When they come into the Japanese marketplace, they are not as competitive or as conscious of quality as we are. The biggest drawback to importing American merchandise into Japan is the problem created by your own industry..."

Michio cut himself off in mid-sentence. "Please understand, I did not come here to debate or to argue this point. I accepted an invitation to speak at UCLA and came only to present our position. I do, however, welcome challenging questions such as these. A frank dialogue must exist between the United States and Japan if we are to continue to have good relations."

For the first time, Sarah displayed a winning, ingratiating smile. Looking at him evenly, she said, "Thank you, Mr. Matsuda, and please forgive me if I have caused you any discomfort."

As their eyes met, the whole room seemed charged with electricity.

Once more, Sam Davidson took the microphone. "Indeed, we thank you for a wonderful presentation, Mr. Matsuda. And thank you, too, Ms. Marshall, for making this a lively debate. Our time is running out so we must bring this question and answer period to a close. I appreciate all of you coming here tonight. We are proud to have been able to present Mr. Michio Matsuda as our guest speaker. We will continue to welcome Japanese investment in our country. And once more, we have reaffirmed the American tradition of airing our disagreements openly. The problems of international trade are by no means simple and cannot be resolved in a single meeting. However, dialogue, such as we have had tonight, is a good, healthy beginning. I am quite sure everyone in this room is now aware that we not only have a global economy, but we are in the midst of a global society. That was the purpose of this forum and once more, I thank you all for coming."

After brief applause, the audience began to file out. Sarah was about to leave when Michio called out to her.

"Sarah." he said, stepping in beside her, "I'm glad I caught you. Listen, can we go have a drink or a cup of coffee? I'd like to talk to you."

Face to face, they searched each other's eyes. After what seemed a long time, Sarah smiled and said, "Okay, let's talk."

Chapte Twenty-Two

▼

Sarah and Michio walked over to a little coffee shop in Westwood Village, a few blocks from campus. They sat across from each other in a faded green leather booth in the back of the brightly lit restaurant and sipped their coffee.

"Sarah, why did you attack me as you did?"

"That was no attack. If I were attacking you, you'd know it. I was merely stating a position." She dropped her eyes and began to twirl a spoon with her index finger.

"You know, Michio, I'm still very angry about the way in which the buy-out was handled."

"But why?" Michio asked with a perplexed look. "Why would you be feeling angry? You and your family received a great deal of money. I would think you'd be very pleased."

"How can you say that?" she cried out in disbelief. "You lived in our home. You and I shared confidences. We were more than just friends. And you knew what was going on but you never said a thing. That's what hurts. And the reason that it hurts is because I have always been honest and up front with you, in everything we've done."

"But it was not my position to say anything," Michio replied defensively. "This program was conceived by my father. I was given strict instructions not to divulge any part, until it was presented by him. He was adamant that it be introduced to your father, with all the respect due him, by my father, and my father alone."

Michio paused, "But, Sarah, that's all in the past, yet we just had a confrontation that sounded like something between adversaries during trade talks. Now you tell me something. Why do you Americans feel antagonistic towards the Japanese? We've come to the United States with quality products and contributed to your economy. We're even buying your treasury bills. Tosui, like many other Japanese companies, contributes to the arts as well as to your colleges and universities. In fact, we're even building special research facilities at certain schools. Why should you be unhappy about that? I'm very puzzled, I must tell you."

"Well, Michio, I guess the reason I'm unhappy—or angry—is because we, in the United States, have allowed so much of our country to be taken over."

"Taken over?"

"Yes, absolutely, 'taken over'. The same way you took over Marshall-Telesonic. You didn't do it viciously or with a knife at anyone's throat, but you took it over nonetheless. And the worst part of it was that the plan had been in place all along. It was just a matter of waiting for the proper time before you executed the decision that had already been made. I'm aware of that and so is my father. That's one of the reasons we formed the Marshall Foundation six years ago—to try and prevent such things from happening again. And to put the United States back into a more competitive position."

"But Sarah!" said Michio anxiously, "that would be welcomed by my country. We have said all along that the problems in the United States were created by Americans, not by the Japanese. To our credit, we have been most sincere in cooperating and working with you to…"

"Wait a minute," Sarah interrupted. "That is utter nonsense! I asked you earlier this evening why the Japanese markets are closed to American products. Why can't we ship rice to Japan? Why can't we ship beef?"

She stopped herself. "Listen, I don't want to get into a debate about a national or international issue with a 'friend.' You came to our house speaking book-learned English, sounding nothing like you do today. You walk with confidence here in the United States because you lived in our home. We introduced you to our friends so you'd learn to interact with Americans. My father took you under his wing and taught you all about American habits, American distribution, sales concepts. And you say you don't understand my unhappiness?"

Michio reached over and took her hand. "Sarah, I meant no disrespect to you, or your family. In our way of doing things, we feel we have been very proper. Although I have great autonomy here in the United States, running the company as I see fit, I am still tied to Yoshikazu Matsuda. He holds the reins as the head of the family, the head of the company, and the man to whom I am expected to give my loyalty and respect. This is part of a long tradition in our family, which started with my great-grandfather. Not only is it difficult to break those traditions, but I don't feel that I can break them. They're too deeply imbedded in me.

"I am speaking to you now, Sarah, as I speak to no one else because I have great feeling for you…because I have missed you. And please understand, it is almost impossible for a Japanese man to admit this—but I have missed you."

The look in Michio's eyes was the same one she'd seen on their last night together and it melted her anger away. Taking his hand in her own, she squeezed it gently. "I've missed you, too, Michio," she whispered softly.

Suddenly, Michio became aware that he was holding hands in a coffee shop in Westwood and he slowly slipped his hand away.

"Sarah," he said, "would you do me the honor of having dinner with me tomorrow night? Perhaps we can try to recapture some of our past relationship. I would consider it a great honor."

"I would like that very much," she answered, quietly.

"Wonderful!" he said, his face beaming. "I will prepare a Japanese dinner for you at my home. Will that suit you?"

She smiled at his use of such a colloquial expression. "It will suit me just fine."

"Here is my address!" he said, removing a card from his wallet. "If you will drive to the front entrance, the doorman will take your car and direct you. Will seven o'clock suit you?"

"It will suit me just fine."

The next evening, promptly at seven, Sarah pulled her shiny black Porsche convertible into the circular driveway of a six-story brick building on Burton Way in Beverly Hills. She had driven along the Wilshire corridor heading east, past the towering glass and steel apartment buildings and condos that line the streets. The simple, unpretentious building where Michio lived was distinctly different from the others.

As she pulled into the driveway, an attendant quickly appeared. The red jacket he wore had the address of the building stitched in gold above the breast pocket. When he opened her car door, Sarah gracefully slid her long legs out of the car. Her pale apricot silk dress flowed as she moved. Smiling at the doorman who had walked over to greet her, she said, "I am here to see Mr. Matsuda."

"Yes, ma'am," the doorman said. "Mr. Matsuda is expecting you. If you'll follow me."

They walked past the main elevator in the lobby to a private elevator, partially hidden in the corner. Pressing a small black button to his left, he announced into the speaker, "Mr. Matsuda, your guest is here."

"I will send the elevator right down," came the reply.

Moments later, the door opened and the doorman motioned for Sarah to step inside. He pressed another button and the doors quickly closed. Effortlessly, the elevator rose to the penthouse on the sixth floor. When the doors opened again, Sarah was in Michio's apartment, unprepared for what she saw.

Directly in front of her, in a small alcove, stood an exquisite Cloisonne vase containing several perfectly balanced twisted branches of flowering peach. Alongside the vase was a strikingly simple Tokonoma scroll, ink brushed in black and white. Sarah's eyes continued to wander around the room until she spotted Michio standing by a wide archway, silently watching her. When their eyes met, he walked over, smiling, and took her hand. "Welcome to my home, Sarah-San."

He led her into a large, high-ceilinged living room. Sleek, high-tech furniture gave the room an elegant impression of spaciousness. Combinations of antique and modern art adorned the walls. To Sarah's right was a series of Japanese woodblock prints by Hiroshige, depicting Japanese fishing villages. Alongside these prints, was an original painting by Georgia O'Keefe, which portrayed a lily so vividly sensual, it seemed to rise from the canvas.

In the corner, separating the pictures from the fireplace wall was a tall bronze sculpture on a marble stand. "Is that a Giacometti?" asked Sarah.

"Yes, it is," Michio replied with a smile, pleased by her knowledge. "It is the one of his brother, Rodrigo."

On the wall above the fireplace, was a sequence of shapes in soft, subdued colors that moved along the wall.

"What is that?"

"That is a hologram." Michio explained. "It's a technique we developed in our laboratory that transmits figures which change in shape and produce a feeling that is somewhat indescribable."

He then led Sarah out onto a terrace that seemed to wrap itself around the entire apartment. Exotic plants in beautiful hand-painted pots were perched along the railing. In the corner were two gold wrought iron chairs which stood beside a small, glass-topped table where a bottle sat chilling in a silver ice bucket.

Glancing up at the sky, Sarah noticed that twilight was beginning to descend. On her left was the Pacific Ocean and on her right, a mosaic of lights that was Beverly Hills.

I have taken the liberty of chilling a bottle of sake for us," Michio said, lifting the bottle from the bucket. "However, if you would prefer something else, I will be happy to bring it."

"Cold sake?" she asked.

"Oh, yes, it makes an excellent drink."

"Well, what do I have to lose?" Then, she added, "Perhaps I shouldn't ask that question."

Michio poured the cold sake into two champagne flutes and handed one to Sarah. The two glasses clicked softly and Sarah took a sip. She rolled her eyes comically. "This stuff could revolutionize east-west relations," she laughed.

"Look, Sarah," he said, "The sun is about to set. Each night you can see the most startling colors, different each time."

They watched as the sun, now a huge orange ball, became surrounded by shades of blue, purple and yellow. At sunset, it touched the ocean where the sky and the water met.

"I almost expect to hear it sizzle," Sarah said, as the sun slowly disappeared, leaving a profusion of colors in its wake and the first signs of darkness.

"Your home is beautiful," she continued, as Michio bowed in acknowledgement. Finishing the sake in their glasses, he raised the bottle to refill them.

"It's been almost six years since we last spoke," he said. "You didn't return any of my calls. I tried several times to reach you, than waited six months before I called again. Each time, I left messages on your answering machine, but you never called."

"I couldn't. I was too angry. I felt you and your family had taken advantage of us. More importantly, I felt that you hadn't been honest with me. I also saw the hurt my father was suffering, the pain he felt in watching his friendship with Yoshi end. They haven't spoken since the takeover was completed, you know."

A slightly built middle-aged woman in a kimono suddenly appeared before them, carrying a tray filled with a colorful assortment of sushi. She quietly placed the beautifully arranged platter on the table in front of them. Bowing, she left the veranda as silently as she'd come.

"Where did she come from?" asked Sarah, slightly startled.

"Oh, she's from a small Japanese restaurant that I sometimes have deliver food to my home."

Sarah looked, delightedly at the exotic array of raw fish before her, each piece nestled snugly on a bed of rice. She picked up a pair of the chopsticks that had been set on the table, and expertly snared a piece of albacore tuna. Dipping it first into soy sauce that she'd mixed with hot green radish, she popped it into her mouth, "Delicious!" she said, looking Michio in the eye.

Darkness set in as they finished the sushi. Finally, at Michio's suggestion, they laid their chopsticks down and walked to the dining room. Inside, Michio motioned for Sarah to sit down across from him at a low table on the floor. Unlike the tables in Japan, a well had been carved under this one, leaving room for Sarah's long legs.

Michio smiled. "This is the concession I have had to make for my western friends who refuse to sit on the floor without a place to set their feet."

"You definitely have a most unusual blend of east and west here, but that is, of course, what you have become," Sarah said.

"That's true but I think you'll find that although I love the United States, deep in my heart I am purely Japanese."

"Yes, I think that's pretty obvious," Sarah replied curtly, "from the way you're running Telesonic. Since Tosui has taken over the company, the American management personnel have gradually been removed and replaced with Japanese."

"I wish we could have kept the American managers and middle managers in place, but unfortunately, they did not seem to understand the need for conformity. They just don't have the team spirit that is necessary to run a successful company."

"We were pretty damn successful as Marshall-Telesonic when my father was running things," Sarah replied, angrily.

"That is true," Michio said, "but it wouldn't have lasted. The quality control for our products was developed in Japan. As you know, we are now starting to manufacture in the United States and we must have a specific kind of work force and suppliers."

Sarah's eyes flashed as she jumped up from the floor. Looking down at where Michio was seated, she said, "That was part of the plan all along, wasn't it? First, get rid of the Marshalls and then get rid of the American managers—even though you assured us that nothing would change."

Michio got up and they glared at each other. "We would keep the American managers if they had our proficiency," he said, "but each one of them has his own agenda. In our country, everybody works for the common good. Our workers are proud of Telesonic. They sing the company song and they follow the company line. But the American worker doesn't care about the company. He just wants to collect his pay and get home to his television set."

"We invented the goddamned television set!" Sarah spat out, "and the VCR, and the automobile. And all the other things that you have copied."

"…and have improved upon and made better," Michio finished, condescendingly.

Looking at him with contempt, Sarah snorted, "I don't know why the hell I decided to come here anyway. You're so damned smug and controlling. I feel like I'm suffocating. I hate to eat and run, but I've got to go."

Brushing past him, she made her way to the door where Michio caught up with her, grabbed her arm and twirled her around. Pulling her toward him, he held her tightly and kissed her passionately.

Sarah gasped and started to struggle. But after a moment, her body relaxed. Throwing her arms around his neck, she began to return his kisses with equal intensity. For years, they'd tried to ignore the feelings inside them. Now, their bodies trembled as those feelings sprang to the surface.

Without saying a word, Michio held her close. He kissed her neck, her forehead, her cheeks, her lips. Then, lifting her gently in his arms, he carried her into his bedroom and placed her upon his bed. Tenderly, he caressed her face with his hand. Closing her eyes, she could feel the strength from his body melt into hers.

Michio took off his jacket and their eyes met as he slowly began to unbutton her dress. Sarah reached out and began to unbutton his shirt. In slow motion, they continued removing each other's clothing, piece by piece. When there was nothing left, they looked at each other's naked bodies in silence. Barely touching her, Michio ran his fingers lovingly across her full, round breasts. Sarah reached out to him, breathing rapidly. The invisible barrier had finally been broken. With their bodies locked together in a hungry embrace, they made love, tirelessly and passionately, long into the night.

Later, as they lay in each other's arms waiting for the sun to come up, Sarah turned to look at Michio. Although it was still dark, she could see the brightness of his eyes.

"What happened?" she asked. "One minute I was ready to kill you and the next minute…this."

"My feeling for you is like no other I have ever had," Michio told her, stroking her tussled hair. "It confuses me and makes me feel that perhaps I should be sorry for what has happened."

"Well, I'm not," said Sarah, stretching up to brush her lips against his. "What happened is an expression of everything I feel for you."

"Love and hate do seem to touch at their extreme ends, don't they?" Michio mused.

"It's funny that you should say that. My father's often said that he has a love-hate relationship with the entire nation of Japan."

"Our two countries have so much to offer each other," Michio said in a serious voice.

Sarah pulled back the rumpled sheet that lightly covered them. She ran her hand along Michio's firm, flat stomach and up and down his muscular thighs. She could feel him growing hard again. "You could certainly say that," she giggled.

CHAPTER TWENTY-THREE

▼

"I love him and there's nothing I can do about it. All I know is, I have this feeling in the pit of my stomach that just won't go away."

Sarah sat on the couch across from her mother. A single tear trickled down Sarah's cheek as she gazed out the window at the garden She barely saw the flowers, bursting with color, or the hummingbird hovering over the branch of a Sycamore tree.

Ruth leaned over to brush the tear away and took Sarah's hand in hers. "Let's start from the beginning," she said softly. "When did you first realize you were in love with Michio?"

"Was it that obvious?" she asked, with an embarrassed grin. "Actually, when we first met, I thought he was a little strange. He was so bloody polite! But in spite of his desire to please everyone, he had a strong air of self-confidence about him. He was so completely different from anyone I'd ever met—so exotic-looking! And being fifteen, I was immediately taken with him. I wanted to tell him everything I knew so that he'd tell me everything about himself. I don't know whether it was love or not: I just felt like I wanted to be with him.

"Then, 1982 happened...it's hard to believe it was only six years ago. I was stunned when Uncle Yoshi announced that Tosui planned to buy us out. It was as if the bottom dropped out of my world. Then I realized that Michio had to have been aware of the plan all along. As close as we were, he never dropped a hint of what was coming. You know I'm a pretty tough cookie, Mom, but damn it, I felt like we'd been had. It was also the first time I'd ever seen Dad caught off guard and that really bothered me, finding out that Hank Marshall was as vulnerable as the rest of us."

Sarah got up from the couch and started pacing across the den. Ruth sat quietly, waiting for her to continue.

Looking out at the garden again, Sarah spoke in a voice, barely above a whisper.—"I really love this room—this house, this garden. Ever since I was little, I've found peace and comfort here."

She crossed the room and returned to the couch to face her mother. "I never forgot about Michio…there was no way I could. Two weeks ago, when I found out he was giving a speech to a foreign trade group at UCLA, I had an overwhelming desire to see him, to hear what he had to say. I was just going to stand quietly in the back of the room where he couldn't see me. But I guess it didn't turn out that way."

Sarah chuckled as she glanced up at her mother, sheepishly. She then told Ruth how she'd begun asking Michio challenging questions and how that had turned his talk into a debate. She told of their meeting in the coffee shop and, finally, about what had transpired at Michio's apartment.

"It was like a fairy tale," she said dreamily. "It was Anthony and Cleopatra…Heathcliff and Cathy…Scarlett and Rhett. Oh Mom, it was two people coming together from miles apart. I know it makes absolutely no sense, but we're in love! And there's nothing we can do or say that's going to change that."

Ruth's body stiffened involuntarily as she listened to her daughter's confession. In her mind, she was back at the beach, forty-six years earlier. Yoshikazu Matsuda, handsome and strong, had her wrapped in his arms and they had become lost in the magic of that moment, so long ago.

"Mom, what's the matter? You look so pale!" Sarah said, looking at her mother with concern. "It's hard for me to believe this comes as such a shock to you. I was always sure you suspected what my feelings for Michio were. And somehow, I thought you'd approve."

"I do approve, darling," Ruth said, reassuringly. "I not only love Michio, I admire him. He's been a part of our family since the first day he entered our lives. But Sarah, it's not that simple. Michio's future has been carefully mapped out for him. And that future does not include a 'gaijin'. Whatever Michio feels for you or you feel for him, will not change those things."

"How can you say that?" Sarah asked her face flushed. "We love each other. And after all these years, we finally understand that."

Has Michio told his father yet?"

"No, but I haven't mentioned it to Dad yet either. I wanted to talk to you first. This is 1988, Mother, not the Middle Ages. We all live in one big world now."

"That's true, Sarah, but different cultures see things differently. Are you prepared to become a Buddhist and to be a Japanese wife? Suppose you are accepted by Yoshikazu and the entire Japanese family, are you ready to make the kinds of sacrifices they will expect you to make?"

"You know that's not going to happen, Mom. Can you really picture me as a subservient Japanese housewife? Look, Michio and I have already discussed this. We see no reason for either of us to give up our faith or our traditions. We love each other just as we are and that's the most important thing. I'm quite sure Dad will go along with us. I think he's missed Michio almost as much as I have."

"You talk as if everything has been decided and the two of you are already engaged."

"Well, we know how we feel. The proposal is really just a formality."

The two women stood up at the same time and hugged each other tenderly. Ruth stroked her daughter's hair, and said, "Yoshi will never approve, you know."

Stepping back from her mother's arms, Sarah was vehement. "Well, he damn well better approve! If he doesn't, he's liable to lose a son."

Ruth's eyes grew cold and her voice hardened. "I hate to say this, darling, but when this battle is over, Yoshi may very well be the victor. He's got the spirit of shoguns throughout the ages within him. He's a man with a mission—almost a fanatic. Don't ever underestimate him!"

"But you've always been close to him. How can you say these things?" Sarah stammered, close to tears. "I was hoping you'd be able to use your influence—that you could help us. But you're talking as if we're entering some kind of battlefield. Is that the way you see it, Mom? Is there no hope?"

Ruth took Sarah's hand. "Why don't we take a walk in the garden," she said softly.

Hand in hand, they strolled out into the bright, late morning sun. The flowers and trees were glorious in their color and light. "This is our world," Ruth explained. "It's open and free. There are no hidden agendas here. Your father and I have worked long and hard to reach this place. It's for us and for our children. I guess you could call it the 'American Dream'. And through our foundation, we hope to be able to share it with the rest of the world. Right now, what you need to ask yourself is, 'Am I prepared to give up this dream?'"

"Yes," said Sarah, emphatically. "There's a whole other world out there. It may not be as beautiful or secure as this one, but Michio and I will make it ours. We want to bring our families together, not tear them apart. We know that the two of us can be happy respecting each other's traditions...but can you?"

"That's a foolish question. Of course I'll do everything in my power to help make things work out." Ruth embraced her daughter. "You know how proud I am of you, Sarah, and that I love you very much."

They walked through the garden to the driveway where Sarah's car was parked. "Sorry I've got to run, Mom, I'm meeting Michio for lunch. Thanks again for the shoulder to lean on. You know I really appreciate it. You're a terrific lady."

Sarah kissed her mother on the cheek and gave her a long hug before climbing into car.

"Love you, Mom!" Ruth heard her call out as she drove away.

CHAPTER TWENTY-FOUR

―▼―

"I think that would be a big mistake, Mr. Secretary," said Hank. With this, Edward Mannis, the U.S. Secretary of Commerce, swiveled his chair around to face his Under Secretary, who stood next to a large metal easel to the left of the desk. On the easel was a graph depicting comparative trade figures. The United States was represented by a descending black line and Japan by a red line, spiraling upward.

Stan Blackmore, the Under Secretary, put down the pointer he'd been using to explain the chart. "Mr. Secretary, I've asked Hank Marshall to join us—to get his thoughts on what I now regard as a desperate situation. Nothing we've tried thus far has alleviated our escalating problem—the dollar's continuing drop against the yen. Most of our economists predicted that as the dollar dropped in value, our merchandise would become cheaper, therefore more competitive. This would then help to equalize the balance of trade. At the same time, we were told the high-priced yen would make Japanese merchandise more expensive here in the United States and would therefore lessen the demand for Japanese imports."

"But," interrupted Mannis, loosening his tie, "that hasn't happened. And despite the cheaper dollar, our exports haven't increased and we're buying even more from Japan." Edward Mannis' expression was grave. U.S. and Japanese trade relations had become one of his priorities since taking on the post of Secretary of Commerce,and the deadlock they were discussing had been frustrating him for quite some time. Reflectively, he leaned back in his black leather chair. His hands were clasped together in front of his tanned, handsome face, leaving his index fingers free to tap together in a nervous rhythm.

"Now, what you're telling me is, the reason the Japanese use high tariffs and increasingly complex regulations is so they can keep their borders closed and keep us out," Mannis said. "However, when I suggested a showdown meeting to force them to remove those restrictions, Mr. Marshall told me it would be a mistake."

Hank cleared his throat. "Please allow me to explain. I believe that you've already had several meetings with the Ministry of International Trade—MIT—but nothing's really changed, has it? Their strategy is simple—they stall us until the problem goes away."

Hank continued, "It's been proven many times that direct and public confrontation with the Japanese is not the way to success. In the past, we've tried to seek quick and decisive solutions while the Japanese have continued to follow their philosophy of 'Kaizen' and, as we can see, it's been a mistake."

"What does 'kaizen' mean?" Stan Blackmore asked, moving to the empty chair next to Hank.

Hank remembered how Sandy Gold had first defined the word for him. "It means, 'a little bit at a time', he explained. "It's an evolutionary process. It's the single step that begins a journey of a thousand miles. In simple terms, it's long range planning. 'Kaizen' is not a quick solution, but one that is carefully devised and which employs great discipline.

Hank stood up to make his point. "Please understand, gentlemen, the problems we're having now are as much our fault as theirs. It wasn't the Japanese who made us produce automobiles with high prices and low quality. It's not their fault that we stopped selling American products around the world or that we've paid such little attention to our rapidly escalating debt. The Japanese have simply produced better products at better prices. American industry has now got to heed the wake-up call or we'll be left in the dust."

Hank watched the two men across from him, and smiled inwardly. He had their complete attention. He took a sip from the glass of water.

"I've got to tell you, it scares the hell out of me that the Japanese are now producing such a wide range of products in the United States, using American Labor," he continued. "They get tax incentives not available to American manufacturers and they obtain union concessions that aren't granted to domestic producers. It scares the hell out of me, Mr. Secretary, and it should scare the hell out of you, too."

Stan jumped in. "Now wait a minute," he said, tapping his pen nervously, against the palm of his hand. "I set up this meeting with hopes that we could get some good observations from your long experience working with the Japanese. Sandy Gold has been keeping me advised of your activities over the past six years. We're impressed with your venture capital foundation. It's realizing some remarkable high technology breakthroughs. But I must tell you honestly, I think you're over reacting to the imbalance of trade issue."

Hank tried to control his impatience. "Gentlemen, I'd like to propose a plan, one I believe will make our Japanese friends breathe a sigh of relief at how reasonable we're being. What I propose is that we try our own version of 'Kaizen'. I suggest that we no longer discuss any of the areas of trade that previously brought us to an impasse. I propose that we start the sales ball rolling by concentrating on American products that are not threatening to the Japanese."

"What sort of products do you have in mind?" Ed Mannis asked.

"Well, Mr. Secretary," Hank said, "We've spotlighted several businesses that pose no threat to the Japanese. We can start with jewelry, processed foods, furniture, recreational equipment and apparel. By going in with products such as these, we'll be taking the first step in getting the Japanese to accept our exports as a normal course of events. And, we'll be in a better position to start bringing in major industries,"

Opening his briefcase, Hank removed a large yellow envelope. "I've taken the liberty of outlining a program in detail in this regard," he said. "I would like to respectfully submit this confidential document for your consideration."

Reaching across the desk, Hank handed the envelope to Mannis.

"Inside is a list of companies and people whom I recommend become involved in a special Presidential Trade Mission to market American products in Japan. I also suggest that you, Mr. Secretary, personally lead this expedition and that you invite my wife and me to be your special assistants. I hope you don't think it's too presumptuous of me to make these requests, but I strongly believe that the prestige of a Presidential Trade Mission, headed by the U.S. Secretary of Commerce, would give us the clout we need to get things started."

Stan leaned over and removed a large, black appointment book from his briefcase. He thumbed through it until he found the page he was looking for. Raising his eyes, he nodded at Hank and turned to the Secretary. "I recommend this project. I think it's an excellent idea. We can invite fifteen to twenty manufacturers and send them out on a sales mission, as Hank has suggested. I'd also like to suggest, Mr. Secretary, that Sandy Gold be made a part of this group and actively participate in this project."

Mannis had been gazing thoughtfully at the trees outside his window as he listened. A few moments later, he said, "Okay, I'll take this under consideration. I'll also need to consult with some of our other specialists and to check my schedule to see if I can work this trade mission in."

Rising from his chair, he extended his hand to Hank. "Mr. Marshall, I thank you for your time and your very astute comments. We'll be in touch."

CHAPTER TWENTY-FIVE

▼

When Yoshikazu Matsuda visited the United States, he'd become accustomed to having his important meetings take place in his bungalow at the Bel Air Hotel. Tosui's influence in the U.S. had grown so that anytime its chairman made an appearance, it was cause for speculation. Recent trips to Los Angeles were made in relative secrecy, under tight security, to avoid the need for explanation.

On this particular day, a series of meetings had been in progress since eight o'clock in the morning. With the everpresent Takei Watanabe at his side, Yoshi received reports from Tosui's real estate group followed by updates from the automotive and auxiliary parts divisions.

It was four in the afternoon, and the last group—computers, chips and software—had just left. Michio Matsuda, President and Chief Executive Officer of Telesonic, U.S.A., was due to arrive and give his report before joining his father and Takei for dinner.

The knock at the door brought Takei to his feet. He bowed respectfully as the younger man entered. Walking into the room, Michio nodded to Takei and bowed in the direction of his father. Yoshi, sitting in the throne-like red velvet chair, moved his head slightly in acknowledgment.

Although the day had been long and strenuous, Yoshi's posture remained erect as he sat, waiting for his son. Watching

Michio stride across the room filled Yoshi with pride, and lifted the weariness he'd been feeling minutes before.

His heir had lived up to all expectations, and had in fact performed above and beyond what had been expected. Telesonic was now the foremost name in consumer electronics. Market share had grown as the product continued to improve and profitability had surpassed all projections. There was no doubt in anyone's mind that the son of the chairman would be more than capable of taking over the leadership of Tosui's vast empire when Yoshi eventually retired.

Michio seated himself on the sofa across from his father. Opening his briefcase, he removed two folders, handing one to Yoshi and the other to Takei. "Here are the latest figures on Telesonic, U.S.A. The last quarter was the best in our history. Our new line of laser discs is sweeping the country. I have also submitted a proposal recommending that we acquire a major record company."

Michio's voice was tired and his face looked haggard and thin. Lines had begun to form around his eyes. Yoshi looked at his son with concern.

"The reports you bring are excellent," Yoshi said, "but something seems to be worrying you. Is there some trouble you have not mentioned?"

Michio hesitated. "There is something of great importance on my mind but I must speak to you about it in private. Will you please excuse us, Takei?"

Takei turned to Yoshi, who nodded his consent. Rising to his feet, Takei offered a quick bow and left the room.

As soon as the door closed, Michio turned to his father, who waited for him to speak.

"Father, there is something we must discuss," Michio began. "From my earliest childhood, I have rigorously followed our traditions and accepted the rules that have been set down. I have had the great fortune to be born into a family, destined to be a dominating influence on the economy and the wellbeing of our country and our people. I have accepted the role I inherited with joy. To be the first son of the house of Matsuda is not only an honor but a sacred trust."

Michio began gaining confidence as he spoke, and his voice became stronger. Yoshi observed these minute changes cautiously. Without thinking, his back grew stiff and straight, making him appear taller and even more imposing. His watchful eyes followed Michio as the younger man stood and walked over to the window.

Gathering his courage, Michio could feel his father's eyes boring into him. "I have always followed your orders without question, Father, not only because I felt it was my duty, but because I felt I was performing my role in a manner that brought satisfaction to you and honor to our name. Now, for the first time in my life, I am seeking your permission to part from the course that has been charted for me."

He paused for several moments while his father stared straight ahead, saying nothing. Taking a deep breath, Michio went on. "I know a wife has been chosen for me and that I have delayed in setting a date for the wedding."

Then suddenly, in a burst of anguished words that seemed to be torn from him, Michio turned from the window and blurted out, "Father, I am in love with Sarah Marshall and wish to marry her!"

The expression on Yoshi's face never changed. They did not look at each other for quite a while, and their silence filled the room.

At last, in a low voice, Yoshi said, "I am afraid that is not possible. For centuries our bloodline has remained pure. Each of our forefathers produced a son to carry on the family name and the family traditions. After three daughters, I almost despaired of ever having a son. Every day, I prayed to the gods to send a male child to fulfill our destiny. Now, you stand before me, the embodiment of my prayers.

"It is without question that you are to succeed me as head of the Tosui Empire. In each of our companies and throughout the world, you are recognized, respected and acknowledged as my successor. A perfect Japanese mate, with correct bloodlines and a family that is steeped in power and tradition, waits patiently for us to set a date. But now you tell me that you are willing to disregard all of this for a 'gaijin'. I am afraid that is impossible."

Michio knew well what his father's expectations for him were. In the past, they had not only been acceptable to him, they had been in full accordance with his own feelings. Then, he'd seen Sarah again and suddenly, his life changed. He felt now like a king about to abdicate his throne.

Michio turned to his father and said, "Papa-San, I cannot just walk away from my feelings for Sarah. They are too deep…and too strong."

Yoshi flinched when he heard the name Michio had called him as a child, but he did not falter. "Is it easier then, for you to turn your back on your ancestors and on your obligations to your family and your country? No, that cannot be. In fact," he spat out, "I forbid it!"

Michio could hear the venom in his father's voice. When he first confronted Yoshi, he'd felt sure of himself—full of confidence. But the weight of his ancestor's ghosts and the love and respect he had for his father now cast doubts on his ability to make the right decision. He felt small and insignificant. Michio turned again to look out the window, as if hoping to find answers in the darkening shadows that were moving in to replace the brightness of the day.

He couldn't imagine his life without Sarah, but neither could he reject the burden of his father's wishes and also those of his grandfather, Yukio, and of every first son of a first son who had come before him. No, he could not abandon them all in this moment.

When at last Michio spoke, his words came slowly as he continued to stare out the window. "I have spent many years in the United States. There are times when I feel as American as I do Japanese. It was your decision that I live with the Marshall family. They took me in and accepted me without question. I wonder now if my mission was to learn or to spy. Six years ago, when you decided to take over Marshall-Telesonic, I understood that was as it should be. Deep within me though, I felt I had betrayed the Marshalls, but because I am your son I pushed those feelings aside. I have been trained to accept without question—to follow the path that has been chosen for me. For the past six years, I have worked diligently, without thought for anything but the needs of the company."

Twilight melted into darkness as Michio paused, searching for the right words. He turned to face his father.

Yoshi had not moved. Erect in his chair, his body was as motionless as a statue.

Michio sighed deeply before going on. "Last month, when I met Sarah again, my life changed. Now, there is joy in my heart such as I have never known before. I'm torn, Father," he said, miserably. "I can't give up my heritage but I can't walk away from my passion either."

Passion…Michio was startled by his own use of the word.

Yoshi looked at his handsome son standing before him—tall, straight and tormented. The memory of his own experience with Ruth so long ago forced its way into his mind. There was one difference, though. Despite what he'd felt during that summer of 1941, it had never occurred to him to question his father's orders. He now felt torn between rage and compassion. How could his son question his decisions? But how could he ignore the pain his son was experiencing?

Yoshikazu Matsuda had spent his life being strong and decisive. Everyone who knew him looked upon him as a reincarnation of the ancient Shoguns, endowed with wisdom, patience and strength. He knew he could not abandon his tradition, but neither could he exile his son.

Tosui's corporate symbol—a bamboo bending in the wind flashed before his eyes. That is it, he thought to himself. I must be like the bamboo. I must bend but I cannot break.

"There are times," Yoshi said, shattering the silence, "when the act of not making an immediate decision is, in itself, a decision. What I ask of you is that you continue to perform as you have. You will remain in the United States, pursuing our business interests. For a period of time, you may not marry. Events and the passing of time have a way of resolving many conflicts. Let us meet again six months from now to further discuss this subject. Then, whatever decisions are made will come as a result of contemplation rather than from acting in haste."

Relief flooded through Michio's body. He and Sarah could certainly wait six months. Their feelings for each other had survived so long, time would only increase their desire to be together.

Bowing formally to his father, he said, "I agree to this and am hopeful that you will give us your blessings six months from now. I thank you, Father, for your patience and your wisdom."

CHAPTER TWENTY-SIX

▼
——————————————————————

Two weeks had passed since Sarah had confessed her love for Michio to her mother. Then suddenly she called, saying she had to see both Ruth and Hank right away. She sounded so upset that Ruth told her to come to the house right away.

Sarah arrived in less than an hour. She wore no makeup, faded jeans and a sloppy, baggy sweater. Opening the door, Hank took one look at her face and gathered her in his arms, holding her tightly. Immediately, Sarah began to sob. They remained standing in the doorway that way for several minutes, until finally, Sarah pulled herself together.

Entering the warm living room, holding onto Hank's arm, Sarah laughed nervously. "Can you believe this?" she said. "Here I am—a grown, sophisticated woman, and I'm acting like some dumb school kid."

Walking over to her, Ruth welcomed her daughter with a reassuring hug. But concern was written all over Hank's face. After they sat down, he demanded, "Okay, what's going on?"

In a monotone voice, Sarah repeated the story of how she and Michio had found each other once again, how they planned to marry and that Michio had asked for Yoshi's blessings.

"Well, I'm glad you decided to tell your father," Hank interrupted, annoyance in his voice. No sooner had he spoken, however, than he wished he could have taken his words back.

"Honey, I'm sorry," he said. "This just comes as such a shock. I can imagine what Yoshi's response was. He's already arranged a marriage for Michio with the daughter of a prominent Japanese family."

This time, Sarah interrupted. "But I thought Yoshi loved and accepted me, the same way you accept Michio."

"It doesn't work that way in Japan," Ruth said quietly. "A proper match is made by the families in order to perpetuate bloodlines and increase business power. Love has nothing to do with it."

Hank glanced at Ruth sharply when he heard the hard edge that had creeped into her voice. He'd lost none of his bitterness toward Yoshi, but the rancor in Ruth's voice surprised him.

Turning to Sarah, Hank said, testily, "Okay, so tell me, how did the little bastard respond to Michio?"

"They had some strong words," Sarah replied carefully. "And they agreed to delay making a decision for six months. I guess Yoshi figures that will give Michio enough time to come to his senses, kiss me off and return to the Japanese girl they picked for him."

Sarah looked from her mother to her father imploringly. "Please believe me…I know our love is right and that we belong together. But sometimes, I get frightened. I think that something terrible might happen to stop us. I must find a way to reach Uncle Yoshi—to convince him that Michio and I belong together. He has to understand that we love each other and that he cannot drive us apart!"

Sarah began to plead, "Mom and Dad, you're leaving for Japan tomorrow. Will you please talk to Yoshi? Will you try to make him understand that this is 1988, not 1945? Will you tell him that the time has come for him to change?"

Sarah caught the cynical look on her father's face.

"Dad, I know how you feel, but remember, you and Yoshi were once very close friends. I think you miss him, even though now you consider him the enemy. If you really analyze the situation though, you'll see that under the circumstances, we were treated fairly. They gave us just about everything we asked for. And Yoshi knew how much he stood to lose. He knew how bitter you'd be."

"If you're asking for my permission to marry Michio," said Hank, "which I know you're not, then please understand I am only interested in your happiness. If this had happened before the takeover, I would have been delighted. You know how highly I thought of Michio. We used to talk all the time. Since the takeover, however, I haven't heard a word from him."

"Now just a minute," Ruth chimed in. "We can't keep looking back with anger."

She turned to Sarah. "Perhaps Yoshi had the right idea when he said you should delay your decision for six months. But, on the other hand, he might very well be setting the stage to make sure things work out the way he wants them to."

Ruth stopped and thought a moment. "Okay, we will see Mr. Matsuda in Japan. And we might even have a few surprises for him," she added with a smile.

The following morning, Ruth and Hank boarded a plane in Los Angeles headed for Washington, D.C. There, they would meet the rest of those involved in the mission before heading on to Japan.

Hank sighed deeply as they settled into their seats. "We really have a hectic schedule ahead of us," he said. "I feel like a producer who's spent years preparing a show that's about to open on Broadway. The only problem is, the script isn't finished yet, so there's no way of knowing how the story will end."

"But that's just it," Ruth interrupted. "It doesn't end. It's too big to end. If we hadn't taken the position we did six years ago, we would have been able to just fade into the sunset. We'd be lying on the beach somewhere— going on cruises, or just contemplating our navels."

Hank laughed. "'Yes, but that's not the kind of people we are, are we? I had to stay in the arena. I had to try to make a difference. Do you really think we could just sit back, knowing what we know about a Japanese plot to take over the United States?"

Ruth was thoughtful for a moment. "Do you really think that a bunch of old men who swore vengeance forty-three years ago have that kind of power? It could be that the Japanese are just making good, sound investments in the global marketplace."

"Ruth, you don't understand these people. Although most of the original members of the group are probably dead, the plot continues. And now two generations later, our daughter wants to marry the grandson of the man who masterminded the whole thing. It's ironic, isn't it?" Hank, smiled wryly and shook his head.

Ruth looked out the window at the great landscape of the United States below. "How many people down there have any idea there's a battle going on?"

"And more importantly," Hank added, "How many people care?

"But let's get back to our schedule," he said. "When we arrive in Washington, we barely have time to change before the Presidential Trade Commission cocktail party. It's important that we get to know the people who are going on this trip. It's quite a group—nineteen entrepreneurs and twelve bureaucrats. The Secretary of Commerce will have four of his staff with him. And don't forget Sandy Gold."

"Who could forget Sandy Gold?" said Ruth, sarcastically. "Well, we're fortunate that the reception is being held at the Madison Hotel, where we're staying. That'll give us some break."

By seven o'clock, the cocktail party was over. Ruth and Hank left the others and went directly to their room. They were looking forward to relaxing after their long day.

The phone was ringing as they walked into their suite. Picking it up, Hank heard Sandy Gold's voice on the other end.

"I know we just saw each other at that dog and pony show they called a cocktail party," Sandy said, "but I figured you were returning to your room and I need to talk to you. It won't take more than fifteen minutes. Do you mind if I come up?"

"Can't it wait until we get together tomorrow?"

"There are some things I can't discuss in front of the others and we may not have another chance to speak privately. I'll be there in two minutes."

Before Hank could protest further, Sandy hung up.

Ruth looked up questioningly. "That was Sandy Gold," Hank said. "He's on his way up."

"And we don't have a choice, do we?" Ruth sighed.

Seconds later, there was a sharp knock at the door. Hank opened it and Sandy entered. His suit was in its usual rumpled state and his jacket was open, revealing several greasy stains on his shirt and tie, the result of poor hors d'oeurves maneuvering.

In his hand was a double oldfashioned glass, half-filled with bourbon. "I hope you don't mind," he grinned, "I brought my cocktail with me."

Loosening his tie and unbuttoning his collar, he plunked himself down in the sitting room on the first chair he saw.

"Boy, they sure keep this place hot," he said. "Or maybe I'm just getting old. Lately, I'm finding Washington tougher and tougher to take."

He took a long sip from his drink and let out a loud "Aaahhhhh", smiling at Ruth and Hank, who were seated across from him. "Have you had a chance to walk through the Department of Commerce yet? It's the biggest government building in Washington. It must warm your heart to think that your tax dollars are paying for the largest concentration of freeloaders in the world."

Hank was tired. Looking over at Ruth, he noticed that circles were beginning to form around her eyes. The strain of the past two weeks was taking its toll. Irritation crept into his voice as he looked at Sandy sprawled out on the chair.

"I know you didn't come here at this hour to talk about taxes. So what is it you have to say that can't wait until tomorrow?"

Straightening up, Sandy's face got serious. "Okay, here it is in a nut shell. This entire trade mission is pure bullshit. Looking at Ruth, he added, "Excuse my language, ma'am. There is just no other way I can describe what's going on.

Sandy took a drink from his glass. "When you folks arrive in Japan, they are gonna dance around all the key issues. They'll promise to take everything under consideration but nothing will happen. Oh, they may see that some of these yokels get a token order but there won't be anything of real consequence accomplished. The Secretary of Commerce will ultimately declare the mission to be an unqualified success and everyone will return home with big smiles on their faces. That's the way it works in Washington. Once they decide to do something, it's a success before it even gets started. That way, no one in this town ever makes a mistake."

He drained the last drop of bourbon from his glass and looked at Ruth as if to say, 'Hey, my glass is empty'.

Ignoring the look, she lashed out angrily. "If that's the case, then why did you get us involved? And who the hell are you anyway?"

With sarcasm dripping from her voice, she added, "Please excuse my language, sir. It's the only way I know to express myself."

Sandy laughed at the implied insult. He was enjoying the exchange. "Okay, I guess it's time to tell you…I'm with the CIA. I'll even show you my badge if you'd like. But although I work for the organization, I don't always follow their prescribed approach. I'm more interested in results than procedures. You might say I'm one of the last true patriots in the world. I just cannot accept half-assed solutions or the bungling of so-called professionals.

"A large percentage of the people in this town are political hacks, bureaucrats or heavy campaign contributors who've been paid off with political appointments they're not qualified to fill. Those with good connections become foreign lobbyists when they leave office. Half of them wind up working for the Japanese, who now spend more than one hundred million dollars a year in the U.S. on the most powerful lobby in Washington."

Sandy looked longingly at his empty glass. Realizing no one was going to refill it, he sighed. "Basically, this is the situation: our world consists of enemies and friends. The problem is that their positions keep shifting. Yesterday's enemy is today's bosom buddy and it's getting harder to keep track of the players without a scorecard. Forty-three years have passed since the Great War—when the United States emerged as the greatest power the world has ever seen. Then, it was our ballpark, our bat and our ball. We dominated militarily and economically. We were the largest creditor nation in the world. Today, we are the largest debtor nation in the world and we go deeper into debt every day. The two dominant powers are now Japan and Germany. But once again, the world is changing and industrial might is going to give way to high technology."

Zeroing in on Hank, Sandy continued. "This has been your arena for the last six years, my friend, and the Japanese are well aware of the progress you and a few others have made. They are going to try and make a deal with you. They're nervous right now. Their plan for the economic takeover of the U.S. is in jeopardy and they're going to have to re-think their strategy.

"As you can imagine, this is a very frustrating time for the Japanese, but they keep plugging away on all fronts. Wherever there are factories you'll find the Japanese are there. They follow the trail of low-priced labor from Taiwan to Korea to the Philipines, because they understand the global market and worldwide production.

"But here's the rub," Sandy continued. "The Japanese don't originate new products. It's the lazy Americans who produce the geniuses that create new industries. We invent basic products like airplanes, automobiles, radios and televisions. The Japanese then improve upon our inventions and manufacture them faster and cheaper."

Hank was becoming irritated. "Look, I'm too damned tired to listen to a lesson in Economics one-oh-one, 1988. The high-tech venture capital groups, being financed by The Marshall Foundation, are on the verge of major breakthroughs. Super chips and digital technology are going to make many of the present industries, obsolete."

Sandy rose to his feet, grinning. "Then here are your orders for the mission. This week, you'll be wined and dined. The American entrepreneurs will sell some products and the Japanese will make sounds like they're going to throw open their economic borders at long last. But the important deals are going to be made behind closed doors. Our Japanese friends know all about what you've been doing in your laboratories and in your pilot plants. They want to make a deal with you—to joint venture or to buy you outright. Yoshikazu Matsuda, himself will want to renew old acquaintances and we suggest that you meet with him. Be amiable. Find out what they've developed, than agree to another meeting. Don't make any commitments. Just play it cool like they do. Remember, time is on our side. Our goal is to break down the barriers to free trade—sell more and buy less. To do this, we will unleash our secret weapon."

"What do you mean, secret weapon?" Ruth asked.

"The Japanese consumer!" Sandy cried. "They've been traveling around the world—to the United States in particular. They've been buying up a storm on Rodeo Drive, the Rue St. Honore and Kings Road. After all their years of hard work and saving, they're now discovering that things are cheaper everywhere else in the world than they are in Japan. The Japanese distribution system has been set up to keep the competition out and Japan's prices high. If the Japanese were forced to allow our major discount retailers—like Walmart or Toys R Us—to operate in Japan, local competition would be destroyed. And our exports would automatically increase. Then, the new high technology controlled by the United States would systematically overpower the stranglehold the Japanese have on our economy."

"This is incredible," said Hank. "Are you telling us that the point of this sophisticated plan is to get the Japanese to shop at Walmart? And are you also saying that because Yoshikazu Matsuda has become one of the most powerful people in Japan, we should resurrect our old relationship to get his cooperation?"

Sandy looked at his watch. "Look folks, I'm also tired and you have it just about right. Japan's official policy is to keep out our retailers, and our investment people, our banks and our products. If we publicly threaten them with sanctions and heavy punitive tariffs on their exports to the U.S., we'll force an all-out trade war that could be very destructive. The Japanese could not stand to lose face in a public confrontation. Besides, they're convinced that we won't carry out our threats -that in reality we're just paper tigers. Matsuda knows both of you well and knows that you don't bluff. It will be up to you to convince him that if he does not level out the playing field, the results will be disastrous to Japan. This must be done quietly but forcefully."

Sandy paused, allowing his words to register. He knew the hour was late and that they were all tired. But he needed to be sure that they fully understood the importance of their participation in this program. "You should know that the situation in Japan has changed dramatically since Tosui bought out your interest in Telesonic," he said. "To put it in simple words, your high tech achievements scare the shit out of them. They realize they could lose control and they don't like it. When you meet with Yoshikazu Matsuda in Tokyo, you will be on equal ground. That meeting should be a real doozy! And now, since no one is offering me a drink and I have said all I have to say, I will take my leave."

Ruth and Hank stared in amazement as Sandy left the room and the door closed behind him. Shaking her head in disbelief, Ruth said, "The guy is eerie. He's like tomorrow's headlines today."

"No one should ever underestimate that raunchy little bastard," Hank added with reluctant admiration.

Ruth walked into the bedroom, and as she began to undress, she noticed Hank was watching her every move. "And what are you looking at, buster?" she laughed.

Panting heavily, he lisped in his best Humphery Bogart voice, "You still turn me on, Babe. And I lust for you."

"Talk about raunchy little bastards!" she giggled, falling back on the bed with her arms outstretched. With exaggerated haste, Hank began ripping off his clothes while they both laughed. Slowly, the tension disappeared and hilarity gave way to the soft, sighing sounds of their love.

CHAPTER TWENTY-SEVEN

▼

The red carpet was out for the Presidential Trade Mission of 1988. From the moment they landed in Tokyo, the Americans were received with smiles and bows, exuding goodwill. An official limousine picked up Ed Mannis, Stan Blackmore, Ruth and Hank. Two shiny new buses, each with a friendly hostess and a trade official, picked up the rest of the party. The guests were then sped through passport inspection and on to the Okura Hotel.

Their rooms had been pre-assigned. Ruth and Hank were given a one-bedroom suite with a large living room on the twentieth floor. What made it special was the breathtaking view, overlooking the entire city.

As they entered their quarters, the Marshalls' eyes immediately fell upon an exquisite little Bonsai plant in the center of an elegant crystal table. On one side of the plant was a sterling silver ice bucket cradling a magnum of Mumm's champagne. On the other side was a quart of Johnny Walker Black Label scotch and a smaller ice bucket, filled with ice cubes. Propped up against the bottle of scotch was a white linen envelope. Ruth opened it and read:

> Welcome to Tokyo! The trade group is scheduled to meet tomorrow at three in the Board of Directors room at Tosui Trading headquarters. Later, Tosui will be hosting a cocktail party.

I would be greatly honored if both of you would join Takei and me for a private dinner immediately following the cocktail party.

The note was simply signed, "Yoshi."

The next day began with a flurry of activity. After breakfast, the entire group met at the American Embassy. There, they were greeted with a welcoming speech by the ambassador to Japan, the former U.S. senator, Mike Mansfield. Although in his late seventies, the ex-senator possessed dynamic energy.

"This mission of entrepreneurs is a wonderful idea." Mansfield told them. "It is truly the wave of the future. The American entrepreneur has been a role model for the entire world. While mighty Fortune 500 companies are readjusting to the conditions of 1988, small and medium size companies are a step ahead of the times. And this great Presidential Trade Mission is at the forefront of it all. The world is watching us. Small companies are becoming part of the great global economy at last."

Enthusiastic applause greeted Mr. Mansfield as he walked off the podium to shake hands with all who were present. He remained the consummate politician from Montana, always enjoying the chance to meet the public.

Stan Blackmore, as Under Secretary of Commerce, then outlined the well-planned program which covered the next five days.

"First the delegation will meet with MITTI, the powerful Japanese government office that sets the policies for Japanese business and its role in world trade. Later in the morning, we will split into individual trade groups. Each group will then meet with executives of Japanese companies, prepared to import American merchandise. In the late afternoon we will all meet again at the corporate headquarters of Tosui Trading Company, one of the largest companies in the world. Their revenues are in excess of one hundred billion dollars a year, dwarfing even the largest American companies. After our meeting, we've been invited to attend a cocktail party Tosui is hosting in our honor."

The mood was jubilant and optimistic as the group filed out of the Embassy. The Americans were elated by the contacts they would make and the business they hoped would result. Everyone was going all-out to ensure this trade mission's success.

When the members of the Trade Mission arrived at Tosui's headquarters at three o'clock that afternoon, the mood was sober. The Americans were disappointed with the session at MITTI. The Japanese minister had been blunt in his criticism of the quality of American merchandise.

"We are ready, willing and able to allocate great amounts of business to American companies provided we can count on their quality as being acceptable to the Japanese consumer," they were told.

One member of the group, a manufacturer of high quality furniture, protested angrily. "My wood tables and chairs are of better quality than those being manufactured in Japan and they cost less," he told the MITTI representative. "Yet, despite superior quality and lower prices, my proposals to supply furnishings to Japanese hotels have been turned down."

The minister smiled accommodatingly and promised to look into the matter. "Please keep in mind," he told them, "the reason for this mission is to offer renewed opportunities to American suppliers. Japanese consumers are most eager to be able to purchase American products."

Feeling the situation had been adequately smoothed over, the Minister looked at his watch and said, "I regret that we must now end this discussion. But in due time, we will answer all of your questions."

Bowing as he rose, the Minister briskly walked out of the room followed by his staff. The Americans were then ushered from MITTI's center of operations amidst smiles and bows.

Twenty minutes later, the group arrived at the Tosui headquarters, a towering gray, granite, structure in downtown Tokyo. Entering the lobby, they were overwhelmed by the grandeur that surrounded them. A huge reclining statue by the sculptor Henry Moore greeted them as they entered. On the walls hung paintings by famous artists, both contemporary and traditional.

"Walking into this lobby is like entering a museum of fine art," Ruth whispered in awe.

Japanese guides escorted the Americans through the lobby to softly-lit, lushly carpeted elevators that sped them to the executive offices on the 42nd floor. As they walked into the Board of Director's room, an audible gasp could be heard. A 360-degree view of Tokyo could be seen from the enormous glass windows encompassing the room. Each delegate stood rooted to where he or she was, totally mesmerized by the sight.

A giant oval-shaped conference table made of shiny teakwood dominated the center of the room. Forty gray upholstered armchairs were positioned around it. Behind them were two rows of bleached walnut benches, set aside for advisors, observers and the press.

The room was filled to capacity. As Ruth and Hank walked through the heavy double doors, they were amazed by the size and splendor of the room. "Do you think King Arthur's Round Table was this big?" Ruth whispered.

Hank laughed. "I can't answer that, but I do know this ain't Camelot."

A group of twelve reporters and twenty Japanese business executives and their advisors were waiting for the Americans to arrive. In front of each chair at the table were brass nameplates. American business people were seated across from Japanese business people, and Japanese government officials faced their American counterparts. The room was humming with introductions, conversation and excitement.

After everyone was seated, the front doors briskly opened, causing a hush to fall over the room. Yoshikazu Matsuda entered, flanked on his left by Takei Watanbe and on his right by his son, Michio. They bowed to the group assembled before them, and took their seats at the head of the table.

Ruth's heart began to pound as she looked at Yoshi. His appearance had changed in the last six years. His hair had turned gray, and heavy lines around his eyes had caused them to become narrower. What hadn't changed, though, was his regal bearing.

As usual, Yoshi and Michio were immaculately dressed. Their gray, double- breasted suits seemed molded to their bodies. In contrast, Takei wore a single-breasted navy blue suit that bulged conspicuously, despite its effort to contain his massive chest.

The room was still as Takei rose to his feet and looked around, smiling broadly in friendly greeting. "I would like to welcome our American friends and their Japanese hosts," he began. "We sincerely thank you for making the long journey to our country. Here to meet you and answer your questions are the heads of many of our major companies, well known in the United States."

He proceeded to introduce the Japanese executives who were present, stating their positions and the names of their companies. Each stood when his name was called and offered a smile and a bow. Honda, Sony, Matsushita and Mazda were among those represented.

Finally, Takei said, "And now, I would like you to meet the chairman of Tosui Trading Company, Mr. Yoshikazu Matsuda."

Yoshi rose to the sound of applause. He nodded to different members of the group until the room became quiet once again. His low, powerful voice, with only a slight trace of an accent, seemed to caress the microphone.

"I would like to add my thanks to those of Mr. Watanabe. This is truly an historic occasion. We meet here as a community of business people, not only to discuss our problems, but to find their solutions and to explore the many ways in which we can work together.

"The lines of communication we establish here today will be the most important results of these meetings. We do not want to indulge in rhetoric. We want action. We want to purchase and import many of the items that Americans produce and that the Japanese need. It is my goal and the goal of my Japanese colleagues to find ways in which to expand opportunities for bringing more American products to Japan."

Yoshi continure, "We are not just interested in making deals. We are interested in forming relationships. In this regard, I would particularly like to welcome Ruth and Hank Marshall to this gathering. Together we formed Telesonic thirty-six years ago. I would also like to take this opportunity to now publicly thank them for all they did to make Telesonic the respected name it is today."

With a half smile, Yoshi extended his palm in the direction of Hank and Ruth, who were sitting across the room. They rose in acknowledgment to the sound of applause. Ruth smiled and nodded graciously. Hank turned his gaze toward Yoshi, looking at him evenly. Yoshi returned the look. During this exchange, Michio sat stiffly in his chair, his eyes darting back and forth between Ruth, Hank and his father.

When Ruth and Hank sat down, Yoshi continued. "I would now like to introduce you to our company through a special television presentation. It will show you some of what we do here and around the world."

Ruth looked around for the television monitors but didn't see any.

"They'll probably drop a screen from the ceiling," Hank said. But as he spoke, individual screens began popping up on the conference table all around them.

"I'll be damned," said Hank, "pop-up television!" Two larger screens also appeared in front of the benches, so that the visitors and advisors could see as well.

The fifteen-minute film dramatically illustrated just how far-reaching Tosui's influence was in everything, from heavy industrial equipment to micro chips.

"I'm impressed," Hank muttered at the film's conclusion, "but after all of this, I think I'm starting to go into overload. Isn't it cocktail time yet?"

As though he'd heard the whispered comment from across the room, Takei stood up and grinned. "We thank you for watching our presentation. We now invite you to join us for cocktails and hors d'oeuvres."

The Americans and Japanese mingled freely as they walked down a long hall to another large room. The room was decorated with red, white and blue banners and scores of American and Japanese flags. The guests were greeted by fifteen smiling Japanese hostesses, who were dressed in tights and leotards, and who looked like Asian Playboy bunnies.

"What a spread! Exclaimed Hank, as he and Ruth entered the room. "Tosui really knows how to throw a party."

An abundance of hot and cold serving tables had been set up along one side of the room. Platters were garnished with little flags, naming the country originating each dish. German flags were displayed next to bite-sized frankfurters resting on a bed of sauerkraut and an assortment of plump, juicy sausages. Italian flags were positioned proudly beside three different varieties of pasta and a steaming platter of sauteed calamari. Close by were four tables bearing Japanese flags and featuring an array of sushi, sashimi, and exotic seafood. The two American tables spotlighted sumptuous Maine lobster and slices of roast beef served on toasted buns. The French table displayed sizzling platters of garlicky frogs' legs and an assortment of quiches.

Three bars had been set up around the room, tended by serious bartenders in uniforms. Drinks of all nations were being served: French champagnes, California wines, German and American beer, Japanese sake, and Russian vodka. Irish and Scotch whiskies were also being served in generous quantities.

The room was bursting with life. Ruth and Hank continued to be dazzled by the sheer opulence surrounding them. They looked at each other, shaking their heads, not quite knowing where to start.

Suddenly, as though he'd been dropped from the sky, Sandy Gold appeared beside them. His suit was in its standard rumpled state, but his shirt was fresh and clean. Smiling maliciously, he said, "Is this the most elaborate 'dog and pony show' you've ever seen or what? This time they've gone balls-out to impress everyone." His customary glass of bourbon was in his hand.

"Where did you come from?" Hank asked. "I didn't see you in the meeting room."

"That's because I wasn't there. Fact is, I just arrived. I'd already seen the Tosui promo film and was duly impressed. There are, however, more important things for me to do than go through this foreplay. Now, this here is the seduction room and soon they will drop the net over us. That means you don't want to waste your time here with me. It's important that you meet all these leaders of Japanese industry. I just showed up to make sure you accept Mr. Matsuda's dinner invitation. It could be a crucial meeting."

Ruth looked at Sandy in amazement. "How did you know that we received an invitation?" she asked, in a puzzled tone.

He looked back at her innocently. "A little Japanese birdy told me," he said with a wink, before walking away.

There was movement everywhere. Animated conversation could be heard throughout the room. Buffet tables were constantly being replenished and held what seemed to be an endless supply of food and drinks. Smiling hostesses moved about silently and efficiently, catering to each guest's every wish.

Ruth looked up from her plate to see Michio making his way toward them from across the room. When he reached her, she smiled warmly and kissed him on the cheek. The unrestrained show of affection embarrassed him and caused Ruth to chuckle at the uncomfortable look on his face.

"I'm sorry, Michio," she grinned, "I'm just so happy to see you!"

Taking his arm and giving it a squeeze, they turned to face Hank.

It was obvious that Michio felt ill at ease standing next to Hank after so many years of silence. With a stiff half bow, he held out his hand and said, "It is very good to see you again,
Sir."

Then, suddenly, as if the dam had broken, he blurted out, "I have really missed you! You both look wonderful! I'm so pleased that you've come to Japan. I have wanted to speak with you so many times. I hope we can now be friends again."

Ruth looked at him coyly. "It seems that you've been much more than friends with Sarah," she said.

"We love each other," Michio said simply, without apology. "And I hope very much that you approve. It is most important to me that you do."

Hank looked at him and bluntly said, "Six years ago I would have been more than pleased, Michio. Today, however, I have many mixed emotions."

Switching to a lighter tone, Hank continued, "We received a note from your father inviting us to dinner, but it didn't mention your being here."

"I am aware of that," said Michio. "Unfortunately, I cannot join you this evening. It is my great hope, however, that tonight will bring about a renewal of our close friendship. It would mean a great deal to me," he paused, "and to Sarah."

"Wounds don't heal that quickly," Hank replied, icily. "But we are here on a mission of goodwill, to bring about a better understanding between our two countries, and that's a first step."

"Hank-San," Michio said softly, "you once taught me that all business is personal. You said, 'Companies do not make deals nor do countries. When people want to agree they find a way to make it happen'."

Hearing his own words come back to him, Hank smiled. "You've learned well," he said.

Michio smiled back. Bowing, he said, "I apologize, but I must leave now. I look forward though, to seeing both of you again soon." Shaking Hank's hand firmly, he looked around quickly before leaning down to kiss Ruth's cheek.

"Good luck," she whispered softly in his ear.

No sooner had Michio walked away, than Takei appeared wearing a smile so wide it seemed his face would burst. He bowed and seized Hank's hand, shaking it heartily. Turning to Ruth, he bowed very low, took her hand and kissed it lightly.

"Thank you both so much for coming. It is a great pleasure to see you again," Takei said. "Matsuda-San is currently involved in another meeting, but he was most happy to see you earlier and is looking forward to our dinner at eight o'clock. He has asked me to escort you to the club and he will meet us there. I must tell you, too," said Takei, still grinning happily, "that I am personally very pleased we are spending time together once again."

From all outward appearances, Takei had not changed. It was only when his face relaxed that the deep lines around his mouth and eyes became visible. He, too, had begun to show signs of age.

From their first meeting at the Trans-Pacific Traders offices, over forty years before, Hank had had a special feeling for Takei. And the bond had deepened between them over the years. After six years of silence, it seemed that their relationship might have ended, but looking at Takei now, Hank realized how he had missed that constant smile and reassuring presence.

"We have missed you, too, Takei," he said. Ruth nodded in agreement and patted Takei's hand.

"Please," said Takei, smiling, "let us meet here again at seven-thirty. The car will then take us to the dinner club where we will meet Matsuda-San. We both are looking forward to a fruitful visit." Bowing slowly and deeply to show his respect, he turned and walked toward the door.

At eight-o'clock, Ruth, Hank and Takei were seated in the dinner club, at the same table Hank had shared with Yoshi, Takei and Yukio, thirty-six years before. Looking around, Hank experienced a feeling of deja vu. The place seemed even more luxurious to him now than it had then. The aging furniture had taken on a patina of elegance with the years, lending the room an air of beauty and refinement.

Hank noticed another change, too. In 1952, there had been no women dining there. Now, the tables were sprinkled with glamorous looking ladies, dressed in the latest western fashions.

Yoshi had not yet arrived, and Takei had ordered a bottle of French champagne. The wine steward popped the cork with a flourish and poured the sparkling liquid into crystal champagne goblets. Takei lifted his glass. "On behalf of Matsuda-San and my own personal pleasure, I thank you once again for honoring us with your esteemed presence."

Reluctantly, Hank raised his glass. He found it difficult to forgive and forget so quickly. Ruth, however, joined in eagerly, helping to create a festive mood. "It is our pleasure to be here and we look forward to a bright future," she said.

Just as they placed their glasses to their lips, the waiter approached the table. Bending his head down to Takei's ear, he spoke in a hushed voice. The smile faded from Takei's face and he stood up quickly. "Please excuse me for a moment, Hank-San and Ruth-San. There is a phone call I must take. I will soon return." And he abruptly left the table.

Several minutes later, Takei returned. He sat down heavily, his body limp. "I have just been advised that Matsuda-San has had a heart attack. He has been taken to the hospital. You will please excuse me, but I must go to him now. The driver will return you to your hotel. I will be in touch as soon as we have more information."

With that, Takei stood, bowed to them quickly and left the restaurant.

Ruth felt paralyzed. She told herself to remain calm and not let her emotions betray her. Looking at Hank, she saw that he was stunned, too. Since neither of them could speak, they sat in silence. Finally, Hank reached over and touched Ruth's arm. Mutely, she got up and followed him out of the club.

Three hours later, they were sitting in their hotel suite, still numb, when the ringing of the phone jarred them to their senses. Hank quickly reached over to answer it.

"Yes," he said, practically yelling into the receiver. Takei's calm voice was on the other end.

"Matsuda-San is resting comfortably. They have stabilized his condition and will be administering tests in the morning. He has suffered a heart attack, which may require a bypass operation. He is conscious now and has asked me to extend his apologies to both of you. He is hopeful that he will still be able to meet with you before you return to the United States. I will keep you advised."

The next day, Yoshikazu Matsuda had an emergency quadruple bypass while the Presidential Trade Mission went on as scheduled. The days were long and filled with meetings of all kinds.

The American manufacturers had come prepared with catalogues, samples and prices. The Commerce Department had arranged meetings for them with prospective Japanese buyers. Everyone was cautiously optimistic that a breakthrough would be achieved. The hope was that they would come away with bonafide orders rather than just vague promises.

The news of the Tosui chairman's heart attack had been kept a secret. Takei had asked Ruth and Hank to say nothing, and they had honored his request. They were both deeply disturbed by the turn of events and found it difficult to concentrate on the meetings they attended. They waited anxiously each night for Michio's call to report on Yoshi's condition.

Yoshi was removed from the critical list on the third day after the operation and the by-pass surgery was declared a success. Ruth and Hank were overjoyed when Michio called to tell them the good news.

"Do you think there's a possibility that we can visit Yoshi before we leave for home?" Hank asked.

"That is my wish, too," was Michio's reply.

On the last day of the mission, Michio had agreed to join the Marshalls for breakfast in their hotel suite. Ruth jumped up as soon as she heard the knock on the door. Opening it, she saw Michio, impeccably dressed as usual. But his beautifully tailored clothes could not hide the haggard look on his face. Deep circles had formed under his eyes and his complexion was sallow and pinched looking.

Ruth held out her arms and they embraced. As she held him, she thought she detected a faint sigh of relief escaping from his lips. Several moments later, she stepped back with a smile and motioned for him to enter.

"How is your father doing today?" she asked, as Michio crossed the room to where Hank was standing. He waited until Ruth and Hank were both seated before answering.

"My father is doing very well, I'm happy to report," Michio said with a smile. He sat down in the chair across from them.

"And he has asked to see you. He is only allowed one visitor at a time—for no longer than ten minutes. I was able to visit him yesterday, and his spirits are good. I'm very grateful that he is now recovering. My father is a very special man. It is only now that I understand the greatness that lies within him."

Abruptly, he changed the subject, as if he realized he might have revealed too much.

"I spoke with Sarah last night and told her I would be seeing you this morning. She is very concerned about my father and me. And about the affect this may have on our marriage."

"What kind of affect do you think it might have?" asked Hank. "And what do you think will happen if your father can no longer carry out his duties at Tosui?"

If Hank's directness startled Michio, it didn't show. "Sarah and I plan to be married," he said. "As for your other question, we must not speak of that now. I have taken the liberty of arranging for you to visit the hospital this morning at eleven o'clock. If that is convenient for you, I will have our car pick you up in front of the hotel at ten-thirty."

"That will be fine," Ruth told him. "We'll be ready. Now, how about a cup of coffee? Or perhaps you'd prefer tea?"

"Thank you but I must go. There is so much I have to do," Michio said. He turned to Hank apologetically. "There are many things I wish I could speak with you about. There are so many questions now for which I must find answers. And many decisions to be made in areas in which I am unfamiliar."

Hank had to smile. "There are some things they just don't teach you in business school, aren't there? Like how to make decisions in the real world when there are no right or wrong solutions. I know it sounds like a cliché but sometimes there isn't any black or white. There are only shades of gray. And the question isn't whether or not you'll compromise. It's a question of how much."

Michio got up and walked to the door. He paused with his hand on the knob. "When I first came to your home as a student, I remember you said to me, 'Ease up, kid. It will be all right.' At the time, those words were both strange and wise. But I understood what you meant then and I appreciate your wisdom even more now."

He waited, as if wanting to say more, but said only, "Thank you both. We will meet again at the hospital at eleven o'clock."

CHAPTER TWENTY-EIGHT

▼

Michio ushered Hank into Yoshi's room as soon as they arrived at the hospital. Ruth waited in the adjoining room, gathering her thoughts, preparing for her visit. Try as she might, she couldn't keep her eyes from filling with tears.

Hank felt an eerie sense of the unreal as he sat stiffly in a plain wooden chair, facing Yoshikazu Matsuda. He was surprised to see that Yoshi was sitting almost upright in his narrow hospital bed, eyes alert, watching Hank.

Yoshi wore a pair of light blue silk pajamas, covered by a dark blue silk robe. His face had been freshly shaven, his silver hair neatly combed. In spite of all that he'd gone through, his voice was still strong.

"Please forgive me for not keeping our dinner appointment," he said with a wry smile. "But there are times when the gods change the plans we so painstakingly make. This is the first time in many years, I have had to face my own mortality. It is a very sobering moment when one realizes that time is not without limits. I am therefore pleased that we have this opportunity to discuss some issues that need to be resolved."

"I wonder if this is the time or the place to discuss issues," Hank said. "I came here because I was anxious to see you and to express my best wishes for your speedy recovery."

Yoshi impatiently waved the comment away. "There is no need for delay. I am feeling strong. My heart has been repaired and my doctors tell me there is no reason why I should not be able to return to my duties very soon. They say that I can now live a long and productive life. We may discuss any subject without fear. This attack came without warning and if there is another, I am sure it will come the same way. No one can predict what will happen. In the meantime, we must continue with our lives."

Yoshi adjusted himself in his bed. "I was pleased that you accepted my invitation to dinner for several reasons. After having worked so closely together for so many years, it was time to bring the silence between us to an end. I am aware of the anger you felt toward me when I proposed buying out your interest in Marshall-Telesonic. But, as it turned out, the transaction was of great benefit to us all. You received much more than your shares were worth at that time and we made Telesonic the number one company in consumer electronics.

"We know you have invested your money wisely because your foundation has been leading the way in the development of a new generation of high technology. I am referring specifically to your interactive television, made possible through digital technology. Our experts see a merging of computers and television. They call it the new 'information highway'."

Yoshi paused and rested his head against the pillow, gathering his strength, waiting for Hank to respond. Hank just laughed out loud.

"Yoshi, you never cease to amaze me! I came here expecting to find you frail and weak, valiantly trying to recover from a major heart attack. Instead, I find a roaring lion, shaking off the experience the way most people slap at a bothersome flea. Instead of weeping for you, I'm rejoicing in your strength and determination."

Yoshi smiled and nodded.

"And you're absolutely right," Hank continued. I was deeply disturbed by the takeover. The decision wasn't made after a discussion by two friends and partners. It was made behind my back. The only option I had, was to sell out. And the only gratification I could gain was to bounce back bigger than ever. By doing that, I knew that when this day finally arrived—and I knew that it would, you and I would be able to face each other as equals in the battle for control. As usual, I am very impressed by your knowledge of our progress. Yes, we are on the verge of some major breakthroughs. Yet, I must tell you, Yoshi, I wish I knew as much about your progress as you do about mine. You've always managed to know about my activities, starting from the time I first met our old friend, Jack Strong. What ever happened to him anyway?"

Yoshi smiled. "He still does some work for us but his effectiveness has been diminished by age, whiskey and women. He has done well for himself, though. He has increased his wealth through wise investments in Japanese stocks and real estate."

Hank felt anger welling up inside of him. He'd never be able to forget Jack's duplicitous role in the takeover. "Well, I'm sorry I can't rejoice at his good fortune," he said, testily. "But I still haven't figured out which was worse—realizing that I trusted a man like Jack Strong, or finding out that my good friend, Yoshikazu Matsuda employed a Judas to spy on me."

Yoshi sat up in his bed, his eyes blazing. "Jack Strong worked for me long before you met him. Your anger is based on a sophomoric code of ethics, used by Americans to make themselves feel self-righteous as they rape and plunder those who fall under their domination. You've never known the humility of defeat or suffered the senseless destruction of the atom bomb. To this day, yours is the only country to have ever used this weapon to incinerate two cities. Even now, forty-three years later, our people are dying of cancer caused by your bombs."

Hank could barely contain his own fury. "Do you recall Pearl Harbor? It was your country's sneak attack that started the war!"

"Oh no, my friend." Yoshi said bitterly, "It started long before Pearl Harbor. It started the moment Admiral Perry anchored his gunboats off our shore and pushed us to the wall. You forced us to open our country to the outside world. And yet, isn't it amazing that after the devastation of war, we have been able to rise from the ashes and beat you at your own game? That we now dominate the world with our industry?"

Hank sat transfixed. He had no idea Yoshi had hidden so much anger for so many years. Now I see the real man, he thought to himself.

"In our country we have a saying—'It's not over till the fat lady sings', Hank said. "As far as you and I are concerned, I think you know that I have always been honest and fair with you. I've always held you in high esteem. I would have risked my life to protect you, but obviously, the reverse wasn't true."

Yoshi leaned back on his pillow, eyes half closed. His voice was so soft that when he finally spoke, it seemed to be coming from a dream. "Do you remember April 4th, 1945, Hank-San? When you and your squadron of B-29's launched the biggest air raid of the war against Tokyo? Halfway back to your base in Saipan lay the battlescarred island of Iwo Jima. Although we Japanese, were still fighting, the airfield had already been secured. Yours was the first B-29 to make an emergency landing there. After you landed, you and your crew came out of the plane and surrounded it with your guns drawn."

Hank's stomach muscles tightened and his head began to ache as memories of that day flashed vividly in his mind. His eyes closed involuntarily as he relived the scene that had haunted him a thousand times before. Once again he saw the rutted landing strip and felt the oppressive heat and the fear that had gripped his insides when he'd seen the movement in the bushes.

Yoshi's voice was low and steady as he continued. "You had just dropped to the ground from the pilot's compartment. Your pistol was drawn and ready. You were standing very still, staring into the bushes, thinking you saw or heard a sniper."

"How can you know this?" Hank asked in a whisper.

"Because, Hank-San, I was the sniper. I held your head in my gun sight. I was just starting to pull the trigger when I recognized it was you. I could not fire then. For forty-three years, I have asked myself, 'Why did you not kill him on that day?' And now, for the first time, I know the reason why."

The two men looked at each other, their faces tight with emotion.

"But why?" Hank asked, barely able to get the words out. "Why didn't you pull the trigger?"

"Because it was not our destiny to die on that day. Had I killed you, I would have been discovered and shot by your comrades. Then, everything we have done or been since then would have been left in the sand at Iwo Jima. And that was not meant to be."

Hank could no longer sit still. He jumped up from his chair and began to pace the room. Yoshi lay motionless in his bed, seemingly drained of all energy. The tension that had permeated the room had disappeared with the revelation of the long-kept secret.

The visions that were appearing in their minds were as fresh to them now as when they'd first experienced them—the young American pilot standing apprehensively in the sand at Iwo Jima, his head about to be blown off by the young Japanese soldier.

"Isn't it strange," Hank said at last, "that after all that has happened, our children have fallen in love with each other? I've been told you won't consent to their marriage and I must admit, I, too, have my doubts. In our culture, however, I wouldn't have the power to prevent their marriage, even if I wanted to."

Yoshi sat up quickly. "But I believe that you agree, Hank-San, that it cannot work. Our cultures are too different. Michio must fulfill his destiny, which is here in Japan as the head of a Japanese family. Our tradition is too inbred in him to set that aside."

Shaking his head obstinately, Yoshi added, "I do not believe we need to discuss this any further."

Hank made no effort to hide his irritation, and got up abruptly. "I'd better go now. I've stayed way past my allotted ten minutes," he said.

As if on cue, a tentative knock was heard at the door. The nurse entered and whispered, "Matsuda-San, you must rest now."

Yoshi waved his arms impatiently. "We will be a few more minutes. Please leave us!"

The nurse started to respond, then, thinking better of it, quietly closed the door behind her.

Adjusting his position on the bed, Yoshi looked at Hank with bright, lucid eyes. "Please pardon the interruption. Doctors think that life travels on a convenient time schedule, but we know the windows of opportunity are soon closed and so must be examined the minute they're opened."

"Your new ventures are at a critical point. It will take a great deal of money to bring these products and processes to the marketplace. Raising vast sums of money is very time-consuming and can delay your bringing these projects to their ultimate end. I would therefore like to propose the discussion of a joint venture whereby we would provide the funds and research and you would provide the technology you have already developed."

Hank was taken by surprise. He hadn't expected to receive a business proposal now and certainly not one with this magnitude. His first impulse was to reject any kind of business arrangement with Yoshi. The bitterness from their last association was still too fresh.

But he shook that feeling off. Being handed a proposition of this kind sent a surge of excitement through him. Yoshi's attempt to make a deal from his sick bed only confirmed the importance of what the Marshall Foundation had developed. We've really got them worried! Hank thought, gleefully.

But as usual, Yoshi had put his finger right on the crux of the problem— developing high technology products had all but exhausted Hank's funds. Yet, the Japanese man was now offering a solution that would be very tempting under normal circumstances.

Assuming a poker face, Hank said in a flat, emotionless voice, "You do realize you're talking about literally billions of dollars?"

The answer was matter-of-fact. "This is a high stakes game, Hank-San. We understand better than anyone else the vast resources and disciplines needed to develop the lifestyle and products of the future. We have already budgeted large sums of money. By combining our resources, we would be able to minimize costs and greatly improve our chances for success."

"But, Yoshi," Hank asked with a devilish grin, "who would control this venture?"

"Equality is possible..." Yoshi began, but Hank interrupted him.

"...but not very likely. Besides, where would you find another Jack Strong to swing the balance of power? And that is what this is all about, isn't it? Power?"

Yoshi ignored the pointed barb. "Hank-San, please be reasonable. We have an enormous lead in almost every field, including the areas you are developing. We virtually control the capital markets. And, even more importantly, Hank-San, you and I are no longer young. We do not have the convenience of time. If you insist on continuing to fight alone rather than joining forces, you will not win."

In spite of all that had happened, Hank had to admire this old warrior who had been his friend. He got up from his chair and stood next to Yoshi, who sat taut and straight in his bed. They held each other's eyes in the silence that followed.

Finally, Hank said in a soft voice, "Tell me, is this another part of the plan to take over the United States?"

"Where did you hear of such a plan?" Yoshi asked, startled.

"It doesn't really matter," Hank replied confidently. "You might come close but you won't succeed. I thank you for your kind offer, Yoshi, but I don't need any partners this time. I thank you, too, for sparing my life so many years ago. We have been enemies and we have been friends. And we may yet face another great battle together."

Hank realized it was time to leave. "But there is one thing I would like you to know, Matsuda-San," Hank said. I have great feeling and enormous respect for you." He reached out and shook Yoshi's hand. "I also wish you a speedy recovery and a long life."

Yoshi returned the handshake firmly. "Thank you for your kind wishes, Hank-San. I, too, hold you in high esteem and have great admiration for your honesty and courage. I must tell you, though, in the battle for control, while you may make a strong effort, you are too late."

Bowing to his adversary, Hank walked out of the room. As he left, both men realized with heavy hearts that this could be their last meeting.

Ruth sat in the waiting room, red-eyed. She noticed immediately how pained and drawn Hank's face was. "You look as if you've just gone through a war," she said, her voice filled with concern.

"I think I have," he replied, softly. "Don't expect to see a weakened warrior when you walk in there. That's vintage Yoshikazu Matsuda in that room."

She put her arms around her husband's neck and gave him a reassuring hug. "I won't be long," she whispered.

Knocking softly on the door, Ruth opened it without waiting for a reply. Stepping in, she closed the door quietly behind her.

Yoshi's eyes were clear and his gaze direct as he watched her walk shyly over to the bed. Leaning down, Ruth placed her hand gently on his shoulder and kissed his cheek. Yoshi remained impassive as she looked at him with a worried expression on her face.

"You look fantastic! It's hard to believe you've just come through a major operation. Are you in any pain? Is it all right for me to visit with you for a few moments?"

Her sweetness and concern made him smile, and his face became gentle.

"I am fine. The operation was a complete success. I'm told I am in even better shape than I was before." Yoshi studied her carefully. "And you are more beautiful than I remembered."

"How much do you remember?" she asked boldly. "Now that we're older and you've made it through this terrible ordeal, perhaps we can speak of our earlier days when you were so kind to me."

"But you were the one who was kind," he interrupted. "It was you who made a complete stranger, far from home, feel comfortable. While others had no understanding of our traditions or respect for who we were, you showed me much of what was good in your country. I will never forget what you did."

Tears came to her eyes as she caught a sudden glimpse of the shy, gentle Japanese student she'd known forty-seven years before. "You know that I've always thought that too much is made of people's differences. After you scratch away the dirt on the surface, we're all pretty much the same. Deep down, we all want the same things—love, happiness, a feeling of self-worth, recognition. In fact, when you drop your Shogun image and Hank stops acting like an AllAmerican football player, you're both very much alike. You both have power, compassion, intelligence, understanding, and respect for other people—the stuff great leaders are made of. And that, my dear Yoshi, is why I find it difficult to understand your refusal to accept the marriage of your son and my daughter."

His body stiffened at her words, the muscles in his face growing tight. "This subject is between my son and me and thousands of years of tradition. The ghosts of my ancestors would not rest if I were to waiver in my resolve. I understand your concern, but it is not your place to speak of this."

Ruth fought to hold her tongue. Taking a deep breath, she forced herself to speak calmly. "The strength of a man with vision is his ability to discard useless traditions in a modern world. My daughter has asked me to remind you that this is 1988, not 1941."

"And is your daughter aware of what happened in 1941?" he shot back.

"You mean besides Pearl Harbor?" Ruth responded with sarcastic sweetness. Immediately, she wished she could take her words back.

Yoshi closed his eyes and leaned his head back against the pillow. In a tired voice he said, "This is the second time today I have heard Pearl Harbor mentioned. Am I supposed to cringe at those words and retire in shame? I am proud of our history and make no apologies."

Ruth reached over and took Yoshi's hand in hers. The gesture sent an electric shock through them and their eyes met in mirrored surprise. In a hushed, husky voice, she whispered, "If you cared for me at all and for what might have been, you will give these young people your approval. Then, they will be able to pursue their lives without guilt or regret."

Yoshi lay there stone faced and implacable. With her hand still on his, Ruth asked shyly, "Yoshi, do you remember that night on the beach?"

His answer could barely be heard. "We must not talk of this. I cannot change. Please, I am tired now. I must ask you to leave."

Ruth removed her hand from his and got up slowly. "With all my heart I wish you a speedy recovery, Yoshi. And I will never again speak of anything personal with you."

She walked to the door, then turned and looked back at him once more. His eyes were closed and his head lay heavily on the pillow. In a choked voice, she said softly, "Goodbye, Yoshi," and left the room.

Yoshi opened his eyes when he heard the door close and stared at the void where she'd stood. Faintly, as if to the shadows, he said:

The morning glory

Even as I paint it

Fades away

His eyes closed again and a peaceful smile appeared upon his face before he drifted into a deep sleep from which he never awakened.

CHAPTER TWENTY-NINE

▼

There was little conversation between Ruth and Hank as the limousine drove them back to the hotel. And although the streets of Tokyo were teeming with activity, they saw nothing as they stared blankly out the windows.

In their minds, they kept replaying their visits with Yoshi. Ruth could still feel the sensation from the touch of his hand. It had been so natural and spontaneous. If he could feel that way, why then was he so unrelenting where Sarah and Michio were concerned? Perhaps, she thought, when he was feeling stronger, he would see things more clearly and rethink his decision.

She looked over at Hank and studied his handsome face, so serious now as he sat lost in his own thoughts. There had never been a question of her unconditional love for him. Yet, Yoshi had always held a very special place in her heart and always would.

Hank was in his own world. He couldn't stop thinking about what Yoshi had told him. Everything he had, everything he had done, he owed to Yoshi's one moment of hesitation. All the bitterness he had felt inside these past six years! And now to find this out. He needed time to think things through.

As the car pulled up to the hotel, Ruth reached for Hank's hand. "He looked better than I thought he would," she said.

"The man is a fighter. He has got that Samarai spirit that refuses to let go."

The phone was ringing as they entered their room. Hank rushed over to pick it up. The voice on the other end was low, almost a whisper. "Hank-San, my father is dead."

He stood there, unable to react. Finally, he mumbled, "No, this cannot be. When did this happen? Where are you now?"

"I'm still at the hospital. Preparations are being made to bring him home. Arrangements must be made for the burial. Our family will be gathering at our home. You and Ruth are welcome to join us there after five-o'clock. I must go now. There is much to do, but I wanted you to know."

"Michio, we are so sorry." Hank said. "Of course we'll be there. It will be an honor. I thank you for calling. I know how difficult this is for you." He put the receiver down slowly and stared vacantly at the phone. Lifting his head, he caught sight of Ruth's stricken face and held out his arms. She rushed into them as he whispered, "Yoshi is dead."

"How can that be?" she sobbed, her body sinking limply against his. "He said he was feeling fine. And he looked strong, almost as if he hadn't been sick. He's always seemed so indestructible. Oh, Hank," she cried mournfully.

He held her tightly and said, "I guess this proves that none of us are indestructible." His eyes traveled the room without seeing, as tears ran down his cheeks.

It was just after 6:00 when Ruth and Hank arrived at the Matsuda residence. They removed their shoes at the door where they were received by a somber, Takei. His trademark smile had been replaced with bloodshot eyes in a grief-stricken face. After Takei bowed low to them in greeting, Hank shook his hand and Ruth reached out to embrace him. Takei nodded his head in thanks, than gestured for them to walk in ahead of him.

The strong, sweet smell of burning incense filled the air as they entered. Yoshi's body lay in an open casket in the middle of what appeared to be a large receiving room. A Buddhist priest and three monks stood in front of the coffin, softly chanting prayers. Directly behind them sat Yoshi's wife, Kimi, surrounded by her three daughters and two sons-in-law. The women were dressed in black silk kimonos, making their faces appear even paler in the muted light. The men wore conservative black suits with white shirts and black ties.

Kimi was sitting very straight and still. She greeted Ruth and Hank with a wan smile. "My husband is pleased that you are here," she said in her soft voice.

Ruth looked at the sad, elegant woman before her. They'd met at business- related functions several times over the years. Neither had expressed a desire to broaden the relationship, so they had remained distant and polite. Now, though, Ruth felt an unbearable closeness toward Kimi, whose lovely face was etched with weary lines of mourning.

Seeing the sadness in Ruth's face, Kimi offered her hand. Ruth held it with both of hers and the two women looked deeply into each other's eyes. Several moments later, they smiled in silent understanding and released each other's hands.

Hank leaned over and kissed Kimi on the cheek. "Your husband was an exceptional man," he told her. "He will be greatly missed."

Kimi responded passively. "Although his spirit has left his physical body, it remains here with us. This allows us the chance to visit and to say our farewells." She motioned to a table laden with tea, sake, sushi, sashimi and rice cakes.

"Please, help yourselves to our simple repast. And please join us in prayer. Tomorrow, my husband will be taken to the temple where a service will be performed before the cremation."

The words brought forth a low, haunting sob from deep inside the grieving woman. Ruth knelt down and placed her arms around her, rocking her gently.

Leaving the two women to console each other, Hank walked over to the foot of Yoshi's casket where Michio was standing quietly. He placed his left hand on the younger man's shoulder, and they silently shook hands.

Hank then moved to the head of the casket and looked down at the face of the man with whom he'd shared such an intense relationship for so many years. Yoshi lay in quiet repose. His arms were folded over his chest, and his hands rested on the fabric of a luxurious black silk kimono that covered his lean body. Even now, an aura of power emanated from him.

He wondered what would happen now to the plan to take over the United States. Would that dream simply fade away without Yoshi's life force?

Visions of the experiences they'd shared raced through Hank's mind. And this is our final farewell, he thought. Without any warning, it's suddenly all over.

We could have been brothers, he mused, and in a deeper sense, we were. It could very easily have been me lying here, and Yoshi saying his farewell. In that instant, Hank realized the precariousness of his own mortality. He wondered if the soul really did remain alive. And if Yoshi was looking at him from some other place, watching as he gazed at the face in the casket.

Perhaps he was. And perhaps he knew.

"Goodbye, old friend," Hank said, his throat tightening. And slowly, he turned away.

Ruth approached the casket as Hank left. She embraced Michio, who returned her hug gratefully. For years, Ruth had seemed like a second mother to him. It was only right that she and Hank should be with him now. "My father would have been most pleased that you are here," he told her.

She smiled, acknowledging the compliment, and patted his arm before walking to the casket. A sudden wave of panic came over her. How could she stand over Yoshi's dead body and gaze at his lifeless face? Nausea welled up inside of her. She closed her eyes and swallowed hard, waiting for the moment to pass. She knew that she must perform this final ritual to say goodbye for the last time.

Gathering up her courage, she moved into place. Taking a deep breath, she looked down. On Yoshi's face was a look of peace she'd never seen before. For as long as she'd known him, he'd always seemed to be in the midst of some inner conflict. Now, it was as if his stern, serious face had been transformed back into the handsome twenty-year-old boy she'd met so many years ago. Once again, she could see the earnest young student trying to learn as much as he could, as fast as he could. She smiled, remembering how she could make him laugh and how unused to the sound of laughter he was.

Softly, she spoke to him. "You were right about my love for Hank. That instinctive intelligence of yours proved correct once again. But I wonder if you ever knew how deep my feelings were for you. I will never forget, as long as I live, the emotions you awakened in me. I will never forget your words either, dear Yoshi, for they were like no others I had ever heard before."

Lowering her face, closer to his, she whispered, "Goodbye, dearest friend. The morning glory has faded away."

With tears streaming down her cheeks, Ruth walked off.

CHAPTER THIRTY

---▼---

Michio and Sarah stood in front of the family plot where Yoshi's ashes rested in a white ceramic urn. Michio visited this spot often. He felt the spirit of his father strongly here and came to seek his guidance and counsel. Sometimes, the connection was so strong he could see his father's face in front of him.

Today was an important day, and Sarah had flown in from the United States to be with him. With her at his side, he began to speak.

"Father, it is exactly six months since I told you of my love for Sarah and sought your blessings for our marriage. In your great wisdom, you asked us to wait six months before making a final decision, which we agreed to do.

"I feel you are always with me in spirit, Father. I'm therefore certain that you have witnessed the grand outpouring of love and respect that has been bestowed upon you and the many tributes that have been made, recognizing your magnificent accomplishments. The memorial services, held in your honor, were attended by more than four thousand grief-stricken people. Our honorable ancestors must have been smiling as they met you at the gates of heaven. Yet, no one can feel as I do. I learned all I know at your feet. I only pray I am worthy of your faith in me.

"Last week, Tosui's Board of Directors elected me to succeed you as president and chief executive officer. While it is a great honor, I will only accept after I consult with you and fully explain the feelings I carry inside."

Michio paused for several seconds as though waiting for a response.

"As I promised," he continued, "Sarah and I have waited six months. She arrived in Tokyo today so that we might visit you together. Our separation has caused our feelings for each other to become even stronger. I have no doubt of our love. I do have one question though…if we marry, can I, in good conscience, accept the presidency of Tosui?"

Sarah had been standing by silently, watching him, her eyes never leaving his face. She could feel the conflict he was experiencing, and his pain hurt her as well.

She looked down at the headstone, marking the spot where Yoshi's ashes lay, and with tears in her eyes, said, "Uncle Yoshi, I still can't believe that you're gone. It seems like you've always been a part of my life. I must admit that it did hurt me a great deal when you objected so strongly to our marriage. I've always loved you and could not believe that you'd reject me. I was very angry at first but I understand things better now. Michio and I don't know if it's right or wrong to go against thousands of years of tradition. We only know that we love each other and something that feels so right can't be wrong. I wish you were here! I would put my arms around you, call you Papa-San and ask you to have faith in Michio and me…and in the future."

Michio put his arms around Sarah's waist and tried to quiet her sobbing. She laid her head against his shoulder and he could feel the wetness of her tears through his shirt.

"Don't worry," he said, soothingly. "He is listening to us and he will give us a sign. Let us go now. I know you're very tired."

Sarah was in fact exhausted. The long flight from Los Angeles had seemed endless. She'd spent restless hours playing out the different scenarios of what might happen. Gratefully, she accepted his suggestion that he take her to the hotel, and they turned from Yoshi's grave.

As soon as they were inside the car, Michio took her in his arms and kissed her. "Sarah, I have missed you more than you will ever know," he whispered.

"I love you more now than ever," she answered with a sigh.

Remembering the driver in the front seat, Michio quickly sat up straight, though he continued to hold Sarah's hand tightly in his.

"I thank you for coming here today, Sarah. There is so much we need to discuss."

She turned in her seat to face him and gently stroked his face with her fingers. Looking into each other's eyes, they knew the magic was still there. With a knowing smile, they leaned back contentedly and let the driver do his job.

Arriving at the Okura Hotel, Michio took Sarah directly to her suite. Once in the room, he put his arm around her shoulders and gave her a squeeze. "It is now one o'clock. Why don't you get some rest and refresh yourself. I will return for you at six."

A knock sounded at the door and a porter walked in, carrying her bags. He brought them into the bedroom, put them down and after bowing to Michio, he left.

As the door closed, Michio kissed Sarah softly on the lips. "Rest now," he told her. "I will see you soon." Then he, too, departed.

Stepping out of the car, Michio looked up at the huge granite Tosui building. His eyes traveled to the top where the company flag waved proudly. He'd grown up with the symbol of the bamboo and the subtle strength it represented. He knew that it symbolized more than the company; it symbolized the country and the soul of the Japanese people.

Michio was proud of the powerful and successful enterprise the Matsuda family had built. In terms of revenue and net worth, Tosui was the largest company in the world. And now, Michio had been asked to become the fifth generation Matsuda to lead this global giant.

Entering the building, he felt the strong presence of his father all around him. Crossing the lobby, he entered a private elevator that took him directly to the penthouse floor. Nodding to the receptionist as he passed, he stopped at the desk of his secretary, Itsuku. She stood up respectfully and said, "Good morning, Sir," bowing slightly as she handed him his messages. "Watanabe-San asked if he could see you immediately upon your arrival."

Glancing over his messages quickly, Michio said, "I will see Watanabe-San now." Entering his office, he sat down at his large mahogany desk where several folders lay, neatly stacked. He thumbed through them briskly, stopping when he heard a rap at the door. After calling out, "Hai," Takei entered and bowed.

"I thank you for seeing me now. I would not have troubled you if it was not most important."

Michio waited patiently for Takei to continue. He'd always had great affection and respect for the person who had been his father's right hand man for so many years. In Michio's eyes, he'd hardly aged at all.

But there were some noticeable changes in Takei. His smile wasn't as ready since Yoshikazu's death. And he'd lost a considerable amount of weight, causing his trademark bulge to disappear from his clothes. Although he was still the same Takei, the pain of his loss was visible.

Michio-San, I wish to congratulate you on the decision made by the Board of Directors to elect you the new president and chief executive officer of Tosui," Takei said. "It is an indication of the high esteem in which you are held, both inside the company and out.

"Many of my associates here have asked me about my future plans. I have just passed my seventieth birthday and there are those who expect me to retire. It is true that I can live most comfortably on the generous pension provided by your father. But rather than make that decision now, I would like to place myself at your disposal."

Takei hesitated for a moment. "That is, if you would find my services useful."

Michio sat quietly, making no attempt to reply. He knew Takei well enough to know he had more to say before a response was required.

"I was at your father's side from the first day he returned from the army. I watched him grow and mature into the greatest industrialist in all of Japan and perhaps, in the entire world. In a very small way, I assisted him in carrying out the decisions he made. Many agreements have been made that do not exist on paper, yet they are honored without hesitation. I am aware of the letter and spirit of every deal your father generated and the thinking behind each of them. I believe I can be most helpful to you, particularly during this time of transition."

Takei paused again, this time waiting for an answer.

Michio studied the familiar face sitting before him. "Takei-San, I have known you since I was a baby. One of my earliest recollections is of you, carrying me on your back. Even then, I was impressed with your great strength. Later, I also came to know your great loyalty, wisdom and devotion, which you gave to my father without question. I am deeply honored that you now wish to work with me. I must first decide, however, if I am prepared to accept the position offered to me by the Board."

Takei looked surprised. "Is there a question of this? It was determined years ago that you would take control of Tosui when the time came and would follow in the footsteps of your father and his father and the past generations from the house of Matsuda. Aside from this, you have demonstrated by your own actions that you are more than capable of leading the company into newer areas and greater glory."

Takei stopped suddenly, as if he had a recollection of something. "Before we go any further, however, I would like to tell you of a meeting I had at the hospital with your father before he died."

Michio leaned forward anxiously. "Yes, please go on," he said.

"As you know, I stayed at the hospital so that I would be available any time he needed me. After the operation, he seemed to regain his strength very quickly. Even the doctors were surprised by his rapid recovery. Although his body was weak, his mind remained alert. If anything, his illness seemed to enable him to bring his own ambitions more clearly into focus.

"Early in the morning of the day before he died, he called me to the side of his bed. He was propped up against a pillow, but his eyes were bright and he was bursting with energy. 'Takei', he said, 'bring me my stationery and my fountain pen.'

"He always liked to write important letters with his old fashioned fountain pen." 'I am going to write a very personal letter to my son,' he told me. 'Should I not survive until October 23rd, you are to deliver it to him precisely on that date.' I protested. 'But you are getting stronger every day. There is no reason why you won't be here for many years to come. Then you can tell Michio yourself, all he needs to know.'

"Matsuda-San graced me with his wise smile. 'Takei, you have been my strong right hand,' he said. I have depended upon you for many years, and you have always surpassed my expectations. I thank you now as I have never done before. I must also make one more request of you. If I do not survive, you are to stay with Michio for at least two years. You are to guide him through the many problems and conflicts he will face. Only you, Takei-San, are aware of the agreements I have made, written and unwritten. And, despite the secrecy surrounding it, others now know of The Plan. You must never discuss it with anyone else but you must reveal all you know to Michio. I have already shared my knowledge with him, but have never asked for his commitment as my father asked for mine. There is still work to be done but from what we have seen, we are moving ahead on schedule.'

"He seemed to tire in that moment but he had the strength to shake my hand with a firm grip. 'Thank you, my friend,' he said, 'for always being at my side'."

Takei reached inside his jacket pocket and removed a sealed manila envelope. Without a word, he handed it to Michio and walked out of the room quickly, so that Michio would not see the tears that filled his eyes.

As soon as Takei departed, Michio buzzed Itsuku. "Please do not allow anyone to disturb me," he said. Then, he sat back in his chair and opened the envelope.

When he'd finished reading the letter, he slumped back in his seat, emotionally drained. He never knew exactly how long he remained that way. The next thing he was conscious of was reaching for the phone. He had to speak to Sarah. He needed to hear her—to see her. As soon as she picked up the receiver, he told her simply, "I must come to you immediately."

Although the urgency in his voice disturbed her, she asked no questions, saying only, "I'll be waiting for you, Michio."

Twenty minutes later, Michio knocked on the door of Sarah's suite. She greeted him wearing a blue kimono and no makeup. Her dark blond hair cascaded loosely around her shoulders.

Seeing the distressed look on his face, she gave him a quick hug and took his hand, leading him toward the couch. Sitting down next to him, she waited expectantly for him to talk.

He looked at her for a long time without speaking. In his right hand was the manila envelope, which he lightly slapped, over and over again, against his left palm.

Finally, in a low voice he said, "I would like to share this letter with you, just as it was written. Because it is in Japanese, I will read it to you."

Michio cleared his throat several times, trying to get rid of the lump that did not want to leave.

"My dear son Michio, if you are reading this letter, it is because I have left this life and am now with our ancestors. I am writing to you even though it is my fervent hope that we will speak of these things together at the appointed time. My heart attack has shown me that one can never be sure of the time that is allotted. But one way or another our date of October 23rd must be kept.

I have led a very full and complete life. Should it end tomorrow., I will have few regrets. I have fulfilled all of my obligations and have kept all of my promises. I am of a generation that is steeped in tradition, one that demands strict adherence to the rules. When you told me of your decision to marry Sarah Marshall, I was shocked. It had never entered my mind that you would choose to marry any one other than the Japanese girl we had so carefully chosen. I was, in fact, most patient with you—allowing you to choose your own time for the union to take place.

When I was a student in Los Angeles, I, too, met American girls who were brilliant and beautiful. But they could have never fulfilled the duties and obligations required of the wife of the head of Tosui. As you know, I have great affection for Sarah, having known her since her birth. Yet, I must ask myself: would this woman be willing to convert to Buddhism?

Give up her career? I think not.

I also wonder what will happen to the Matsuda role in our grand plan if you and Sarah should marry. The Plan is moving along as scheduled. Remember, I gave my promise to your grandfather that I would work toward that goal. I would now like to share my innermost feelings with you, my son. I feel that I walk in two worlds. I have allowed my heart to be penetrated by deep feelings for certain Americans. It was most difficult for me to sacrifice my friendship with Hank Marshall, even though I knew the changes to be made were both necessary and wise. But one cannot dwell on one's own personal pain when there is a larger mission to fulfill.

Japan and the United States have shared a special relationship for more than a century. The Americans are resourceful but unpredictable and undisciplined.

We must continue to move on our predetermined course because we know that if we do not dominate them, they will control us. Perhaps we could have the best of both worlds if we could forget the past, concentrate on the future and learn to trust each other. This is not possible, however. We, of the older generation, carry too many bitter memories within ourselves.

In life, my thoughts have always been clear and unyielding. As I approach my end, I can allow myself the luxury of other thoughts and ideas that might otherwise be impossible to accept in the throes of my unshakeable principles.

This leads me to the reason we were to meet on this day. There is no doubt in my mind that our Board of Directors will elect you to succeed me as the head of Tosui. In addition to your being my son and the grandson of Yukio, you have more than earned the confidence of our associates around the world. More than that, I am very proud of you and all you have accomplished. You are everything I prayed for when I asked the gods to bless us with a son."

Michio's voice broke as he spoke the words his father had never said to him aloud. With tears streaming down her face, Sarah reached for his hand and held it in hers. They sat that way for a long time. Finally, he regained his composure and was able to continue.

"I want you to accept the nomination of the Board. At the same time, I release you from any promises made to me with regard to your marriage and future decisions. I have complete faith in your wisdom and your integrity. The past is history. The future belongs to you.

I am sure you will read this letter to Sarah and so I address my next comments to her:

Sarah, you have many of your father's abilities. You have also inherited your mother's beauty and her great heart. For years, I smiled inside when you called me 'Uncle Yoshi'. If you marry Michio, as I am sure you will, there will be many problems, most of which you cannot now anticipate. If I live, you will never see this letter. I would then proceed on the course that was outlined for me long ago. It is probable that you would not be happy with many of the decisions I would be compelled to make. If, however, my life force is stilled, I will no longer have the power to alter lives—or the course of history. You will find your own way to guide you. It will be up to the two of you to find solutions to the many problems that will face you.

I have one last wish. I ask that you please destroy this letter. I have revealed to you my innermost thoughts—my soul. They are for no other eyes.

I welcome you, Sarah, to the house of Matsuda and wish you both a long and happy life, one that is filled with great accomplishments.

With love,
Papa-San